Velocity

Jules Ashford

Northshore Noir Press

Northshore Noir Press
Toronto, Canada
northshorenoir.com

ISBN: 978-1-998648-05-4

eBook ISBN: 978-1-998648-06-1

For more information visit: julesashford.com or northshorenoir.com

Contents

7:32 a.m.	1
7:51 a.m.	25
8:31 a.m.	44
8:52 a.m.	55
8:55 a.m.	65
9:33 a.m.	86
9:36 a.m.	116
10:07 a.m.	144
10:42 a.m.	169
10:53 a.m.	186
11:45 a.m.	200
12:02 p.m.	211
12:52 p.m.	238
1:28 p.m.	254
2:06 p.m.	267
2:42 p.m.	278
2:58 p.m.	308
3:31 p.m.	324
4:17 p.m.	340

5:19 pm 355

6:40 p.m. 370

Day 285 383

7:32 a.m.

Wren Hubbard stirred in her bed, the shrill sound of the alarm clock piercing through the small apartment like a banshee's wail. She groaned, her arm flailing out from under the covers, searching for the source of the offensive noise. Her fingers found the clock, fumbling for a moment before smashing down on the snooze button with force.

Silence descended once more, broken by the faint hum of traffic outside and the distant whistle of a train. Wren buried her face back into the pillow, inhaling the scent of lavender fabric softener and last night's hair product.

The room remained dimly lit, morning sunlight creeping in through the gaps in the blinds like an unwelcome intruder. Dust motes danced in the pale beams, swirling with each of Wren's exhales.

"Five more minutes," she mumbled into the pillow, her voice muffled and thick with sleep.

Her legs tangled in the sheets as she shifted, trying to find a comfortable position. The coolness of the fabric against her skin sent a shiver down her spine, goosebumps rising on her arms.

A car horn blared outside, followed by the angry shouts of pedestrians. Wren's eyes cracked open, revealing a sliver of striking violet. She glared at the window, as if her gaze alone could silence the world beyond.

"Shut up, shut up, shut up," she chanted, pulling the pillow over her head.

The alarm clock, unimpressed by her attempts at further slumber, began its infernal racket once more. Wren's arm shot out from under the pillow, her hand connecting with the clock and sending it flying across the room. It hit the wall with a satisfying crack, bits of plastic scattering across the hardwood floor.

"Fuck," Wren groaned, pushing herself up onto her elbows. Her short black mohawk stood at odd angles, the purple dye faded and in desperate need of a touch-up.

Wren stretched her arms above her head, her joints popping and muscles tensing. She rolled her neck, feeling the satisfying crack as tension released. Her body hummed with renewed energy, shaking off the last vestiges of sleep.

With some effort (and significantly more reluctance), she swung her legs over the side of the bed until they met the cold hardwood floor. Another shiver ran through her body as she sat there for a moment gathering momentum—or pretending to gather momentum—to stand up fully.

Eventually, she wandered over to the window and yanked open the blinds with all the delicacy of an irritable toddler demanding snacks. Sunlight flooded into the room instantly, making her wince and squint against its sudden brightness. Outside lay what always lay outside: a sprawling mess of concrete structures buzzing with human activity even at this ungodly hour.

She glanced back over her shoulder at what used to be an alarm clock before sighing dramatically and nudging a stray piece of plastic casing with her toe. "Rest in pieces," she said flatly. "You earned it."

Just then, a familiar sound interrupted her morning routine—or lack thereof—the distant wail of sirens weaving their way through traffic down below. She paused mid-thought (or mid-non-thought), tilting her head toward the noise like a dog hearing its owner's car pull into the driveway.

A slow smile spread across Wren's face—mischief flickering behind tired eyes that weren't quite awake but were clearly intrigued all the same.

"Well," she said softly, stretching both arms overhead until something popped satisfactorily in her shoulder joint. "If that doesn't scream 'get up,' I don't know what does."

She rolled her neck next—another pop—and let out a deep breath between pursed lips as energy began creeping back into dormant muscles despite herself. Groggy or not, there was just something about sirens that called to Wren in ways coffee never could.

And so began another day in Wren Hubbard's life: chaotic by necessity but propelled forward by curiosity—and maybe just a little bit of spite against anything resembling an alarm clock ever again.

Wren stood barefoot on the cold hardwood floor and wiggled her toes against its smooth surface. The simple act triggered a memory, vivid and unasked for—the kind that sneaks up on you when you least expect it.

She lifted her right foot and propped it on the kitchen chair, studying her toes, flexing them rhythmically. To most, it would have been an unremarkable movement, something barely worth noticing. But for Wren, those small motions carried weight.

Her mind drifted back to a hospital room—the sharp tang of antiseptic in the air, the kind of smell that lingered too long in your nose. She'd been five years old, swallowed up by a bed far too big for her tiny body. Her right leg had been encased in a clunky white cast, stiff and immovable. The faces around her were blurred now, faded by time, but she could still hear the syrupy voice of a nurse bending down over her.

"Let's see if you can wiggle those toes for me, sweetheart."

Little Wren had furrowed her brow like it was the most important job she'd ever been assigned. She'd stared hard at her toes sticking out of the end of the cast—stared so long that the room seemed to hold its collective breath. At first, nothing happened. Her foot stayed still, stubbornly disobedient. Then there it was—a twitch. Small and shaky but real. Slowly and with great effort, her toes began to wiggle, jerking awkwardly back and forth.

The room lit up with cheers that were too loud for the small space. Doctors smiled at one another; nurses beamed as though she'd done something miraculous. They clapped; they encouraged; they praised with easy dexterity. In Wren's memory—or maybe just in the version she'd pieced together later—her parents had been there too, smiling wide with relief. It wasn't much of a victory in hindsight, but at the time, it had felt enormous.

Back in her apartment now, Wren smiled faintly as she wiggled her toes again—not because they needed coaxing anymore but because they could. She knew better than to believe her own memories entirely—she'd filled in gaps over the years: painted warmer smiles onto faces that weren't there at all; imagined applause from people who had been noticeably absent. Her parents hadn't stood by her bedside during those small victories—they'd left her in someone else's care without much ceremony or fuss because they had other things to tend to: jobs, siblings—they always had an excuse lined up neatly like dominos waiting to fall.

Still, she wiggled her toes once more—just because she could—and marveled at how something so ordinary could once have felt impossible. If nothing else, it reminded her just how far she'd come since then.

She crossed the room slowly on bare feet that left faint imprints on battered wood with every step. When she caught sight of herself in the full-length mirror leaning precariously against the wall, she paused longer than usual to take herself in.

A worn band t-shirt hung loosely from her frame—the logo faded to near obscurity after years of wear—but it still clung stubbornly to life despite its age. Boxer shorts slung low across her hips revealed not just hints of toned muscle but also snippets of ink peeking out beneath fabric edges—a tattoo half-hidden but deliberate all the same. She ran a hand through her mohawk as though smoothing it might make sense of its jagged angles or its defiant purple streaks—though admittedly "sense" wasn't what she'd been aiming for when she dyed it that color anyway.

Her violet eyes stared back from beneath heavy lids still weighted by sleep while sunlight caught on a nose ring glinting faintly—a small rebellion against... well... everything really.

When Wren turned back toward the bed behind her, something softened within her—not much but enough to notice. Maggie was still sleeping soundly under their shared duvet; strands of chestnut hair spilled across the pillow like loose threads on a halo gone askew. Each rise and fall of Maggie's breathing made subtle waves through the blanket covering them both—a rhythm so steady yet delicate that Wren found herself holding still just to match it unconsciously.

She sat carefully on the edge of the mattress where springs groaned softly beneath even light pressure—it was familiar now though: part annoyance and part comfort depending on mood or moment—and let her hand trail idly over rumpled sheets cool to touch despite Maggie's warmth beneath them somewhere close enough to reach but far enough not quite touching yet.

Wren's eyes traced the familiar contours of their bedroom, a landscape of organized chaos. Maggie's cycling gear hung neatly on hooks by the door, each item meticulously placed as though part of a display in a museum of order. Wren's gear, on the other hand, had declared war against the concept of neatness, collapsing in an unruly heap on the floor as if staging its own rebellion. The bookshelves were overcrowded and unapologetic about it, their spines jutting out in mismatched colors and fonts, forming what could generously be called a "mosaic" but more accurately resembled a bookstore after an earthquake.

A potted plant perched on the windowsill, its leaves stretching hungrily toward the sunlight filtering through. Maggie had insisted on the plant—"It'll keep us company," she'd said—but Wren suspected its survival had far more to do with spite than care. The walls held their usual patchwork of posters and photographs: cityscapes teeming with life, open roads that promised freedom, candid snapshots from their adventures together—Wren grinning mid-wheelie as Maggie struggled not to tip over; both of them drenched in mud after a particularly poor route choice. Every image whispered fragments of their story back to her.

Wren turned her gaze toward Maggie, still bundled snugly in the duvet like some kind of sleepy burrito. One stray strand of hair fell rebelliously across her face, shifting with each exhale. Without thinking—because there wasn't much thought required anymore—Wren reached over and brushed it away, her fingers hovering just long enough to feel the faint warmth radiating from Maggie's skin.

The soft ripple of movement from Maggie's body was pulling Wren out of sleep's lingering haze like slow waves lapping at an anchored boat. She blinked hard once, then again, until her vision sharpened enough to take her in properly: Maggie lying there, lips parted, breaths spilling out in a rhythm so steady it almost felt rehearsed. The morning light did what morning light always does and bathed her girlfriend in gold: across her cheekbones, down the slope of her shoulder—all those lines Wren knew by heart.

A year together now—that realization landed softly but still managed to set off a ripple effect inside her chest. One year since they'd nearly collided during a ride through traffic—her fault entirely—and ended up laughing over too-strong coffee at some hole-in-the-wall café neither could remember the name of later.

They hadn't spent much time apart since then, but it hadn't been without its complications.

Wren sighed quietly enough not to disturb her. The problem—or maybe just *their* problem—wasn't love; they had that part covered. It was time—or more specifically, their utter lack of it. Both worked as bike couriers for rival companies (though "rival" made it sound far more dramatic than reality). They loved their jobs—deadlines didn't drive them; velocity did. The electric pull kept them both moving forward, faster and faster. It made everything sharp and vivid. It made them feel alive. Missed dinners and postponed plans had become routine; sometimes all they managed was a half-asleep kiss in passing before being swallowed back up by schedules that refused to align.

Maggie stirred suddenly next to her, her eyelids fluttering open like she instinctively knew she was being studied. She stared at Wren for a second or two longer before breaking into one of those smiles—the ones that started slow but always ended up taking over her entire face.

"Morning," she mumbled through half-closed lips.

"Morning," Wren replied softly.

Maggie stretched dramatically before collapsing back into her pillow fortress with exaggerated defeat. "Five more minutes?" Her voice was low and raspy with sleep.

Wren fought back a grin. "That's what you said yesterday."

"And that's what you said this morning. I heard you, woman," Maggie shot back without opening her eyes.

"And I meant it when I killed the alarm clock." Wren gestured toward the remains scattered across the floor—a pile of plastic shards that bore silent witness to her talent for violence before coffee.

Maggie cracked one eye open just enough to glance at the evidence before chuckling softly and burying her face in the pillow again. "You're impossible."

"That's why you love me." Wren smirked but got no reply beyond Maggie's theatrical snore.

She watched as Maggie drifted back toward sleep almost effortlessly—not quite awake enough yet for responsibility but not fully lost to dreams either. Wren knew this particular expression well: relaxed features edged with total vulnerability. Even now—even after knowing this woman intimately for an entire year—that level of trust still made something shift inside her.

Maggie curled deeper into herself like she always did when asleep—knees pulled up toward her chest while chasing whatever warmth was left on this side of dawn. It reminded Wren vaguely of a cat soaking up sunlight by a window sill or maybe just someone who understood how fleeting moments like these could be.

And really? That was fine by Wren. Just look at that woman.

The sheet had slipped, leaving Maggie's shoulders exposed, her collarbone catching the soft morning light. Wren's gaze followed the curve of her neck, tracing it downward until it landed on the gold cross. The delicate chain had shifted overnight, leaving the cross perched awkwardly on Maggie's shoulder instead of resting, as it usually did, at the center of her chest.

Wren reached for it, her fingers hovering just above the tiny pendant. They were calloused from years of gripping handlebars—hands that rarely showed restraint—but now they moved with a carefulness that felt foreign even to her. She hooked the chain lightly and flicked it back into place. The cross settled neatly against Maggie's breast, rising and falling with each steady breath, like a small boat bobbing on a quiet tide.

She let her hand drop but didn't look away. Her gaze lingered on the necklace, then drifted across Maggie's skin where the morning sun fell in slanted streaks through the blinds. Two freckles caught her eye—small and faint against Maggie's sun-warmed skin. They were close together but off-center, forming a constellation only Wren knew.

Her fingers twitched with the urge to trace them, to connect those dots like stars in an imagined sky. Instead, she stayed still, holding herself back. Disturbing Maggie's sleep wasn't worth it; besides, this was enough—this quiet moment where time felt paused. She filed it away in some corner of her mind reserved solely for Maggie: a private collection of details no one else would ever notice or care about.

Wren had asked Maggie to stop wearing the necklace once. It had been early in their relationship, when familiarity still came with sharp edges and missteps were common. She couldn't remember exactly how she'd said it—it didn't matter really—but she could still feel the charged silence that had followed.

"It's not you," Wren had told her, running a thumb over the tiny pendant where it rested against Maggie's throat. "You're so much more than whatever outdated crap that thing represents."

Maggie hadn't answered right away. Her hand had gone reflexively to the chain as though to shield it from Wren's words. For a long beat, neither of them moved or spoke. Then Maggie nodded once—a quick dip of her chin—and tried for a smile that didn't quite reach her eyes.

"You're right," she'd said softly, almost too softly to be believed. "I'll take it off."

At the time, Wren had taken this as a victory—not over Maggie but for her—or so she'd told herself anyway. She remembered feeling oddly triumphant as Maggie unclasped the chain later and dropped it onto her bedside table without ceremony. That night Wren had kissed her deeply in gratitude or maybe reassurance; only later would she taste something salted on Maggie's cheek and dismiss it without question.

It was the next day when things shifted.

Wren had come home early—earlier than expected—and found their apartment unusually quiet, almost stifling in its stillness. She'd called out for Maggie once, twice—her voice echoing back like an empty joke—and finally heard something muffled from behind the closed bathroom door.

She opened it slowly and found Maggie perched on the edge of the bathtub with her shoulders pulled inward like armor she couldn't make fit anymore. Her head hung low; in one hand was the cross necklace tangled around trembling fingers.

"Mags?" Wren dropped to one knee in front of her without thinking or hesitating—it was instinctive almost—and tried to catch her eye.

Maggie looked up eventually through red-rimmed eyes that seemed stretched too wide and tired all at once. "I'm sorry," she whispered hoarsely before any explanation could be asked for or offered unprompted.

"For what?" Wren kept her voice level but felt some unnamed weight settle uneasily at the base of her ribs.

"I know I said I'd take it off, but I... I can't."

The guilt hit Wren like a sudden gust of wind to the chest—sharp, unexpected, and impossible to shake. She hadn't meant for this to happen. "Hey," she murmured, her voice softening. "It's okay. Just talk to me."

And Maggie had talked. Between hiccups and shaky breaths, she had explained what the necklace meant to her—how it wasn't just about faith, though that was part of it. It was about her family, about tradition, about having something solid and familiar in a world that constantly felt like it could crack and crumble without warning.

"It's..." Maggie cleared her throat and dropped her gaze toward the floor, as though the moment was too much for her to bear. "It's part of how I was raised. It's part of who I am."

Wren had reached out then—not knowing exactly what else to do—and taken Maggie's trembling hands in hers. She could feel the little cross pressed between their palms, its edges cool against her skin as though it wanted to remind her of its importance too. "I didn't get it before," Wren admitted after a beat. Her throat tightened so much that she barely managed the words that followed: "But now I do. And if it means that much to you... you should keep wearing it."

Maggie had looked up at Wren then, something unspoken yet undeniable passing between them, and Wren had said one more thing: "I'm sorry I asked you not to wear it."

The memory unraveled itself as quickly as it had surfaced—as though Wren was waking from a vivid dream where emotions lingered long after the scenes themselves evaporated. She blinked hard and shook her head like that might clear away the tightness coiling in her chest. Her gaze shifted back toward Maggie now, sleeping peacefully with the little cross on its chain resting quietly against her chest.

But just like that—because minds are rarely good at staying where they're supposed to—her thoughts veered sideways again. This time landing on yesterday's race: the Alleycat event. The rush hit first—the adrenaline flooding back like a tide she hadn't entirely been prepared for—and then came the sharp clarity of every sound, every sensation.

The starting signal hadn't fully faded before Wren launched herself forward into the chaotic pack of riders. Legs pistoning beneath her, lungs already starting their rhythmic burn; each inhale felt alive with purpose but also razor-edged with effort. The air streaked cold against her face as she weaved through competitors with precision that felt borderline reckless but necessary if she wanted any chance of staying ahead.

Her mohawk—purple strands flying wild behind her like some kind of war pennant—whipped around in the wind as she took a corner. Wren didn't just feel alive in the velocity of the ride; she thrived in it. Every second was a gamble, an unspoken challenge to gravity and fate.

She shot through alleys littered with life doing its thing: dumpsters cluttering paths like obstacles no one cared enough to move; startled pedestrians leaping aside mid-scream; neon signs flashing dirty light onto wet bricks by her head—all noise and chaos along the street telling graffiti-smeared tales.

Main Street was where everything turned dangerous.

Traffic snarled loud enough to rattle bones—horns blaring endlessly over brakes screeching protest—and yet somehow none of it was louder than the blood pounding through Wren's veins or the low hum-whir-click cadence coming from her wheels spinning too fast for comfort or caution.

And Zak—Zak had been right there ahead when everything narrowed down again into an alleyway that seemed darker than most others in memory or reality combined.

Wren could still feel how sharp every muscle felt in those moments; legs straining until they burned so bright-hot they may as well have been on fire. The alley walls blurred on either side—a moving tunnel made entirely from grime-coated brick and graffiti scrawls bleeding stories no one cared enough anymore even try decoding—and all Wren could see clearly was Zak up ahead, his blonde hair catching just enough light here and there so he seemed almost glowing: some deceptive kind of beacon promising safety while delivering exactly none.

Then came his tell—a hand dipping quick into his jersey pocket—and right behind came hers: eyes widening just far enough that time slowed itself down.

The plastic baggie came next—a small thing torn open quick-as-lightning—but what tumbled free clattered loud enough inside Wren's head anyway because their meaning struck harder than anything she'd ever heard or seen mid-race before: tacks gleaming wicked-sharp under weak alley light scattering everywhere too fast/far across pavement suddenly hostile beneath tires threatening betrayal at every rotation forward now.

"Shit," she hissed under breath already held too tight inside lungs begging release while jerking handlebars hard-left simultaneously praying blindly half against impact half against falling outright straight into Zak's dirty gamble laid plain right there across unforgiving ground below them both.

Her bike wobbled violently before steadying itself back beneath instinct-driven balance alone somehow mostly intact—but anger drove itself upward even faster/hotter/heavier than relief soon after realization: Zak wasn't playing dirty—Zak put people directly at risk without care beyond winning alone making him something lower than low.

Zak's laughter reached her, faint but deliberate, the kind that didn't just mock—it itched. Itching in a way you couldn't scratch. Wren clenched her jaw. He thought it was over. Thought he'd outpaced her. But Zak should've known better. Wren didn't lose. Not to him. Never to him.

"Tacks! Watch out!" Her voice bounced off the alley walls, jagged and hoarse, a warning flung behind her to riders she couldn't see. She wasn't sure if they'd hear or even care, but she had to yell it anyway. The tacks gleamed under thin slivers of dim light—crude little spikes scattered like caltrops in an ancient battlefield. She gritted her teeth, wondering just how many more Zak had decided to leave for them.

The alley was a blur, shadows pooling like spilled ink. Her tires slid and scrambled on the slick pavement beneath her, threatening treachery with every sharp turn. She leaned deeper into each curve, becoming one with the machine beneath her, every motion calculated instinct over thought.

Sweat clung to her skin, salted beads slipping dangerously close to her eyes. She blinked rapidly, keeping vision sharp and trained on the ragged trail ahead.

Her pulse pounded thick and heavy in her ears, like war drums driving soldiers forward into battle. The distance between her and Zak melted away inch by inch until the stiff slope of his shoulders sharpened into view. Even from behind him, she could tell he was glancing back too often now—could almost feel the nervous energy vibrating through his frame.

Wren's lips twitched into a smirk—sharp and toothy enough to cut glass if it had to. He knew she was closing in on him. More importantly, he hated it.

The adrenaline kicked through her in waves: searing heat under her skin, raw electricity arcing through every nerve ending. It didn't numb a thing—instead it made everything brighter, louder, clearer—the hiss of breath between clenched teeth, the rhythmic hum of spinning wheels slicing pavement—and somewhere further back, the chorus of shouts from riders as they dealt with Zak's mess.

The bricks gave way again up ahead; this alley spat them out onto city chaos—cars honking their protests and pedestrians frozen mid-step as cyclists surged past like restless ghosts slipping through the cracks of reality where traffic laws held no sway.

Zak hesitated at the threshold—just for a second—but a second too long for someone like Wren not to notice. She took that gap without hesitation, diving headlong into moving cars and weaving through gaps so tight they felt custom-made for her alone.

The street was hers now—her stage. Where Zak faltered, Wren thrived without pause or doubt. Every horn blare or shouted curse fed fuel into her veins as she carved paths between vehicles with surgical precision.

Ahead loomed salvation—or damnation—with its gaudy banner stretched high above pavement littered with oil stains and discarded wrappers: the finish line.

She could see him fully now: his face losing its cocky veneer moment by moment as Wren crept closer still—her breath hot against chapped lips but steady enough for one final shot across his bow.

"Choke on this, asshole!" The words came out raw and jagged-edged as she launched herself forward with everything left inside—a final burst so reckless it felt stolen from someone else entirely but wholly necessary regardless.

Her tires screeched against asphalt when momentum wasn't quite ready to let go yet—but there it was—she'd crossed first by what might've been millimeters but felt like miles.

The noise around them erupted—not quite deafening but loud enough that trying to dissect individual cheers felt futile—but none of it mattered right then because all Wren could hear was air rushing into lungs desperate for relief after being denied so long.

Zak rolled up beside her slower than before—as if disbelief weighed heavier than anger right now—and opened his mouth once words finally came back around looking for him: "How the hell did you—"

But Wren silenced him before he could finish forming sentences destined for nowhere good anyway: "Next time," she bit out between gulps of air big enough they practically hurt; "you want to win? Try not sucking so bad."

His expression shifted—anger mutating briefly toward sheepishness before settling somewhere closer toward shut-mouthed acceptance he wouldn't admit aloud anytime soon—but then again maybe silence suited Zak best after stunts like today's anyway.

The thrill of victory was dulled, as it often was, by Zak's underhanded tricks. Two couriers had gone down because of his stunt, and instead of triumphant wheels across the finish line, they dragged themselves and their battered bikes behind them like war-weary soldiers retreating from battle.

The first courier, a wiry guy with dreadlocks, had hit the pavement hard enough to make Wren flinch at the sight of his road rash. His bike had spun out behind him in a chaotic tumble of wheels and metal. His exposed skin—knees, elbows, forearms—looked raw enough to sting just from a glance, streaked with crimson and dust. His shirt hung in shreds, revealing red patches that would soon bloom into painful scabs.

The second casualty, a girl distinguished primarily by her neon green helmet (and Wren couldn't remember her name because she hadn't been around long), had fared better. She'd managed to roll with the impact but ended up in a heap nonetheless—a heap that took its time moving.

Wren had been there in an instant—adrenaline doing most of the driving—her heart pounding loud enough to drown out everything else for those first few moments. The guy with the dreads hobbled off to the side, grimacing as he held up scraped palms for inspection. The girl hadn't even made it halfway upright yet, groaning as she wrestled with what remained of her mangled bike.

"You guys okay?" The words came automatically. Wren's eyes darted over their injuries, searching for anything broken or unnaturally twisted. Road rash and bruises—not ideal but better than broken bones or worse. Relief washed over her like a cold compress on a fevered forehead... right until she caught sight of the girl's bike frame twisted grotesquely out of shape. That thing was dead on arrival.

The dreadlocked courier shook his head in disbelief, muttering through clenched teeth. "Just some road rash... but seriously, what the hell happened?"

"Zak," Wren spat without hesitation, her anger bubbling back up before she could tamp it down. "That asshole dropped caltrops in the alley."

At that, Green-Helmet Girl finally managed to pull herself upright enough to yank off her helmet, revealing an angry bruise already forming high on her cheekbone. Her voice came out sharp and incredulous: "Tacks? Are you serious right now?"

From somewhere nearby Zak piped up defensively: "It wasn't me! It was the guy in front of me! I almost wiped out too!" His voice cut through like nails scraping glass—and just as easily ignored by everyone present.

Wren's mind replayed it again now—the crashes, the bruises, Zak lounging on the sidelines like nothing had happened—and found herself biting down on the inside of her cheek hard enough to taste iron. Sure, no one had been *seriously* hurt this time—but how long until "this time" turned into something far worse? Zak's recklessness wasn't just infuriating—it was dangerous.

* * *

Mornings weren't normally an enemy for Wren—not even when the alarm clock blared too early—but today she allowed herself five minutes after silencing it before reaching for her phone on instinct. All these memories, emotions, anger. In just five minutes.

There wasn't much waiting for her on her phone: no urgent messages or missed calls demanding attention. She half-curled under the blanket, stealing the residual warmth, she glanced left at Maggie.

Maggie still slept. Wren had lived a lifetime of memories and that chick was still sleeping.

A grin spread slowly across Wren's face—the kind that started small but couldn't be stopped once it gained momentum—and before she could think better of it, she leaned over closer until her lips brushed against Maggie's bare shoulder.

She followed Maggie's spine downward with deliberate kisses soft enough not to wake her *immediately*, pausing occasionally as though savoring some invisible map etched across Maggie's skin. By the time she reached Maggie's arm, gently peppering it with small pecks along its length like raindrops hitting pavement, movement stirred beneath blankets.

"Mmm..." Maggie shifted—but only slightly—pulling more fabric over herself rather than bothering with full consciousness quite yet.

"Morning," Wren whispered as though letting Maggie stay asleep wasn't already clearly off today's agenda.

"Five more minutes..." came Maggie's muffled reply from beneath layers of cocoon-like bedding.

Wren chuckled softly—though sympathy wasn't exactly high on her list right now—and tugged at the edges of Maggie's fortress until daylight started creeping through like an uninvited guest.

"Time's up," Wren informed her lightly before yanking away what little remained between Maggie and reality—or more specifically cool morning air that earned immediate protests.

"You're *evil*," Maggie mumbled groggily—not quite awake yet still managing indignation—as Wren trailed teasing kisses down from forehead past collarbone toward less mentionable stops until giggles replaced complaints entirely.

"Effective though," Wren countered cheerfully while sliding out from bed herself onto hardwood floors chilled by autumn mornings seeping through thin walls poorly suited for insulation purposes.

"Rise and shine, sleepyhead!" Wren's voice boomed through the small apartment, bouncing off walls that hadn't yet shaken off the quiet of dawn. "Breakfast won't eat itself!"

From the bed came a muffled groan. Maggie, face buried in her pillow, muttered something unintelligible, though by tone alone it was safe to interpret as an insult. Wren smirked and headed to the kitchen, her stride as cocky as ever. "A menace who's about to make you eggs," she called back over her shoulder.

The kitchen wasn't much—a stove too close to the fridge, a single window covered by security bars and the remnants of a galvanized window well—but Wren moved around it like she had trained for this exact choreography. Fridge door open, carton of eggs and butter in hand, pan on the burner before the door swung shut again. She cranked the heat a little higher than medium because patience wasn't her strong suit. The butter hit the pan with a sizzle sharp enough to cut through any lingering sleepiness in the air.

Wren cracked three eggs into a bowl, whisking them briskly—efficiently—like this was some culinary mission she needed to accomplish before any distractions arose. Her eyes stayed fixed on the mixture as she poured it into the shimmering butter. The hiss and pop of eggs hitting heat filled her ears as she stirred.

"Maggie!" Wren didn't look up from her work; not ruining breakfast required vigilance. "You better be getting dressed!"

There was a pause—no reply—then Maggie's voice drifted from the other room. "I'm on it!" Her casual tone suggested otherwise.

Wren stirred methodically, scraping the pan just before anything had the chance to stick. From behind her came the faint rustle of fabric and soft steps on hardwood—a sound that normally wouldn't warrant much attention but now pricked at her awareness like a static charge before lightning strikes.

She turned her head but immediately froze. Maggie stood in the doorway—not quite dressed, not quite undressed—with her courier uniform bunched loosely in one hand and an unmistakable glint of mischief lighting up her eyes.

"Well," Wren said after a beat, arching an eyebrow in mock appraisal as she leaned one arm against the counter for effect. "This is shaping up to be dinner *and* a show."

Maggie smirked but said nothing. Instead, with deliberate intention, she began pulling on her cycling shorts—the kind that clung like they'd been painted on—as though dressing required choreography only she knew. Her hips swayed subtly with each movement, unhurried yet calculated enough to dare someone to look away.

Wren did not look away.

She might have burned breakfast right then if not for spitting hot butter hitting her hand. A well-timed stir saved both her eggs and perhaps her pride, though neither emerged entirely unscathed. Still half-distracted—because who wouldn't be?—she called out toward Maggie without meeting her gaze: "You're killing me here, babe."

From across the room came an exaggerated laugh—not quite mocking but close enough. Maggie zipped up her jersey slowly now—and clearly for effect—the faint metallic rasp somehow louder than even Wren's agitated stirring.

Turning back toward the stove, Wren exhaled sharply through her nose and gave herself a mental shake—all focus now on salvaging what remained of breakfast before it was too far gone in more ways than one.

Moments later, Maggie padded toward her with that same smirk still playing on her lips—not growing or fading but simply existing there like it had found permanent residence—and slid an arm casually around Wren's waist. The gesture was warm but light enough to make someone wonder whether affection or teasing had been its primary purpose.

Then came Maggie's voice: low, near-whispered next to Wren's ear but clear enough to snap anyone fully awake: "Damn. Your ass is *ridiculous*. What's your secret?"

Wren felt rather than saw Maggie's grin widening as she reached back instinctively with one hand—not so much pushing Maggie away as pretending she might—but only muttered dryly while flexing under Maggie's touch: "Good genes and bad decisions."

The laugh that escaped Maggie turned real then—not performative anymore—and before long Wren found herself laughing too despite everything (or maybe because of everything). For a few seconds neither spoke; they just stood there in their too-small kitchen with its too-close counters pressed up against whatever space existed between them while their poorly contained giggles filled every remaining inch.

Eventually—because some things could only wait so long—the eggs were scooped onto plates while Maggie busied herself pulling tortillas from the pantry shelf above their heads like it was all part of some unspoken pact about balance: one person starts what another finishes until everything—including them—falls together just right.

"Avocado?" That was all she said without looking up as shredded cheddar spilled over tortilla edges onto countertops no one would bother wiping down until at least tomorrow night.

Wren nodded automatically before realizing no one could see nods when their back was turned and instead reached into the fruit bowl where avocados always sat like small green promises, each one whispering about ripeness but almost always delivering a damn lie.

The knife sliced cleanly through peel first then flesh—a single twist revealing pale green perfection beneath tougher exteriors (a metaphor if ever there was one)—before fingers worked deftly at peeling skins away altogether until nothing remained hidden anymore.

Wren sliced through the avocado halves with mechanical precision. The soft flesh gave way easily to the spoon, leaving behind clean, hollowed shells. She placed the smooth, green mounds onto the cutting board, her knife rhythmically chopping them into uniform slices. The blade moved deliberately, each motion precise and controlled. Wren liked tasks like this, things she could masterfully execute without much thought. It left room in her mind for other matters.

Some of the avocado clung stubbornly to her fingers. She noticed it absently at first, the cool slickness of it against her skin a subtle contrast to the warmth of the sunlit kitchen. As she wiped her hands on a dish towel, an idea surfaced, unbidden and mischievous.

"Hey, Mags." Wren held up a finger smeared with avocado and wiggled it in Maggie's direction. "Want a taste?"

Maggie looked up from grating cheese, her brows raised in curiosity until she saw Wren's finger extended toward her like some kind of slick offering. A slow grin crept across Maggie's face—one of those playful smiles that always left Wren wondering what exactly was going on behind those sharp blue eyes. Maggie set down the grater and crossed the small kitchen space with a measured step.

Without a word and without breaking eye contact, Maggie leaned in close and took Wren's finger into her mouth. Her lips sealed around it as if this were perfectly normal breakfast preparation behavior. Her tongue flicked lightly against Wren's skin as she licked off every trace of avocado, deliberate but unhurried.

Wren stopped breathing—or she thought she did—her pulse stuttering in response to this unexpected turn of events. Maggie finally released her finger with a soft pop before straightening up with that same infuriating grin.

"Mmm," Maggie murmured approvingly. "Tastes better off you."

"Tease," Wren muttered under her breath, though there wasn't much weight behind it. Her voice had dropped an octave she hadn't intended.

Maggie winked at her before turning back to finish assembling the burritos as though nothing had just happened. Wren blinked herself back into focus and returned to slicing avocados, though now her movements were less steady than before.

They settled at their narrow kitchen table—with its perpetually wobbly leg that no amount of folded napkins ever seemed to fix—and tucked into breakfast. Sunlight poured through the windows and pooled onto their plates like honey. The homemade cheese-and-avocado-and-jam-the-egg-in-there-too burritos came together perfectly—simple food elevated by fresh ingredients—but for all their culinary success, they ate almost too quickly to appreciate it.

"So," Wren said mid-bite, catching a drip of salsa with the back of her hand before it hit her plate. "You ready for tonight?"

Maggie's face lit up like someone had flipped a switch inside her. "The Vista?" Her smile widened into something near childlike excitement. "Hell yes—I've been counting down all week."

Wren grinned back at her partner's enthusiasm—it was impossible not to get caught up in it. "I know! And did you see they added DJ Spindle Sister last minute?"

"No way," Maggie gasped through a mouthful of food before choking on her own excitement.

"Whoa—careful there," Wren said as she leaned forward to pat Maggie's back once firmly in case needed assistance was required. "Don't die before we even get there."

Wren finished up the dishes and finally dressed. She walked over to the dresser, her toes curling against the cool hardwood floor. She peeled off her oversized t-shirt, tossing it onto the cluttered floor.

"Use the laundry basket!" Maggie protested.

Wren shimmied out of her baggy boxers, kicking them into the laundry basket. The morning air kissed her skin, raising goosebumps along her arms and legs. Wren rummaged through her drawer, fishing out a clean pair of underwear.

She slipped them on, the soft cotton hugging her curves. Next came the socks, thin and moisture-wicking. Wren sat on the edge of the bed, rolling them up her calves with care, smoothing out any wrinkles.

Standing again, she grabbed her cycling shorts from the back of a chair. Wren stepped into them, tugging them up her legs. The spandex was a second layer of skin, compressing her muscles. She adjusted the waistband, making sure it sat just right on her hips.

Finally, Wren reached for her cycling jersey. She pulled it over her head, the fabric sliding down her torso. Her arms snaked through the sleeves, the material stretching to accommodate her muscular build. She tugged at the hem, straightening out any bunches.

The jersey fit snugly, like a glove molded to her body. Wren rolled her shoulders, feeling the fabric move with her. She flexed her arms, testing the range of motion. Satisfied, Wren zipped up her jersey, her fingers lingering on the collar. The familiar fabric hugged her body, but it didn't bring the usual comfort. A nagging unease gnawed at her gut, a leftover from yesterday's wild chase.

She glanced at Maggie and forced a smile, not wanting to worry her girlfriend.

"You okay?" Maggie asked.

"Yeah, just thinking about work," Wren replied, avoiding eye contact.

She busied herself with packing her courier bag, double-checking her gear. Helmet, check. Gloves, check. Water bottle, check. Her hand brushed against the jumbo auto body marker tucked in a side pocket. A small smirk played on her lips as she remembered the satisfying squeak it made against car windows.

"Thinking about the race again?" Maggie probed, always perceptive.

She thought back to yesterday's race, the scatter of tacks on the pavement, the swerve of her bike. The memory sent a shiver down her spine.

"I just... I can't stand working with that cheating bastard," Wren muttered, zipping her bag with more force than necessary.

Maggie wrapped her arms around Wren's waist, resting her chin on her shoulder.

"You can't let him get to you," Maggie said softly. "You're better than that."

Wren leaned back into the embrace, letting out a long sigh. "I know, I know. It's just... the city's dangerous enough without assholes like him making it worse."

Maggie pulled away and flopped onto the bed. "I don't wanna go. Let's stay in bed all day," she said as seductively as she could with her courier bag jammed into her back.

Wren stood in the doorway, her gaze settling on Maggie sprawled across the bed. One leg dangled off the side, and her courier bag—her ever-present companion—now sat nestled beside her like a loyal pet waiting for its next command. She was fully dressed for work, but there she lay anyway, flat on her back as though getting out of bed was again an insurmountable task. Wren let her eyes linger.

"You planning on moving anytime today?" Wren asked, stepping closer. Her voice carried that teasing lilt Maggie had come to expect—half playful, half challenging.

Maggie groaned in response but didn't bother opening her eyes. "Maybe," she said at last, dragging out the word as though even speaking required monumental effort.

Wren crouched down and lifted Maggie's dangling foot onto the bed with deliberate carelessness. The movement jolted Maggie just enough to make her sigh dramatically, but not enough to spur her into action. Without waiting for an invitation, Wren dropped onto the mattress beside her. The bed bounced under the added weight as Wren shifted to prop herself up on one elbow.

Maggie turned her head toward Wren, a lazy smile lighting up her face. "You're awfully cozy for someone who was just lecturing me about getting up," she murmured.

"Don't tempt me," Wren countered, brushing a stray curl away from Maggie's face. "I'd love nothing more than to stay here all day with you. But those bills? They don't pay themselves."

That earned another groan from Maggie—this one louder and more theatrical. She threw an arm over her eyes like some tragic figure in an old movie. "Why did we pick careers that keep us broke and bruised?"

"Because deep down we thrive on chaos," Wren said dryly, absentmindedly drawing circles across Maggie's forearm with the tip of her finger.

Maggie peeked out from under her arm, one eyebrow quirking upward. "Speak for yourself. I just like biking through the city without getting stuck in traffic."

Wren grinned at that—a mischievous grin that made Maggie's stomach flip even after all this time. "Sure you do," she said. "Is that why you once outran a cop car?"

"That was *one time*," Maggie shot back quickly, though laughter danced in her voice now. "And it happened because *someone* dared me."

"Best dare I ever made," Wren replied softly, leaning closer until their faces were only inches apart. "Well... second best."

Before Maggie could ask what the first was—or maybe she already knew—Wren closed the distance between them and pressed her lips to Maggie's in a tender kiss that stretched out longer than either of them intended.

When they pulled apart, they stayed there for a moment longer, faces so close their noses almost brushed. Neither of them spoke; there didn't seem to be any need to fill the silence between them as they lay tangled together on the bed. Outside, faint morning sounds filtered through the thin apartment walls—the distant honk of a car horn, someone slamming a door—but they felt far away and unimportant.

The buzz of Maggie's phone cut through the stillness like a knife. It vibrated angrily against the nightstand until Maggie reached over to grab it. She squinted at the screen as if it might go away if she stared hard enough.

"What is it?" Wren asked without looking up.

Maggie frowned and held up the phone so Wren could see for herself. On the screen glared a new text message—from Karen.

Still wasting your potential on that ridiculous bike job? When are you going to grow up and get a real career?

Wren read it twice before sitting up abruptly. The soft fondness in her expression hardened into something much sharper, much angrier.

"Your mom's an asshole," she said flatly.

"She means well," Maggie mumbled automatically, but there wasn't much weight behind it—no real conviction in defending Karen today.

"She means to control you," Wren snapped back without hesitation. Her fingers found their way into Maggie's hair again—soothing this time instead of teasing—and stayed there, anchoring both in place. "You're amazing at what you do. You love it."

Maggie didn't respond right away, but when she finally did look back at Wren, there was gratitude shining in her tired eyes—a quiet kind of warmth that didn't need words behind it.

"Thanks," she whispered simply.

Wren answered by pressing a kiss to Maggie's temple—a lingering gesture meant more as reassurance than affection this time—and then leaned back with renewed energy.

"Come on," she said briskly as she stood up and offered Maggie a hand. "Let's go show Karen exactly how much potential you're wasting."

For once, Maggie smiled at that name—not because anything about Karen had changed but because standing here now with Wren reminding her what mattered most felt like enough to drown out even Karen's loudest disapproval... at least for one more day.

Maggie groaned but eventually swung her legs over the side of the bed, standing beside Wren by the door. "I hate mornings," she mumbled, grabbing her helmet. She always said this, as though declaring it daily might somehow change the cruel fact of mornings existing.

Wren just grinned. She couldn't resist. Before Maggie could settle the helmet on her head, Wren hooked her fingers into Maggie's messenger bag strap and pulled her close, her lips capturing Maggie's in a kiss that started as sweet and ended somewhere more mischievous. Her hands wandered, predictably and un-apologetically, to Maggie's backside until Maggie swatted them away with mock indignation. "Save it for later," Maggie murmured, but there was no real heat behind the words. She smiled. "Please."

Wren turned next to Argo, her bike leaning against the wall like an old friend waiting patiently for adventure. "Morning, beautiful," she said under her breath, running a hand along its frame. Argo never slapped her hands away. The black aluminum tubing gleamed faintly in their dim basement light. A smudge on the crossbar caught her attention—a crime against Argo's otherwise pristine condition—and Wren swiftly wiped it away with her sleeve. There. Perfect again.

Kneeling down, she unzipped Argo's under-seat toolkit and gave everything a quick once-over: spare tube, tire levers, multitool, patch kit—all accounted for. It was a ritual by now, one she could perform blindfolded if needed.

Meanwhile, Maggie grabbed Bridger—her own bike—from its usual spot near the laundry hamper. Bridger wasn't flashy like Argo but solid and dependable in a way that fit Maggie perfectly. Wren often teased Maggie about Bridger's lack of personality; Maggie always countered that this made Bridger the ideal partner for long-haul rides—uncomplicated and steady.

Together, they wrestled their bikes up the steep staircase leading out of their basement apartment. The steps creaked ominously under their weight, as they did every morning, though neither of them seemed particularly motivated to do anything about it. Wren took the lead with Argo balanced easily across her shoulder while Maggie followed close behind with Bridger bumping against her hip.

The narrow staircase finally spit them out into open air. Morning light spilled across everything—the sidewalk damp from last night's rain, the dew clinging stubbornly to blades of grass along the fence line. A symphony of urban noises greeted them: distant car horns blaring in frustration, pigeons shuffling on wires overhead, a jogger's rhythmic footfalls echoing faintly against asphalt.

7:51 a.m.

They guided their bikes along a gravel path beside the house that Fannie Severina—their landlady—insisted remain gravel despite all logic suggesting it would be easier paved over. The crunch of tires on loose stone blended with muted birdsong as they rounded toward the front yard.

And there she was: Fannie Severina herself, perched on her porch rocker like some benevolent queen surveying her bustling kingdom of tenants and patchwork gardens. Her silver hair glinted in the sun, catching highlights that seemed almost too perfect to belong to anyone not starring in a shampoo commercial. Her knitting needles clicked rhythmically in her lap—a metronome keeping time with nothing in particular except maybe life itself.

"Morning!" Wren called out cheerfully as she wheeled Argo up near the porch steps.

Fannie peered over her glasses at them with mock suspicion before breaking into an indulgent smile. "Well now," she said warmly. "If it isn't my favorite rabble-rousers." She inspected them both like someone appraising auction items before adding dryly: "Out saving Brooklyn one delivery at a time?"

Maggie leaned Bridger against the porch railing and grinned as she wiped sweat off her brow despite barely being awake long enough to generate any reason for sweating yet. "Something like that," she replied before nodding toward Fannie's lap. "What're you working on now?"

Fannie held up an absurdly colorful bundle of wool—emerald green tangled with fiery orange knotted alongside streaks of sapphire blue so bright you half-expected them to glow after sundown—which gave off strong vibes of something plucked straight from an acid-induced fever dream circa 1968.

"Just something cozy for these old bones come winter," Fannie said with a wink while tugging lightly at one strand to tighten it just so.

Wren tilted her head theatrically while squinting at Fannie's creation like someone puzzling over abstract art at MOMA: intrigued but alarmed. Then she let out an impressed whistle that wasn't entirely sarcastic. "Wow," she said finally. "That looks... groovy? Psychedelic? Should we be worried you're about to dust off some tie-dye shirts and break out into protest songs?"

Fannie raised an eyebrow without missing a single click of her needles. "You say 'worried' like it'd be a bad thing."

Maggie laughed while Wren smirked before shaking her head fondly—because if anyone could pull off reliving their hippie days while still scolding tenants about late rent checks—it was Fannie Severina without question or competition.

Fannie's eyes lit up, the deep creases in her face softening as though someone had turned back the clock just a little. She beamed at Wren and Maggie, the kind of smile that felt like sunshine after a long, gray stretch. "You two be careful out there," she said, tilting her head, her voice laced with the unmistakable edge of motherly concern. Then, with a sly grin: "And Wren, keep those ears open for anything juicy, will you? This old lady needs her daily fix of neighborhood drama."

Wren smirked and gave an exaggerated salute. "Consider me your official gossip courier."

Fannie chuckled softly, but then her expression changed in an instant. Her brow furrowed deeply, her lips pressing into a tight line as she jabbed a knotted finger toward the end of the block. "Speaking of drama—have you seen that monstrosity?"

Wren turned to follow Fannie's gaze and immediately spotted it—a garish sign standing boldly at the corner like an unwanted guest overstaying its welcome. The bright letters screamed: *COMING SOON: LUXURY CONDO-MINIUMS—INVEST IN YOUR FUTURE TODAY!*

"Can you believe it?" Fannie huffed, her knitting needles clicking sharply now, as if they too shared her outrage. "They're planning to tear down half this block for some ridiculous condos. Just what we need—more yuppies swarming in like they own the place."

Anger sparked in Wren's chest—not fiery exactly, but hot enough to sting. "Are you serious? That's bullshit."

Fannie nodded emphatically, her knitting needles clacking with renewed energy. "You said it, honey. Forty years I've been here—you hear me? Forty years—and now they wanna shove us out like we're last week's garbage to make way for their overpriced shoeboxes." She shook her head slowly and sighed, shoulders sinking as though the fight had already begun to sap her strength. "It's a shame is what it is... A real damn shame."

"That's awful," Maggie said quietly from beside Wren, her forehead creased with worry. "Is there anything you can do about it?"

Fannie sighed again and waved one hand dismissively while the other kept right on knitting. "We're trying. We've got a petition going—door-to-door signatures and all that—but you know how these things go." Her voice was heavy with resignation. "Money talks. The rest of us? We're just background noise."

Wren's jaw tightened as her mind whirred into overdrive. Ideas tumbled in—most of them bad, a few downright illegal—but before she could even hint at one of them aloud, Maggie caught her eye and gave a small shake of her head. Subtle but firm enough to stop Wren mid-thought.

Instead, Wren nodded solemnly and said, "We'll keep an eye out for anything that might help." She paused and glanced sideways at Fannie before adding with a wry smile: "But seriously... Are you sure this neighborhood can get any worse? I mean, Maggie and I already live here."

Fannie froze for half a beat before throwing back her head and laughing—a sound so full-bodied it seemed to ripple through every inch of her frame until even the colorful wool in her lap bounced along merrily with it.

"Oh!" she gasped between bursts of laughter as tears gathered at the corners of her eyes. "Oh, you! Always running your mouth." She reached up to dab at her eyes with one shaky hand.

Maggie groaned in mock exasperation beside them while swatting Wren lightly on the arm. "Speak for yourself," she said dryly. "I'm clearly the model citizen here."

Wren winked at Fannie while Maggie adjusted the strap on her helmet with deliberate precision. There was an ease in these moments—the kind that made

Wren feel unexpectedly grounded despite everything happening just outside their crumbling home.

Finally satisfied with her adjustments, Maggie swung one leg over the bike frame and straightened up just enough to fix Wren with what could only be described as *the look*. Her eyes were steady now—not harsh exactly but serious enough to make it clear she wasn't about to let Wren brush off whatever was coming next.

"Be careful out there," Maggie said firmly as she settled onto the seat and planted both feet on either side for balance. Her tone softened when she added: "No crazy stunts today."

Wren pressed one hand flat against her chest as though mortally offended by the implication. "Who—me?" she asked innocently before letting a grin break through anyway. "I'm always careful."

Maggie raised an eyebrow—the skeptical kind—and didn't even bother replying before continuing anyway: "Just... Look out for yourself, okay? And watch for taxis—and potholes—and—"

"Okay! Okay!" Wren interrupted with a laugh that filled the small space between them easily enough to cut Maggie off mid-list. She threw up both hands dramatically as though surrendering under duress and added quickly: "Scout's honor—I'll be good."

Maggie didn't look entirely convinced but gave Wren one last lingering glance before pedaling away down the street at an easy pace that still managed to exude control somehow—like everything else she did.

Wren stayed where she was for another long moment watching—noticing how effortlessly Maggie weaved around early morning traffic without hesitating once or losing focus even when distracted drivers honked impatiently nearby.

The silence stretched thin until Fannie cleared her throat loudly behind Wren's shoulder again.

"Well," Fannie said at last while gesturing faintly toward where Maggie had disappeared into traffic, "...if she doesn't come back later complaining about *you*, then I'll eat my yarn stash."

Wren pushed off hard, and there it was—that first jolt of exhilaration, a sensation that uncoiled through her like static electricity. The wind found its way into her hair, teasing loose strands across her face, a reminder of freedom disguised as chaos. Ahead, the stop sign stood defiant, its red octagon unwavering like an authority figure Wren refused to acknowledge.

She leaned forward, body low over the handlebars, her feet pressing harder against the pedals as she picked up speed. The stop sign blurred past her, ignored and forgotten almost as quickly as it came. A familiar heat spread through her chest as adrenaline surged—the kind of high that made everything sharper: the hiss of tires on asphalt, the distant droning of a car alarm somewhere down the block, even Fannie's predictable expression in Wren's peripheral vision. She dared a glance in her rearview mirror and there it was. The exact look she expected—an exhausted shake of the head with just enough fondness to keep it from becoming scolding.

Wren smiled at that She didn't wave or acknowledge Fannie further; there was no time for that. Her mind had already shifted forward to the next turn, the next stretch of road, the next thrill waiting just a few blocks away. Another day had begun—an unpredictable collision of chaos and rhythm—and Wren had every intention of meeting it head-on.

Traffic was dense but alive—almost sentient in its movement—and Wren wove herself into it like thread through fabric. Her heart kept time with her legs: steady pushes and pulls countered by the shallow breaths she took to keep pace. Around her, the city blared out its usual morning soundtrack—a discordant composition of honking horns and voices raised in anger or urgency—and yet she absorbed it all with something close to joy.

Out of nowhere (or perhaps not—these things rarely came out of nowhere if you were paying attention), a yellow taxi swung into her lane too quickly for comfort. Its bulk loomed closer than Wren would have liked, but still she didn't flinch. Instead, she leaned to one side and slipped into the impossibly narrow space between the cab and a parked sedan—a calculated risk executed with precision. The driver shouted something after her, but his words were lost before they reached her ears; all that lingered was their texture—rough around the edges but already forgotten.

Ahead, traffic slowed to an ugly standstill—a bottleneck without explanation. Wren's gaze darted instinctively left and right until it landed on salvation: an alley tucked between two squat brownstones, its mouth dark and narrow but undeniably inviting. She veered toward it without hesitation, tires spitting gravel as she made the sharp turn onto uneven ground.

The alley wasn't forgiving—not that Wren expected it to be—but she rode through its challenges like someone who knew all its tricks by heart. Overstuffed trash cans crowded around corners made tighter by sagging fire escapes overhead; shafts of aggressive sunlight blinded her through gaps wherever they could find an opening. Her focus narrowed with each obstacle conquered until finally she emerged on another street altogether, startling pigeons into sudden flight.

Their wings beat arrhythmically against each other in protest before scattering into disorganized freedom above her head—a momentary burst of gray feathers drifting back toward earth long after Wren had left them behind. She grinned at their indignation but didn't slow down; instead, she scanned ahead for options and saw one immediately: a sidewalk clear enough to promise a shortcut past snarled cars stretching for blocks.

A quick glance confirmed no cops in sight—not that they usually cared—but there were pedestrians aplenty. Wren hopped onto the curb anyway because hesitation would make things worse. Shouts followed as people scrambled out of her way ("Watch where you're going!" "Hey! Slow down!"), but she tossed apologies behind her without turning around or slowing down—it counted if you said sorry whether they believed you meant it or not.

A particularly irate voice called louder than others, something about irresponsibility or danger or whatever else people always said when they didn't understand what drove someone like Wren to keep moving forward at any cost. She laughed lightly—not mockingly but out of something closer to relief—and let herself be carried away by momentum once again.

The park offered a reprieve from concrete monotony—a stretch where grass struggled valiantly against cracking pathways riddled with weeds poking through wherever they could find space. Kids played nearby; their laughter brightened something inside Wren briefly before fading back into background noise like everything else tended to do eventually. She popped a wheelie without planning to—just muscle memory responding automatically—and their cheers followed even long after she'd passed them by.

Then it was back onto another main road where traffic thinned just enough for rhythm rather than chaos to take hold again momentarily: legs pumping steadily; lungs working in harmony; sweat rolling unnoticed along temples until caught briefly by wind gusts smelling faintly (if improbably) of both fresh bagels and exhaust fumes mingling together.

The bike lane narrowed ahead thanks to some oblivious delivery truck blocking part of the lane. But obstacles never stopped being opportunities if viewed correctly, and so when Wren noticed a flatbed stopped in traffic parallel nearby? A chance presented itself clearly enough: build speed first...then launch skyward...stick the landing beyond the obstacle...because some mornings simply demanded proper punctuation marks before moving forward once more.

Adrenaline hummed in Wren's veins, the faint shouts of scattered bystanders barely registering over the pounding rhythm in her chest. These were the moments she craved—not just freedom, but the kind of unfiltered chaos that sharpened her senses and blurred everything else into static.

Velocity wasn't just speed; it was something sharper, something more calculated—a delicate threading of the needle through Brooklyn's anarchic streets. She needed it in her veins. The buildings loomed around her, a jagged, indifferent skyline of glass and steel. Wren leaned into the pulse of it all, her legs pumping, her breath coming fast and shallow, until—

The sedan came out of nowhere. Silver, hulking, impatient. It cut into the bike lane as though she didn't exist.

"Shit!" she hissed through clenched teeth, veering hard to avoid its lumbering bulk. The tires wobbled dangerously beneath her for one sickening second before steadying again. Anger flared hot and fast in her chest. Without thinking—because thinking was always too slow—she lashed out, swinging her shoe into the car's rear panel. Her foot hit solid metal with a satisfying thud that reverberated up her leg, but the car didn't even flinch. Damnit.

Before she could savor it—or regret it—the guttural growl of another engine pulled up beside her. A black sedan this time, its driver leaning halfway out of his open window. His face was red, his mouth working furiously even before she heard him shout.

"Watch where you're going, you crazy bitch!" He spat the last word like venom, flecks of saliva catching the light as they flew toward her.

Wren's righteous fury burned brighter now—it always did when faced with men like this one, puffed up and furious in their suits like over-filled balloons waiting to burst. Her hand moved to her pocket without hesitation; by now it was muscle memory. Fingers found smooth plastic—her trusty black jumbo marker—and pulled it free.

The man was still yelling when she leaned in close and struck with one bold stroke across his half-raised window: a thick, unmistakable black smear that scrawled across the pristine glass like an angry signature. His words cut off mid-insult as his face twisted into wide-eyed outrage.

He fumbled for his door handle while Wren was already moving again because standing still wasn't an option anymore—no matter how tempting it might have been to watch him sputter like a deflated tire. She hoped he hadn't put the car in park.

Her bike shot forward as she swerved sharply toward the sidewalk, slipping between startled pedestrians who yelped and scattered in her wake. She didn't bother apologizing; there wasn't time for niceties when everything behind you felt like it might collapse if you stopped moving for even a second.

Up ahead: stairs. She caught sight of them just beyond an office building entrance—a daunting stone gauntlet lined with cold precision—and aimed herself toward them on impulse more than strategy. The first jolt nearly threw her off balance; after that came another bump and another until each pedal stroke burned deep into her thighs.

She didn't look back when she reached the top—not until she'd slipped inside behind someone exiting through a set of heavy glass doors. The air conditioning hit her like a slap as she wove through the lobby with reckless abandon, darting between clusters of startled office workers clutching their coffee cups too late to save them from spilling.

"Hey!" somebody shouted as liquid hit tile floors and shoes squeaked in protest. Behind her voices rose louder: security guards yelling now—but yelling wasn't catching.

She rounded a corner at full tilt before bursting through a sliding door on instinct alone; daylight shattered across her vision like an explosion as she emerged onto a completely different street.

For half a block all she could hear was laughter bubbling up uncontrollably from somewhere deep inside—a release valve turned loose after too much pressure building all at once. It wasn't just adrenaline; it was something sharper than joy but softer than despair—something alive that thrived on edges most people avoided.

Brooklyn traffic swallowed her whole again almost instantly but Wren didn't care because this felt right—or at least close enough to right for now—and that had to be enough.

The morning rush stretched out ahead of her like an obstacle course designed specifically for survivalists or thrill-seekers or fools depending on your point of view (Wren figured she qualified as all three). Cars honked aggressively at nothing in particular while delivery vans blocked bike lanes entirely without apology or acknowledgment.

One such van loomed just ahead—white paint dulled by grime and indifference—as though daring someone to call it out on its blatant disregard for anything resembling order or fairness.

Those things mattered so much to Wren.

"Fucking hell," Wren muttered under her breath without breaking stride—not because she expected anyone else to hear but because words sometimes helped smooth over frustration long enough to keep moving forward anyway.

Excitement coursed through Wren's veins as she threw a glance back at the offending truck. "Hey, asshole!" she yelled, her voice cutting through the cacophony of honking horns and engine rumbles. "This look like a damn loading zone to you?"

The driver—a burly guy with an eternal scowl etched into his face—responded by flipping her off. Wren responded in kind, raising her middle finger high and proud as a grin cut across her face.

She veered back into traffic with nonchalance and didn't flinch when horns blared angrily around her like some kind of urban symphony composed entirely from rage and impatience.

It was close—an SUV skimmed past so near that air rushed against her skin—but close didn't count unless you let it stop you altogether.

And Wren never let anything stop her altogether—not yet anyway.

The city blurred around her as she gained speed, weaving between cars as though it were second nature. Her mohawk slashed through the wind like a violet banner of rebellion, a bright streak against the monotony of concrete walls and dull skies. Her bike hummed beneath her, wheels spinning in tune with the rhythm of her pulse.

And then it happened—the thing that always seemed inevitable in a city full of people who thought they were alone in it. A man stepped off the curb directly into her path. Head down, eyes glued to his phone, he might as well have been walking on another planet. Wren's breath hitched as she dinged her bell frantically—once, twice, three times.

"Move it, dickhead!" she shouted, her voice raw with fury. She gritted her teeth as adrenaline flooded her system and narrowed her focus on this intruder in her lane—or rather this intruder in *her* city.

The man didn't hear—or if he did, he chose ignorance over self-preservation—and continued ambling into danger like some zombie mindlessly seeking brains but finding likes instead. At the last possible second, Wren jammed on the brakes with all the force of someone trying to halt time itself.

Her tires screeched loudly enough to make pedestrians on either side flinch. The front wheel stopped just short of turning his legs into collateral damage.

Finally—*finally*—the man looked up from his screen. His face was pale now, all color drained by delayed comprehension of how close he'd come to an unplanned hospital visit. Wren glared at him hard, as though she could drill common sense directly into his skull through sheer force of will.

"Get your head out of your screen, loser!" she snapped, pulling each word taut with anger until they felt sharp enough to slash across any remaining delusions of invincibility he might have harbored.

His startled expression faltered just long enough for him to lose grip on his phone—it slipped from his hand and clattered uselessly onto the pavement below—and Wren seized that moment like a sprinter off the starting block.

Before he could recover or stammer out some half-hearted apology (or worse yet, justification), she was pedaling away again, leaving him behind in a gust of wind laced with fumes and frustration. She didn't glance back; she didn't need to know how stunned he looked or whether he'd bent down to retrieve his precious device off dirty asphalt—it wasn't like it mattered anyway.

For maybe two minutes—three tops—the ride turned smooth again: no cars swerving too close to clip her handlebars; no jaywalkers pretending traffic laws didn't apply when their coffee cups ran low; no oblivious tourists clogging up bike lanes like cholesterol in an artery. The sun even managed to break through the smog for half a second or two and touch her face with faint warmth before disappearing behind clouds again.

Wren dared to breathe deeply—not that fresh air was ever on offer here—and let herself revel in those rare moments when riding wasn't an exercise in dodging idiots or fighting chaos but simply existing within it.

Which made what happened next all the more inevitable.

She saw them before they saw *her*. A cluster of tourists huddled together near the curb—prime offenders decked out in matching "I ♥ NY" T-shirts and weighed down by overstuffed fanny packs that bounced against their hips with every aimless shuffle forward or backward they took as they debated picture angles for reasons only they understood.

"You've got to be kidding me," she muttered under her breath as she scouted for any possible gap between them—a sliver wide enough for both bike and rider to squeeze through without incident (or casualties). She gritted her teeth and adjusted course leftward before angling sharply right toward what looked like just enough space between oblivion and impact.

It wasn't clean—these things never were—but it worked well enough: She threaded herself between two particularly unaware culprits: a couple whose shopping bags seemed swollen beyond reason. She narrowly avoided clipping their matching elbows as she slipped back into open space beyond them.

Someone yelled "Hey!" after her—not one of hers but theirs—and maybe there was indignation behind that single syllable or maybe just surprise at having been brushed aside by something moving faster than their collective thoughts ever could.

Wren twisted halfway around just long enough for one parting shot cast over one shoulder: "Go back home already! Jersey misses you!"

Wren's phone buzzed against her thigh, the vibration insistent. She groaned—loudly this time—and fished it out of her pocket without breaking stride. Balancing her bike with one hand, she darted between a parked car and an old truck belching exhaust, her movements fluid and practiced.

Sure enough, Willie's name lit up the screen. "ETA?" read the message, curt and characteristically impatient.

Wren rolled her eyes and let out a dramatic sigh, though there was no one to hear it. With her thumb, she quickly tapped out, "OMY. There soon," before switching her focus back to the road.

She was about to pocket her phone when another notification popped up. This one was from Dennis, one of her regulars—a guy with deep pockets and simple tastes who always tipped well.

"Usual breakfast order. ASAP if possible," it read.

A grin ripped across Wren's mouth. Dennis was reliable in a way most of her life wasn't. She sent back a quick "Got it" and veered off course, her legs pumping harder as she rerouted toward his favorite diner.

The city unfurled like it always did, loud and alive and utterly indifferent to her presence. Wren weaved through the mess with ease—dodging potholes, skirting jaywalkers, and squeezing past a lumbering delivery truck hogging two lanes.

She calculated her route on the fly, leaning into her pedals as she veered into an alley. The narrow space reeked of garbage and piss, but it shaved precious seconds off her time. A startled orange tabby bolted for cover, its yowl of protest echoing as Wren shot past.

Back on the main street, she spotted the diner ahead: a small, weathered joint tucked into the corner, easy to miss if you didn't know it was there. The smell hit her first—grease, coffee, and something vaguely sweet.

Wren slowed, coasting to a stop in front of the walk-up window. "Two blueberry muffins and a large black coffee," she called out as she propped her bike against the wall with one hand. Her other hand fished out her phone, tapping it against the payment terminal while the teenager behind the counter punched in her order with all the enthusiasm of a brick.

While waiting, Wren opened her FonBill app and fired off a message to Dennis with his total, adding her usual $5 delivery fee. She was pocketing her phone when it buzzed again. A notification flashed: **Payment received—$10 tip included.**

"Nice," she murmured as she glanced at the kid handing her the bag. She stuffed the muffins and coffee into her insulated carrier, secured it to her bike, and hopped back on.

The city was chaos, but it was *her* chaos. And with Dennis's breakfast secured, Wren felt like she'd just won a small, private victory.

Wren kicked off at a steady pace, her legs pumping rhythmically as she merged into the chaos of the morning traffic. The smell of freshly baked muffins wafted up from the bag hanging off her handlebars, teasing her. She ignored it. Dennis was waiting, and Wren had a reputation to uphold.

Argo, her trusty bike, glided through the mess with the same effortless precision she demanded of herself. They were a team, navigating potholes and the occasional rogue cab cutting across two lanes.

She arrived at Dennis's building five minutes later: a sprawling brown brick monolith stretching nearly two blocks. Wren swung off Argo in one practiced motion, her sneakers hitting the pavement with a soft thud as she locked the bike to a nearby rack. The building loomed over her, weathered but sturdy, its cracked paint and creeping ivy bearing the scars of decades of city life.

She adjusted the bag on her shoulder and headed for the entrance, fingers jabbing Dennis's name. Her finger hovered for half a second before pressing down. The harsh buzz echoed in the quiet morning air, followed almost instantly by the click of the door unlocking. Efficient, as always.

The lobby greeted her with a faint chill of air conditioning, a welcome break from the heat outside. Cream-colored walls lined with scuff marks and faded linoleum floors stretched before her. A sagging leather couch occupied one corner, flanked by a rickety side table stacked with crinkled magazines that no one ever read. Wren barely spared the decor a glance.

She ignored the elevators and made for the stairs. Elevators weren't her style—they felt slow, like they dulled the edge she constantly chased. Her feet pounded against the concrete steps, each echoing thud like a drumbeat pushing her forward. Two at a time came naturally now, her thighs burning as she ascended, the bag swinging lightly in rhythm with her movements.

By the time she reached the third floor, her breathing was quickened but steady. Dennis was waiting in the doorway, leaning casually against the frame as though he had all the time in the world. His tall frame and sharp blue eyes gave him an air of quiet detachment, and he watched her approach without a flicker of emotion.

"Two blueberry muffins," Wren said, holding out the crumpled paper bag and the oversized cup of coffee, its lid already slick with condensation. "And your giant black coffee."

Dennis nodded, his signature response, and took the items with a quiet "Thanks." No small talk, no banter, just business as usual. The door clicked shut behind him before Wren had even turned to leave.

She spun on her heel, already retracing her steps. The descent down the stairs was faster, her sneakers slapping the concrete with urgency. She burst out into the sunlight moments later, squinting as the brightness hit her full force.

Wren made a beeline for Argo, her fingers flying over the lock as she freed her bike in record time. With one fluid motion, she was back in the saddle, pedaling hard as she merged into the relentless tide of traffic.

The city swallowed her whole again, its chaos a constant, unyielding force. But to Wren, it wasn't chaos—it was a challenge, a rhythm she knew by heart. As the wind streamed past her face and her pulse quickened, she felt it again: the rush.

She couldn't put a name to it, but it was the reason she did this. The speed, the movement, the city alive around her. It filled her veins with a purpose that had nothing to do with Dennis, Willie, or blueberry muffins.

This was freedom. This was life.

Maggie's voice lingered in the back of Wren's mind, a gentle murmur beneath the roar of the city. *Be careful,* Maggie had said, her tone heavy with worry, as though her words could plant caution where it didn't belong. But careful didn't live here—not in Wren's world, and certainly not when she was on her bike.

The risks? She knew them. Too well. Gravel scars still marked her palms from past spills, and she'd lost count of the close calls. But fear didn't weigh enough to tip the scale against this rush. The speed, the precision—it was an addiction, one she had no intention of quitting.

She flew through a red light, threading between cars like a thread through a needle. Tires screeched, but she didn't glance back. This wasn't recklessness; this was mastery. Control at its most exhilarating.

Maggie didn't see it that way. Wren could still picture her face this morning, the faint crease between her brows as she'd said goodbye. *Why doesn't she understand?* This chaos wasn't reckless—it was salvation. The city might chew people up and spit them out, but on her bike, Wren was untouchable.

Her thoughts skipped, fragmented by the rhythm of her ride. *Puppy! Damn, that's cute.* A basset hound, ears flopping, paused at the curb. Wren swerved instinctively, narrowly avoiding an open car door. *Focus. The street art here—amazing. Have to come back tonight, take it in properly.*

An SUV veered into her lane without warning, snapping her back to the moment. Reflex took over. She jerked her handlebars, her heart lurching as she skimmed past the car's fender. "Watch it, jackass!" she shouted, her voice raw with adrenaline.

The driver flipped her off, but Wren was already ahead, weaving back into the flow. The city surged around her, relentless and alive, matching her heartbeat with its unceasing rhythm.

The Cyclista Bike Courier office came into view, its weathered sign jutting out like a beacon. Relief mingled with the lingering high of her ride as she slowed, coasting into the bike parking area. She swung off Argo in one fluid motion, her legs shaky but her grin unshaken.

The faint scent of coffee and grease wafted from the building. Inside, her coworkers' chatter and the clatter of bike chains would greet her, grounding her in a different kind of chaos. For now, though, Wren stood still for a moment, letting the energy of the ride ebb.

Her body hummed, her pulse thrumming with life. She knew she'd do it all again tomorrow.

The office buzzed with energy. The air hung thick with the scent of bike grease and rubber, mingling with the aroma of fresh coffee. Dispatch radios crackled, their disjointed chatter a constant backdrop to the organized chaos.

"Yo, Wren! Cutting it close again, huh?" Jake called out from where he was adjusting his bike chain.

Wren flashed him a grin that was part mischief, part challenge. "I don't cut it close, Jake. I *own* it." She gave her bike a hard, confident pat.

"Hey, hotshot!" Lena greeted her at the door. "Heard you crushed it at the Alleycat. Again."

Wren shrugged, a cocky smile playing on her lips. "What can I say? The streets are my playground."

As she strode into the main office area, the energy in the room seemed to shift. Conversations paused, heads turned. Wren's arrival was like a jolt of electricity, sparking the atmosphere.

"Look who decided to grace us with her presence," Willie's gruff voice cut through the chatter. He stood by the dispatch desk, arms crossed, a hint of irritation in his eyes.

"Aw, Willie, did you miss me?" Wren quipped, her tone light but with an edge of challenge.

Willie's frown deepened, but before he could respond, Wren was already moving past him, high-fiving colleagues and creating chaos.

"Alright, you maniacs!" she announced, clapping her hands together. "Who's ready to fucking own these streets today? Let's tear it up and show the losers at SycleSwift how it's done!" Everyone laughed—they all knew Maggie worked there.

Couriers darted back and forth, some strapping on helmets, while others pored over their phones as they sat at mismatched tables. Wren spotted Massimo adjusting his bike seat near the storage area. She sauntered over.

"Hey Massi, leave any speed records for us mortals today?" Wren called out, leaning against a workbench.

Massimo looked up, a slow grin spreading across his face. "Only because I thought I'd give you a chance, Wren."

She snorted, shaking her head. "Dream on, buddy. I'll smoke you any day of the week."

Across the room, a flash of color caught Wren's eye. Thanh stood by the dispatch desk, their hair a vibrant kaleidoscope of hues. Wren weaved through the crowd, dodging a courier carrying a stack of packages.

"Thanh, loving the new hair colors!" Wren exclaimed, giving a low whistle. "What's the inspiration—rainbow on steroids?"

Thanh ran a hand through their technicolor locks, beaming. "Just trying to keep up with your wild personality, Wren."

"Ha! Good luck with that," Wren retorted, playfully punching Thanh's shoulder.

The office door swung open, and Jones stumbled in, looking flustered. Wren couldn't resist the opportunity for some good-natured ribbing.

"Late again, Jones?" she called out, crossing her arms. "Did you take a scenic route?"

Jones rolled his eyes, but a smile tugged at the corners of his mouth. "Nope, just got stuck behind a herd of tourists. You know how it is."

"Rookie mistake," Wren teased. "Next time, use the sidewalk. That's what it's there for, right?"

Wren sauntered over to the dispatch desk, her eyes scanning the chaos of the office. "Got any deliveries today that won't try to kill me?" she asked, her tone dripping with sarcasm.

The dispatcher, a burly man named Frank, looked up from his computer screen. His eyes twinkled with amusement as he played along with Wren's game.

"Sorry, Wren. Only death-defying routes left for you," he shot back, matching her playful tone.

Wren threw her head back and laughed, the sound echoing through the bustling office. "Perfect. Just how I like 'em."

As she turned away from the desk, Wren spotted Ellen, a fellow courier known for her cautious riding style. Ellen was meticulously checking her bike, her movements slow and deliberate.

"Ellen, if you ride any slower, you'll start growing roots," Wren called out, her voice laced with good-natured mockery.

Ellen looked up, unfazed by Wren's jab. She rolled her eyes and retorted, "Better than being a human bullet like you. It's called savoring life!"

Wren snorted, shaking her head. "Savoring life? More like watching it pass you by, grandma."

As she scanned the room, Wren's eyes landed on an unfamiliar face. A young man stood near the lockers, looking overwhelmed by the chaotic energy of the office. His wide eyes darted around, taking in the scene with a mixture of excitement and apprehension.

Wren strode over to him, stopping directly in front of the newcomer, hands on her hips.

"Hey, who the fuck are you?" she demanded, her voice sharp and direct.

The rookie's mouth opened and closed, but no words came out. He seemed speechless, caught off guard by Wren's wild, chaotic energy. His eyes widened even further, if that was possible, and he took a small step back.

Before Wren could continue her interrogation, Willie's gruff voice cut through the air.

"Wren! Calm the fuck down and stop scaring the newbies," he barked from across the room.

Wren turned to face Willie, a defiant grin spreading across her face. "Aw, come on, Willie. I'm just giving him a proper Cyclista welcome."

Willie's frown deepened as he approached. He glanced at the rookie, then back at Wren. "We need fresh blood, and your antics aren't helping. Give the kid a break."

Wren raised an eyebrow, her grin not faltering. "Fine, fine. I'll play nice." She turned back to the rookie, who still hadn't uttered a word. "Welcome to the madhouse, kid. Hope you can keep up."

Willie sighed, pinching the bridge of his nose. He looked at the newcomer, his brow furrowing. "Sorry about that... uh..." He paused, clearly struggling to remember the kid's name.

Wren couldn't help but laugh. "Smooth, Willie. Real smooth. Can't even remember the newbie's name? Kinda pathetic." Wren rolled her eyes at Willie's exasperation, a smirk playing on her lips. She leaned against the dispatch desk, her posture casual but her eyes sharp.

"Alright, boss man. What've you got for me today? Anything exciting? Dangerous? Potentially life-threatening?" she asked, her tone a mix of sarcasm and genuine enthusiasm.

Willie's frown deepened to the point where Wren wondered if his face might actually cave in on itself. His arms crossed tightly over his chest, a defensive shield against her, as his eyes narrowed into slits sharp enough to cut glass.

"If I had any orders for you, Hubbard," he began, his voice low and growling like an annoyed dog just shy of biting, "I'd have handed them over the second you walked in. Maybe then you'd be out of here instead of terrorizing the rest of the staff."

Wren placed a hand on her chest in an exaggerated pantomime of shock, staggering back half a step as though Willie's words threatened to knock her flat. "Willie," she said, drawing out his name with mock heartbreak. "I'm hurt. Truly. Here I am—your most loyal employee—ready to risk life and limb for Cyclista, and you're telling me you've got nothing for me?"

Willie's jaw tightened so visibly it was almost audible. If clenched teeth could start a fire, Wren figured she'd be standing in the middle of a blaze by now. "Nothing yet," he ground out, each word carefully sharpened to inflict maximum irritation with minimum effort. "And when I do have something, believe me, you'll be the first to know. Until then, why don't you go make yourself useful? Oil your chain or something."

Wren pushed off the edge of his desk with a smirk that widened at his thinly veiled irritation. "Oil my chain?" she repeated, her voice light and lilting like Willie had just confessed his undying love for her. "Willie, you old softie—I didn't know you cared."

She whipped around to face the rest of the office, spreading her arms like a preacher addressing her flock. "Did you hear that? Willie wants me to oil my chain! Anyone wanna watch? Surely someone here can lend a hand."

The room responded exactly as she'd expected: groans from those trying not to laugh and chuckles from those who didn't care about hiding it. Behind her, Willie pinched the bridge of his nose as though trying to banish a migraine that only she could cause.

"Just sit down already, Hubbard," he muttered through grit teeth before sighing with what sounded suspiciously like defeat. "I'll let you know when something comes in."

8:31 a.m.

Her phone chimed—a sharp ding that sliced cleanly through the buzzing hum of office chatter. Wren dug it out of her pocket, glancing at the screen as her brows furrowed. The number staring back at her was unfamiliar. The message? A food pickup request.

She hesitated for a moment, thumb hovering over the screen like it might bite if she pressed too hard. New numbers weren't unusual—friends passing along requests or desperate contacts cobbling together last-minute favors—but something about this one prickled at the edges of her instincts. Could be nothing. Could be trouble.

And trouble... well, trouble might as well have been Wren's middle name.

She glanced up toward Willie's desk across the room, catching him mid-scowl—not that he ever seemed to be anywhere else emotionally when she was in his line of sight. He looked exactly how he always did when she annoyed him: like he wanted nothing more than to toss her out onto the curb but couldn't bring himself to admit how much worse things would be without her around.

"Hey, Willie," Wren called out sweetly, letting just enough syrup drip into her voice to guarantee he'd hate whatever came next. "Any orders ready for pickup?"

The effect was immediate—and glorious. Willie's face darkened by several shades until it settled somewhere between beet-red and maroon. His jaw tightened again; honestly, if it were possible for someone's jaw muscles to snap under pressure alone, Wren thought this might finally be the moment.

"If I had any orders," he barked, each word clipped and razor-sharp as though wielding them against an imaginary foe (or maybe not-so-imaginary), "don't you think I'd already be dispatching them? What part of 'sit down and wait' is so hard for your brain to process?"

Wren held up both hands in a practiced gesture of mock surrender—one that felt more like muscle memory after years honing it in situations just like this one. "Alright, alright," she said with faux contrition laced into every syllable. "Just checking! Wouldn't want to miss out on any heart-pounding package deliveries or nail-biting document runs."

Sliding back toward Massi's desk with deliberate nonchalance (and knowing full well that Willie wasn't done muttering dire threats under his breath), Wren dropped into the seat beside him and leaned closer until their shoulders nearly touched.

"Willie's such a piece of work," she whispered conspiratorially, though loud enough for anyone paying attention to hear anyway. Her tone was light but dripping with amusement as she added: "I swear he's got a stick up his ass big enough to support scaffolding."

Massi shook his head but couldn't hold back a snort of laughter—the sound short and sharp but accompanied by crinkled eyes that gave him away entirely. "Tell me something I don't already know."

The office door swung open with a startling bang, drawing heads like a magnet. Zak strolled in, shoulders back, chin lifted, as if he were the star of a movie only he was watching. His blonde hair was an unruly mess, sticking up in jagged peaks that hinted at either rebellion or sheer indifference to mirrors. His small frame didn't seem to bother him; he moved with a kind of buoyant swagger that made you wonder if he ever doubted himself—though clearly, he should.

Wren glanced toward Massi, catching the faintest twitch of amusement in his expression as they both tracked Zak's progress. Never mind that their boss Willie—who could practically sniff out tardiness like a bloodhound—didn't so much as flinch at Zak's late arrival. It was like Zak existed in some alternate dimension where rules dissolved around him.

"Unbelievable," Wren muttered, just loud enough for the words to carry across the office din. "Fairness? Forget it."

Massi leaned back in his chair, voice dripping with mock outrage. "Yeah, seriously. We get an eyebrow raise for sneezing too loud, but he shows up whenever he feels like it? Nothing."

Zak's head turned sharply at the sound of their voices, his smirk faltering before snapping back into place like a shield.

Wren's gaze locked on him, her lips curving into a slow grin that promised trouble. "Guess Willie doesn't waste his energy picking on anyone who doesn't even come up to his waist."

Massi erupted in laughter so loud and sudden it startled Betty from accounting in the back office. "His waist... good one! I mean, seriously though"—he gestured broadly as if presenting evidence to an invisible jury—"Zak here doesn't even register on Willie's radar."

Zak froze mid-step, his face flushing pink under the freckles scattered across his nose. "Watch it," he snapped, though the crack in his voice took any bite out of the retort.

Wren leaned back in her chair like she had all the time in the world. "Oh come on, Zak. What's wrong? Can't handle a harmless joke?" She let her grin widen before delivering the final blow with deliberate sweetness: "Or is that just another thing you're too dumb for?"

The laughter bubbled out of her then—sharp and unapologetic—but fizzled almost as quickly as it started. The air around them seemed to shift suddenly, heavy now with something unspoken amidst the hum of computers and soft ring of phones. The smell of stale coffee hit her nose again—overpowering and oddly claustrophobic this morning—and Wren decided she needed to move. Needed anything other than sitting here watching Zak try to piece together his shattered cockiness.

"I'm heading out," she announced abruptly. "Coffee."

Massi raised an eyebrow but said nothing. Across the room, Willie's hawkish eyes snapped up from whatever spreadsheet had consumed him. He glared hard enough to bore holes into her from behind his thick glasses.

"There's coffee right here," he barked without looking away from her for even a second. "Don't leave."

Wren stopped at the edge of her desk but didn't sit back down. Instead, she turned to meet Willie's glare head-on with an arched eyebrow that practically dripped defiance. "What's wrong?" she asked coolly, folding her arms over her chest like she had all day to wait for an answer. "Afraid I'll enjoy myself too much out there? You have nothing for me, Willie. Nothing."

Willie's face flushed crimson beneath his near-permanent scowl. "You're not leaving," he finally growled through clenched teeth.

"Why not?" Wren shot back immediately, voice sharp enough to slice through tension hanging over them both now like a storm cloud about ready to burst open wide. She jabbed her thumb toward the empty clipboard near Betty's desk—the one reserved exclusively for order pickups they hadn't received yet today—and said flatly: "There's nothing happening here anyway."

For once Willie seemed utterly at a loss for words—it wasn't exactly common for him—but watching him open and close his mouth wordlessly might've been satisfying... if it weren't also painfully awkward somehow watching someone lose so much steam so fast right before your eyes.

Wren waited. One beat. Then two. Willie didn't answer, his gaze fixed on the same spot on his desk like it might suddenly offer him salvation. Wren let the silence stretch, savoring it for a moment before shrugging, a smirk tugging at the corner of her mouth. "Well, this has been fun," she said lightly, though neither of them looked like they were having much fun. "I'm leaving."

She didn't bother waiting for a reaction—there wouldn't be one anyway—and strode out the door without so much as a backward glance.

Outside, the city greeted her with its usual sharp slap to the face: air thick with exhaust, tinged with something greasy and tempting—street food, of course. Wren took a deep breath and felt the tension in her shoulders loosen just enough to remind her it had been there in the first place. New York City was many things—grimy and relentless and loud—but it was also freedom, if you knew how to claim it.

She walked toward where Argo sat waiting patiently, locked to its post like some loyal steed tethered outside a saloon. Her fingers moved automatically as she worked the combination—three turns right, one left, one more right—and the lock popped open with a satisfying click. She stuffed it into her bag without ceremony and swung her leg over Argo's frame in one fluid motion.

The streets beckoned—chaotic, alive—but Wren hesitated anyway, one foot still on the ground as though something unseen held her back. She glanced over her shoulder at Cyclista Couriers' dull gray facade. Maybe she thought Willie would be there in one of those grimy windows, glaring down at her like some vengeful specter trying to pull her back inside. But there was nothing staring back at her except empty glass panes reflecting an equally empty sky.

"Good riddance," she muttered under her breath, shaking off whatever had crept up on her in that moment. She was leaving for an hour, not a lifetime. She dismounted Argo and began to walk instead of ride, pushing the bike alongside her as she put more distance between herself and that suffocating little office.

Wren pulled out her phone when she was halfway down the block, thumbing through notifications until she found it: the unusual order ping she hadn't had time to think about earlier amid Willie's brooding silence. Breakfast burrito with hash browns from Golden Bites—an unfamiliar name—with delivery all the way up on 164th Street.

"The hell is Golden Bites?" Wren muttered to herself as she tapped furiously into Google Maps only to find...nothing. No hits, no helpful red pins showing an address or even a hint of its existence.

She sighed heavily and fired off a text: "Address?"

The reply came almost instantly: "188th and 45th. Deliver to 17-164th."

Wren stared at the message because what it implied didn't sit right—it was way out of range for Cyclista deliveries. A different borough practically! Willie would blow a gasket if she went through with it...which made Wren smile as she weighed her options.

Fingers flying across the screen again: "$15 extra for the distance." Her thumb hovered briefly over "send." She hadn't meant $15; she'd meant $5—still cheeky but not quite reckless enough to raise eyebrows.

Too late now—her thumb pressed send almost of its own volition.

"OK," came the simple response mere seconds later.

It took another second for Wren's brain to register what had just happened—and when it did, surprise quickly melted into amusement. They'd agreed without hesitation? They hadn't even tried haggling? A slow grin spread across her face at how absurdly easy that had been.

Her number was available to her regular off-the-books clients and to people her regulars had passed it on to. She looked up 17-164th Street. It was real. A quick check of online ownership records showed an Anne Cantu.

"Fuck yeah," she murmured as she pocketed her phone with satisfaction that bordered on glee. Breakfast delivery miles out of bounds for triple the usual payout? It was shaping up to be an excellent day—and bonus points for sticking it to Willie while doing so.

Wren mounted Argo again, this time with purpose, and pushed off into traffic. The first few pedal strokes were stiff—her muscles adjusting—but soon enough they found their rhythm like always: tense then relax then tense again as momentum took hold.

The city blurred around her as she moved through its veins—the endless flow of cars and buses and pedestrians all vying for space they couldn't share but somehow managed not to destroy entirely (most days). Reeson Avenue stretched ahead of her like a challenge laid bare; every gap between vehicles begged to be threaded by someone bold—or foolish—enough not to hesitate.

The wind whipped past her face, tangling strands of hair that escaped from beneath her helmet while carrying smells both rancid and delicious in equal measure (because New York could never pick just one). Her thighs burned with effort—a burn that felt good—and when Hardy Fenner Expressway loomed ahead in all its sprawling gridlock splendor, Wren laughed like someone who'd never been warned against stupid risks.

She darted into the fray without flinching—a flash of blue-green weaving through stagnant reds and silvers. A horn blared somewhere behind her—or maybe beside; hard to say—but Wren didn't bother looking back because what was done was done.

Her heart raced alongside Argo's wheels against pavement—a rhythm steady yet urgent—as she leaned into turns so tight they felt carved just for her alone amidst this chaos masquerading as order.

Today really *was* looking up.

Taking the slight right onto 64th Avenue, Wren's eyes narrowed as she spotted the traffic circle ahead. Without hesitation, she aimed straight for the park at its center. Her tires hit grass, then dirt. She bounced over roots and rocks, the jolt of each impact reverberating through her body. She cut across the circle and was spit out the other side in no time.

Emerging on 188th, Wren slowed her pace, scanning for the restaurant. Her chest heaved as she caught her breath, sweat trickling down her back. The thrill of the ride still hummed in her veins.

Golden Bites came into view, nestled between a laundromat and a vacant storefront. The restaurant's facade was unremarkable—just a printed sign on a covered window. No flashy neon, no inviting decor. It looked more like a pop-up than an established eatery.

As Wren pulled up to the curb, a sudden shiver ran through her body. The hair on the back of her neck stood up, and an inexplicable sense of unease settled in her stomach. She frowned, shaking off the feeling as she dismounted Argo.

Wren parked Argo, securing the bike. She approached the takeout window, her eyes scanning the sparse menu taped to the glass. The smell of grease and spices wafted through the air, making her stomach growl.

A woman appeared at the window, her dark hair styled in a sharp, no-nonsense bob. Brown eyes met Wren's, and the woman's athletic build was evident even in her casual jeans and shirt.

"What can I get you?" the woman asked, her voice carrying a hint of amusement.

Wren leaned against the counter, a crooked grin spreading across her face. "Breakfast burrito and a side of hash browns, please. And make it snappy, I've got places to be."

The woman snorted, her fingers flying over the register. "Don't we all? You in some kind of race?"

"Always," Wren quipped. "Life's one big Alleycat, and I'm winning."

The cashier laughed, shaking her head. "Whatever that means. That'll be twenty bucks, speed demon."

Wren fished out her wallet, eyebrows raised. "Twenty? Damn, these better be gold-plated hash browns."

"Nah, just seasoned with the tears of slower cyclists," the woman shot back, her eyes twinkling.

Wren barked out a laugh, slapping the money on the counter. "Well played. I might have to come back here just for the banter."

"We aim to please," the cashier said, sliding the receipt towards Wren. "Food'll be ready in three."

Wren pulled out her phone, tapping the FonBill app icon. She punched in the customer's call-back number and the amount: $35.00. A smirk played on her lips as she hit send, thinking about the extra cash she'd scored through her little typo. The app dinged almost immediately, confirming payment.

"Damn, that was fast," Wren muttered, pocketing her phone. She drummed her fingers on the counter, impatient energy thrumming through her body.

The cashier reappeared, brown paper bag in hand. Steam wafted from the top, carrying the mouthwatering scent of spices and grilled meat. Wren's stomach growled again, reminding her she'd skipped breakfast in her rush to leave.

"Here you go," the woman said, sliding the bag across the counter. "Good luck."

Wren's hand froze halfway to the bag. She cocked an eyebrow at the cashier. "Good luck? What's that supposed to mean?"

The woman shrugged. "Just a saying. Have a nice day."

Something about the exchange felt off, but Wren couldn't put her finger on it. She grabbed the bag, the warmth seeping through the paper into her palm.

"Right. Thanks, I guess," Wren said, backing away from the window. The uneasy feeling from earlier returned, settling like a lead weight in her gut.

She shook her head, trying to dislodge the creeping sense of paranoia. It was just a weird interaction, nothing more. Probably some new customer service bullshit they were trying out.

Wren strode back to Argo and swung her leg over the bike, ready to push off, when her phone buzzed. A text from the customer:

"ETA?"

Wren rolled her eyes, firing back a quick reply: "10 mins. Chill."

Wren secured the warm paper bag in her courier pack. She pushed off, her legs pumping as she maneuvered Argo back onto 188th Street. The unease from her interaction at Golden Bites lingered, but the familiar rush of adrenaline as she picked up speed pushed it to the back of her mind.

She hit Roosevelt Turnpike, weaving through the morning traffic. Wren cut across to 186th Street, her body leaning into the turn. She could feel the warmth of the food against her back. The streets flew by as she zagged onto 73rd Avenue, her muscles working in perfect harmony with Argo's gears.

As she approached 180th Street, Wren spotted a delivery truck blocking the bike lane. Without missing a beat, she veered into traffic, narrowly avoiding a taxi's side mirror. The driver leaned on his horn, but Wren was already gone, a fleeting middle finger her only response.

She hit 69th Avenue hard, her tires screeching as she made the sharp turn. The street signs blurred as she pedaled harder, her breath coming in controlled pants. The thrill of the ride coursed through her veins, pushing away any lingering doubts about the strange order.

164th Street loomed ahead. Wren stood up on her pedals, pushing for one final burst of speed. She flew past rows of brownstones and parked cars, her eyes scanning for the customer's address. The wind whipped through her hair, carrying the sounds of the city.

Wren slowed Argo to a stop in front of 17-164th Street, her eyes scanning the charming Craftsman-style house before her. The two-story structure stood out among its neighbors, painted in soft, earthy tones with dark wood trim that gave it a cozy, inviting feel. A welcoming front porch stretched across the facade, complete with a pair of vintage rocking chairs and potted plants that added a homey touch.

Large windows with decorative shutters caught the morning light, their reflections bouncing off the pristine garden that framed the front walkway. Wren took in the black metal fence encircling the yard, waist-high and a little too perfect—like a wedding cake topper meant to impress but not actually touched.

She swung a leg off Argo, her bike, her calf muscles still humming from the ride. A glance up the street, then down. No movement, no sound. Just glossy cars parked neatly along the curb like they were part of some suburban showroom. She shrugged and propped the bike against the fence without locking it. Who'd be bold (or dumb) enough to swipe a courier's ride in a place like this? Nothing bad ever happens in picture-perfect neighborhoods, right? Sure.

Reaching into her courier bag, Wren found the warm paper sack holding someone's overpriced breakfast—an artisanal burrito with hash browns that had truffle oil or some crap. The spicy smell wafted up, hitting her stomach like a sucker punch; she still hadn't eaten. She pulled out the bag and tucked it under one arm as she made a mental note to grab something—anything—to eat.

With her free hand, she unlatched the gate. The latch gave way with an obedient click, and as she pushed it open, it creaked softly like it'd been rehearsing in secret. The stone path to the front door was too clean—not just neat but unnervingly immaculate—and felt cool underfoot compared to the warm sun heating her back.

As she stepped forward, Wren's gaze darted over the house and yard like an involuntary reflex. Everything here screamed deliberate—the perfectly aligned flower beds, not a single blade of grass out of place. It was unsettling in its perfection. She couldn't say why exactly, but something didn't sit right. The house looked lived *in* if you imagined that life itself had been carefully staged for an expensive real estate catalog.

Wren rolled her shoulders back and shook off whatever weird vibes were crawling up her spine. Probably just residual tension from Golden Bites—the sort of place where everything looked great on the surface but left you quietly queasy afterward. She bounded up the porch steps two at a time. They groaned faintly under her weight, their old wood betraying their years despite any fresh coats of paint slapped on top. Two rocking chairs flanked either side of the porch, swaying lightly in some unseen breeze like they could sense a storm a-brewin'.

At the door now, she raised her hand to knock when... there it was. That feeling again, sharper now—like ice water poured straight down her back on an otherwise sunny morning. Wren froze mid-motion and forced herself to focus on what was throwing her off this time: silence. Not just quiet—the kind you welcome after a loud day—but silence so heavy it felt unnatural. No birds chirping in those trees overhead; no hum of traffic from a block away; no distant lawnmower or barking dog to break up all that oppressive stillness.

Pushing through her unease, Wren rapped her knuckles against the door anyway—firm enough for whoever might be lurking inside to hear but not loud enough to seem confrontational (she hoped). The knock echoed louder than expected in all that emptiness around her. She stepped back a little and shifted her weight awkwardly between feet as irritation started building alongside unease.

A few beats passed—no sound of shuffling footsteps approaching from inside or calls of "one second!" Impatient now—and maybe just wanting to leave this place sooner than later—Wren shook her head and muttered under her breath: "Okay then... Guess you don't care about your fancy five-star burrito."

Pulling out her phone from her back pocket with one hand while holding up the paper bag with the other, she swiped open her camera app for proof-of-delivery duty—a standard CYA move for sketchy drop-offs like this one.

She bent down to drop the food when her head touched the door. That's when she heard it: first faint, then louder as realization settled cold into her chest—the soft groan as the door cracked open.

She stumbled back half a step before catching herself, heart thudding hard against ribcage walls now trying very hard to cage something wilder growing behind them. Her grip tightened instinctively around both phone and bag as if either could serve as protection against... what? Against who?

"What *is* this?" she whispered harshly into no one's ear but hers because there was no one else here—or at least none she could see yet—and somehow speaking aloud made things momentarily less terrifying.

But then came the voice—not hers—low and stretched thin by something beyond exhaustion: "Help me."

It wasn't loud—it didn't need volume to rattle every nerve ending in Wren's body at once like they were live wires exposed to air too suddenly sharp for comfort or sanity anymore.

Her eyes darted between the narrow opening at that door and everything behind/around/beyond—the empty street stretching endlessly blank behind fences painted too white against skies feeling wrong-blue now somehow... All logic dictated running right then—dump burrito; pedal fast—but curiosity? Or fear disguised as bravery?

"Hello?" she called out, her voice sounding unnaturally loud in the silence. "Anyone there?"

8:52 a.m.

Wren pushed the door open, her heart pounding in her chest. The paper bag crinkled in her grip as she stepped into the dimly lit foyer. The smell hit her first—a sickly sweet odor mixed with something metallic that made her stomach churn.

Her eyes adjusted to the gloom, and she froze. The entryway was a mess of overturned furniture and shattered glass. A trail of dark, sticky liquid led deeper into the house.

"Holy shit," Wren breathed, her voice barely above a whisper.

She took another tentative step forward, her cycling shoes crunching on broken glass. The sound echoed through the eerily silent house.

"Hello?" she called out, louder this time. "Anyone here?"

A weak groan answered her from somewhere to her left. Wren's head snapped in that direction, her eyes widening as she saw a figure slumped against the wall in the adjacent room.

She rushed forward, food forgotten, nearly slipping on the slick floor. As she entered the living room, Wren's eyes widened as she took in the gruesome scene before her. A woman lay sprawled on the floor, her hair matted with blood. Her brown eyes, wide with fear and pain, locked onto Wren's face.

The woman's chest heaved with shallow, gasping breaths. Blood pooled around her overweight frame, soaking into the old wooden floorboards. The rich, golden-brown color of the wood turned into a gruesome, dark crimson.

"Fuck," Wren breathed, her heart pounding in her ears. She dropped to her knees beside the woman, her hands hovering uselessly over her.

"What happened?" Wren asked, her voice cracking. "Who did this to you?"

The woman's lips moved, but no sound came out. Her brown eyes darted frantically around the room, as if searching for something—or someone.

Despite the chaos in her mind, Wren's keen eyes quickly took in the scene. The woman appeared to be in her early forties, with short brown hair now matted with blood. Wren could see a gaping wound on her stomach. Shot? Stabbed? It was clear that the woman was losing blood rapidly, her face pale and pale pink foam bubbled on her lips.

What the actual fuck? Oh shit, oh shit! Blood—there's so much blood! Fuckfuckfuck! Move, Wren, MOVE! Help her! God, what do I do? Towel, towel, get a towel! The kitchen—right there! Got it, got it! Here, press—where? Her stomach? Yeah, she's clutching her stomach. Fuck, it's pouring out! She's saying something—what is she saying? Should I talk to her? What do I say? Call for help, Wren! Call for fucking help!

"Hold on," Wren said, trying to keep her voice steady. "Help's coming. Just... just hold on."

The woman's hand shot out, grabbing Wren's wrist with surprising strength. Her mouth opened and closed, struggling to form words. The woman's grip on Wren's wrist tightened, her nails digging into the skin. She nodded once, her eyes filled with a desperate urgency.

Wren pressed the kitchen towel against the wound, feeling the blood seep through almost immediately. It was warm, sticky—too much of it, too fast. The woman groaned, a low and guttural sound that made Wren's stomach twist.

"I'm sorry," Wren whispered, her voice quivering as she glanced at the woman's face. "I'm trying to help. I'm so sorry."

The woman's eyes, wide and wet with pain, locked onto hers. Her lips moved, but a wet gurgle emerged. Wren leaned closer without thinking, her ear hovering just above the woman's mouth.

"What is it? What are you trying to say?"

The blood-tinged air smelled metallic and sharp as shallow gasps escaped the woman's lips, hitting Wren's cheek in damp bursts. She didn't pull away—her focus stayed pinned on catching whatever words might still come out.

"R-run," the woman finally choked out between ragged breaths. Her eyes flicked past Wren, toward the shadowy hallway at her back.

Wren froze. The word sat heavy in her chest like a stone dropped into water. Slowly, she turned her head to look over her shoulder, bracing for... what? Someone? Something? She didn't know what she expected to see.

Nothing was there.

Just the hallway stretching out into darkness. But somehow it felt deeper now—darker around the edges, like shadows pooling together to hide something unseen.

"Who did this to you?" she asked, turning back quickly. She halted mid-sentence. "Are they still here?"

The woman didn't answer—or couldn't answer—but blood continued to flow freely from the wound beneath Wren's hands. Warmth seeped through the towel and onto Wren's fingers, dripping steadily down into the fabric of her cycling shorts until it clung cold and damp against her skin.

"Hey!" Her voice softened unexpectedly, almost a whisper now as she tried to keep herself steady for this woman—this stranger in her kitchen who had been bleeding out on the floor only minutes after Wren burst through the door without warning or explanation. "Hey, can you hear me? Stay with me."

She pressed harder on the towel even though she wasn't sure if it was helping anymore—wasn't sure of anything except that there was blood everywhere, far more than there should be—and still it kept coming.

The woman stirred faintly beneath her touch. Her eyelids fluttered open just enough for their gazes to meet again for a fleeting moment of clarity before her lips parted once more.

"My work." The words were faint but deliberate this time.

Wren blinked at her in confusion before leaning closer again until their faces were nearly touching.

"What about your work?" she asked quietly.

No response came—not really—but the woman's frantic gaze darted across the room as though searching for something invisible among its corners and shadows.

Her eyes fluttered shut again just as quickly as they'd opened.

"Help me," the woman breathed weakly this time instead—and that did something to Wren, broke something inside her chest that hadn't already been shattered by fear or shock or whatever panic-driven instinct had taken hold since all of this began unraveling so suddenly.

"I'm trying," Wren said aloud—not just for the injured woman now but possibly for herself too—as sweat began trickling down from her forehead and into her eyes despite how cold everything else seemed to feel around them both now.

Her hands fumbled clumsily for her phone; when she finally managed to grab hold of it again through trembling fingers slick with blood, streaks smeared red across its touchscreen surface almost immediately.

Wren's fingers slipped on the touchscreen as she punched in 911, the blood making everything slick and unsteady. The phone rang once. Twice. Three times. Four. Twenty? Each ring stretched out, too long, too loud, filling the silence with something that felt unbearable. Her gaze was locked on the woman's chest, rising and falling in shallow, uneven breaths—each one a battle that seemed destined to be lost.

"911, what's your emergency?" The voice, calm and professional, crackled through the speaker.

Wren's breath caught. "I need help!" The words tumbled out in a rush, disorganized and panicked. "There's a woman—I found her—she's bleeding. Oh god." She pressed a shaky hand to her mouth for half a second before pulling it away again. "There's so much blood."

"Ma'am, I need you to stay calm," the dispatcher said, her tone steady in a way that made Wren feel both reassured and entirely inadequate for this moment. "What is your location?"

Her location? Her mind skidded blank for a moment, useless and spinning in place like tires on ice. A memory surfaced—the fence. White. Black? The house number hanging crooked near the mailbox. "Uh... uh... 164th Street," she stammered out at last. "I don't know the exact number—it's near a fence—and..." She squeezed her eyes shut as though doing so could squeeze out the answer she needed. "Seventeen! It's 17-164th Street."

"That's good," the dispatcher replied calmly, like they were having an ordinary conversation on an ordinary day. "We can work with that. Can you tell me what happened?"

What had happened? Wren didn't know how to answer that question because she wasn't sure herself. Her gaze flickered around the room—the upturned chair near her feet, shards of smashed glass scattered like jagged confetti across the floor, streaks of red smeared on random surfaces like some horrific Pollock painting—and landed back on the woman sprawled there, barely breathing.

"I don't know," Wren admitted finally, her voice cracking under it all. "I'm just a courier—I was delivering food—and when I walked in...it's broken, all broken. She's bleeding..." She took another look at the room but couldn't find anything else to say about it that wasn't already obvious: broken furniture, bloody streaks, shattered glass—and now this dying woman clutching at life with fingers so pale they looked translucent.

"She's been stabbed, I think," Wren added after a beat—or maybe longer; time was doing strange things right now.

"Is the attacker still there?"

The question made her stomach drop like she'd missed a step going down stairs. Was the attacker still here? Suddenly every corner of this room felt darker than it should have been, every shadow turned threatening.

"I..." Her voice faltered as her eyes darted toward those shadows, flicking from one suspicious patch of darkness to another before snapping back to the dispatcher for safety, even though that voice was just distant noise coming out of her phone speaker. "I don't know."

"Okay," said the dispatcher like they were working out simple instructions for assembling flat-pack furniture instead of processing what might be life-or-death information. "Listen carefully: I want you to look around you—without moving anywhere—and see if it seems safe for you to stay with the victim." A pause followed where Wren could almost hear gears turning on this stranger's end of the line before more words came through: "If you see or hear something unusual—you leave immediately. Do you understand?"

She nodded instinctively before realizing how useless nodding was over a phone call and whispered instead: "Yes."

But even as she said it—the yes—her hands were already trembling harder than before because Anne (that was her name—Anne; she'd read it somewhere earlier) had started moving again—just slightly, but enough for Wren's focus to shift entirely onto her now.

Anne's fingers twitched once near her side before disappearing slowly into one pocket like they were caught up in molasses or underwater or maybe both at once somehow impossible yet happening anyway right here in front of them both while all other sounds faded except strained breathing... whose breathing? Both theirs, probably.

"T... take..." Anne rasped suddenly through lips barely capable of forming words anymore.

"What?" Wren asked automatically without thinking whether asking mattered anymore because Anne wouldn't last long either way judging by everything around them adding up horribly.

There wasn't time left—not much anyway—and yet Anne didn't rush. Anne's trembling hand reappeared holding something small metallic shining faintly under dim light where fingerprints smeared blood.

Wren hesitated, her hand hovering in the air. Her mind was racing, careening between questions she couldn't untangle. What was so important about this thing? Why did it feel like it carried more weight than its size should allow?

With a deep breath that didn't quite steady her, Wren reached down and plucked the USB drive from Anne's blood-slicked palm. It was small, cold, and somehow felt as though it might burn her. The blood made it slippery in her hand. She tightened her grip.

"I have it," she said quietly, her voice thick and unsure. "What... what do you want me to do with it?"

Anne didn't answer. Her eyes had closed, her chest barely moving now—a fragile whisper of breath that might stop at any moment. As that realization struck, panic began to claw its way into Wren's thoughts.

"Hey!" She placed a hand on Anne's shoulder and gave her a shake—firm but not rough. "Stay with me! The ambulance is coming; just hold on a little longer, okay?"

"Is she still breathing?" The 911 operator's questions were soundly ignored.

Anne's eyelids fluttered weakly before cracking open. When she spoke, each word came out slurred and faint, barely louder than the sound of air leaving her lungs: "He's... still here."

Wren froze as those words entered the room and settled over everything like a shadow, heavy and unwelcome. Still here? Who was here? But before she could ask or make sense of what Anne meant, the woman's eyes fixed on some distant point beyond Wren—beyond anything—and then they dulled completely. The light left them, not quickly but gradually, like the slow extinguishing of a flame that had fought for too long against the dark.

Her arm slid limply off Wren's wrist and hit the floor with a sound softer than Wren expected—a muted little thump that still managed to echo in her ears.

The voice from her phone cut through the silence so sharply that Wren nearly dropped it. "Ma'am? Are you there? What's happening?"

Reality rushed back all at once like a hard slap. Wren fumbled to bring the phone closer to her face. "Yes! Yes, I'm here!" Her voice broke as she said it. "She's—she's not breathing anymore! He's...What do I do?"

Her gaze dropped back down to Anne's still form on the floor. Every detail burrowed into Wren's brain—the unnatural angle of Anne's head, the blood smeared across her own trembling fingers, the metallic taste of fear sitting bitter on her tongue. In her other hand was the USB drive pressing uncomfortably into her palm, as if reminding her it existed when everything else seemed unreal.

One moment she'd been dropping off breakfast; now this.

The hallway stretched endlessly behind Wren—or at least that was how it felt as she glanced back over her shoulder again and again. Shadows crept along walls but didn't move in ways they shouldn't have; nothing shifted in the corners or brushed against doorframes. Just hold still for one second, she thought uselessly to no one but herself.

"She's dying." The words came out unbidden—cracked and raw—and hung awkwardly in the air as though waiting for someone else to claim them.

The operator responded calmly—too calmly given how completely everything seemed to be unraveling for Wren: "Ma'am, I need you to perform CPR right away. I'll walk you through it step by step."

Perform CPR? Could she even do that? Her hands were shaking badly now—not lightly trembling but vibrating like leaves caught in a windstorm—and yet despite herself, despite every part of her screaming that she wasn't ready for this moment, Wren nodded.

She looked down at the USB drive again—a stupid little thing covered in blood but somehow carrying all the gravity of something bigger than herself—and without thinking too much about why or what it meant or even whether it made sense to do so, she shoved it into her sock and let it press sharply against her ankle bone.

She placed the phone on the floor beside her with great care—as though setting down anything too loudly might shatter whatever composure she had left—and whispered into its speaker: "Okay." Then louder: "Okay! What do I need to do?"

The operator replied with cool precision: "First thing—check for breathing. Look at their chest. Tell me if it's rising or falling."

Wren leaned over Anne slowly—not because there was any point in hesitation but because every movement felt leaden, magnified by dread pressing on every inch of her body. She stared at Anne's chest until all she could see was its stillness, unbroken and unnerving.

"No," Wren whispered hoarsely after a pause too long for comfort but far shorter than what felt like forever.

"Alright," came back through from the phone speaker, steady as ever even if nothing else was: "We're going to start compressions now."

Start compressions now? Start saving this woman who'd just died right in front of her? Wasn't that impossible?

"Push hard and fast," the voice on the phone urged, calm but firm. "About 100 compressions per minute. I'll count you in. Ready? Begin."

Wren interlocked her fingers and hovered over Anne's motionless chest, preparing to start. But before she could press down, a sound reached her ears—soft, almost imperceptible, but enough to snag her focus. She froze, her head snapping up toward the hallway.

Someone was there. *Fuck!*

A uniformed cop stood at the far end of the corridor, his figure looming against faint streaks of light spilling through a cracked door. Wren's breath caught somewhere between her lungs and throat—a raw tangle of relief and unease. Her pulse quickened.

"There's someone here," she blurted into the phone, barely aware of how loud her voice had gotten. "A cop." She flung a hand up in the air, waving frantically toward him, her palm slick with blood from Anne's still frame. Her movement left streaks in the dim light—dark red slashes that seemed to linger in midair more than they should have. "Hey! Over here!" Her voice pitched higher than intended. "I need help!"

The officer turned toward her, his body moving slowly, deliberately. He stepped forward without speaking; his footfalls landed heavy enough that Wren swore she could feel them even across the distance between them.

Her phone made its way to her ear. Blood smeared across the screen where her fingers clutched at its edges, desperate not to lose it as she stammered into the receiver: "Did you hear me? There's an officer—I'm looking right at him. He's coming over now." The operator's response crackled faintly in her ear, but Wren barely noticed it anymore; everything else around her had started to blur away except for those looming footsteps echoing louder and closer with each step he took.

Something wasn't right.

She knew she should feel relieved—help was here—but an uneasy hum stirred somewhere low in her chest instead: muted, insistent, growing louder with every inch this man drew closer down that darkened hallway. His stride was off somehow—too measured—or maybe it was his posture or how his eyes glinted under weak light as though they weren't fully looking at anything but saw too much all at once.

And then recognition clicked, sharp and intrusive like a shard of glass cutting through fog.

It was Dennis.

Dennis: the same guy who always ordered breakfast. A regular. She saw him that very morning. Quiet Dennis who was a little standoffish but that was okay. Dennis was a cop?

"Dennis!" The word burst out before she could think twice about saying it aloud; just seeing a familiar face made something inside her loosen for half a second too long. Relief flared hot enough that it cracked briefly through layers of fear weighing heavy on everything else still hanging unsaid behind clenched teeth. "Thank God—it's you! Please—" Her voice faltered mid-air as if words themselves had decided not to cross whatever invisible threshold separated safe ground from where things slid sideways fast—

Because Dennis raised his gun.

Not casually—not cautiously—but fast enough that there wasn't room left inside Wren's mind for anything resembling reason anymore except for white-hot static crashing into itself over and over again until nothing coherent stood steady beneath waves slamming down faster than thought could shape around them.

This didn't make sense.

Dennis tipped well—and smiled too easily—and was so much more polite than her other regulars...

Time didn't slow—it never did, not really—but everything felt sharper, stretched thin as Dennis's finger tightened on the trigger. Wren's body moved before her mind caught up. She flinched hard, instinct curling her in on herself like a crumpled piece of paper. Her head jerked to the side, eyes clamping shut, bracing for the inevitable.

The gunshot tore through the room, splitting the air with a crack so loud it swallowed everything else. It wasn't like in movies—neat and distant—it was chaos wrapped in sound, shaking her bones from the inside out. Her ears rang, high-pitched and relentless, blotting out even her own ragged breaths. The only thing she could feel was her heartbeat battering against her ribcage, each thud a frantic reminder: Alive. Alive. Still alive.

Something snapped—a sudden sharp crack that didn't belong to her—and Wren's eyes flew open. Time didn't make sense again yet but there it was: splinters of wood erupting from the floorboards inches from her sneaker, a starburst of jagged edges where the bullet hit.

Move.

8:55 a.m.

Her muscles woke up first—hard jolts of electricity firing through her limbs—yanking her out of place before she had time to think about what came next. She scrambled upright, her feet slipping and skidding in the blood pooling around Anne's body. Warm and sticky, it smeared underfoot, thick enough to make bile rise in her throat as she fought to stay upright.

The rest of her had caught up now: twitches in her legs ready to spring into action, adrenaline turning every nerve into a live wire sparking wildly under skin. Without thinking about anything but forward—just forward—she lunged for the doorway.

The ringing was still there too—the muffled cocoon of an aftershock wrapping around everything—but she could hear just enough to know another gunshot was coming before it came: another explosion splitting open that fragile bubble of noise around her head. Something hot and wrong whizzed past too close, brushing air against the side of her face so sharp it almost cut her hairline open without touching it at all...Air displacement wasn't something Wren had thought much about before today—but oh god did she know it now; oh god she felt its exact shape against her cheek now.

The bullet struck something behind Wren—ping! She flinched again reflexively but barely noticed anymore because now suddenly suddenly (!) outside noise... Cars honking faintly further away than they should be...real people's voices somewhere? Hadn't seemed *likely* they'd exist while under threat indoors.

Wren burst onto the sidewalk, her breath sharp and uneven. Her eyes darted around, cataloging every detail—every possible threat or escape route. She caught sight of three pedestrians, their reactions unfolding in a chaotic display. To her left, a middle-aged man in a business suit crouched behind a parked car, his briefcase abandoned on the pavement like some sad casualty of the moment.

Ahead of her, an elderly woman froze mid-step, her cane suspended just above the ground. Her face was a study in shock—eyes wide and unblinking, mouth forming a perfect 'O,' as though trying to catch an answer from the air that wouldn't come.

To Wren's right, a teenager stood utterly still despite the thump of music escaping from his headphones. His hand hovered near his pocket where his phone buzzed insistently. The heavy bassline leaking from his ears underscored the scene in an absurd way—a strange beat to the mayhem.

Wren ran toward the fence. Her muscles tensed, wound tight like coiled rope about to snap free. And then they did: she vaulted over the metal barrier, her body curving through space with a speed and grace that seemed almost instinctive. She landed silently on the other side—knees bent to absorb the impact—and lunged for her bike in one motion that felt inevitable, the way falling feels inevitable once you've stepped off a ledge.

Her hands knew exactly where to go—the familiar grooves of the handlebars were cool under her fingers, grounding her for one fleeting second before reminding her of another sensation: the tacky warmth of blood still drying on her skin. She shoved it out of her mind.

"Police! Freeze!" The voice—Dennis's voice—shattered through the street noise like glass against concrete.

Wren turned instinctively, snapping her head back toward him. There he was, framed by the doorway like some grim painting brought to life. His gun was up, arm steady, barrel aimed directly at her chest. For what felt like forever but couldn't have been more than a heartbeat, she watched him tighten his grip on the weapon and thought: This is it.

Then he faltered. Dennis wasn't one to hesitate—it wasn't in his nature—but his eyes flicked sideways and took in the chaos she'd just registered herself: The businessman half-hidden behind the car with white knuckles grasping its hood for balance; the elderly woman rooted to her spot like she'd forgotten how legs worked; the kid with music loud enough for everyone within twenty feet to hear but no real sense of what was happening.

Dennis hesitated because he had rules—or maybe it was the idea that the witnesses would have something to say about him shooting a young woman in cold blood. Either way, that hesitation was hers now. Wren didn't waste it. She threw herself onto her bike in one fell swoop—one leg swinging over while muscle memory did all the work of positioning her body just so—and then she launched into action.

The pedals were underfoot before she even realized she was moving again. Her legs churned mechanically as if powered by something beyond effort or pain or fear—though all three surged through her veins anyway—and she shot forward down the street.

Behind her came Dennis's voice again: "Stop! Police!" But no gunshots followed this time. No sharp cracks cutting through air thickened by adrenaline and exhaust fumes; no bullets slicing past her ears with that terrifying sound you somehow always recognize even if you've never heard it before.

There was only wind now—cold against her cheeks—and noise: honking cars, tires screeching because drivers weren't expecting someone like Wren weaving recklessly between them at speeds reserved for things with engines rather than chains and pedals.

She didn't look back. Couldn't look back. Every nerve screamed at her to focus forward—to focus on escape—while chaos sharpened at its edges behind her and pressed harder against who she used to be.

The USB drive tucked into her sock burned against her ankle—not literally but close enough that she kept imagining scorch marks on skin beneath frayed cotton threads. It wasn't heavy—not really—but its weight was unbearable; it carried everything she'd seen moments earlier along with an unspoken understanding about what would happen if Dennis got hold of it instead of her keeping it safe—or buried—or gone forever.

Her muscles screamed louder now than nerves ever could: Slow down! Stop! Rest! But stopping wasn't something Wren could do yet—not after everything—not until streets blurred into nothingness behind miles thick enough to feel impossible to retrace backward later.

So onward she pedaled through intersections barely missed by turning cars whose drivers shouted curses muted by distance too quickly gained; onward past buildings whose windows reflected someone too familiar yet unreachable; onward until movement itself became both destination and purpose merged into one fragile thread pulling taut across time measured by breathlessness.

She reached for her phone, her fingers trembling as she pressed them against the sticky surface of the shattered screen. "Hello? Can you hear me?" she rasped, though deep down, she already knew there'd be no answer. The display was black, a spiderweb of cracks radiating from a neat hole—not large, but precise, like punctuation—a bullet marking the end of her last connection to help.

Wren let out a bitter curse under her breath and stuffed the useless device into her bag. Her eyes darted to the street ahead, searching for an escape route. That's when she saw it: an alley, narrow and cut deep between two brick buildings, half swallowed by shadow. There wasn't time to debate whether it was her best—or worst—option. She jerked her handlebars sharply to the right and plunged in without hesitation.

As soon as she entered, the walls seemed to close in on her, narrowing impossibly with every rotation of the pedals. The dim light barely reached this far back, leaving piles of garbage and broken glass scattered like traps across the cracked asphalt. Her heart thundered in her chest, a relentless hammering that drowned out nearly everything else—the skittering of something small through a tipped-over trash can, a door slamming somewhere above—as each new sound sent fresh jolts of electricity up her spine.

When Wren burst out the other side into open daylight again, it felt as though she had breached the surface after being underwater too long. She didn't stop to catch her breath or take comfort in surviving one small moment. Instead, she propelled herself straight into traffic without even glancing sideways. A car horn erupted in a sharp blast just inches away from her shoulder—the warning bark of some sleek blue electric two-door pipsqueak screeching to a halt—and when she flicked her head toward it for just a second too long, she locked eyes with its driver: middle-aged man, face frozen halfway between outrage and disbelief at the sight of someone streaked in red and ragged desperation cutting him off mid-commute.

But she didn't pause. She couldn't afford to. Wren shoved down on the pedals harder than before, dodging between honks and side mirrors in a chaotic rhythm that seemed bound to collapse at any second under its own recklessness.

The sirens were close now—close enough that they began to separate themselves from all other noise: There were three distinct ones layering together into an urgent chorus ahead of her somewhere down this labyrinthine urban maze. Were they for her? For Anne? For Dennis? It didn't matter what logical answer came next; Wren's gut had already decided that they were coming because everything was falling apart.

Her muscles burned as though fire had replaced blood in her veins; every gasp dragged shards of air into lungs that no longer wanted to work. But those things—painful as they were—were manageable compared to what looped endlessly inside her mind: Dennis lifting his arm and aiming carefully; his finger curling on the trigger; two bodies crumpling instead of one; Anne's eyes wide even as they went glassy; Wren bolting before either hit the floor completely.

She cursed under her breath again when a big yellow taxi swerved unexpectedly into her path like it had been summoned just to test how much more chaos could fit into this day. Wren swerved hard to avoid it, veering against parked cars at the edge of the street with nowhere else left to go. Her hip slammed brutally against one side mirror as she passed—a sudden explosion of white-hot pain tearing through layers of adrenaline buzz—and though she heard something snap beneath all those sounds (the mirror hitting pavement behind her), she refused even then to slow down.

The ache in her side was notable but secondary—a dull bass line underneath all the sharper edges: screeching tires here; car horns there; every new breath a knife stabbing inward—but up ahead emerged something new enough to refocus all attention forward again: Flashing lights weaving their way closer through packed lanes farther ahead—police cruisers clearing paths easily where bikes couldn't—and they were unmistakably heading toward Anne's house... maybe.

There wasn't time anymore for assumptions or doubts—not when panic grabbed hold of everything logical inside Wren and twisted it past breaking point until instinct took full command again. She yanked hard left without warning herself first—narrowly avoiding another collision—and angled toward sliver-thin space between two old buildings braced stiffly against each other like weary bookends near collapse.

The gap barely seemed wide enough for anything larger than memory or regret to pass through unscathed… but somehow Wren wedged herself into it anyway; handlebars brushing rough brick on both sides while elbows grazed close behind before slipping forward deeper still.

It smelled worse than anything prepared properly ever could—the scent rising hotly humid around rot layered atop grease layered atop something far worse left undefined beyond pure revulsion alone—and Wren gagged twice whole-heartedly before gritting teeth harder still beneath clenched fists clinging tighter now onto grips threatening constantly never quite fully letting go yet managing miraculously moment-by-moment somehow anyway continuing onward forward always forward.

Wren felt the sick give of something soft beneath her bike tires. She didn't look down. She couldn't. Her feet hit the ground, and she stumbled forward, finally stopping in the grimy alley that smelled like spoiled grease and old urine. Here, at least, she was hidden—or as hidden as she could hope to be.

Her breath came in jagged bursts, chest rising and falling like an overtaxed bellows. She reached for her phone again but fumbled it, her blood-slicked fingers skidding uselessly across the cracked glass. No response. Dead as…

No. Don't go there.

She squeezed her eyes shut, squeezing out the image that had burned itself into her mind: Anne's face tipped to one side, eyes fixed on something far away—something Wren couldn't see or follow. Her fingers trembled as she pried open the side compartment of the phone and popped out the SIM card with a desperate sort of violence. She held it between her teeth like a lifeline, its faint bitter tang mixing with the metallic taste already coating her tongue and throat. Blood? Her own maybe? Hard to tell anymore.

Wren glanced down at herself for the first time since she'd taken off—and immediately wished she hadn't.

Anne's blood—because whose else could it be?—clung to her cycling jersey in darkening patches like a grotesque mosaic, twisting its bright colors into something unrecognizable. Her sleeves were streaked from elbow to wrist with sticky crimson tracks that had started to dry, tightening against her skin like old varnish on wood.

"Shit." The word escaped before she realized it had formed, quickly followed by another "shit" and another as if one wasn't enough to convey the mess she was in. The SIM card clicked against her teeth as she muttered curses around it, her gaze darting wildly up and down the narrow alleyway for something—anything—that might help her figure this out.

She rubbed at her arms absentmindedly, smearing rather than cleaning them, which somehow made things worse—it made *her* worse too because now there wasn't any denying what she'd done or where she'd just come from or why this blood wasn't hers.

The sirens wailed faintly in the distance at first—far enough away that maybe they didn't matter yet—but even that small comfort faded as they grew louder and sharper by the second. They hadn't found her yet, but they would soon enough unless...

Unless what? Wren felt desperation claw its way up through her lungs and throat until it pushed tears into her eyes—not quite spilling over but close—so close that if someone even looked at her sideways, she'd fall apart completely.

Her eyes landed on him then—the man perched casually on an overturned bucket near an open service door, a cigarette balanced between his fingers in that lazy way people hold them when they aren't thinking about smoking so much as passing time. He wore a tired expression paired with hooded eyes that slid toward Wren with no particular alarm or urgency despite how she must've looked: wild-eyed and gasping like something cornered and feral.

His brow arched when his gaze took in the blood trailing down her arms and splattered across her legs. But instead of fear—or judgment or pity or any of those more complicated reactions people usually have when faced with someone like Wren—his face registered nothing more than mild surprise. Maybe curiosity too; yes, definitely curiosity.

"Rough day?" His voice was gravelly but even-toned, almost warm in its detached way.

Wren froze for half a beat before common sense (or what passed for it right now) kicked back in; whatever he saw when he looked at her didn't seem to bother him much—or if it did, he wasn't showing it—and so maybe... Maybe he wouldn't bother calling anyone about it either.

"You could say that," Wren managed finally; though "managed" might be generous considering how raw and uneven those words sounded coming out of her throat.

She hesitated again before blurting out: "It's not my blood." That wasn't what she'd meant to say—it wasn't even close—but once it was out there hanging between them like smoke curling off his cigarette tip.

He tilted his head—not enough to suggest disbelief exactly but enough that she knew he was considering everything he saw versus everything she said and weighing those two things carefully against each other in his mind.

"That's worse for you then," he said after another beat had passed—a flicker of dark humor threading through his words while still somehow managing not to come off cruel or careless either.

The sirens were closer now—were they circling her?—and panic flared fresh inside Wren's chest as though someone had struck a match next to gasoline-soaked nerves. She dropped down without thinking onto hands shaking harder than they should've been beneath all this adrenaline coursing through them while scooping dirty water from a shallow puddle nearby; cupping it awkwardly between palms stained red-black-brown-green depending on how light hit everything wrong all at once under neon glow spilling from above dumpsters nearby.

She scrubbed furiously—the grit stung almost immediately but barely registered because nothing washed off properly anyway—not blood—not doubt—not fear—and certainly never anything important enough ever gets cleaned away by effort alone does it?

He spoke again just then—in between slow deliberate pulls off smoke disappearing faster now than before because time *was* running thin here, wasn't It?

"Those sirens," he began casually—half-sigh half-murmur—as though stating facts nobody cared enough disputing today anyway "...they for you?"

Wren froze, her hands slick with the murky mixture of water and blood. The metallic tang of it lingered in the air, mingling with her ragged breaths. She glanced up at him, her chest shuddering with each inhale. "No," she said finally, her voice unsteady. "I was trying to help a woman when...when a cop shot at me."

The man's eyebrows lifted, though his expression stayed neutral. He didn't flinch, didn't so much as shift his stance. Instead, he just watched—watched as Wren resumed scrubbing at her legs with frantic urgency, each movement more erratic than the last.

"That's not gonna work," he said after a moment, his tone maddeningly calm. Wren looked up sharply, frustration flashing across her face like lightning before giving way to open exasperation. The man reached into the bag beside him and pulled out a plastic bottle of water. He shook it once for emphasis, the liquid sloshing against its sides. "Here," he said, holding it out.

Her fingers trembled as she grabbed it from him. She twisted off the cap and tipped the bottle without hesitation, cool water spilling down over her thighs and pooling on the cracked pavement below. The blood thinned instantly, running in weak pink streams that clung stubbornly to her skin.

The man gestured toward the restaurant behind them, a place that had seen better days long before Wren's current troubles had begun. "Rags inside," he said simply. "Door's open."

Wren followed his gaze and spotted a bundle of cloths tossed haphazardly just past the doorway—dirty ones by the looks of it. Before she could second-guess herself, she made a break for them. Her hand shot out to snatch up a handful of fabric, coarse and stiff against her palms. Back on the ground outside, she scrubbed violently at her legs again, as if sheer force might erase what had been done.

"Did I hear you right?" The man's voice cut through the tense silence between them like a blade dulled with use but no less sharp for it. He took another drag from his cigarette before exhaling smoke that curled lazily upward into the morning air. "You said a cop shot you?"

Wren stilled again, mid-swipe this time. Her gaze darted to him briefly before falling away, like someone ashamed to meet an accuser's eyes—not that he was accusing her of anything specific yet. "Shot at me," she rasped. "He missed."

He chuckled then—a low sound that felt true here amidst all this scrubbing and blood and panic—and flicked ash onto the ground between them. "Guess those sirens are for you then," he said.

Her reaction was immediate: shaking her head furiously as though trying to chase away bees swarming too close for comfort. She bent back over herself and resumed scrubbing with even greater intensity now, each stroke desperate and unrelenting. "I didn't do anything wrong," she muttered under her breath, almost like a prayer—one meant more for herself than anyone listening.

The man raised an eyebrow but didn't laugh this time; instead, he studied her before speaking again: "Yeah? Since when's that ever stopped them?"

His words landed heavier than they should have—heavier than Wren was prepared for—and all at once something cracked open inside her chest where panic had already taken root hours earlier. It came rushing back now in full force—the kind that pressed down on your lungs until breathing felt impossible and left your hands moving faster just for something to do.

The filthy rags were turning pink beneath her relentless scrubbing—blood diluted but not gone entirely—and yet she couldn't tell whether she was making progress or spreading guilt-colored stains further across herself.

She needed options—and fast—but none presented themselves readily except one: communication.

"Is there... Is there somewhere nearby I can get a burner phone?" Her question tumbled out hurriedly while she tried desperately not to choke on how tiny her voice sounded compared to everything else happening right now—sirens swelling louder somewhere far too close by.

The man pointed lazily down toward an alley stretching deeper into darkness beyond them both—just two fingers extended mid-cigarette drag like directions weren't worth wasting words on anymore tonight unless absolutely necessary: "Couple blocks that way," he said finally after taking another pull first because apparently timing wasn't nearly high enough up his list of priorities compared against nicotine cravings.

Wren nodded, the relief flooding through her body in a slow, tentative wave. She'd barely shifted to move when the man's gravelly voice cut across the moment.

"Something wrong with your phone?"

Her hand froze mid-motion as if caught doing something incriminating. Hesitation flickered briefly before she reached into her bag, fingers brushing against the jagged edges of her shattered device. She pulled it out, holding it up for him to see. The bullet hole gaped at its center like an accusatory eye, an ugly souvenir of how close she'd tiptoed to disaster. The man's gaze snagged on it, his expression betraying a flicker of surprise—subtle enough to make Wren think he was used to this sort of thing. Whatever "this sort of thing" was.

"Huh." He dragged the word out lazily before cocking his head. "You still want that phone?"

Her fingers tightened instinctively around the broken device, though she wasn't sure if it was from protection or possession. "Yeah," she said shortly. "It's got the bullet in it."

If the man thought this was a strange reason to cling to a useless phone—and surely he did—he didn't say so outright. His eyebrows rose incrementally, amusement glinting faintly in his eyes, but he kept his tone conversational. "Tell you what," he said, leaning forward just enough so that his cigarette dangled precariously close to ash-dropping territory, "how about I take the phone off your hands—you keep the bullet—and I'll trade it in for an upgrade? They take them in any condition these days." A brief pause, followed by what was clearly an afterthought: "Consider it a reward for me helping you out."

Wren blinked at him, struggling to process what felt like a bizarrely casual offer given the circumstances. It wasn't the worst deal she'd ever heard—her mind quickly cataloged worse—but still, she hesitated. The phone wasn't just damaged; it had become a kind of talisman in her grip, proof that she'd survived whatever chaos had tried to claim her hours earlier. But then again—the bullet might matter more later.

"You serious?" she asked warily.

The man shrugged like he'd just offered her half his sandwich instead of proposing some mildly suspicious trade involving gunshot electronics. He flicked ash from his cigarette with nonchalance. "Sure. Fair trade, right?"

Wren's grip on the phone loosened before tightening again in some last tug-of-war with herself. Finally, she nodded once and murmured an uncertain "Okay." The words came out quieter than expected, hesitant even as they left her lips. "I've got the SIM anyway."

It took longer than it should have for her trembling hands to pry at the edges of the bullet hole—it turned out removing embedded projectiles wasn't exactly a skill they taught you in school—and her nails scraped awkwardly against shards of shattered glass until finally, with a soft but oddly satisfying pop, it came loose. She turned it over in her palm once before quickly pocketing it like someone might snatch it away if she lingered too long.

"Here," she said at last, extending the ruined device towards him while carefully avoiding eye contact. Then came another murmur: "And... thanks."

The man whistled low as he took the phone from her—a sound that somehow felt like both admiration and mockery all at once—and flipped it over in his hands as though appraising something valuable despite its obvious wreckage. "No problem," he said lightly before adding with a half-smirk: "Be careful out there."

Be careful out there? As useful as the woman who told her 'Good luck.' Wren swallowed hard against whatever sharp retort had sprung to mind and glanced down at herself instead as though reminding herself why no one would take well-meaning advice seriously from someone who looked like... well... this. The blood-stained clothes were still doing her no favors despite that haphazard scrubbing session earlier—a literal washout—but at least now she resembled someone who'd taken a nasty fall rather than fled fresh from a crime scene.

"It'll have to do," she muttered under her breath before throwing him another quiet "Thanks" and swinging one leg over her bike seat with far less grace than intended. Her muscles screamed complaints immediately—not indignantly but earnestly, as if questioning every foolish decision that had led her here.

The man gestured vaguely behind him with his cigarette hand toward where daylight just barely illuminated distant storefronts beyond the alley mouth. "Phone store's two blocks up," he said simply. "Can't miss it."

Wren pushed off without another word—what else was there to say?—and felt gravel crunch beneath her tires as she pedaled slowly from shadow into sunlight that hit harder than expected on skin still tender from everything recent memory had thrown at her.

The alley seemed less heavy now somehow; maybe it was something about leaving parts of yourself behind (a broken phone here or whispered gratitude there). Or maybe sunlight alone could dissolve things like suspicion and threat if you let yourself believe that long enough.

She squinted ahead toward where storefronts blurred together and focused all remaining energy on moving forward rather than thinking backward: one pedal stroke after another toward something small but necessary—something like clarity—or failing that... just a burner phone that wouldn't betray her secrets any further than life already had done today.

Wren pedaled slowly down the street, her gaze darting around as though every shadow might spring to life. Her heart had yet to find a normal rhythm, hammering at her ribs like it was trying to escape. The adrenaline that had kept her upright was ebbing now, leaving behind a hollow shakiness in its wake. She kept her head low, chin nearly grazing her chest, trying her damnedest to vanish into the chaos of New York.

Two blocks felt more like twenty miles. Each stroke of the pedals added to her velocity, building to a crescendo that drowned out the distant wail of sirens somewhere behind her. Did the goddamned sirens ever stop? Every flash of blue—whether a jacket sleeve or someone's jeans—sent a fresh jolt through her already frayed nerves. But no one paid the slightest attention to her. That was New York for you—bloodstained clothes and wild eyes didn't even register. The city churned on, indifferent, swallowing Wren whole while ignoring everything she brought with her.

Then she saw it: a bodega wedged between a liquor store that blinked "OPEN" in defiant neon and an old mattress shop where the "FOR LEASE" sign hung tilted and sad. The bodega's window boasted a hand-written sign in thick black marker: "Unlocked Phones Sold Here." Relief didn't so much wash over Wren as crash into her like a breaking wave.

She swung off her bike awkwardly, her legs wobbling under the sudden weight of gravity. Her hands felt clumsy as they fumbled with the lock, looping the chain twice as though double security would somehow reassure her. It didn't.

The bell above the door jingled when she stepped inside, and immediately Wren felt ensnared by the sensory overload—a sharp contrast from the relative quiet of the street outside. The smell hit first: burned coffee tangled with spices that prickled the back of her throat. The narrow aisles stretched on forever—or maybe just three or four paces—crammed full with shelves stuffed to collapse with snacks, canned goods, cleaning supplies. Pretty much anything you never thought you'd need until you did.

To her left stood a glass display case, its shelves lined with neatly arranged unlocked phones ordered by brand and size like some exhibit at a tightly packed museum of outdated tech. Above it dangled rows of phone accessories—chargers, SIM cards, cases in garish colors no one in their right mind would buy but everyone somehow ended up owning anyway.

Wren shuffled forward on legs that felt more foreign with every step. A red-eyed old man swayed near the ice freezer, watching her without much interest or coherence. He reeked of stale cigarettes and cheap whiskey even from across the room. She ignored him and forced herself to take slow breaths through clenched teeth. Stay calm, stay invisible, stay normal—or at least as close to normal as someone covered in blood could manage.

Reaching the counter, she fixed her eyes on the row of phones behind glass like they were lifeboats drifting just out of reach. Her pulse started to settle for half a second before panic kicked down the door again; instinctively, she reached for what wasn't there—her back pocket—and came up empty-handed. No phone. No wallet. No cash folded neatly for emergencies because there hadn't been time for planning or packing or anything resembling foresight.

"Fuck," she muttered under her breath—not loud enough to draw attention but still loud enough for the clerk to glance up briefly, brows knitting together before he shrugged it off and returned his focus to his register tape or phone screen or whatever else clerks busy themselves with when they're pretending not to notice you.

Wren plastered on what she hoped passed for an absentminded smile and pretended to browse along one of those endless aisles filled with things neither she nor anyone else needed right now—a can of Spam here, a dog toy there. Her mind raced ahead into dangerous territory: She needed that phone *yesterday*. She needed Maggie on speed dial—or at least within shouting distance—and she needed answers fast.

An idea came suddenly—an idea so simple it almost felt laughable if laughter had any business existing here right now. Without pausing long enough to sec-ond-guess herself (or smarter still abandon this plan entirely), Wren spun on her heel and strode out of the bodega, past that same bell jingling its goodbye behind her.

Her bike sat where she'd locked it—or rather slumped against its pole like it had given up hope—its seat hiding exactly what she was looking for: the toolkit Suze had given her years ago when she still thought biking would make everything better between them (spoiler: it hadn't). Wren flipped open one grimy latch after another until she found what she needed—the multi-tool glinting faintly under weak fluorescent light spilling from somewhere overhead.

Perfect.

She headed inside again.

The old man chose this exact moment to shuffle past her toward freedom—or maybe just deeper oblivion—and their shoulders brushed accidentally-on-purpose as he slurred something incoherent under his breath—the kind of soundless curse only bored drunkards could perfect. Wren caught herself wrinkling her nose at his smell but shook it off quickly; he was irrelevant noise compared to what mattered right now.

Back in front of that glass case filled with phones promising salvation (or at least some temporary connection), Wren squared herself up for Step Two: making this work without completely losing control—or worse yet giving away how desperately close she'd come already.

Wren stepped up to the counter, her pulse thudding in her ears. The man behind the clouded Plexiglas gave her a once-over, his gaze lingering on the streaks of dried blood smeared across her shirt and the edges of her shorts. Suspicion flickered across his face—brief, but unmistakable.

"I need a phone," Wren said. Her voice sounded steadier out loud than it felt in her chest, which was something. "I don't have cash, but I've got this." She held up multi-tool, the weight of it solid in her palm.

The guy raised an eyebrow, skepticism softening into something closer to mild interest. Without speaking, he gestured toward the opening at the base of the barrier. Wren hesitated for half a second—long enough for doubt to whisper its usual warnings—but then she pushed the tool through and watched as it skidded across the scuffed metal counter on his side.

The cashier picked it up with hands too quick and methodical for someone who worked in a place like this. His fingers flipped open each attachment as if testing its potential worth: a blade here, a file there, hex keys glinting beneath the washed-out buzz of fluorescent lights. For a moment, Wren forgot to breathe. She didn't move, didn't blink, not even when his inspection slowed over one particular piece.

"This?" he asked, holding it up between his thumb and forefinger as though it were a puzzle he intended to solve.

"Chain breaker," she replied quickly—too quickly—and forced herself to add after a beat, "For bike repairs."

He grunted softly at that, an ambiguous sound that could mean just about anything. His focus shifted back to the multi-tool while Wren's focus stayed locked on him.

After what felt like an eternity but was surely no more than thirty seconds, he shrugged. "It'll do." He set the tool down and nodded toward a modest display case near his elbow. "Pick one."

Three flip phones sat inside: no-frills designs with scratched exteriors that looked two software updates overdue for retirement. The sight of them sent a wave of relief coursing through her chest so fast and sharp that she nearly swayed under its weight.

"Fine," she said too eagerly. "Yeah, fine."

The cashier turned away to grab one of the phones. Wren's fingers tapped an uneven rhythm on the counter now—tap-tap-tap-tap—in time with every harsh beat ricocheting off her ribcage. The tapping grated against her nerves almost as much as waiting did: first seconds stretched thin like pulled thread; then those same seconds snapped all at once into spiraling urgency.

"Can you hurry?" Wren blurted before she could stop herself. The words hit harder than planned, edged with something close enough to panic to make her grit her teeth in regret.

The man glanced over his shoulder briefly but said nothing. He simply plucked a phone from wherever he'd been deliberating (deliberating why? What was there even to deliberate about?) and placed it on the counter alongside a prepaid SIM card still sealed in plastic packaging.

"Here," he said flatly.

Wren's hands shot forward like reflex—grab first; think later—a survival instinct honed sharp over too many years of needing exactly what she couldn't afford to lose. But before her fingers could close fully around either item...

"Wait."

Her whole body stiffened at that single word—wait—and without turning toward him again completely (because why look when instinct already screamed Run), she froze mid-motion while blinding spikes shot upward from gut-level dread straight toward conscious thought-level fear.

The man emerged from below, holding a tangled mess of phone chargers that looked as though they had been wrestled from the belly of some electronic beast. The cords were looped together like a bird's nest, hopelessly knotted, and Wren felt her chest tighten. Every second he spent fumbling with the pile stretched painfully long, like her own private eternity. Her fingers tapped an uneven rhythm against the counter—tap, tap, pause, tap—as her teeth caught the corner of her bottom lip.

Through the grimy bodega window, Wren's gaze swept the street outside. Nothing but the daily chaos of New York: men in suits rushing with coffee cups in hand, tourists craning their necks to peer up at buildings, delivery bikes zigzagging past pedestrians who barely noticed their own near misses. No flashing red-and-blue lights. No uniforms weaving through the crowd. That should have calmed her down. It didn't.

"Got it!"

The cashier's voice jolted her back to reality. He held up a single charger, battered and frayed but still intact enough to cling to life.

Wren didn't hesitate. Her hand shot out and grabbed it, along with the phone and SIM card on the counter before he could even blink. She mumbled something that vaguely resembled "Thanks," but whatever tone she used was lost because she was already pivoting toward the door.

The bell jingled overhead as she pushed out onto the sidewalk in a burst of motion, her courier bag thumping heavily against her hip as she jogged to where her bike was chained up outside the store. She dropped to one knee beside it, yanking her bag open with trembling fingers and shoving everything inside—charger, phone, SIM card—all crammed into one pocket without ceremony or care.

Her hands moved quickly on instinct now, muscle memory taking over where panic threatened to creep in again. The lock clicked open after one failed attempt, and Wren swung a leg over the frame easily before pushing off with a forceful stroke.

The bike jerked forward like a wild thing released from a cage, wobbling for just a moment before surging into motion. She hunched low over the handlebars as if that might make her invisible—or at least harder to recognize—and wove through clusters of pedestrians who mostly ignored her except for an annoyed shout here or there when she came too close for comfort.

The wind hit her immediately—cold and biting and sharp against her cheeks—but it did wonders to clear some of the fog from her brain. With each pump of her legs against the pedals, more tension seemed to drop away—not all of it but enough so she could think again without every thought being drowned out by sheer noise inside her skull.

She had no plan yet beyond going somewhere else—anywhere else—but at least she had something now: a phone (broken or not), a charger (frayed or not), and that tiny slip of plastic that might help her figure out what was happening or reach someone who could explain it all to her.

None of that changed what was behind her—or ahead of her for that matter. She pedaled faster anyway.

She stuck close to side streets and weaved through alleyways when she could, staying away from anything wide enough for someone watching from above—or behind—to spot easily. Her usual casual disregard for road rules—darting through traffic lights just as they turned red or taking pedestrian-only paths be-cause they shaved seconds off travel time—was overshadowed now by something more careful than fear: survival instinct.

At an intersection thick with honking cars and impatient drivers leaning too hard on their horns as though sheer volume would force things to move faster, a sleek black SUV cut directly across Wren's path without warning or apology. It came so close that its side mirror grazed empty air where just seconds earlier her front wheel had been.

For one long second too many, Wren wanted nothing more than to lash out—to take aim at its stupidly shiny bumper with one well-placed kick or let loose every curse word she'd ever learned (and there were plenty). But she didn't—not even when anger surged hot through every nerve ending like acid in her veins.

Instead, she swallowed hard past the knot forming in her throat and forced herself back under control because lashing out—even if deserved—wasn't an option right now.

Her knuckles turned white around the handlebars; every muscle in her body flexed tight as though bracing for another hit that never came while she watched tail lights disappear into distance ahead like nothing had happened at all—as though none of this mattered except getting wherever they were going faster than everyone else around them did.

Eventually—slowly—her grip eased up again enough for circulation return properly while breath steadied itself back into something resembling normal pace instead jagged gasps between clenched teeth.

After several more blocks of navigating with care—too much care, if she were honest, each turn feeling like a gamble—Wren spotted a parkette wedged between two office buildings that seemed to claw at the sky. Her legs throbbed, a rhythmic reminder of the morning's chaos, and everything she'd tried not to think about pressed on her chest like a stone. She needed this moment. A reprieve. Just enough time to breathe, to steady herself.

She rolled into the little park, her bike tires crunching faintly on the gravel path. The sound was oddly satisfying, though it was swallowed almost immediately by the hum of buses, shouting pedestrians, and all the other auditory graffiti of city life. The parkette was trying its best to be an oasis—trees leaned protectively over a small circle of grass, scattering sunlight in broken patterns across the ground. Wooden benches traced its edges, their paint long past its prime but still managing to look oddly welcoming, as though peeling didn't mean unloved.

In the middle stood a fountain no bigger than a kitchen table, water burbling lazily from its spout like it couldn't quite muster the energy for anything more dramatic. Pigeons milled around it like gossipy regulars at their favorite café, oblivious to Wren's arrival—and really, who could blame them?

Wren swung off her bike and stayed still for a moment, feet planted on solid ground. She rested her hands on the handlebars and closed her eyes briefly, letting the semi-quiet settle over her like some kind of secondhand calm. The smell of freshly cut grass tangled with the usual city bouquet—car exhaust, distant hot dogs on portable grills—and she hated how comforting she found it.

Her gaze landed on an elderly woman crouched near one of the benches. The woman's hands were knotted with age but quick and precise as they worked through a small flower bed—a weed here, a tuck of soil there. A guerilla gardener doing battle against neglect and concrete. For just a moment—a flicker—Wren felt envy. How nice it must be to focus on that: flowers needing tending and nothing else.

But Wren couldn't stay still long enough to let that thought linger. Her hands were trembling again—was it adrenaline? Fear? The caffeine from hours ago?—as she pulled out the new phone from her bag. It felt alien in her grip, too square and too unfamiliar. She fumbled with it awkwardly until the back popped off, revealing the SIM card slot inside. Whatever tiny prayer she still dared to believe in slipped through her lips as she slid the burners prepaid chip into place.

The phone lit up with a faint buzz when she pressed its power button—the screen flickered once, then again—and Wren held her breath as though exhaling might shatter whatever fragile bit of hope remained intact inside her chest. The startup animation dragged itself across the screen in slow motion; every passing second stretched taut as wires between panic and impatience.

Her heart hammered against her ribs as she scanned the park automatically—even though she knew better than to think Dennis or anyone else would just appear right now (but wasn't that always how these things played out?). When finally—finally—the home screen blinked into view like some reluctant guardian angel had taken pity on her for once in this whole mess, Wren let out an audible breath she hadn't realized she'd been holding.

Her fingers flew over the keypad—unfamiliar buttons tripping under muscle memory that didn't quite fit this outdated thing—as she punched in Maggie's number and pressed call before hesitation could creep in. The phone felt heavy against her ear as it rang once... then twice... then three times... each ring louder than it should have been against the fountain's lazy burble and rising din from beyond the trees.

A jogger passed by—a man in neon running shoes who glanced at her too long before moving on—and Wren turned away from him without thinking about why exactly she felt exposed sitting here like this.

The fourth ring ended in Maggie's voicemail—the sound of her girlfriend's voice spilling out crisp and warm and painfully normal even now: "Hey, you've reached Maggie! I can't come to the phone right now, but leave me a message—I'll get back to you as soon as I can."

There was a beep.

Wren just stood there gripping this stupid little phone while something sharp twisted low in her gut. Then finally—finally—she forced herself to speak:

"Call me," she said roughly into that tiny plastic void where Maggie's voice had just lived seconds earlier. "Call me back with a redial."

A sudden, involuntary tremor hit but she steadied again for what came next: "Someone's dead."

9:33 a.m.

Wren straddled her bike, the cool steel frame steady and familiar beneath her weight. She drew in a deep breath, filling her lungs with the sharp tang of freshly cut grass and the faint sweetness of blooming flowers. It was one of those postcard-perfect moments. Birds chirped somewhere unseen. A butterfly drifted by on lazy wings, catching a glint of sunlight as it passed.

"Damn," she muttered under her breath, letting herself sink into the rare feeling of quiet. "This is nice."

Her gaze wandered across the small parkette. The riotous colors of tulips and marigolds dotted the flower beds like spilled paint, and sunlight filtered softly through a canopy of leaves overhead. For just a second, it felt almost possible to forget everything.

Almost.

The blood came back to her first—dark, almost black beneath the weak glow of her memory, spreading in slow, viscous tendrils across the floor. Then the sound: a wet, rasping gurgle as lips moved to form words that never reached the air. Finally, there were the eyes, wide and glassy and locked onto hers in terrified desperation.

Wren's stomach flipped. Her fingers clenched at the handlebars so hard that her knuckles went pale against sun-bronzed skin. She shut her eyes briefly—but that made things worse because now she could hear it again too clearly: the sharp crack of gunfire splitting open the air; bullets slicing so close she could feel them zip past her head; the rhythmic pound of her feet against pedals as she pushed herself faster and harder than she thought possible until—

"Shit." Wren shook her head hard enough to make strands of hair whip against her cheeks. As if that would help. As if shaking could force out what was now etched onto the backs of her eyelids, playing on repeat like some sick highlight reel every time she blinked.

Her hands fumbled for her phone, fingers jerky as they hit redial. The chipper ringtone buzzed faintly against her ear while panic coiled tighter in her chest with each unanswered ring.

"Come on," she hissed through gritted teeth, one leg bouncing impatiently against the bike frame. "Pick up."

But Maggie didn't pick up. She hadn't picked up on Wren's earlier call either—and this time was no different. Voicemail again.

"Babe, it's me," Wren said when the beep came, though she already knew Maggie wouldn't answer this message either. Her lips quivered as she pushed out more words: "I—I need help." A long pause followed while Wren clenched her jaw tight enough to hurt before adding quietly: "Just... call me back, okay? Redial, not my old number."

She ended the call without waiting for an answer that wasn't coming and shoved her phone back into her pocket like it had personally offended her. The mid-morning sun beat down relentlessly now, its earlier warmth having turned oppressive somewhere along the way without permission—it pressed against her skin in thick waves, turning sweat into sticky rivers down between her shoulder blades.

She stood abruptly then—sitting still wasn't working anymore—and began pacing aimlessly beside where she'd propped up the bike moments earlier so carefully like none of this mattered yet (when clearly all of it did). Her movements were choppy now; restless energy bristled through every step forward or backward or sideways because there didn't seem to be any direction that felt right anymore—not here anyway.

The parkette felt too open—too exposed—with its meandering paths crisscrossing at odd angles like targets painted over green lawns dotted by benches and playgrounds meant for quieter lives than hers had ever been capable of holding onto for long stretches at once anyway.

Are they staring at me? That thought prickled suddenly across Wren's mind as someone jogged past. A man strolled by walking his dog lazily enough not even noticing *her,* probably—but God did it feel otherwise inside her head despite knowing better altogether rationally speaking always somehow still far too late after already twisting tighter around spirals unraveling—

Stop.

She was in trouble again (and not the fun kind of trouble that left her laughing and exhilarated). No, this was the wrong kind of trouble, the kind that left a bitter taste in her mouth and a knot in her stomach. The kind that made her wonder if she'd finally pushed her luck too far.

Wren wriggled her toes inside her sneakers. She watched them press against the leather, a movement so small it was almost imperceptible, but she felt it. The sensation grounded her. Proof that everything still worked, that she was here and alive and capable. There had been a time when she couldn't do this—when her toes just sat there like they belonged to someone else and refused to listen.

The smell came first. That sterile, hospital disinfectant smell that crept up her nose and lodged itself in her memory for good. Suddenly, she was back there: a hospital bed too big for her small body, wires snaking out of machines that beeped in rhythms she didn't understand, adults whispering things they didn't think she could hear. "Nerve damage," one had said. "Recovery uncertain," another murmured. Wren hadn't cared much about the words themselves. All that mattered was that her legs wouldn't move and neither would her toes, no matter how much she willed them to.

The weeks after that had stretched on forever. Endless hours of therapy where nothing happened until, one day, something did—her big toe moved. Just once, just barely. She remembered staring at it for a full minute before bursting into tears so loud the nurses came running. A single twitch of one toe shouldn't have felt like such a victory, but oh, it had.

Now Wren flexed those same toes with ease. It wasn't exactly miraculous—not to anyone else—but it meant everything to her. She smiled faintly, a tiny gesture for what felt like a massive triumph. Her body worked now: legs strong enough to run and jump and bike through traffic-clogged streets without hesitation or fear. The gratitude coursed through her like sunlight breaking through clouds.

But the warmth didn't last long.

She stilled suddenly, the smile slipping off her face as if it had never been there at all. Gratitude gave way to something heavier—something darker—and Wren dropped onto the nearest bench as though she might sink under its weight if she didn't sit down immediately. She rubbed at her temples as memories began swirling in faster than she could stop them.

Her eyes shut tight against it, fists clenching so hard her nails pressed little crescents into her palms—not that it helped. Some memories weren't willing to leave you alone just because you wanted them gone.

She was nine again and standing barefoot in the front yard—the first time in years she'd felt grass between her toes or sunshine on legs pale from being hidden beneath blankets and hospital gowns for too long. The shorts she wore were unfamiliar; they made her skin feel exposed and strange.

Her legs trembled under her weight—a jelly-like wobble that betrayed how weak they still were—but Wren didn't care about any of that right then because she was outside and standing upright all on her own. She took one shaky step forward, then another, marveling at each new sensation: grass poking gently at the soles of her feet, warm air brushing against bare skin.

"Well, look who's finally up and about."

The voice froze her mid-step as effectively as if someone had grabbed both shoulders and yanked her back into place. Officer Thomas Goldfinch stood leaning casually against his side of the fence like he always did, one boot crossed over the other at the ankle. He smiled as he spoke again: "Didn't think I'd ever get to see you out here again."

Something about his tone—or maybe his eyes—made bile rise in Wren's throat even though they were separated by several feet of neatly trimmed lawn and wood planks painted white.

"Why don't you come closer? Let me see how you're doing?" he added with what passed for friendliness but wasn't even close to real kindness; Wren could tell even then—even at nine years old—that whatever sweetness coated Goldfinch's words hid something rotten beneath.

Wren's instinct wasn't courage exactly—she stepped back instead of forward—but it was enough for now because stepping backward meant not stepping toward him like he wanted. Her toes curled into the grass as though anchoring themselves there despite legs too weak yet to run anywhere fast or far.

Goldfinch tilted his head and chuckled low enough to sound private even though there wasn't anyone else around to overhear him say: "Careful now—you wouldn't want those pretty new legs of yours giving out already."

Wren didn't answer him—not aloud anyway—but all these years later just thinking about his words made everything inside tighten painfully: throat clamped shut; hands gripping anything solid nearby; chest rising faster than usual while lungs forgot how breathing worked properly.

Back then though? Back then she hadn't screamed or cried (even though part of her wanted desperately to do either or both). Instead, nine-year-old Wren turned slowly away without saying goodbye—not because politeness dictated anything so formal but because speaking felt dangerous somehow—and started wobbling carefully toward home again instead.

Wren glanced toward the front door, measuring the steps. Too many, she thought. Her legs, trembling beneath her like loose scaffolding, weren't ready for this. They complained with every second she remained standing, muscles straining, knees buckling. But standing felt better than staying close to Goldfinch.

"I should go inside," she murmured. Her voice came out weak, barely more than a breath.

Goldfinch's smile didn't budge. He leaned against the porch railing, casual as could be, but his eyes stayed fixed on her like a predator waiting for its prey to falter. "Now, don't sell yourself short," he said, his tone dripping with false warmth. "Your parents told me you wouldn't ever walk again. But here you are."

Her jaw tightened. Wren's parents had said a lot of things about her over the years—most of them when they assumed she couldn't hear—but that particular comment stung more than usual now. Not because it was cruel (it wasn't even close to the worst of it), but because it might have been true if she hadn't pushed herself every day just to prove them wrong.

"Show me," Goldfinch coaxed, tilting his head as though he were talking to a skittish colt instead of a girl who wanted very much to be anywhere but here. "Take a few steps for me."

His words lingered in the air between them like bait, sweet and sticky and impossible to ignore. Wren swallowed hard and shifted her weight toward the house. Her legs screamed their objections immediately, but she gritted her teeth and took a step anyway—the first real step she'd taken since... well, since before everything had changed.

Then another step came. And another after that.

"That's my girl," Goldfinch crooned when she faltered and then righted herself again, as though sheer stubbornness alone kept her upright. His grin widened until it split his face in two.

Wren fought back the wave of nausea that hit her at those words: *my girl.* She wasn't his anything—not anymore than she was anyone else's.

With one final burst of willpower—or maybe desperation—Wren pivoted on shaking legs and bolted for the house. Her coordination left much to be desired; each stride felt precarious, like skittering across broken glass on stilts. But she didn't stop moving.

The cool grass blurred beneath her bare feet as her breath came in short bursts that didn't seem nearly enough to fuel this reckless escape attempt. The wooden porch steps loomed ahead like salvation itself.

"Well now!" A booming voice cut through the pounding of her heart and startled her enough that her hand slipped off the doorknob mid-reach.

Wren turned slowly toward him, dread pooling low in her gut before recognition caught up with reality: Thomas stood close—he'd moved much faster than she could. A tall figure gleaming under the midday sun in full uniform, badge flashing brightly enough to make her wince just looking at him.

"Didn't I always tell your folks there was fight left in you?" Thomas called cheerfully before stepping closer into what Wren had come to know as *his zone*—friendly enough on paper but never quite safe enough in practice.

Before she could calibrate some kind of response (or at least muster a polite excuse), footsteps scuffed behind her as her parents appeared at last—drawn outside not by concern for their daughter so much as curiosity about whatever scene she'd caused this time.

Her mother's expression shifted instantly into something warm and familiar reserved exclusively for interactions involving people who weren't family members—or more specifically when interacting with men like Thomas who carried authority around like cologne.

"Thomas! What brings you by?" Wren's mother asked brightly despite having practically ignored Wren altogether seconds earlier when passing by indoors.

"Oh nothing special," Thomas replied easily while gesturing toward Wren still teetering awkwardly near doorway liminality somewhere between triumph and collapse altogether. "Just lending a little encouragement to our newest miracle."

Her father draped an arm across her mother's shoulders, his voice warm with relief, though he missed the mark entirely. "I swear, you'd never know she was hit by a car. Kid's up and about like nothing ever happened."

Thomas was there before the words even finished settling, his grin wide enough to eclipse the moment. "I was just telling Wren how proud you must be," he said, clapping her father on the back like they were old friends. "This calls for a celebration!"

The next few moments blurred together in a flurry of nodding and enthusiasm. Her parents, buoyed by their joy and Thomas's easy charisma, latched onto his suggestion as though it had been their own idea all along. He was Officer Goldfinch, after all—a pillar of the community, a man in uniform who knew everyone's name and always stopped to say hello at supermarket checkout lines.

"Why don't you bring Wren over to use our pool?" Thomas suggested casually, as though the thought had just come to him. "It'd be perfect for her recovery—water therapy works wonders. Plus, the neighborhood kids are always splashing around over there."

Wren's parents didn't just agree—they practically leaped at the offer, their heads bobbing in unison as if synced to some invisible rhythm only Thomas conducted. Plans were made before Wren could even open her mouth.

At first, it wasn't so bad. The water felt good—weightless and freeing in a way nothing else had since the accident. She could drift there without being afraid of falling or stumbling or seeing her parents' worried (disgusted?) faces hovering over her every time she took a misstep. Other kids were always around too, their laughter echoing off the backyard fences as they cannonballed into the deep end or raced across inflatable floats.

And then there was Thomas.

Thomas with his relentless cheerfulness. Thomas with his camera always slung around his neck like a permanent fixture. "For the scrapbook!" he'd joke with an easy laugh, snapping photo after photo of kids mid-splash or mid-sunbeam without ever missing a beat.

She didn't like him, but couldn't say why. He was friendly; he was funny; he had her parents wrapped around his finger with every polite word or passing compliment. But slowly—so slowly that Wren couldn't even pin down when things started to shift—she began to sense it.

The way his lens seemed to linger on her just a moment longer than on anyone else. The way he'd wave her over while she floated aimlessly near the shallow end, asking for "just one quick photo" but never stopping at one. "Let's get a shot of our miracle girl," he'd say with that honeyed tone that coated his words too thickly, his smile stretched tight across his face like something barely held in place.

"Smile bigger," he'd urge softly but insistently when she gave him anything less than perfection on her first try. "Turn this way—yeah, like that." His fingers hovered near her shoulder once—just once—but long enough for her skin to prickle beneath his touch.

She wanted to tell someone—it felt wrong not to—but how could she? Her parents adored him; everyone did. "He's got your best interests at heart," they reminded her whenever doubt flickered across her face like static on an old TV screen. "Listen to Officer Goldfinch."

Yet Wren couldn't shake it—the clench in her stomach whenever Thomas singled her out from the crowd of other kids splashing happily nearby; the odd pitch of his voice whenever he said things like "You're my favorite subject" too close to her ear; or the way he'd wait until no one else was watching before asking for "special photos." Special photos where she stood alone while everyone else played behind them in soft-focus backgrounds.

"Our little secret," he whispered once when no one was close enough to over-hear him.

Her stomach twisted hard now—not from injury but something sharper and icier—as droplets rolled off her arms and legs after pulling herself out of the pool one afternoon. She stood there dripping wet on concrete gone uncomfortably warm under midday light but couldn't summon herself back into that feeling of weightlessness anymore—not when Thomas stood waiting nearby.

There he was: camera in hand, gaze fixed on hers with an intensity that made bile rise unchecked in her throat.

"Come on," he said lightly—too lightly—as though coaxing wasn't really coaxing if done under bright sun and clear skies. His hand gestured toward a spot near where water lapped against smooth tiles at pool's edge—a spot carefully chosen out of range from any prying eyes except his own.

Her feet stayed rooted firmly where they were despite everything inside her screaming run—but where would she even go? The water beckoned behind her like some slim promise of safety compared against whatever waited ahead near Thomas's shadowed figure beneath blinding sunlight.

"I... I think I'll get back in," Wren muttered finally after what felt both too long and too short all at once—a crack forming audibly between polished words meant for keeping peace versus frayed instincts desperate enough now to claw through them entirely.

Thomas's smile didn't falter, not even for a second. "It'll only take a minute," he said, holding the camera up to his face. "You look so pretty with the water droplets on you."

Wren hesitated but moved to where he pointed, stiff and clumsy, her arms folded tightly over her chest like armor.

"Perfect," Thomas murmured, his voice smooth as glass. The camera clicked incessantly. "Now, turn to the side for me. That's it. Chin up."

Click. Click. Click.

With every snap of the shutter, Wren's skin prickled, her discomfort deepening with each frame he captured. She felt his gaze crawling over her, lingering on places it had no business being, and all she wanted in that moment was to dive back into the water and never surface again.

"Alright," Thomas said finally, his tone heavier now—too heavy—and it made Wren's stomach twist. "Last one. Give me a big smile."

Her lips pressed into something resembling a grin, but there was nothing genuine about it. As soon as Thomas lowered the camera, Wren spun on her heel and bolted for the pool like her life depended on it. She jumped in with a cannonball that sent water flying in every direction, a desperate attempt to wash away everything—his voice, his eyes, the way he'd looked at her like she was something small and trapped under glass.

That night, Wren lay flat on her bed staring at the ceiling fan as it spun lazy circles above her. She wasn't thinking about school starting soon or what to do over the weekend—no, all she could see when she closed her eyes were Thomas's eyes: roving and hungry. All she could hear was his voice carrying that strange weight when he asked for a smile.

Enough was enough.

She decided then and there: no more pool parties.

The following week when her parents mentioned Thomas's name—the casual way they always did when they wanted her to head over there for another one of his get-togethers—Wren shook her head firmly.

"I don't want to go," she said.

Her mother tilted her head in confusion. "But you love swimming," she said like this was some immutable fact of nature.

Wren shrugged. "Not anymore."

Her father glanced up from his tablet and raised an eyebrow. "Is this about the photos?" he asked in that casually dismissive tone parents reserve for things they don't want to deal with. "Thomas is just trying to document your recovery—it's a miracle you're even walking again, after all."

He knows about the photos?

"I don't like having my picture taken," she said quietly but firmly.

This time her parents exchanged one of their patented looks—the kind that only came after years of shared shorthand communication—before turning back to their daughter.

"You're being ungrateful," her mother said sharply after a moment's pause, shaking her head as though Wren had disappointed them both profoundly without saying much at all.

Her father nodded along like an echo chamber of denial. "What's wrong with a few fun photos? He does this for all the neighborhood kids—he cares about their growth."

Growth? Growth toward what?

Wren bit down hard on her lip because if she started yelling now, she might not be able to stop herself until all the ugly truths spilled out onto their perfectly polished hardwood floors—the truths they clearly refused to see.

That summer became an endless game of avoidance punctuated by craftily constructed lies and careful balancing acts: feigning headaches one day or planning imaginary outings with friends on another; retreating into quiet rebellion as though licking wounds no one else could acknowledge but herself; whatever it took so long as she didn't have to feel those eyes behind the lens ever again—or worse yet hear another snide reprimand disguised under neighborly smiles coming from people incapable (or unwilling) to read situations correctly.

Wren had never been one to break the rules—not real rules, anyway—but that afternoon, something in her snapped. She decided to try her brother's bike. If she wasn't there, if she could just disappear for a little while, maybe all her problems would disappear with her. It was a naïve thought, sure, but Wren didn't care. She swung a leg over the bike and felt a wobble of uncertainty before her feet found the pedals.

Her legs moved furiously—pump, push, pump, push—and the bike surged down the street. The wind lashed at her face, whipping through her hair like it was trying to untangle all the chlorine-stained memories and scrape away Thomas's voice from where it clung like mold. She pedaled harder. Faster. More and more and even faster. Anything to put as much distance as possible between herself and that suffocating neighborhood.

Her brother wasn't home to stop her—not that he ever was. Wren didn't miss him. How could she? Not once had he visited her in the hospital. None of them had—her siblings, that is. Only her parents came, but even then, their visits were rare enough to feel like charity. She supposed she should be grateful he left his bike unattended. Wren had no bike of her own, no skateboard like other kids her age, nothing with wheels except for that old wheelchair collecting dust in the garage.

What started as aimless rides up and down her street quickly turned into something else entirely—longer rides, harder ones that left her muscles trembling and sweat pooling in the hollow of her neck by the time she finally stopped to rest. Yet no matter how far she rode or how fast she pushed herself, something inside her always screamed for more distance, more speed.

In those early weeks, Wren played it safe. Her uncanny sense of direction helped; she stuck to straight lines at first—out and back again—with a methodical system: when she turned, it was only ever to the right. The plan worked well enough in theory—turning right meant home was always waiting if she retraced each step backward—but it wasn't long before the lure of discovery outweighed caution.

As she grew bolder, Wren ventured further—past quiet cul-de-sacs into neighborhoods where people didn't know who she was or why they should glance twice at the girl on a too-big bike with scuffed-up sneakers pumping furiously against gravity's pull. She wound through quiet parks with trees older than time itself and streets with shops bustling so loudly they drowned out everything else: memories of chlorine pools and eyes that lingered too long.

And then came that day—the sweltering afternoon when everything changed.

It started like any other ride: legs pumping, tires spinning on sun-baked asphalt. But something about the heat made Wren reckless; it fanned whatever flames burned inside her until she felt drunk on freedom itself. Turn after turn blurred together until familiar landmarks melted into alien streets filled with faces she did not recognize.

The sun began its slow descent before Wren noticed how far gone she was. By then it was too late—the comfortable edges of what she knew had dissolved completely into unfamiliar corners and foreign shadows stretching across cracked pavement like they'd always been waiting for someone foolish enough to stumble into them.

She was lost.

A cold knot formed deep in Wren's stomach as panic crept closer with each passing second. Her instincts screamed at her to do something—anything—but all those somethings tangled together uselessly in her head until remembering became impossible: Which way had she come? What turns led home? Did these houses look familiar before?

She forced herself to think past the rising tide of fear swelling inside her chest—a lesson from school came clawing its way through distant memories about getting lost in forests: stay put; wait to be found; don't wander deeper into places you can't find your way out of again.

Wren spotted a bench near what passed for a park—if you could call three spindly trees and one sad patch of grass "a park." She steered toward it with trembling hands gripping handlebars slick from sweat.

Once seated on that wooden bench—her legs swinging nervously above cracked dirt paths below—it became easy enough pretending everything would fix itself somehow: surely someone would notice eventually... right? They'd come looking soon—it wasn't possible not noticing someone missing altogether... Was it?

Wren spotted Officer Goldfinch's cruiser as it pulled up to the curb, its headlights slicing through the growing shadows of the park. The sun had nearly set now, stretching the trees' outlines across the cracked pavement, making everything look colder, darker. Her fingers gripped her brother's bike handles tighter, knuckles whitening against the rubber grips. She squinted, trying to make out his face through the glare.

"There you are!" Goldfinch called out, his voice too loud, too cheerful for the dusky quiet around them. "Your parents are worried sick about you."

The words hit Wren like a jolt. She hadn't thought about her parents much at all, not until this moment. The anger on her mother's face as she realized Wren was missing flashed in her mind, followed by a dull ache of fear that twisted into something heavier when paired with the unease that had been gnawing at her ever since she'd gotten lost.

"I... I didn't mean to be gone so long." The words came out quieter than she meant them to, like they wanted to hide.

Goldfinch walked closer, smiling wide—too wide. "No harm done. Let's get you home," he said smoothly.

The cruiser's engine idled behind him as he reached out and took hold of her bike. His fingers brushed hers in passing—a fleeting touch—and Wren jerked her hand back like she'd been shocked. If he noticed the movement, or even cared, it didn't show on his face.

"Here," Goldfinch said casually, wheeling the bike with one hand toward the trunk of his car. "Let me take care of this for you."

Wren stood frozen where she was, her sneakers not even scuffing the pavement beneath them as she watched him lift her brother's bike with ease and slide it into the trunk like it belonged there. He slammed the lid shut without looking back at her. The noise echoed louder than it should have, rattling in her eardrums and making her stomach lurch unpleasantly.

"Alright," Goldfinch called over to her again with a wave toward the passenger door of his cruiser. "Let's get going. Hop in up front—don't want anyone thinking you're some kind of criminal sitting in the backseat, do we?"

The laugh that bubbled out of Wren's throat wasn't real—it barely sounded like it came from her at all. She shifted awkwardly on her feet but didn't move any closer to the car yet. Something wasn't right here; that thought had been circling in her head ever since he arrived. But then again, what could be wrong? He was a cop; this was exactly what police officers were supposed to do.

Wasn't it?

Her hesitation must've shown because Goldfinch closed the gap between them in a split second. His hand landed on her shoulder lightly at first but settled there quickly with more weight than seemed necessary. He gave what might have been meant as an encouraging squeeze—it didn't feel like one.

"Come on now," he urged softly but firmly enough that there wasn't room to argue or even think about doing so. "Your folks are waiting for you."

The pressure from his grip left no room for choices; before she knew it, Wren found herself being steered toward the car like someone else was moving her legs for her. Her steps faltered anyway when they reached the door he'd opened for her.

She looked inside and froze again. The interior of Goldfinch's cruiser seemed impossibly large yet claustrophobic all at once—vast enough to swallow her whole but compressed by shadows pooling deep into every corner where they shouldn't belong.

And then there was the smell.

It hit before anything else: thick and sour and clinging to everything inside—sweat and something sharper mingling with a faint metallic tang Wren couldn't place but didn't like one bit either way.

Goldfinch leaned across her suddenly—not roughly but not gently enough either—to grab hold of the seatbelt and drape over where she sat frozen against the upholstery now pressed firm against her back as though trying desperately to disappear into it altogether.

"There we go," he murmured just inches away from where she could feel his breath warm against her cheek when he clicked the belt buckle into place slowly—deliberately—like fastening shackles instead of providing safety measures.

His hand lingered just long enough afterward that she felt it more than saw it brushing too close against her thigh along one arm before pulling away again as though nothing unusual had happened at all.

"I could have done that myself," Wren muttered, her voice barely rising above the hum of the idling engine. If Thomas heard her, he pretended not to.

Instead, he chuckled—a low, rasping sound that crawled under her skin and settled there, unwelcome. "Just looking out for you, kiddo. That's my job, after all."

He shifted in his seat, casually resting one hand on the wheel as the other lingered on the gear shift. His eyes caught hers. Wren held his gaze for a fraction of a second too long—long enough to feel her muscles tense as though preparing to spring. But there was nowhere to go. The doors were locked with an audible click when they'd gotten in. You don't just exit a cop car on your own. Not that it would matter; Thomas's hand hovered just close enough that she imagined him grabbing her wrist if she tried.

The cruiser eased away from the curb, leaving the park—and any notion of escape—in the rearview mirror. Wren turned toward the window, watching unfamiliar streets melt into ones she recognized. The route home should have been comforting in its familiarity, but instead it felt like a slow tightening noose. Every turn brought her closer to an inevitability she couldn't quite name.

Behind her, Thomas broke the silence. "Your parents were worried sick about you." He let out a small sigh. "Out all day without telling anyone where you were going? That's so unlike you."

Wren didn't turn her head. She watched streetlamps blur by instead, streaks of light against the darkening sky. "I lost track of time," she murmured.

Thomas hummed in response—an ambiguous sound perched somewhere between amusement and reproach. "Lost track of time," he repeated slowly, turning the phrase over like a coin he didn't quite believe was real. "Well," he added after a beat, his tone lighter but still carrying an edge sharp enough to cut, "I'm sure your folks will be so relieved to see you, they might just forget all about grounding you."

There was movement from his side of the car—a small shift—and then his hand landed on her knee with casual weight. Wren jerked away faster than she thought possible, pressing herself against the door as though she could slip through its cracks and disappear into thin air.

Thomas pulled his hand back easily enough but not without a tiny laugh under his breath. "Now, now," he said softly, his tone laced with mock concern that made every hair on her body stand on end. "No need to be scared, Wren. You're safe with me—you know that, don't you? I'm here to protect and serve."

Wren's stomach tightened into knots as they turned into her driveway. The house was brightly lit; her parents must have been pacing at every window while waiting for any sign of headlights pulling up outside. As soon as Thomas shifted into park, they burst through the front door in tandem—her mother rushing ahead with frantic energy while her father followed more slowly behind.

"Oh, thank God!" Her mother's hands flew up toward her face before darting back down again like unsteady birds unsure where to land. "Where's the bike? Did she lose it?"

Thomas stepped out first. His smile had morphed into something big and benevolent—the kind of thing that might've belonged to a politician or a preacher who had just done some grand public service for free publicity alone.

"No need to worry," he called out reassuringly as he walked around to pop open the trunk. "Found our little adventurer safe and sound—for now anyway." He hoisted Wren's brother's bike out with exaggerated care, handling it like it was made of glass instead of cheap aluminum tubing from a department store clearance rack.

The bike was freed before Wren was.

Her father nodded awkwardly at this display of goodwill; whatever anger he'd been nursing earlier seemed to evaporate under Thomas's steady string of reassurances. He looked harder at the bike than at Thomas releasing his daughter from her cop car prison.

"Thank you so much for bringing her home," her father said gruffly but sincerely.

"All part of the job," Thomas replied modestly—or at least what passed for modesty when someone kept repeating how humble they were being while doing it. He glanced over at Wren then with an odd mix of authority and expectation in his eyes.

"Come here," he said suddenly—and too cheerfully—spreading his arms wide like a conquering hero returning from battle expecting flowers and applause along with gratitude he hadn't earned yet. "Give your hero a hug!"

Wren hesitated for half a second too long—that strange liminal space where decisions are made but not yet acted upon—and it was enough for Thomas to step forward and take matters into his own hands quite literally.

His arms enveloped her tightly before she could react; fabric pressed against fabric until there was no space left between them except for all the words caught in Wren's throat—words she couldn't force herself say because every nerve in her body had short-circuited into silence born out of shock.

And then it happened: The hand sliding lower than it ever should—the unmistakable squeeze disguised poorly as affection—and suddenly everything inside Wren snapped.

Her blood seemed to boil and freeze simultaneously; she couldn't tell whether what surged through veins now was courage or sheer adrenaline alone—but either way—it propelled her arms forward before logic could catch up entirely or hold them back altogether

Her palm connected hard against cheekbone with satisfying impact—so loud even crickets lurking somewhere beyond porch lights seemed startled momentarily silent afterward

"Don't touch me!"

Her mother gasped, one hand flying to her chest as though Wren's words had physically struck her. "Wren! What has gotten into you? Apologize to Officer Goldfinch this instant!"

Her father's face darkened, his jaw tightening as he took a step forward. "Ungrateful brat," he said, his voice low and simmering. "We've raised you better than this—"

But Thomas raised a hand, his expression so calm, so magnanimous that it turned Wren's stomach. "No, no," he said, the corners of his mouth pulling into a smile that was supposed to look understanding but didn't quite reach his eyes. "She's just a little girl. You know how they are. Still shaken up from her little adventure."

Wren didn't wait for more. She spun on her heel and bolted for the house, the slap of her sneakers on the pavement merging with the sound of her parents calling after her. Their voices—a chaotic tangle of anger and confusion—faded as she reached her bedroom door. She slammed it shut behind her, leaning against it with all the force of her small frame, as though she could keep them all out by sheer willpower alone.

Her legs gave out beneath her. She slid down until she was sitting on the floor, knees pulled tight to her chest. Her breath came in short gasps, sharp and uneven like she'd been running far longer than just across the yard. Tears stung at the corners of her eyes, but she squeezed them shut and willed them not to fall.

From downstairs came the muffled murmur of voices—her parents' laughter mingling with Thomas's smooth baritone. It rose and fell in rhythm like a melody no one had taught Wren how to follow. They were chatting amiably now, as though nothing were wrong—as though they couldn't feel the palpable knot of dread coiling tight in Wren's stomach.

"She's just a little girl," he'd said.

She was a little girl—Wren knew that much—but why did *he* care? The thought slithered through her mind like something alive and cold-blooded. It made her skin crawl worse than when she'd accidentally touched the snake that summer by the creek.

The stairs creaked and she retreated to the wall opposite the door.

Every muscle in Wren's body stiffened as she heard measured footsteps padding closer to her room—the kind that tried too hard to sound casual but wasn't fooling anyone. Three soft knocks followed, then her mother's voice, artificially cheerful: "Wren? Honey? Officer Goldfinch is here to see you again. Why don't you come say hello?"

Wren pressed herself tighter against the wall, as if somehow fusing with it would make her invisible.

"Wren?" The knob rattled once before turning completely. Her mother stepped aside—and there he was.

Thomas stood in the doorway, framed by the soft golden light of early evening spilling in from behind him. His camera hung around his neck like part of his silhouette—a permanent attachment that seemed as natural to him as breathing might be to anyone else. He smiled at her then—a slow, deliberate smile that showed teeth without warmth.

"There's our shy girl," he cooed as he lifted the camera to his eye. "How about a smile for me? A rescue photo—something for posterity."

Click.

"Isn't this nice?" Wren's father appeared from somewhere behind Thomas, grinning wide enough to match him shot for shot. "Look how thoughtful Officer Goldfinch is—making sure we remember everything! Smile big for him now."

Click.

And then another.

Thomas lowered the camera but not his gaze—it drilled into hers with an intensity that made Wren want to shrink into herself until she disappeared entirely.

"It's my pleasure," Thomas said softly, almost reverently now. "She is such a special girl."

The visits started coming more often after that—or maybe they always had been regular and this was just when Wren started noticing them more because she couldn't *not*. Every time she turned around, there he was: standing in their kitchen holding his camera like some kind of trophy or setting up shots in their living room where light pooled through the curtains just so.

Her parents never questioned it—not once—not even when Thomas lingered longer than any polite guest should or when she flinched away from his hand brushing against hers during one too many posed family photos.

He always brought that same look with him—the one he gave right before pressing down on the shutter button—and no matter how hard Wren tried describing it later (to herself mostly), words like "hungry" or "sharp" never felt quite enough because they didn't capture how much space it took up inside rooms too small for what he carried with him everywhere he went.

The school nurse had visited Wren's classroom one day, her smile warm and practiced, her voice lilting with the kind of rehearsed empathy that adults often used when speaking to children. She talked about privacy—how every person's body was their own and how it was okay to set boundaries. Wren didn't listen at first; the words felt like background noise, like static on a radio station you weren't tuned into. But then the nurse said something—something about speaking up if someone crossed those boundaries—and Wren sat up straighter.

A small flicker sparked inside her chest. Maybe, just maybe, this woman might understand.

Wren waited until the other kids filed out of the room before she approached the nurse. Her hands were clammy, and her throat felt tight, as though her words might choke her before they escaped. "There's... uh... there's a neighbor," she began, barely above a whisper. "He... he likes to take pictures of me."

For a moment, the nurse's face softened in a way that made Wren think she had done the right thing by speaking up. "Oh, sweetie," she said, crouching so they were at eye level. "That must make you uncomfortable."

Wren nodded quickly. Too quickly. Her eyes stung, but she blinked hard against the tears. "It does," she managed. "I don't like it."

The nurse placed a hand on Wren's shoulder—a gentle enough gesture but one that already felt dismissive. "You know," she said lightly, almost as though they were discussing nothing more serious than an annoying sibling or a scraped knee, "some girls have it much worse than that." She straightened up and gave Wren's shoulder one last pat—the kind that signaled an end to the conversation. "If he hasn't touched you or anything, I wouldn't worry too much about it. It's probably harmless."

Harmless. Probably.

The spark inside Wren sputtered out so fast it left behind smoke and ash. She muttered some polite response—"Okay" or "Thank you" or something equally meaningless—and walked away feeling smaller than ever.

Years passed in much the same way: quietly and without much fight from Wren herself. By fourteen, she had grown into a girl who still carried herself like she was trying not to be noticed but who couldn't quite manage to disappear entirely.

Officer Don Bardello came to her middle school one day to talk to the older kids about drugs—a presentation full of stern warnings about slippery slopes and bad decisions—but all Wren cared about was what he might say if she told him about her neighbor. There was something fatherly in his tone when he spoke to the class, something steady in his posture as he paced back and forth across the gymnasium floor. He might listen.

When the other students dispersed after his talk, Wren stayed back, lingering near the bleachers until everyone else was gone. Finally, she approached him, each step hesitant and deliberate, like crossing thin ice.

"Officer Bardello?" Her voice was shaky and thin when she said his name.

He turned toward her with a small smile felt genuine enough in that moment. "Yes? What can I do for you?"

Wren bit down on her bottom lip for a second before forcing herself to speak. "There's this neighbor," she began slowly, careful not to stumble over her words this time. "He... he keeps taking pictures of me. For years." Her hands found each other awkwardly at her sides; fingers twisted nervously around one another like they wanted something solid to hold onto.

Bardello frowned—not in anger but in what seemed like concern—and leaned forward as though inviting her to go on. "That doesn't sound right," he said carefully. "Have you talked to your parents about it?"

"I tried." The words came out quieter than she had intended but with more weight behind them because of it. "They don't think it's a big deal."

"Why on earth wouldn't they—" He stopped mid-sentence when Wren added, almost inaudibly:

"He's a police officer too."

The color rose in Bardello's face immediately—not pink with embarrassment but red with something much sharper and meaner—and whatever warmth had been there moments ago froze over so quickly that Wren felt it like a slap.

"A police officer?" His voice was louder now, harsher around the edges as he stared down at her like she'd just insulted him personally. "Are you accusing one of my colleagues of... liking young girls?"

The word hung there—wrong in its phrasing but no less cutting for it—and Wren shook her head frantically even as panic clawed its way up her throat. "No! I'm not accusing anyone! I just thought—"

"You thought what?" Bardello snapped before she could finish. His voice ricocheted off the empty walls of the hallway they stood in now—the hallway that suddenly felt far too long and far too narrow all at once—as he continued: "Do you have any idea how serious an accusation like that is? How dare you make up lies about someone who puts their life on the line every day!"

"I'm not lying!" The protest burst out of Wren with more force than she expected—but even as she said it aloud, even as tears streaked hotly down her cheeks now—she knew there was no point anymore.

Bardello wasn't listening.

His anger filled every inch of space between them until Wren couldn't take another second standing there beneath its weight; without thinking twice—or maybe thinking too much all at once—she turned and ran.

Her sneakers squeaked against polished linoleum floors as she darted around corners blindly until finally collapsing against the side door leading out toward empty soccer fields beyond campus grounds where no one could see how hard or how long or how hopelessly fourteen-year-old girls sometimes cried when everything else failed them too.

She stayed frozen there for what felt like forever while Bardello's shouts echoed faintly somewhere behind her—not words anymore but sounds stripped raw by distance—and all Wren could think through sobs choked quiet was how stupid she'd been for hoping anyone might actually care.

* * *

Wren pedaled furiously, her legs churning like pistons as she streaked down the familiar streets toward school. The wind tugged at her hair, teasing her with a fleeting sense of freedom. It wouldn't last. It never did.

The flash of red and blue lights in her peripheral vision made her stomach twist into a familiar knot. She slowed to a stop, her heart sinking as if weighted by lead. She didn't have to look to know who it would be this time.

Officer Jennings stepped out of his cruiser slowly, deliberately, like he had all the time in the world. That smirk—the one that always made Wren's pulse quicken with a mix of anger and dread—spread across his face. "Well, well. If it isn't our little troublemaker," he drawled, his voice laced with mockery. "Let's see what you've got for me today."

Wren didn't say a word. She never did anymore. Instead, she slipped her back-pack off her shoulders and handed it over, jaw clenched so tight it ached. Jennings didn't bother to take it gently. He turned the bag upside down and shook it until its contents spilled across the sidewalk in a chaotic heap.

"Oops," he said lightly, as though they were playing some kind of game and not trampling over everything that mattered to her. "Looks like somebody's having a bad morning."

He crouched and rifled through the scattered items with exaggerated care-lessness—a carefully annotated library book tossed aside; loose papers bent and dirtied; her brown paper lunch bag crumpled under his boot like it was nothing more than trash.

"All clear," he finally announced with mock authority, tossing the now-empty backpack at her feet without so much as a glance back at the mess he'd made. "Better hustle, kiddo, or you'll get yourself another tardy slip."

Jennings climbed back into his cruiser while Wren kneeled on the pavement to collect what she could salvage. Her fingers trembled as she shoved crumpled papers and squished snacks back into her bag. Her cheeks burned—not just from humiliation but from the sharp sting of helpless rage that simmered under her skin.

The next day, it was Officer Ramirez waiting for her at the corner near the school. His expression was apologetic before he even rolled down his window. He waved her over with none of Jennings' smug theatrics and stepped out like someone resigned to an unpleasant chore.

"I'm sorry about this," he muttered as he opened her bag and sifted through its contents with careful hands, taking pains not to damage anything important. He handed everything back gently enough—her books still intact, no lunch bags crushed today—but his uncomfortable half-smile didn't make it any better.

Wren nodded stiffly without meeting his eyes. She knew Ramirez wasn't try-ing to humiliate her like Jennings did—or Bardello—but even so, the violation gnawed at something deep inside her.

Over time, Wren became almost numb to these stops on her way to school—or tried to convince herself she was numb anyway. They were predictable now: Simmons would make her empty the bag herself while he loomed over her like a shadow; Peterson always seemed unnaturally eager to pat her down for reasons she didn't want to imagine; and then there was Bardello.

Bardello wasn't like the others—not even close.

"What's this little contraband?" Bardello sneered one morning as he held up her It was Wren's science project: a DIY water filtration system—a plastic jug full of gravel, sand, activated charcoal and a coffee filter.

Wren froze mid-step, already knowing what was coming next but powerless to stop it.

"What's in this?" Bardello asked with exaggerated mock innocence as he opened the jug.

Before Wren could even get the words out—"Please don't"—he poured everything out onto the pavement with sickening glee. The strata tumbled from the mouth of the jug, scattering across the earth like shattered teeth.

Wren bit down hard on the inside of her cheek until she tasted copper, refusing to let him see how close she was to breaking right there on the sidewalk. Somehow—she didn't know how—she managed to kneel down slowly and begin scooping the ruined layers while Bardello chuckled above her like this destruction had been nothing more than sport.

That chuckle stayed with her long after he drove away, mixing with all the others that had come before it—a cacophony of voices that reminded her every day just how small she'd been made to feel in a world that wouldn't give her room to stand tall again.

The harassment didn't stop when Wren was at home. Patrol cars crawled past her house at all hours, their headlights slicing through her bedroom window like knives. The officers inside didn't try to hide their stares, the way their eyes followed her silhouette behind the curtains. And it wasn't just at home—at the park, at the mall, even at innocuous school events, there was always one of them. Lingering. Watching. Waiting for her to slip up somehow.

Her parents? They chalked it all up to teenage mood swings and a supposed uptick in local crime. "It's for our safety," her mom would say, like that explained anything. They didn't notice how much smaller Wren seemed lately, how she moved through life like a shadow of herself, shrinking a little more every day as if trying to disappear completely.

When Officer Carlson filled the history classroom doorway with his bulk and trademark scowl, Wren's stomach flipped over on instinct. The room went still as his gaze swept over each student and landed—of course—on her. He didn't smile exactly, but there was something in his eyes, sharp and glittering, that made her skin crawl.

"Wren Hubbard," he said, his voice cutting through the silence like a slap. "Let's go."

The weight of thirty pairs of eyes fell on Wren as she grabbed her bag with trembling hands. She could feel them dissecting her every move, their whispers loud in the otherwise silent room: "What did she do this time?" Her face burned as someone muttered just loud enough for everyone to hear: "Busted."

Carlson didn't wait for her to catch up. His long strides took him into the hallway, where he grabbed her arm without preamble and steered her toward the principal's office. His grip wasn't exactly rough—it didn't leave marks—but it was firm enough to make a point. Wren had learned not to pull away; it made things worse.

She ran through a mental checklist as they walked: homework turned in on time? Yes. Attendance spotless? Yes. Did she even *talk* to anyone who could accuse her of something? No—and yet here she was again.

They stopped outside the principal's office door. Carlson turned toward her then, his mouth set in a grim line that didn't quite hide his disdain.

"We got a report," he started slowly, deliberately dragging out the words like they were some sort of death sentence, "that you shoplifted from the corner store yesterday."

For a second, she thought she'd misheard him. "I what?" The words tumbled out before she could stop them.

Carlson arched an eyebrow like he couldn't believe she was stupid enough to play dumb. "A candy bar," he said flatly. "Ring any bells?"

"No—I mean—" She shook her head hard enough to make herself dizzy. "I haven't even had chocolate in weeks!" The sound came out jagged, like it was being forced through a throat too tight to cooperate.

Carlson's lip curled into an ugly sneer that made him look more like a caricature than an officer of the law. "Save it," he snapped. "You're not fooling anyone." He leaned down so they were almost eye level now, which somehow made him seem even taller and more imposing—a trick Wren hated herself for noticing.

"I'm *not* lying!" She could hear how desperate she sounded and hated that too, but there was no stopping now—not when it felt like the walls were closing in around her. "I swear I didn't take anything!"

Carlson clucked his tongue like he pitied her—or worse, like she amused him somehow—and shook his head slowly. "That's funny." He crossed his arms over his chest and shifted his weight onto one foot as though settling in to enjoy himself. "Because Officer Goldfinch told me otherwise."

Wren couldn't stop the full-body flinch at that name—Thomas Goldfinch—any more than she could stop breathing in oxygen or pumping blood through her veins.

Carlson caught the movement and smiled for real this time—a cruel thing full of teeth but without any warmth behind it. "Yeah," he said softly now, leaning just closer again for effect that bordered on theatricality, "he told me all about you."

Her throat went dry.

"Said you're nothing but a liar." He shrugged casually as if conveying indisputable facts passed down from some higher power above them both—a truth beyond reproach simply because *he* believed it so deeply that reality bent around him when necessary to accommodate such beliefs.

Wren's locker was a war zone. Her books, papers, and gym clothes, once neatly stowed in rows like soldiers in formation, now lay strewn across the linoleum in disheveled heaps. She winced as she watched a particularly fragile notebook land with a sad flop, its pages fanning open like a wounded bird.

Officer Carlson, the self-appointed general of this assault, rifled through the remaining contents with all the delicacy of a bulldozer. His jaw worked like he was chewing on gravel—whether from the effort or from frustration, Wren couldn't tell. Maybe both. The principal stood nearby, arms crossed and eyebrows drawn together in what might have passed as concern—if it wasn't paired with an obvious reluctance to intervene.

"Don't bother trying to talk your way out of this one," Carlson said without looking at her. "We've got our eye on you, Hubbard. One more slip-up…" He paused dramatically before delivering his verdict. "And you'll be in serious trouble."

As they filed out of class and into the hallway, Wren's classmates slowed their pace just enough to gawk while attempting to appear inconspicuous. Whispered exchanges and covert glances flew through the hallway like invisible arrows aimed at her back. Wren bristled but kept her gaze forward. Let them look.

Carlson grabbed another stack of papers and shook them out as if expecting contraband to tumble forth like confetti from a party popper. Nothing did. His expression darkened further, which seemed unfair considering her notes were now scattered like fall leaves beneath her feet.

"Where is it?" he growled, his voice cutting through the murmurs around them.

Wren inhaled sharply through her nose but didn't answer right away. She knew exactly what he meant—of course she did—but nothing irritated Carlson more than having to repeat himself.

"Where's what?" she asked finally, feigning innocence so poorly it bordered on mockery.

Carlson whirled on her, brandishing his accusation like a sword. "The chocolate bar, you little thief," he spat, his voice heavy with contempt. "Or did you already eat the evidence?"

For a moment—just a fleeting moment—Wren forgot how furious she was because *what*? A stolen chocolate bar? That was what this whole pretend scene was about? It took everything she had not to laugh outright.

"Eat it?" she said instead, raising her eyebrows high enough that they practically disappeared into her hairline. "You think I ate a stolen chocolate bar?"

Carlson stepped closer until they were nearly nose-to-nose—or rather nose-to-forehead; Wren wasn't exactly tall—and narrowed his eyes at her in the way adults do when they're convinced they're dealing with someone significantly less intelligent than themselves.

"Don't play dumb with me," he snapped. "We know you took it."

Her pulse quickened—not out of fear but something closer to outrage—as she straightened up under his glare. "There's no proof I ever had a chocolate bar," she said evenly, though inside she felt anything but calm. "You're targeting me."

Carlson scoffed—a short bark of laughter completely devoid of humor—and waved dismissively at her words as though swatting away an annoying fly. "Targeting you? Don't flatter yourself, kid," he said gruffly. "We're just doing our job."

Those words lit something in Wren that had been simmering beneath the surface since this whole mess started: defiance—or maybe indignation or some combination thereof that made standing still impossible. She crossed her arms over her chest—not defensively but deliberately—and tilted her head.

"Oh really?" she shot back coolly. "Then who reported this alleged shoplifting? Which store was it?"

For the first time during their exchange, Carlson faltered—not much, just enough for Wren to notice—and then his face turned an alarming shade of crimson.

"That's none of your business," he said stiffly after what felt like an eternity spent glaring at each other.

"I think it *is* my business," Wren countered without missing a beat, leaning forward as if daring him to argue further. "If I'm being accused of a crime doesn't that mean I have the right to know *exactly* what I'm being accused of?"

The words hung heavily between them until finally—mercifully—the principal cleared his throat loudly enough that even Carlson had no choice but to acknowledge it.

"Officer Carlson," he began hesitantly but firmly—the kind of tone used when speaking to someone whose temper could go off like dynamite at any second—"I think we've taken this far enough." He gestured vaguely toward the empty locker behind them before continuing: "There's clearly no evidence here suggesting any wrongdoing."

Carlson opened his mouth as though preparing some fiery rebuttal but stopped short when the principal raised one hand palm-outward—an almost priestly gesture of finality.

"Wren," he said then before either party could reignite their argument, looking directly at her now for perhaps the first time since this ordeal began, "please go to your next class."

That was all Wren needed—or wanted—to hear. Without waiting for further clarification or permission (not that either seemed forthcoming), she bent down quickly to gather the scattered loot from her locker floor: notes folded crookedly over themselves; textbooks now sporting new scuffs along their edges; gym clothes bearing the marks of Carlson's duty boots—all hastily shoved into bags or folders with little regard for organization anymore.

She didn't speak again—not when Carlson muttered something inaudible yet clearly unpleasant under his breath nor when curious classmates parted silently like waves ahead of where she walked briskly down hallways she suddenly wished were shorter still—or empty altogether.

But despite herself—and despite everything else—a faint smirk tugged briefly at one corner of Wren's mouth because somewhere deep inside amid all those frayed nerves burning hot against raw humiliation lay *relief*.

Wren's hands trembled as she pushed open the classroom door. She kept her head high, though—chin up, eyes forward. She wouldn't let them see how much it rattled her. She wouldn't give them that satisfaction.

Sliding into her seat, Wren felt her heartbeat pound in her ears, drowning out the muffled whispers that buzzed around her. She could feel their eyes on her—sharp and probing, like needles pressing into her skin. The silence didn't last long.

"What happened?" Jenna leaned in close, her voice low but insistent. "Why'd they pull you out?"

Wren hesitated, her mind scrambling for something—anything. The truth wasn't an option; they'd never buy it. They'd twist it into something far worse than reality. So instead, she said the first thing that popped into her head: "My mom accidentally packed a kitchen knife in my lunch bag instead of a butter knife. They thought I had it in my locker."

The words sounded ridiculous out loud, even to Wren. For a second, the classroom fell quiet, like the room itself was holding its breath, before the laughter started—a mixture of half-snorts and muffled giggles spreading like a ripple in water.

"Oh my god," Jenna whispered through a grin, her eyes lighting up with amusement. "That's so funny."

"Wish my mom packed my lunch," Mark chimed in from behind her. His tone carried just enough mockery to sting. "Must be nice to still have Mommy doing that for you."

Wren forced a tight nod and managed to choke out a response. "Yeah. Nice." Her voice betrayed nothing, but inside, she could feel something harden—a shell forming to keep it all out. She didn't bother trying to gauge who believed her and who didn't. It didn't matter. Or at least, she told herself it didn't matter because there was nothing she could do about it anyway.

As weeks blurred into months, isolation gathered velocity, rushing in like an uninvited guest who refused to leave. Wren heard the whispers when she passed by lockers or entered the cafeteria; she saw the sideways glances and smirks exchanged behind cupped hands but said nothing and moved on. Gossip turned sharper with each retelling until what actually happened—and her subsequent lie—was buried beneath layers of speculation and malice.

She stopped caring—or maybe she convinced herself that she had stopped caring because what other choice did she have? The classmates who laughed at her, the police who dismissed her, the family whose concern felt like pity—they were all just background noise now. None of them mattered anymore.

9:36 a.m.

The shrill ring of her phone cut through Wren's thoughts, dragging her away from memories she would rather leave buried. For a moment, she forgot where she was. The sun hung high in the late-morning sky, its glare turning everything too bright, too sharp. Birds chirped somewhere above her, entirely indifferent to the chaos that had taken root in her chest. Wren winced at the screen of her phone, and for a split second, her heart lifted when Maggie's name appeared.

She answered the call before it finished ringing. "Maggie." She let out a shaky breath. "Fuck, I'm so glad it's you."

"Wren?" Maggie's voice sounded frayed around the edges. "What's going on? I got your messages—are you okay?"

Wren gripped the handlebars of her bike until her knuckles turned white. "No," she said finally, her voice trembling despite herself. "I'm not okay, Mags."

"What happened?"

The words came tumbling out—disordered and frantic—as though getting them out faster might make them more bearable. "I made a delivery this morning. One of my regulars called me with an address I'd never been to before." She paused for half a beat to steady herself but failed miserably. "When I got there... Maggie, there was this woman inside the house. She was dying—god, Mags, there was blood everywhere."

On the other end of the line, Maggie sucked in a breath so sharply Wren could almost feel it. "Oh my god," Maggie whispered. "Did you call 911?"

"Of course I did!" Wren snapped without meaning to, but shame didn't have time to settle in. Her voice softened just barely as she added, "What do you think I am?"

"That's not what I—"

"Doesn't matter," Wren interrupted with an unsteady hitch in her breath. "Anyway... Dennis showed up."

There was silence at first—brief but heavy—and then: "Dennis?" Maggie repeated slowly.

"Yeah," Wren said bitterly. "Dennis." She closed her eyes and pressed the heels of her palms against them as though that might make this whole thing disappear somehow. "Except he wasn't Dennis, not really—not today. He was wearing a fucking police uniform."

"So he was able to help you?"

"No. He...he went for me."

Even over the static hum of poor reception, Wren could hear Maggie's disbelief burst through like fireworks cracking against pitch-black skies.

"Went for you? Oh my god!" Maggie gasped loudly enough that Wren pulled her phone away from her ear for just a second before putting it back again. "Wait—what? Did he hit you? Oh my god—is this real? You found someone *dying*? Are you sure she was dead? And Dennis—you're *sure* it was him? Why would he even be there? None of this makes any sense!"

"No shit it doesn't make sense," Wren cut in before Maggie could spiral further into hypotheticals neither one of them had answers for yet—or ever, probably. Her free hand clenched into a fist at her side as she added through gritted teeth: "He shot at me, Maggie."

That brought silence on Maggie's end again—sharp and sudden and suffocating.

Wren forced herself to keep going anyway: "He fucking shot at me."

The words landed like stones dropping into deep water—heavy and slow until they disappeared into nothingness.

"Oh my god," Maggie finally said quietly—too quietly for someone who had been so loud just moments ago. Then, louder: "Jesus Christ! Where are you right now?"

Wren blinked rapidly and looked around for the first time since sitting down; she had been too caught up to register where she'd ended up after running blindly through the streets. The scene should have been calming—the park stretched wide around her under gentle shafts of sunlight filtering through tall trees sway-ing in rhythm with the warm breeze—but instead it felt alien in its serenity.

She knew every street and alley in this city, except this did not feel like her city anymore.

"I don't know," Wren admitted after another moment passed between them like an eternity carved into seconds too small to hold everything pressing down on her chest right now. Her voice dropped lower as something close to panic crept back in: "I can hear sirens everywhere."

A robin hopped onto the path ahead of her, its tiny head twitching back and forth like it knew something she didn't but wasn't telling.

"And I don't know what the fuck to do," Wren finished quietly.

Somewhere nearby, leaves rustled overhead like soft whispers promising things they couldn't deliver while shadows danced across the ground in patterns that wouldn't stay still long enough for anyone to understand them—not even people who needed answers more desperately than breath right now—which meant Wren didn't stand a chance either.

"Okay, let's stay calm," Maggie said, though her voice wavered just enough to betray her unease. "We'll figure this out. Are you safe where you are?"

Wren's eyes darted to the shadows, and she kept herself coiled—ready to spring if the situation shifted. "For now, I think so," she said, keeping her voice as even as she could manage.

Her grip on the cheap burner phone tightened as Maggie spoke again.

"Wait. What number is this? It's showing up as 'Unknown.'"

Wren glanced down at the phone, a flimsy plastic thing that felt like it might crumble in her hand if she squeezed too hard. "Had to buy a new one," she said. "The old one got shot."

There was a pause—long enough for Wren to imagine Maggie trying to process that sentence properly. Then her voice spiked upward. "Shot? What do you mean, shot? Are you saying someone actually shot your phone?"

"Yeah, well," Wren said flatly, because why not lean into the absurdity at this point, "Dennis wasn't aiming *for* my phone. The bullet just hit it instead of me." She allowed herself a humorless little snort before adding, "So I guess yay for small wins."

Maggie sucked in a sharp breath loud enough for Wren to hear through the speaker. "Oh my god. Oh my god. Wren! You're serious? He actually shot at you? You could've been killed!"

Wren opened her mouth to answer but stopped when another voice cut in—faint but shrill, like nails across glass—and unmistakably Karen's.

"Is that her again? That courier? How many times do I have to tell you she's trouble, Maggie? Trouble with a capital T! You need to-"

"Mom!" Maggie's voice was muffled now, like she'd pulled the phone away from her mouth, though not far enough for Wren's liking. "Mom—please! This is private!"

Wren rolled her eyes so hard it was a wonder they stayed in their sockets. "Tell your mom to go to hell, Mags."

"Wren, don't." Maggie sighed, and Wren could picture the way she pinched the bridge of her nose when she got stressed—an image so vivid it almost made Wren feel bad for snapping at her. Almost.

"She's just worried," Maggie continued softly.

"Yeah," Wren said with a bitter laugh, "worried I'm corrupting her precious daughter or whatever story she tells herself late at night." Her knuckles whitened around the phone as frustration seeped into her tone. "You know what? Never mind me almost getting murdered or anything."

There was a rustling sound on Maggie's end—a door closing, maybe some footsteps—and then her voice came back more clearly.

"Okay," Maggie said quietly now. "I'm in my room... Tell me what happened, start to finish."

Wren leaned back against the wall and exhaled hard through her nose—a sharp release she hadn't realized had been building until now. Her thumb idly traced a crack running down the length of the plastic case on her burner phone as she collected herself—or tried to.

"Maggie," she started slowly, like explaining something obvious to someone intent on misunderstanding it anyway, "I told you already: I found a dying woman while making a delivery. Then Dennis showed up and decided to try shooting me instead of helping her." She let out a bitter laugh that had about as much humor as gravel scraping pavement. "That's it—that's the whole fucked-up story in all its glory."

"Okay, okay," Maggie's voice crackled through the phone, uneven like a scratched record. "We need to think this through. Maybe we should call the police—"

"Are you kidding me?" Wren's voice spiked, sharper than she intended. She forced herself to breathe, tried again, slower this time but no less firm. "Dennis is a cop, Mags. They'll never believe me. It's his word against mine, and we both know how that'll end."

From somewhere on Maggie's side of the call came a familiar voice: shrill, persistent, impossible to ignore. Karen. Even muffled by distance, recognition hit like nails on glass.

"Maggie! Who are you talking to? Is it *her* again? I told you—"

"Mom, please." Maggie's tone stretched tight like a wire about to snap. "I need some privacy. This is important."

Wren pressed her fingers against her temple, closing her eyes as though she could block out Karen's intrusive voice through sheer willpower. "Your mom's still there?" She let out a humorless laugh. "Jesus, Mags."

"I know," Maggie sighed into the receiver, the sound carrying equal parts apology and exhaustion. "I'm sorry." A pause hung between them before she added quickly, "Look, maybe you should go back to the courier office and talk to Willie. He might have some ideas."

"Willie?" Wren bit out his name like it tasted wrong in her mouth. "What the hell does Willie know about what to do?"

"I don't know!" Maggie shot back defensively, her frustration peeking through despite herself. "But he's been around forever—longer than either of us—and maybe he's seen something like this before."

Wren opened her mouth to argue when Karen made another entrance, pushing boundaries as usual.

"Maggie! End that call right now! I've told you—she's nothing but trouble! You shouldn't—"

"Mom!" Maggie's shout sliced through the phone so sharply that Wren instinctively pulled it away from her ear with a wince. There was the sound of a scuffle—distant footsteps or perhaps something heavier—and then a door slammed with finality.

When Maggie came back on the line, her voice was quieter but no less strained. "Sorry about that." A heavy breath followed as though she were trying to steady herself. "She followed me into my bedroom, so I'm in the bathroom right now—I can't even with her sometimes."

Wren pushed out a short exhale that wasn't quite a laugh. Her eyes scanned the park where she sat; kids played on rusted swings while joggers shuffled past with earbuds firmly in place. Still, she felt exposed under their oblivious glances—like someone had peeled back her skin for all to see.

"She means well," Wren guessed because it felt like the kind of thing you were supposed to say about mothers who meddled too much but loved too hard.

Maggie didn't answer right away; maybe she knew better than to unpack those words now when time felt thin around them.

"Look," Wren said after another beat of silence stretched too long and too taut between them, "I can't hang around here forever."

"Wren..." Maggie hesitated in that way people do when they're trying not to beg outright but don't have enough faith in words alone. "Just... be cautious? And think about Willie. Please?"

"Fine," Wren said finally as though conceding cost her nothing when it chipped away at something small but vital inside her. "I'll think about it—but no promises."

Her grip on the phone loosened as she leaned forward on the bench and stared at her boots kicking up dirt beneath them.

"I love you, Mags," she murmured into the phone after a moment passed—a quiet confession tucked safely into those four words.

There was softness now in Maggie's reply: warm enough that Wren could feel it despite everything else threatening to burn cold around them. "I know that." A pause lingered briefly before Maggie added with quiet conviction: "I love you too, Wren. More than anything."

A lump formed in Wren's throat. She swallowed it down, though it didn't go easily. "I'll head to the Cyclista offices," she said, her voice rougher than she wanted it to be. "Maybe one of the couriers has dealt with something crazy before. Might be able to give me some advice."

"That's smart," Maggie said. Her tone softened, less frantic now. "Just... be careful, okay?"

"Always am." The words fell out automatically, a reflex more than a statement of truth.

Maggie let out a small laugh, the kind that carried more worry than humor. "No, you're not. But could you try? For me?"

Wren hesitated just long enough for the silence to stretch between them. Then finally: "Yeah, yeah, I'll channel my inner law-abiding citizen." There was a faint smirk in her voice now, a half-hearted attempt at normalcy. "Talk soon, babe."

She ended the call with a tap and slipped the burner phone into her pocket. Her hand lingered there before she forced herself to move again. A deep breath pressed against her ribs as she scanned the park—the empty benches, the jogger with their headphones on, and an old man tossing crumbs to gorging pigeons. Nothing seemed out of place. Not yet.

Swinging her leg over the bike felt mechanical, not instinctive like it usually did. The pedals met her feet with their familiar resistance, grounding her momentarily in the mundane motion of riding.

Automatic muscle memory started up even as part of her resisted it—a slow push-off from the curb followed by steady strokes—but there was no usual rush of speed this time. Wren wasn't tearing through intersections or weaving past traffic like she could outrun herself. Today, every motion was deliberate and restrained. Each turn of the pedals felt unnatural, like holding back a sneeze or forcing a smile you didn't mean. She could not afford to draw attention to herself. Not now.

She stopped at red lights she normally flew through without hesitation. She signaled her turns as though there was someone paying attention to them; no one was paying attention—no one ever was—but that wasn't the point today. The bike lanes hemmed her in like guardrails or steel bars on a prison cell and riding so carefully felt wrong somehow—foreign and uncomfortable—like walking barefoot when you were used to wearing boots.

The city around her blurred into vague shapes of asphalt and concrete, glass and noise. Normally she loved this chaos—the symphony of car horns and distant chatter—but today it all faded into background static behind the thunderous roar in her own head.

Wren's thoughts raced faster than any courier could ever ride. On loop came flashes of what she didn't want to remember: the woman crumpled like paper in front of her eyes; Dennis's face twisted into something monstrous as he raised that gun; her own breath coming shallow and frantic until everything cracked wide open.

She shook her head sharply—not once but twice—to force those fragments loose again. They didn't belong here with her on this bike under this sunlit sky.

The rhythm of cycling should have been comforting—it usually was—but today it just marked time she couldn't reclaim or escape from fast enough. She glanced at the people crossing streets without noticing her and at cars idling at intersections where she waited too—a proper cyclist obeying every rule of the road for once in her life—and none of them looked back at her.

Good.

Her legs kept turning over in tight circles like clock hands winding toward something inevitable—or nothing at all—as block after block slid by unnoticed under tire rubber that never stopped touching pavement even once since she'd started pedaling away from... well... everything really.

After what felt like hours—though it was no more than a few minutes—the Cyclista offices came into view. Wren eased up on the pedals, her legs barely stretched, her breaths coming easy and unhurried. Her eyes scanned the street, darting from one shadowy doorway to the next. Nothing. No flashing lights. No figures loitering where they shouldn't be. Just an empty stretch of asphalt and the buzz of a flickering streetlamp.

She rolled to a stop outside the open bay doors, her heart hammering against her ribs like it was trying to break free. For a moment, she stayed there, one foot braced on the ground, staring into the dimly lit interior. The place looked exactly as it always did: walls cluttered with bike parts, racks stacked with deliveries waiting to go out, grease stains on the floor that no one bothered to clean anymore. But now, it all felt... different. Or maybe she was just different.

Wren sucked in a breath—deep and shaky—and pushed her bike forward.

The familiar tang of rubber tires and bike grease rushed to greet her as she stepped inside, but it didn't calm her nerves like it usually did. Four pairs of eyes turned toward her in unison, freezing her mid-step.

Willie stood behind the dispatch desk, arms crossed over his broad chest, his scowl somehow managing to deepen as he took in her appearance. Zak leaned casually—too casually—against the wall by the lockers, his trademark smirk faltering for a split second before snapping back into place like elastic. Over at the workbench, Thanh and Massi huddled close together, tools in hand and heads bent over some project until now. Their conversation stopped dead as Wren's presence pulled their focus.

"Holy shit, Wren!" Thanh said first, their multi-colored hair catching the overhead light as they straightened up. Their voice started strong, but then dwindled into a whisper. "What happened to you?"

Wren blinked at them before glancing down at herself—at the blood dried in streaks across her shoes and shirt—like she'd just remembered how disheveled she must look. She plastered on a grin that felt far too big for her face and let adrenaline carry her through whatever this moment was about to become.

"You guys are not gonna believe this," she said, forcing something vaguely chipper into her tone even though it came out pitched too high, almost squeaky. "Craziest delivery of my life."

Willie's brow furrowed deeper—a feat in itself—as he leaned forward on the desk. "Hubbard," he growled in that slow way of his that always sounded like both an accusation and a warning, "what did you do now?"

"Nothing!" Wren threw up both hands and let out a laugh that didn't sound remotely convincing even to herself. "I swear! I was just doing my job."

"Your job?" Willie cut back in before she could get any momentum going. He raised an eyebrow so high it threatened to disappear under his hairline. "You were supposed to be getting coffee."

"I *was*!" Wren shot back quickly—or maybe too quickly—but then waved him off like details didn't matter right now even though they totally did. "Okay fine, I got sidetracked! But I had this call come in for a delivery—not my fault! And when I got there..." She paused just long enough to let everyone lean forward in anticipation before dropping the bombshell: "There was this woman on the floor."

Massi's eyes widened first because of course they did; Massi always wore their emotions right out there where everyone could see them without even trying to guess. "For real? Hurt? Like hurt-hurt?"

"Like *bad*," Wren confirmed with an emphatic nod that made some loose strands of hair fall into her face. She shoved them aside impatiently because there were more important things happening here than personal grooming habits right now.

Zak tilted his head just enough to make his smirk look smug again instead of nervous—for all of five seconds anyway. "Wait—you're telling me you went from coffee run dropout straight into playing hero? What'd you do? Call 911?"

"Duh," Wren snapped without missing a beat but then added quickly (because this part mattered too), "And started CPR!"

Thanh's jaw actually dropped at that one while Massi muttered something under their breath that sounded suspiciously like *holy crap*. Zak squinted skeptically and took half a step closer like he needed confirmation he wasn't being pranked somehow.

"You know CPR?" he asked with so much disbelief packed into those three little words Wren almost laughed outright despite herself.

"No, genius," she shot back with enough venom to take some satisfaction from watching him flinch—all bark tonight apparently—with no bite to follow up on it whatsoever. "The 911 operator walked me through it! What am I supposed to do? Stand there twiddling my thumbs while bleeding-out lady needs saving?"

She leaned on those last words harder than necessary but less than she wanted because even now—standing here safe among people who weren't dying—it felt wrong somehow to talk about what had happened so casually when everything about the morning had been anything but casual.

"Anyway." She exhaled sharply through clenched teeth like punctuation at the end of everything swirling around inside her head right now before finishing simply: "I did what needed doing."

Thanh stepped closer, their expression caught somewhere between concern and fascination. "That's... wild, Wren. Is that why you're covered in blood?"

Wren nodded, her voice flat. "Yeah, it got messy." Her eyes darted around the room, taking in every detail: the peeling paint on the far wall, the faded Cyclista logo above Willie's desk, and most annoying of all, Zak's growing smirk. She could practically feel his smugness radiating across the room like heat off asphalt. The temptation to knock it clean off his face flared sharply, but she swallowed it back. There were bigger problems right now—problems she couldn't punch her way out of.

Willie's brow knit tightly together as his lips pressed into a hard line. "Hubbard," he began slowly, each word weighed down with irritation, "I didn't send you any text order. What the hell are you talking about?"

The floor seemed to tilt beneath Wren's feet. "What? No—it wasn't from you. It was from... an unknown number."

A heavy silence fell over the room, the kind that stretched too long and made everything worse. Willie's face shifted from confusion to alarm and finally landed on anger—a deep, simmering kind that turned his face red and tightened his jaw until the veins in his neck started to show.

"You took a delivery call outside of Cyclista?" He leaned forward now, looming over his desk like a storm cloud about to burst. "Are you out of your damn mind?"

Wren opened her mouth to explain but stumbled over the words. "I didn't think—"

"You're damn right you didn't think!" Willie roared, slamming his hand onto the desk with enough force to rattle the dented coffee mug sitting precariously close to its edge. The sharp sound jolted everyone in the room into stillness—everyone except Zak, whose amused chuckle broke through like nails on glass. Wren gritted her teeth as Willie continued.

"How many times have I told you not to take outside jobs? It's against company policy! It's dangerous! It's *illegal!*" His voice rose with each word until it filled every corner of the small office.

Wren felt heat rising up her neck—the kind of burn that signaled her temper was ready to boil over. She clenched her fists at her sides and fired back before she could stop herself: "Oh, come on! Everyone does it. It's just a little side hustle."

"A little side hustle?" Willie's tone shifted, dripping now with sarcasm that cut sharper than his yelling ever could. "A *little side hustle* that ends with you covered in blood and rambling about dying women? Jesus Christ, Hubbard…" He trailed off as though he couldn't decide whether to continue shouting or give up entirely on stringing words together at all.

From his spot by the wall, Zak finally decided he'd had enough fun watching and joined in with a lazy drawl: "Sounds like Wren's finally bitten off more than she can chew." He pushed himself away from the wall just enough to lean forward for maximum effect before adding with an obnoxious grin: "Maybe it's time for a real courier to take over her routes."

Wren spun toward him so fast it was almost instinctual—a reflex honed by years of dealing with guys exactly like Zak who thought they could bait her into losing control at just the right moment. Her hands balled into fists without even thinking about it as she shot him a glare that could've melted steel beams. "Shut your mouth, Zak," she hissed through gritted teeth. "Or I'll shut it for you."

"Enough!" Willie roared again, snapping both of them back into silence like scolded children caught bickering in class. He pinched the bridge of his nose between two fingers and closed his eyes briefly—a man clearly trying (and maybe failing) to summon patience that had been long since depleted today.

"Wren," he said after a moment of heavy breathing meant to calm himself down but failing miserably at hiding how much this whole mess had gotten under his skin, "I want a full explanation—every detail—and it better be good." His eyes snapped open again, cutting straight through any lingering resistance she might've been holding onto for dear life. "Because if it isn't? You can kiss this job goodbye."

The office phone shattered the uneasy quiet with its shrill ring, cutting through the tension like a knife. Wren felt her heart ramp up, a too-familiar drumbeat against her ribs, as Willie reached for the receiver. His movements were deliberate, unhurried, but his frown deepened almost immediately, and Wren's stomach coiled tight like an overwound spring.

"Yes, Wren Hubbard works here," Willie said at last, his voice flat, his gaze locking onto hers. His brow furrowed further as he listened to whoever was on the other end of the line. "Yeah… she's here right now."

The room shifted subtly—couriers glancing at each other in silent unease, the scrape of a chair leg on concrete amplified in the tense stillness. Zak leaned closer to Wren then, his smirk stretching wider across his face like it had been waiting for this moment all along.

"Trouble always finds you, huh?" he said, low and smug. "Guess you're busted now."

Massi stepped forward before she could respond—not that she had any words ready anyway—and there was urgency chasing every syllable out of his mouth. "Wren, you need to leave. Go home. Now."

Thanh barely waited for him to finish before nodding vigorously and pulling their phone from their jacket pocket. "I'll send you some numbers—lawyers," they said quickly, already tapping away at their screen like time was running out. "You're gonna need them."

"I don't have my phone anymore," Wren blurted out before she could stop herself—the words tasting too loud and final in her mouth even as they fell into the room. "It... it got shot."

Massi froze mid-step. Thanh stopped typing long enough to blink at her like they hadn't heard correctly.

"Shot?" Massi echoed after a beat, his voice rising in disbelief as he stared at her hard enough to peel back layers. "What happened out there?"

Thanh stepped closer now too—too close—and their hand found her arm in a firm grip that didn't quite cross into forceful territory but didn't feel optional either. Their voice dropped so low it felt like they were speaking directly into her bones: "Wren—you need to go. Right now."

And then came that feeling again—that sensation where panic wasn't just rising but cresting inside her, a full-on tidal wave breaching whatever fragile walls she'd managed to build against it. The room blurred at the edges; she thought maybe Massi had reached toward her or Willie had said something else into the phone or Zak was still smirking because smugness was practically tattooed onto his face—but none of it mattered anymore.

Her feet found motion before her brain did, and without even processing what direction she was headed in, Wren shoved past the door and stumbled into daylight like escape was oxygen and she'd been drowning indoors.

The city hit her all at once—blaring horns, footsteps clattering down sidewalks—and yet none of it stuck in her awareness beyond the rhythm of her own steps pounding against pavement. She didn't look back—not at Zak's grin or Thanh's wide eyes or Willie's dark scowl—not at anything except forward because forward was all that existed now.

* * *

Wren's lungs felt like they might collapse, each breath scraping against her chest as she turned onto her street. Her legs kept pedaling, though they screamed for relief with every push. The sight of Maggie and Fannie up on the porch made her slow. She half-expected to fall off the bike entirely, but somehow, she managed to stop, planting one unsteady foot on the pavement.

Maggie was on her feet before Wren had even fully come to a halt. She sprinted down the steps, already calling out. "Wren! Oh my God, Wren!" Her voice wavered between relief and panic.

Fannie stayed seated on the porch swing, her weathered face steady but alert—concern showing in small ways, like the way one hand tightened on the arm of the swing. "Kiddo," she called down to Wren without moving. "You look like something a cat dragged in and forgot about."

Wren tried to dismount from the bike but stumbled instead. Her legs barely worked now; all they wanted was to give out beneath her. She fell into Maggie's waiting arms. "It's... it's bad," she gasped between ragged breaths. "They're after me."

Maggie eased her toward the steps, holding her up as though afraid she might crumble completely if let go. "You're scaring me," Maggie said softly, sitting Wren down as if she might shatter like glass.

Fannie shifted over with a grunt and patted the empty spot next to her on the swing. Her expression didn't change much—still calm and steady—but there was something in her eyes now that hadn't been there before. "Come sit here, honey," Fannie said.

Wren collapsed onto the swing beside her, leaning forward to bury her face briefly in hands that wouldn't stop trembling. Sweat plastered strands of hair to her forehead as she tried to piece together words that felt stuck deep in her throat. Finally: "I got this delivery order." She paused for breath but didn't look at either of them yet. "From an unknown number. Figured it was just another outsider gig."

Fannie stayed quiet except for a small shift—her body leaned a little closer to Wren now, though her expression didn't change much beyond narrowed eyes.

"I got there..." Wren stopped again and dragged both hands through sweat-soaked hair like she wanted to rip it right out. Her voice cracked when it came next: "There was this woman." Another pause while she stared at some point far off in the distance, past anything physical—the kind of stare that froze everything inside and out for a second too long. Then: "She was bleeding everywhere."

Maggie sucked in a sharp breath beside her—so sharp it felt like you could hear it echoing all around them—and then brought one hand up over her mouth while still holding onto Wren with the other hand like letting go might send everyone tumbling into chaos.

Fannie simply waited without saying much yet.

"And that's not even... not even the worst part," said Wren hurriedly after looking briefly at both women as though waiting for permission or encouragement before continuing quickly now because once started again there seemed no stopping anymore: "A cop was already there."

"He... he shot at me as I ran."

Wren's voice was shaky, her words tumbling out unevenly. Maggie had heard the story enough times now that it felt etched into the folds of her brain, but still, she stayed quiet. Across from them, Fannie blinked, her expression clouded with confusion. "The cop?"

"Dennis," Maggie supplied gently, answering before Wren could. The name had become bitter on her tongue.

Fannie sat back in her chair, her eyebrows knitting together. "You know the guy who shot at you?"

"Yeah," Wren said, a bitter laugh escaping her lips. Her eyes were hard, flickering with something raw and untamed. "He's a cop. A fucking cop."

Maggie sucked in a breath, trying to piece the puzzle together. It wasn't adding up—not yet. "I don't understand," she said carefully. "Why would he...?"

Fannie's voice cut through, her tone flat and laced with disdain: "Fucking pigs."

Both girls turned to look at her. Fannie didn't flinch under their gaze; she just shook her head slowly, a grim sort of resignation settling over her features.

"The woman," Wren started again, glancing down at her hands like the words might be scrawled there somewhere, waiting for her to read them aloud. "The woman who was dying—she told me to run." She swallowed hard. "Then Dennis shot at me. Twice. Maybe three times."

Fannie's sigh came long and heavy, like it had been buried deep inside of her for decades and now found its way out. She leaned back further in her chair, gripping the arms like they were anchoring her to something solid. Her voice softened—not gentler exactly, but quieter: "Honey, I haven't trusted cops or the government since '68." She paused there for a moment before adding with disillusionment: "Ain't surprised one bit that this Dennis fella's rotten all the way through."

Wren frowned as though trying to push through foggy memories. "But why call me there if he was gonna kill that woman? What's the point?"

Maggie reached out and placed a hand over Wren's—her touch steady but light enough not to startle. "Maybe it wasn't connected," she suggested after a moment of thought. "Maybe the two things aren't related at all... Did you know the woman?"

"No." Wren shook her head vehemently. Her movements were sharp now—almost too sharp—as though rejecting even the idea of familiarity with this stranger might undo some unseen thread tying them together. "I'd never seen her before in my life."

"Her name?" Maggie asked softly.

"I don't remember—Anne something maybe? I looked into her after I got her address; she seemed legit." Wren's lips pressed together tightly.

"Who paid for it?" Maggie asked next.

Wren pulled out a slick new phone from her pocket—the same one Maggie had noticed earlier—and opened an app with swipes of her thumb. The screen cast pale blue light onto Wren's tense face as she scrolled through transactions.

Her hand froze mid-scroll.

"Shit."

"What?" Maggie leaned forward instinctively.

"It was anonymous." Her tone got quieter, darker—each word pressing harder against the silence.

Fannie snorted—a humorless sound that made Maggie flinch inwardly even though she'd seen it coming from miles away: "What kinda app lets folks send money without names attached?"

"It's supposed to—" Wren hesitated here as though swallowing down bile before continuing dully: "It's supposed to be some kind of privacy feature."

Maggie leaned closer now—not because she needed clarity (she had plenty), but because proximity felt important when everything else seemed slippery and uncertain. Her voice dropped low around edges that weren't sharp but firm enough: "So... we've got no way to trace whoever sent you there? And you think her name is Anne?"

"Yeah," Wren muttered reluctantly. It came out almost like an exhale more than an actual word this time around—flat and drained completely dry of hope or enthusiasm alike.

She turned toward the porch railing then—not fully turning away from either woman nearby but definitely not looking directly at either anymore either—and let one final summation slip loose almost under its own weight entirely:

"We've got fucking zero."

"Honey, just be grateful you're so far under the radar that even the cops don't know where you live," Fannie said, her palm gliding gently over Wren's tangled hair.

"Not even Willie knows. We're contract staff to him, he doesn't have my address," Wren said.

"He wouldn't tell anyway, would he?" Maggie asked.

"He already told them I work there. The bastard." Wren leaned heavily against the porch railing. The wood felt rough against her arm, splinters biting through her sleeve. "So... what now? I can't exactly stroll into a police station and report all this crap."

"Certainly not," Fannie replied, her tone as dry as summer grass. "They'd lock you up quicker than you could spit out the word 'corruption.'"

Maggie stood nearby, chewing on her bottom lip like it might help her think faster. "We need more details. Something to work with. Maybe we can find out who the woman was?"

Wren exhaled sharply through her nose and shook her head. "Anne... something. That's all I got. She owned the place, So I'm not even sure it was here." Her voice wavered for a second, then steadied again. "It's not like I stopped to grab her ID while running for my life."

The words hung in the humid air between them until Maggie's phone shattered the silence with an aggressive buzz against the wooden porch rail. Wren watched Maggie glance down at the screen, her expression tensing instantly—as if she already knew who it was and what kind of lecture she was about to endure.

"It's my dad," Maggie muttered under her breath, thumb hovering over the screen before sliding to answer. "Hello?"

Wren didn't have to hear Charles's voice to feel its weight; she could see it in how Maggie stiffened immediately, shoulders inching toward her ears and jaw tightening so much it looked painful. Tinny static and bursts of sharp-edged syllables leaked from the speaker into the warm evening air, each word landing harder than it should have.

"Dad," Maggie finally cut him off mid-rant, gripping the phone so tightly that Wren briefly worried she might snap it in two. "I can't talk about this right now." A pause. Then a sharp exhale, loud enough it could've carried through the line itself. "No, you don't understand—"

Charles's voice rose just enough for Wren to catch fragments of his mounting anger: something about trouble and messes and blaming people who didn't deserve it.

"Whatever mess Wren's gotten you into—"

Maggie didn't let him finish. "I have to go," she snapped, thumb slamming down on the red button before he could fit another word in edgewise. The call ended abruptly, but maybe not neatly—her hand dropped to her side almost as if letting go of the phone entirely would somehow release all that tension still coiled up inside of her.

"He said it's on the news. Police say a female courier is a person of interest. He assumed it was you."

She stared at nothing for a moment, jaw twitching while she worked through silent words she hadn't said aloud yet—or maybe words she'd already decided not to say at all.

"I'm sorry," Wren said softly when she couldn't take sitting in that awkward quiet anymore. The guilt hit hard and fast now that they weren't actively distracted by life-threatening decisions or barely restrained panic spirals. "This is all my fault—dragging you into this mess."

Maggie turned to face her fully then, leaning back against the railing next to her but keeping enough distance so their arms wouldn't accidentally graze each other—not yet anyway—and softened like melted candle wax around the edges when their eyes finally met.

"No," she said firmly but quietly enough that Wren had no choice but to hear every word of it whether she wanted to or not. "We're in this together now. We'll figure it out."

"But your dad—"

"Forget about him." Maggie waved one hand vaguely toward where her phone sat abandoned on top of an empty flowerpot nearby like forgetting was just *that* easy if you tried hard enough or pretended well enough or heard yourself say it often enough first.

"He's always looking for reasons to hate you anyway; this isn't your fault."

"She's right," Fannie chimed in with a sage nod from behind them both before laying one weathered hand briefly across Wren's shoulder like an anchor or reassurance—or maybe both at once because people like Fannie didn't waste effort separating those kinds of gestures out unnecessarily when time was short or pressure high around them anyway.

"Ain't much use wasting energy apologizing over things none've us ever had any control over."

Wren ran her hands through her hair for what felt like the hundredth time that day. Her scalp stung from all the tugging, but she barely noticed. "But what if I can't fix this? What if Dennis comes after me? After us?" The words came out sharper than she intended, but then again, when did anything come out right these days?

Maggie shifted closer on the creaking porch swing, throwing an arm around Wren's trembling shoulders. Maggie always had this way of seeming calm even when everything was falling apart—an infuriating gift, really. "We'll cross that bridge when we come to it," Maggie said in a voice that suggested they had all the time in the world and weren't standing squarely on the tracks of an oncoming train. "Right now, let's figure out what happened."

Wren barely heard her. Maggie's face was already tilted toward her phone, her thumb scrolling quickly as her brow knitted together in that furrow Wren knew too well. It was her problem-solving face. Maggie called it multitasking. Wren called it maddening.

"What was the address again?" Maggie asked without looking up.

"17-164th Street." Wren spat the numbers out like they were something bitter she couldn't quite get off her tongue.

Maggie didn't respond, just gave a quick nod and buried herself back in the glow of the screen. Wren flexed her fingers nervously and then curled them into fists against her thighs. Sitting still seemed impossible, but fidgeting made her feel worse—like a frayed wire sparking just before it snapped.

Her gaze flicked to Fannie, perched like a sentry at the edge of the porch steps. Quiet as always, Fannie didn't so much as twitch, but her eyes swept over the street like radar scanning for debris. A car rolled past at a snail's pace, its engine grumbling low enough to set Wren's teeth on edge. She froze, one hand jerking reflexively toward Maggie's arm before stopping halfway.

Fannie didn't freeze. Her sharp eyes locked onto the passing car with an intensity that made Wren shiver despite herself. It wasn't what Fannie did—it was what she didn't do. No narrowing of her eyes, no clenching of fists or muttering under her breath. Just that stare: steady and unyielding until the car finally disappeared around the corner.

Only then did Fannie speak, though her voice betrayed no hint of worry or unease—just as practical as ever. "Let's go inside," she said with a tilt of her head toward the door behind them. "No sense sitting out here where every nosy neighbor can listen in."

The relief hit Wren like a wave breaking over rocks—she hadn't realized how exposed she felt until Fannie pointed it out. She rose on shaky legs that weren't entirely ready to follow instructions but managed anyway. She didn't want to stay a second longer on that vulnerable porch with its creaking boards and too many shadows. As Fannie stepped inside, holding the door open behind her, Wren followed without hesitation, feeling Maggie trailing close behind with typical single-minded focus on whatever crucial piece of information might be buried in that glowing screen.

Inside smelled exactly like Wren had expected it would—exactly like it always did: sandalwood incense hanging thick in the air like an old habit that refused to die; patchouli winding spicily through it; and beneath both those scents, something deeper and dustier—the unmistakable smell of old books long since resigned to their place on sagging shelves.

The small house wrapped around Wren like a favorite sweater pulled from storage on a cold day—worn in all the right ways yet scratchy in others if you thought about it too much (so she didn't). For just a heartbeat or two, as she crossed into this familiar territory where chaos couldn't quite seep through the cracks yet, Wren found herself breathing easier—for now.

The living room felt like a scrapbook come to life, a mishmash of mismatched furniture that didn't so much match as coexist. Sunlight filtered through faded floral curtains, the kind that had witnessed decades of secrets and small talk, casting everything in a golden haze that made the room look warmer than it was. The walls were lined with shelves—books with cracked spines leaned into dusty vinyl records, which were flanked by trinkets Fannie had picked up on her endless wanderings around the country.

Wren's gaze landed on a leather armchair in the corner, its surface worn and cracked like a veteran soldier's boots. A crocheted blanket spilled over the back, its bright colors out of place but oddly fitting—just like Fannie herself. Beside the chair sat a tiny table piled high with unfinished crossword puzzles and a mug of herbal tea still steaming faintly, its scent mingling with the faint trace of incense in the air.

Maggie sank into an overstuffed sofa, its lumpy cushions putting up a fight before finally giving way under her weight. Wren sat beside her and instantly felt Maggie's thigh press against hers. It wasn't much contact—just fabric against fabric—but it was enough to anchor her, enough to remind her she wasn't alone in whatever storm they'd walked into.

Fannie eased herself into a rocking chair across from them, the wood letting out a long creak as though offering commentary on her arrival. She began rocking slowly—almost absentmindedly—her movements mirroring the lazy swirl of incense smoke rising and twisting toward the ceiling.

Maggie's fingers flew across her phone screen, her face lit not just by its glow but by sudden alarm. "I found something," she said, her voice tight enough to snap. "That woman? Anne Cantu." She didn't look up.

"Anne Cantu?" Wren repeated, leaning forward even as she felt nausea coil low in her stomach. The name meant nothing to her—and yet it did. "Yeah, that was the name."

Fannie stopped rocking—the absence of that rhythmic creaking was stark—and squinted at Maggie like she could untangle this puzzle with sheer force of will. "Lots of coverage, honey?"

Maggie exhaled sharply through her nose like she couldn't believe she was about to say this out loud. "It's all over the news," she said, scrolling again but slower now, deliberately pulling up another page as though searching for confirmation she didn't want. "They're saying Anne Cantu was found dead in her house today." Her eyes flicked up for just a second before dropping back to the screen. "It's already on all the local sites, a couple of state news sites."

Wren felt something cold grip at her insides and twist hard enough to make her wince. Her stomach clenched painfully as two words escaped before she could think better of them: "Oh fuck." She collapsed backward against the sofa, suddenly unable to meet Maggie's gaze or Fannie's curious stare or even the crumpled blanket on that armchair across from them. "It's real," she murmured into what felt like empty space between them all. "It's all real."

Maggie kept scrolling despite how pale she looked; maybe searching for one last piece of tangible truth would make this nightmare bearable—or confirm that there wasn't any making it bearable at all. "She was an investigative journalist," Maggie said after a beat, each word deliberate and slow now like stepping stones across too-thin ice. "And... And a podcaster." Her brow furrowed deeper still as another detail hit home with an audible weight: "She wrote about corruption at city hall."

And just like that—everything shifted again.

"No kidding?" Fannie said, her eyebrows lifting in surprise. "Well, doesn't that just clear a few things up."

Wren's thoughts churned, each one crashing into the next, messy and incomplete. "What exactly are you saying?"

Fannie tilted her head to the side, her lips quirking into a knowing smile—a smile that didn't quite reach her eyes. "Sweetheart, it wouldn't shock me one bit if your pal Dennis is on the payroll. Maybe someone higher up—oh, I don't know, the mayor or one of his lackeys—put him up to keeping this Anne woman nice and quiet."

Wren shook her head quickly, too quickly. "Fannie, come on. You hear how ridiculous that sounds? That's some late-night conspiracy nonsense."

"Is it?" Fannie asked, leaning forward, her voice sharpening like the edge of a knife. "Think about it, kiddo: A cop shoots at you out of nowhere. A woman digging into corruption turns up dead. You don't have to be Columbo to see there might be a connection."

Wren rose to her feet without realizing it and started pacing the length of the small living room. The floor groaned beneath every step she took as though sympathizing with her unease. She glanced at the walls, at Maggie sitting silently by the window, anywhere but at Fannie's pointed gaze. "But why me? Why drag me into all of this?"

Maggie looked up then, the glow of her phone casting faint shadows across her face. She hesitated before speaking softly, almost reluctantly. "Maybe it wasn't about you specifically. Maybe you were just... there at the wrong moment." Maggie trailed off but then added carefully, as if testing whether she believed it herself: "Or... maybe they needed someone."

Wren stilled mid-step, turning toward Maggie now fully focused on her words. "Needed someone for what?"

Maggie hesitated again, chewing on the inside of her cheek until finally she forced herself to say it: "A witness." A pause weighed heavy between them before she went on quietly: "Or maybe someone they could pin everything on."

The air seemed to leave Wren's lungs all at once. The weight of that suggestion hit hard—not like a punch but something colder, heavier, more suffocating that settled deep in her chest and refused to move.

She sank back down onto the couch almost without realizing it and buried her face in her hands for a moment before looking back up again. "God," Wren muttered under her breath finally and then added louder but no steadier than before: "What in the world have I gotten myself into here?"

Wren leaned over Maggie's shoulder, her gaze fixed on the phone screen. The image of Anne Cantu filled the display—a woman with long, chestnut-brown hair that fell neatly to her shoulders and warm brown eyes that seemed caught mid-laughter. Her round face was framed by faint crow's feet, a sign of years of smiles. She looked so alive, so warm, so utterly human. Wren's breath hitched at the stark dissonance between this vibrant figure and the motionless, bloodied body she had found.

"That was her," Wren said quietly, her voice barely more than a murmur.

Fannie shifted in her rocking chair, the worn wood groaning faintly beneath her weight. "Maggie, honey? Anything about her—or about Wren—in the news?"

Maggie sat cross-legged on the couch, one hand steadying her phone while the other scrolled through article after article. Her lips moved silently as she read, her brow drawing tighter with each new line.

"They're looking for a food courier," Maggie said finally. Her voice was clipped, careful—like she wasn't sure whether to finish the sentence or let it hang in the growing tension of the room. "They called them 'a person of interest.' Someone who might've seen what happened."

A bitter laugh escaped Wren before she could choke it down. She dragged both hands through her already mussed hair and let them fall back at her sides. "Seen what happened?" she repeated, shaking her head as though the words themselves were absurd. "I didn't just *see* it."

She pushed herself up from Maggie's side and started pacing the small living room. The floorboards creaked beneath her sneakers in uneven protest, a sound that grated against the frantic rhythm of her thoughts.

"I didn't just *see* it," she said again, louder this time. The words tumbled out too fast now, uncontrolled like water breaking past a dam. "I was *there*. I watched her die—Jesus Christ, I tried to help her." Wren stopped mid-step and spun toward them both, her voice breaking as she threw up an arm for emphasis. "And then Dennis—he shot at me."

She froze for a moment after saying his name aloud. Her breath hitched again, harsher this time, before escaping in something halfway between a sigh and a sob.

Maggie reached out, her fingers wrapping gently but firmly around Wren's wrist as she stormed by. "Babe, slow down. Just stop for a second. We need to think this through."

Wren's gaze dropped to Maggie, who was sitting there so steady and calm—too calm—like the world hadn't just turned upside down. The worry on Maggie's face was clear, though, carved into the corners of her mouth and the faint crease between her brows.

"Think what through?" Wren's voice clutched at the words, thin and brittle like it might shatter entirely if she pushed it any harder. "I'm screwed, Mags. If I go to the cops, Dennis is gonna pin all this on me. If I don't"—she let out a bitter laugh that sounded more like a choke—"I'm on the run for the rest of my fucking life."

Across the room, Fannie leaned forward slowly, her weathered hands resting on her knees as she watched Wren with sharp eyes that seemed to miss nothing. "Now hold on there, kiddo," she said, her tone cutting clean through Wren's spiraling panic. "Ain't no law says you gotta throw yourself on the fire."

That brought Wren's head around sharply, her brow furrowing in confusion. "What are you talking about?"

"I'm saying," Fannie replied, sitting back now and folding her arms across her chest with an air of certainty that defied argument, "sometimes the best thing you can do is nothing at all. Sit tight. Wait it out. Let things shake themselves loose first."

Maggie nodded then—slowly at first, like she was still turning the idea over in her mind but finding something solid there to hold on to—and her grip on Wren's hand tightened, a quiet reassurance barely felt but unmistakably present. "She's right," Maggie said softly. "We don't know enough yet."

The strength drained from Wren's legs then, leaving them wobbly and useless beneath her until she sank down onto the couch like a marionette whose strings had been cut. Her whole body felt heavy now—not just tired but weighed down by something bigger than exhaustion—as if gravity had doubled its hold on her.

"So what?" Wren asked after a long moment, staring blankly at the floor in front of her as though all the answers might somehow be written there in invisible ink. "We just... wait?"

"For now," Maggie said again in that same soft tone that somehow managed to sound both gentle and unyielding at once. She shifted closer to Wren on the couch without letting go of her hand. "We watch the news. We see what comes out—what they're saying about Dennis and Anne. Maybe we can figure out more about what Anne was looking into before..." Her voice trailed off before finishing the thought.

Wren didn't answer right away; instead, her eyes flicked toward Maggie's phone resting on the coffee table nearby—the screen still lit with that picture of Anne smiling brightly back at them like nothing in the world could touch her. Only now that smile didn't feel warm or kind anymore. Now it felt... wrong somehow. Eerie. Like it was hiding something they hadn't seen before.

Finally, Wren swallowed hard and nodded once—not because she felt any better about all this but because nodding felt easier than trying to find words she didn't have right now.

"No," she whispered eventually—so quietly it was barely there at all—but then shook her head as if already second-guessing herself again before continuing in a voice that broke unevenly over every syllable: "I can't just sit here forever doing nothing, Mags... We have to figure out what happened."

"How did Anne get your number, honey? Was she a regular customer at Cyclista?" Fannie asked. Her weathered hands gripped the arms of her rocking chair, the motion slowing as if waiting for an answer might stop time itself.

Wren shook her head slowly, a furrow carving deep between her brows. "I don't know. I've never seen her before today." She exhaled sharply, fists flexing and relaxing at her sides. "It doesn't make any sense."

She shot to her feet, the sudden movement making the rocking chair creak beneath Fannie's stillness. A jittery charge coursed through Wren's limbs as she started pacing the small living room, the wood floor groaning under every step. "I have to go back to Cyclista," she said finally, half to herself. "Maybe someone there knows something."

Maggie, who'd been perched on the arm of the couch like she couldn't decide whether to join Wren in pacing or stay put, stiffened visibly. "Wren," she said, her voice a low plea. "No. It's too dangerous. What if the police are there? You said they called Willie."

Wren stopped mid-stride and turned toward her girlfriend, her jaw tightening as though holding back words too sharp for this moment. Then she rubbed at her temples in quick circles and let out a breath that was more frustration than calm. "I know it's a risk," she said finally, glancing toward Maggie with an expression that softened just enough around the edges to make room for affection. "But it's all we've got right now. Maybe she's a regular for one of the other riders. Maybe a different courier was supposed to be there."

"Okay, we'll go."

Her gaze flicked between Maggie and the window—dark now except for the faint reflection of their dimly lit living room—and then back again like she was weighing something heavier than just words. "I need you here," Wren said quietly, taking a step closer to Maggie. The words felt heavier when spoken aloud.

Maggie stood now, crossing her arms tightly over her chest as though bracing herself against what was coming next. "I'm not staying here while you go off alone," she said firmly, though there was a slight tremble in her voice that betrayed how much it cost to argue this point. Her chin tilted up defiantly. "We're in this together, remember?"

Wren reached for Maggie's hands then—not in desperation, but with purpose—and folded them into hers like they were an anchor tethering both of them to something solid amid all this uncertainty. She held them there for a moment before speaking again.

"I know," Wren said softly, locking eyes with Maggie in that way people do when they need you to feel their words even more than hear them. "And I love you for it." Her lips quirked into something that wasn't quite a smile but carried warmth nonetheless—a flicker of light before diving back into shadowed waters.

"But I need you here," Wren continued gently but firmly, squeezing Maggie's hands as though trying to pass some of her conviction through touch alone. "Someone has to keep an eye on things—social media, the news." She hesitated for half a heartbeat before adding with forced casualness: "We need to know if my picture shows up somewhere or if there's anything new about... about Anne. And I need you safe. \you won't be safe with me."

There it was—the weight behind everything unsaid pressed between them like air too thick to breathe freely.

Maggie's resolve faltered for just a moment—her shoulders slumping under invisible pressure—but she nodded eventually, reluctantly; one quick tilt of her head that carried all the resignation and worry she couldn't bring herself to put into words.

"Okay," Maggie murmured after what felt like too long a pause. Then louder: "Okay." Her arms dropped back down before reaching instinctively for Wren again—one last tethering embrace before letting go entirely. She buried her face briefly against Wren's neck and then pulled back just far enough so their eyes met again.

"Promise me," Maggie said softly but urgently now—like each word had its own pulse running through it—"promise me you'll be careful."

Wren breathed in deeply then—the familiar herb-and-something-else scent of Maggie's shampoo grounding her as much as humanly possible given everything else spiraling around them both lately—and pulled her girlfriend into another hug that felt less like goodbye and more like armor.

"I promise," Wren whispered into the soft curve where Maggie's shoulder met her neck.

Fannie watched the exchange, her eyes sharp with concern. "You need to change your clothes, honey. You can't go out looking like that."

10:07 a.m.

Fannie unlocked the door that separated her living room from the basement apartment she rented out to the girls. Wren and Maggie slipped through, descending the narrow staircase into their own little haven—a space carved out below ground level, connected to the backyard.

Wren wriggled out of her cycling shirt, grimacing as the fabric clung stubbornly to her skin where blood had seeped through. The vibrant jersey was now defiled with dark maroon stains, and she tossed it onto the floor without ceremony. Her fingers fumbled at the waistband of her shorts. They slid down her legs and pooled around her ankles before being kicked aside to join the crumpled heap.

"Shit," she muttered under her breath, catching sight of red splotches blooming on her underwear. They followed suit, leaving her standing there in nothing but socks.

Maggie, sprawled on the bed, glanced up briefly from her phone. Her eyes widened—just for a flicker of a moment—and then dropped back to the glowing screen as though nothing had happened. "Anne Cantu," she said after a beat, scrolling through whatever article had captured her interest, "was kind of a big deal in journalism. She did all these exposés—like on environmental disasters and shady corporate stuff." Her voice softened as if speaking those words carried some kind of weight.

Wren flopped down beside her on the unmade bed, making it sag under her weight. She bent over to tug at her socks, wrinkling her nose as waves of sweat odor wafted up from them. One came off easily; the other proved more stubborn.

Then came a faint metallic tink—small but sharp enough to cut through their otherwise quiet bubble. Something hit the floor.

Wren froze mid-motion, one sock hanging limp in her hand like an after-thought.

"What was that?" Maggie asked, peering over the edge of the bed with mild curiosity that bordered on concern.

But Wren's mind was already elsewhere—hurtling backward to that blood-soaked scene in the woods: the woman's clammy hand reaching out, clutching something small and urgent—a USB drive pressed into Wren's palm during those final breaths she'd thoughtlessly tried to outrun.

How had she managed to forget about it?

Wren's fingers curled around the small silver object. It felt slick against her skin, tacky with dried blood that left faint, rusty smudges on her fingertips. She straightened and held it up, watching how the USB key caught the dim light of the apartment. The stains across its surface were dark, nearly black, like old secrets refusing to fade.

"The woman—Anne," Wren said, her voice flat but steady, "she gave me this."

Maggie was staring now, her eyes locked on the bloody device. Her lips parted before a quiet "Jesus Wren" escaped, almost too soft to hear. Then louder: "What the hell have you gotten yourself into?"

Wren didn't answer right away. Maggie's eyes darted up to meet hers now, wide and accusing. When she finally spoke again, her voice hitched somewhere between anger and disbelief. "You forgot to mention this? Are you serious? A dying woman handed you a USB drive—covered in blood, I might add—and it just slipped your mind?"

Wren's jaw tightened; she could feel heat prickling at the back of her neck. "Hey, cut me some slack," she said sharply. "I've been kinda busy dodging bullets and trying not to die out there. Sorry if I didn't get around to giving you a full play-by-play."

She tossed the USB key onto the bed with a flick of her wrist. It landed between them with a dull whisper. Maggie flinched before reaching for it gingerly with two fingers, as though it might bite her. She turned it over in her hand and grimaced at the streaks left behind on her skin.

"Christ, Wren," Maggie muttered after a pause. Her tone carried exhaustion more than anger now. It sounded like defeat—or maybe resignation.

Wren exhaled slowly and pushed herself to standing. Every muscle in her body protested the movement, stiff from hours of tension and adrenaline. She ran a hand through her tangled hair, half-conscious of how matted it felt under her palm.

"I need a shower," she said finally. Her voice lacked its earlier edge now, quieter somehow—it wasn't a request or even an announcement so much as an acknowledgment of how far gone she felt in this moment. "I smell like d—."

Maggie wrinkled her nose but said nothing for a second or two before nodding toward the bathroom door. "Yeah," she replied softly. "You do. Go ahead—I'll figure out what's on this thing."

Wren didn't linger for long after that exchange—there was no point—but even as she shuffled toward their cramped bathroom, Maggie's words chased after her like shadows she couldn't escape entirely.

She turned the shower handle slowly, the old pipes groaning as though protesting the effort. A stuttering spray of water burst forth, tepid and thin, hardly deserving of the word "shower." Still, it would have to do.

Wren stepped under the weak stream, feeling its uneven warmth strike her skin. She watched as pale rivulets of diluted blood trickled down her legs, winding their way to the drain. The water turned a faint pink, swirling briefly before vanishing into the gurgling darkness below. She reached for the shampoo bottle on the sill, tipping a sticky glob of purple into her palm and rubbing it between her hands before working it into her hair. As she massaged her scalp, she could feel the accumulated grime of the day—the grit of sweat, dirt, and something darker—dissolve beneath her fingertips.

The water rinsed through her hair in streaks of violet and red, creating a messy kaleidoscope at her feet. Wren caught herself staring at it—those vibrant colors mixing and fading together on the shower floor like some macabre tie-dye experiment. Her hands slowed; her thoughts did not.

The almost-warm water ran over aching shoulders and tired limbs. Her muscles eased under its touch, but not enough to wash away the tension coiled inside. It was a poor balm for everything that weighed on her mind.

She squeezed her eyes shut, letting the steam gather around her like a fog. The heat felt good—almost good enough to distract her from everything else—but not quite. How had it all unraveled so quickly? She thought back to earlier: handing Maggie the USB drive, watching Maggie's expression as she took it from Wren's hand. Had she opened it yet? Was she staring at whatever files were hidden inside right now? What had they stumbled onto?

Reports... photos... videos? Wren couldn't shake the flood of what-ifs crowding in on her: What if it was bigger than she had imagined? A cover-up? Corruption? Something worth killing for? Because Dennis had shot at her—to *kill* her—and that still didn't make sense. Why Dennis?

Her brow furrowed as questions piled up faster than she could untangle them. Did Dennis know about the USB? Had he thought she killed Anne—that he was arresting a murderer? No... that didn't track. He hadn't come through the entryway like someone making an official move; he'd emerged from deeper in the house—from one of the bedrooms maybe. Waiting for her? Or had something spooked him after he got there?

Her head tilted forward under the stream as though that might help clear it somehow, but nothing came into focus—not really. The steam seemed to settle in her brain too, clouding everything further even as it promised release from tension. Dennis didn't add up. None of this added up: Anne's death, that USB key, Dennis pulling that trigger—it all twisted together in a knot Wren couldn't loosen no matter how hard she tried.

She rinsed out the last of the shampoo and pressed a palm against the tile wall to steady herself when dizziness crept in—not from exhaustion exactly but from trying to make sense of something senseless.

At least Maggie had the drive now—Maggie could dig into it, maybe find some answers there amidst all those files Wren hadn't dared look through herself yet—but how much time did they have before this spiraled out even further?

And Dennis... what if he wasn't just covering something up? What if he'd legitimately believed Wren was some kind of threat? But no—that didn't sit right either.

The more she tried to sift through possibilities, reconstruct moments with new angles and assumptions laid over them like layers of tracing paper—the less any of it made sense.

Wren exhaled sharply, shaking droplets from her chin as though they might carry some clarity with them when they fell away from her skin.

The shower sputtered again and cooled—its tepid warmth fading fast—and she realized how little good it was doing now; how little good *any* of this water had done except stall for time under false pretenses.

She turned off the tap abruptly—the whooshing sound echoing dully against tiled walls—and stepped out onto cold tile floor without reaching first for a towel.

She needed answers more than warmth right now.

And Maggie was waiting with that drive.

Wren wrapped the towel tightly around herself. The mirror was fogged over, her reflection nothing more than a purple-tinged blur. She swiped a hand across the glass, carving a streak clear enough to meet her own gaze.

"What the hell have you gotten yourself into this time?" she asked, her voice low, almost conspiratorial. The woman staring back at her didn't have an answer. Same damp hair, same vivid purple dye bleeding onto pale shoulders, same worried crease between her brows. Wren held her stare for a moment longer before letting out a sharp breath and turning away.

She opened the bathroom door, releasing a rush of steam that spilled out into the apartment like smoke escaping from a fire. Cool air met her skin in a sudden, bracing contrast. She crossed the small room to the dresser she shared with Maggie and tugged open the second drawer from the top—her drawer. Fresh cycling gear lay in neat folds, untouched since yesterday's laundry run. Wren grabbed underwear and shorts first and slipped them on; they clung snugly to her hips as she adjusted the waistband. The jersey came next—soft but firm fabric that stretched as she pulled it over her head, catching briefly on damp hair before settling into place. She stretched absentmindedly, rolling her shoulders until they gave two quiet pops.

Behind her, there was movement—a faint creak of bedsprings followed by the metallic click of Maggie's laptop being opened. Wren turned in time to see Maggie shift against the headboard, pulling the slim computer onto her lap while reaching for something on the nightstand: the USB key.

That USB key.

It glinted faintly in Maggie's hand as she hesitated for just a second—a hesitation so brief that if Wren hadn't been watching so closely, she might've missed it altogether—and then slid it into one of the laptop's ports. A soft whir filled the room as the machine took hold of its new task.

Maggie leaned forward, narrowing her eyes at the screen while navigating with deliberate clicks of the trackpad. Her brow furrowed deeply; whatever she was seeing wasn't making sense yet—or maybe it made too much sense.

"There's only one file," Maggie murmured after another moment of silence, tilting her head as though viewing it from another angle might change something fundamental about what was there. "It's... just numbers? A couple of long ones." Her voice grew quieter still, as though reluctant to finish what she was saying: "Maybe it's a phone number."

Wren had been standing near the dresser until then—standing but not entirely still—and now something about Maggie's words made motion impossible to resist any longer. She crossed to the bed in three long strides and launched herself onto it with so much force that the ancient springs groaned in protest beneath both their weights. The mattress dipped beneath them but didn't break—the kind of resilience earned through years of enduring similar abuse.

Settling beside Maggie with one leg tucked under herself and their shoulders brushing lightly together now that they were close enough to share warmth again even without thinking too hard about whether either wanted such proximity right now or not—Wren glanced at the screen.

Wren tilted her head, peering at the laptop screen. Her eyes flicked over the string of numbers, and slowly, a grin curved her lips. "These aren't just random digits," she said, leaning closer. "They're GPS coordinates."

Maggie squinted at the screen, her brow knitting in confusion. "GPS what now?"

Wren chuckled softly and nudged Maggie's arm with her elbow. "Come on, Miss Bike Courier. You're seriously telling me you don't know latitude and longitude when you see it?"

Maggie's cheeks went pink as she crossed her arms defensively. "Hey, I'm not some kind of navigation nerd," she shot back. "I input addresses into my phone—like a normal person. No numbers."

"They tell you where to go," Wren said lightly, still smiling as she tapped the screen. "And yeah, coordinates are basically that—just... less user-friendly." She leaned back in her seat and added with a wry laugh, "Probably if someone had GPS coordinates for Hell, they'd lead straight to here."

Maggie frowned, considering something. "But what if you're one number off?" she asked after a beat. "How easy would it be to miss your destination then?"

"Pretty easy," Wren admitted with a little shrug before turning toward Maggie with a teasing glint in her eye. "Aw, don't get flustered about it. Not everyone gets to be a genius like me."

Maggie rolled her eyes hard enough that Wren would have sworn she heard it. Still, there was the smallest tug at the corners of Maggie's mouth—a reluctant smile fighting its way through.

"Whatever, smartass," Maggie muttered under her breath. "So what are we supposed to do with these coordinates?"

Wren's smirk faded, her face growing serious again as she sat up straighter. "Text them to my new number—the one I called you from earlier today." She hesitated just long enough for the gravity of her next words to settle in the air between them. "We might need to check them out later... but I don't want to risk keeping that USB lying around."

Maggie gave a small nod and reached for her phone without another word. She carefully transcribed the numbers onto the screen, triple-checking each digit before hitting send. Her thumb hovered for half a second before pressing down.

"Done," Maggie said quietly, setting her phone on the table like it might burn her fingers if she held onto it any longer. She looked back at Wren expectantly. "Now what?"

For a moment, Wren didn't reply. Instead, she turned toward Maggie and leaned in close—close enough for their foreheads to almost touch—before pressing her lips gently but firmly against hers. The kiss was brief yet heavy with meaning, like something between them had been sealed or reassured. When Wren pulled back, she caught sight of Maggie's expression: worry etched into every line of her face but softened by something else—something unspoken but shared.

Wren exhaled slowly, lowering her voice until it was little more than a murmur meant only for Maggie's ears: "Now we figure out our next move."

She rose from the bed with a groan, the mattress springs letting out a protest loud enough to make Wren freeze. How could something so small seem so amplified? The sound felt like a flare shot up into the stillness, and for a moment, her breath caught. Exposed. Vulnerable. She hated that feeling.

Her eyes swept the cramped, cluttered apartment, skimming over discarded jackets, half-empty mugs, and the uneven stack of cycling magazines on the table. On top of them sat Maggie's sunglasses—the good pair, the ones Maggie guarded like treasure. Wren crossed the room and plucked them up without hesitation, sliding them onto her face. The lenses gave everything a cool gray haze, dimming the edges of the world and cloaking her thoughts behind dark glass.

"Borrowing these," she said, adjusting them on her nose with exaggerated care.

Maggie looked up from her laptop, her brow creasing. "For what?"

Wren shrugged. "Disguise."

That seemed enough explanation for now. She moved toward the closet, pulling its door open and bracing herself for its usual avalanche of chaos inside—jackets half-hung or not at all, spare bike parts stacked precariously on shelves that weren't designed to hold much weight. A few moments of digging yielded what she was looking for: a helmet in crisp white, starkly pristine compared to her usual scuffed and scratched gear. She hefted it triumphantly and turned it over in her hands.

"Can't be too careful," she added as though it were obvious, fitting it onto her head and fastening the chin strap with a deliberate *click*. The snug fit felt foreign—her old helmet had molded to her shape over years of wear—but there was something strangely satisfying about this pristine one.

"How do I look?" she asked Maggie, turning toward her with a theatrical tilt of her head.

Maggie didn't even pause to pretend thoughtfulness. "Like someone who got lost on their way to join the Tour de France."

"Perfect." Wren smirked as she searched the shelves.

"Water bottle," she muttered aloud as she picked it up and gave it a quick shake; full enough. "Protein bars…" She unwrapped just enough of one end to confirm its chocolate coating hadn't melted into mush. "Check." Then there was the flashlight—or rather there wasn't.

Her hand fumbled through the detritus again before pausing mid-search.

"Shit," she murmured under her breath, glancing back at Maggie like she might somehow be responsible for this latest annoyance. "Where's my flashlight?"

"Looking for this?" Maggie's voice sliced through the stillness, sharp enough to make Wren flinch. She glanced up to find her girlfriend twirling the mini LED flashlight between her fingers.

"You left it on the kitchen counter," Maggie continued, eyebrows raised as if to chide her. "After that epic hunt for whatever was making noise outside last week. Remember?"

"Oh, right." Wren forced a smile and reached out, snagging it from Maggie's hand. "Thanks, babe. Total lifesaver."

She turned to Argo, snapping the flashlight into its holder beneath the seat. The motion was automatic, her hands moving on their own. But then her gaze drifted, landing squarely on the blood-stained USB key lying there on the rumpled bedspread like some small, incriminating ghost.

Wren froze just long enough to feel that twinge of unease twist in her gut, then snatched it up with fingers that trembled more than she cared to admit.

"One more thing," she murmured, mostly to herself as she snatched the key off the bed and stuck it in her sock again. It had been safe there the first time, so, she reasoned, it would work again.

Her movements grew quicker now, hurried as she crouched by the shorts she'd dropped on the floor last night—discarded in a heap at midnight when exhaustion had overtaken her—and started rummaging through their pockets. A moment later she pulled out two small objects: one plastic, one metal. Her old SIM card sat in one hand; in the other rested a warped bullet casing, heavy despite its size and dull except for where faint light gleamed along its battered surface.

"These can't just stay out," Wren muttered under her breath. She wasn't sure if Maggie caught her words or not—probably not—but they were spoken more for herself anyway.

The bullet still smelled faintly of gunpowder—it always did, no matter how many times she convinced herself otherwise—and just holding it brought back too much: smoke in the air, heat against her skin, a phone shattered instead of a ribcage punctured or a heart stopped mid-beat.

"What is that?" Maggie's voice yanked Wren out of the memory like a hook catching flesh.

Wren glanced up and saw it then—Maggie's wide eyes fixed on what she was holding, her brow furrowed as confusion gave way to something harsher.

Wren swallowed hard against the lump forming in her throat; she could feel it sitting there like lead weighing her down. Her fingers clenched around the bullet reflexively before unfurling, leaving tiny indentations in her palm where edges had pressed too sharply against skin.

"It's..." Wren hesitated for just a second before forcing herself to meet Maggie's gaze. "It's the bullet," she said finally, her voice low and rough like gravel turning over in an engine too long neglected. "The one that hit my phone."

The bullet sat in Wren's palm, glinting faintly in the dim light of the apartment. For a moment, nothing moved. The air felt thick, like it had been sucked from the room, leaving behind what that small piece of mangled metal represented. Maggie didn't speak. She just stared at it, all the color draining from her face until her skin was nearly as pale as the walls behind her.

When she swayed, Wren dropped the bullet without thinking, hands shooting out to steady her before she could collapse. The sudden motion sent a sharp pain slicing through Wren's ribs—bruised, cracked—but when weren't they? Of course Maggie noticed none of this; her focus remained fixed on the bullet now sitting forgotten on the scuffed floorboards.

"Easy," Wren said, trying to sound calm even though her body protested every movement. She caught Maggie by the elbows, guiding her away from the center of the room toward something solid: the bed with its worn mattress and sagging frame. Maggie resisted for half a second before her knees buckled completely, forcing Wren to take more of her weight than she should've been able to handle.

By the time they reached the bed, Maggie was trembling so hard Wren could feel it through both their clothes. Her breaths came in sharp little gasps—too fast and too shallow. "Oh my god," Maggie whispered, barely loud enough to hear over the pounding in Wren's ears. She blinked rapidly, like she was trying to clear some fog that refused to lift. "Oh my god. Someone... Someone actually tried to kill you."

The words seemed to crack something inside her because a moment later Maggie just... folded in on herself. Silent sobs shook her small frame as tears spilled freely down her cheeks, leaving shiny tracks that caught what little light there was in their cramped space.

Wren eased onto the bed beside her, moving carefully so she wouldn't jar anything that already hurt (which was basically everything at this point). She slipped an arm around Maggie's hunched shoulders and pulled her close—not tight, just steady, grounding—and felt how warm Maggie was through the thin cotton of her shirt despite how much she shook.

"It's okay," Wren murmured softly into her hair or maybe into empty space—it didn't matter who heard it first: Maggie or herself. "I'm okay."

Maggie turned then, burying her face against Wren's chest so suddenly that Wren almost lost balance for a moment but managed not to tip them both off the edge of the mattress entirely. The damp heat of tears soaked through Wren's shirt almost immediately; it clung uncomfortably to her skin now but she didn't flinch or shift or say anything about it because none of that mattered right now—not when Maggie's world had clearly tilted sideways.

Instead, Wren rubbed slow circles up and down Maggie's back while flickering thoughts tumbled through her head like static on an old radio. But none of those thoughts made it past whatever filter kept them from spilling out loud because right now wasn't about any of that either.

It was about this: two people on a bed too small for comfort with too much fear between them but also enough love (or hope or something equally fragile yet binding) to keep holding on despite everything pressing hard against them from all sides—the past whispering warnings neither could ignore anymore and whatever came after waiting far too close for comfort.

So they sat there together—flexed and braced—waiting for some kind of equilibrium neither was sure would ever come back fully again.

"I could have lost you," Maggie said, the words jagged and raw, like they barely made it past the lump in her throat. Her sobs came in waves, uneven and relentless. "You could have died, and I wouldn't have known. I wouldn't have even..."

"Shh." Wren pressed her lips softly to the crown of Maggie's head. "I'm here. I'm fine. We'll figure this out, okay? Together."

The sobs slowed, tapering off into hiccupping breaths. Maggie's face was blotchy now, her cheeks flushed and streaked with tear tracks that glistened faintly in the dim light. She leaned back just enough to meet Wren's gaze—red-rimmed eyes locking onto hers with something too heavy to name. Fear? Love? Probably both.

"You won't run from this, will you?" Maggie whispered, her voice rasping under the strain of crying.

Wren shook her head. "No. They taught me every lesson except the one they meant to—how to stay down. I'm fighting it. Him. Them."

Maggie's hands gripped Wren's arms like that determination was the only thing tethering her to solid ground. "Promise me you'll be careful."

There were a million ways Wren could've answered that—half-truths, deflections—but none of them felt right. Instead, she cupped Maggie's face gently in her hands, thumbs brushing away the tears that still clung stubbornly to her skin.

"I promise," Wren said, and even as she said it, she wasn't sure if it was true. But what else was there to say? She leaned in and kissed Maggie's forehead softly—one of those quiet gestures meant to reassure but never quite reaching deep enough.

Maggie nodded—not convinced exactly but resigned—and Wren slipped away from her side with a kind of purposeful urgency that didn't leave room for doubt. By the time she returned with a tissue box—brightly decorated with flowers trying too hard to cheer up whoever needed them—Maggie had settled into an exhausted calm.

"Here," Wren said, holding out the box like it might help erase everything that had just happened. "C'mon now. It's not all that different from your close call with the bus a few months ago."

Maggie sniffled into a tissue and glared at her through swollen eyes. "Yes, it is different. Of course it's different."

Wren shrugged, trying for nonchalance but falling short by a mile. "Not really," she said quietly as though saying it softer would make it truer somehow. "A near miss is a near miss."

She didn't wait for an answer and padded toward the kitchen instead, each step landing softly against the worn linoleum floors that squeaked faintly beneath her weight. The bullet caught the light where it rested on the floor—a stark reminder of what they were dealing with—and Wren snatched it up before she could think too much about it.

The cutlery drawer protested as she yanked it open; its hinges groaned under years of neglect while forks and spoons rattled against one another noisily inside. Wren pushed them aside with deliberate care until she'd carved out just enough space at the back of the drawer—a small gap no one would think twice about unless they knew exactly what they were looking for.

The SIM card went in first: small, unassuming, easy to lose or forget about entirely if you weren't paying attention. Then came the bullet—cold metal meeting warm skin one last time before disappearing into obscurity among butter knives and soup spoons.

She paused for half a second before nudging everything back into place as though rearranging utensils could also rearrange the mess her life had landed in.

It couldn't. But it was something to do while she thought about what came next.

Wren crossed back to the bed and let herself fall into its embrace, landing heavily enough to make the mattress groan in protest. Maggie didn't move, just watched her with an expression that was part curiosity, part worry. Wren turned the phone over in her hand, staring at it like it might suddenly give her answers.

"The SIM card might have something," she said finally.

Maggie's brow furrowed. "Like what?"

"The FonBill app could show who paid for Anne's meal," Wren explained, though her tone had no confidence in it. "Problem is, FonBill's public app is anonymous. It doesn't track anything useful. But if they have the order number, they must be able to track who paid."

Maggie chewed on her bottom lip—a habit Wren noticed more when Maggie was trying not to say something—and glanced between the phone and Wren's face before speaking tentatively. "Maybe... maybe we should go to the cops? They might know how to—"

"No." The word shot out sharper than Wren intended. Maggie flinched, and immediately Wren softened her voice. "Sorry, babe," she said gently, but firmly. "No cops. Not ever."

The refusal landed like a stone between them. Maggie nodded slowly, her lips pressed into a thin line. "Right," she said after a moment. Her voice had dropped, more resigned now. A pause, then: "So what then?"

"I don't know," Wren admitted, her head tipping back against the headboard with a dull thud that made her wince. She stared up at the ceiling like it might reveal some grand plan she hadn't thought of yet. It didn't. "Maybe lawyers? Or a private investigator?" She waved the idea away almost as soon as she said it. "But that's later—right now we need to focus on staying alive and figuring out what all this even means."

She let out a breath and felt Maggie shift beside her. Without warning, Maggie's arms wrapped around her waist, pulling her close in one swift motion that left no room for argument or retreat—not that Wren wanted either option right now anyway. The warmth of Maggie's body seeped into hers, chasing away some of the cold that had buried itself deep under her skin ever since... well, ever since everything fell apart.

For a moment, they stayed like that without speaking.

"You know," Maggie murmured finally, her breath soft against Wren's ear, "I'm proud of you."

Wren blinked at the words—simple enough, but they hit harder than she expected them to—and tried to deflect with a shrug and a forced snort of laughter. "It wasn't anything special," she muttered.

But Maggie wasn't having any of it. She pulled back just enough so their faces were inches apart and locked eyes with Wren in that way she always did when she wanted to make sure there was no brushing off or dodging involved—just raw honesty hanging there between them.

Her gaze pinned Wren where she sat—steady and unrelenting—and for once, Wren didn't have anything clever to say back.

"I mean it, Wren." Maggie's voice didn't waver. It was steady, resolute. "You are incredible. I... I just need you to know how proud I am of you. How much I love you. Being with someone as brave and resourceful as you—it's everything to me."

Wren felt the words land somewhere deep, somewhere tender and unguarded. Her chest tightened, a pressure she couldn't quite name rising up like a tide. She swallowed hard and blinked fast, trying to keep everything in its proper place, but her throat betrayed her—the lump growing larger with each passing second.

"Mags..." The sound came out jagged, like it was being forced through a throat too tight to cooperate. She coughed lightly, forcing herself to push through it. "I love you too," she managed, voice low and raw around the edges. "More than anything. I honestly don't even know who I'd be without you."

Maggie smiled at that—not big or flashy, but soft and warm, the kind of smile that steadied Wren even as it unraveled her all at once. She leaned in then, their foreheads touching in an almost imperceptible movement, so close that Wren could feel the faint rhythm of Maggie's breath against her skin. For a moment, there was nothing else—no noise, no chaos creeping in from beyond them—just this fragile bubble where they could both simply exist.

Wren tilted her head, closing the small distance between them. Their lips met softly at first—a careful gesture full of unspoken promises—but it didn't stay soft for long. The kiss deepened quickly, the undercurrent of fear and adrenaline surging up between them like a current neither could resist. Wren's fingers wove tightly into Maggie's hair as if letting go wasn't an option; Maggie's grip on Wren's hips was firm enough to leave marks—not painful exactly, but grounding, anchoring.

When they finally parted, their breaths came heavy and uneven like they'd both run miles together instead of standing perfectly still. Wren rested her forehead against Maggie's again briefly before shifting—her cheek finding Maggie's shoulder almost instinctively. She stayed there for a moment longer than she should have, listening to the steady cadence of Maggie's heartbeat beneath her ear and memorizing the way it felt pressed against her own skin.

But time wasn't on their side—it never was.

With what felt like immense effort, Wren pulled herself back just far enough to meet Maggie's eyes one more time. The loss of contact hit immediately; cold air rushed in where warmth had been seconds earlier.

"It's time," Wren said quietly, though not without effort—the words clung to her throat like they didn't want to be spoken aloud. "I have to go now."

Maggie nodded once—small but certain—her own eyes already glistening as tears hovered on the brink of falling but never quite spilled over. She reached up anyway, brushing gentle fingers along Wren's cheek as if committing even that small touch to memory.

Wren leaned into the touch, letting it linger just a moment longer than might be wise. "Love you too, Mags," she said, her voice low. "And you stay safe, okay? No heroics while I'm gone."

Maggie's lips quirked into a smile that didn't quite reach her eyes. "This is insane."

A laugh slipped from Wren—a thin, brittle thing that broke the stillness of the room. "Insane stopped being accurate a long time ago." She tried for a wink, hoping it might soften the weight in Maggie's gaze. "But I'll try not to do anything too stupid."

She leaned in for one last kiss, her hand brushing Maggie's as she pulled away, fingers hesitating like they had more to say before finally letting go. Wren turned toward the door with measured steps, each one feeling harder than it should. Her hand found the doorknob, and there she paused, staring at it as though it held secrets she wasn't ready to learn. She drew in a deep breath, then another, willing herself forward.

The door creaked faintly as Wren eased it open just wide enough to peer through the slim gap. Her eyes darted across the backyard—left, right, then left again. Stillness. The hum of distant traffic played its constant song in the background, but nothing stirred nearby.

She pushed the door further and pulled Argo with her, her every movement deliberate. Wren ran a hand over the familiar frame as though reassuring herself that it was still solid beneath her touch. She slipped onto the bike and guided it along the side of the building toward the street.

At the corner, she stopped again. Listening. Watching.

The air carried muffled murmurs: footsteps of strangers blurred by distance, cars whooshing past blocks away, someone's laughter caught by the wind and tossed aside before reaching her fully.

Wren stepped out onto the sidewalk at last; it was brighter here but no less oppressive under thick clouds swollen with rain they had yet to release. Gloomy daylight bled across shuttered windows and gray pavement while pedestrians hurried past with shoulders hunched and collars pulled high against the wind's sharp bite.

Her gaze swept over everything—the cars parked haphazardly along the curb, the faint shapes moving behind curtains in second-story apartments above store-fronts—and cataloged them without thought. She swung her leg over Argo's saddle and settled into its worn comfort like slipping on an old pair of boots—no magic in it but some small steadiness all the same.

With one last glance down the empty stretch of street ahead of her, Wren pushed off into what was next.

As Wren pushed off, the first drops of rain tapped against her helmet. A warning, maybe. She ignored it and pedaled harder, eager to put as much distance as possible between herself and the apartment. The streets were waking up now, the traffic thickening as she cut deeper into the city. Cars grumbled at red lights. Horns barked in frustration. She kept her head down and her rhythm steady, weaving through it all.

The rain began to fall in earnest—fat, cold droplets bursting against her cheeks and arms. She hunched closer to the handlebars, her legs moving like a machine, all pistons firing. The tires kicked up a spray that soaked through her sneakers and left her shivering, but it didn't matter. At least rain didn't leave stains.

Buildings blurred past in streaks of gray and steel as she slipped between cars, taking every gap without hesitation. There wasn't time to hesitate—not that she ever bothered with it. Her heart pounded in sync with her legs, adrenaline flooding her system in waves that almost drowned out everything else: the noise, the fear, the mess she'd left behind in that apartment. Almost.

Anne's face flashed in her mind—pale, lifeless—and Wren pressed harder on the pedals like she could outrun it. Fear and uncertainty had been clinging to her like a second skin since she'd discovered Anne's body, but here—here in the chaos of rain-slicked streets and towering skyscrapers—she felt some of it start to peel away. Here she was no one special, just another speck lost in a crowd of hurried strangers. The anonymity was a balm for nerves rubbed raw.

Wren flinched as cold needles of rain pierced through her shirt, biting at her skin. Great. Fucking rain. Just what she needed right now—like things weren't bad enough already.

Then came the pothole. It appeared without warning, a sudden threat to her velocity. She swerved instinctively, muscle memory saving her from calamity—the kind of grace that could only be honed through endless repetition.

She swerved again as a car beeped angrily behind her. "Fuck!" she muttered under her breath but didn't look back. Stay focused, Wren told herself. Keep moving forward, faster now—you have to get there before the questions catch up with you.

Rainwater dripped into her eyes as she dodged a dog darting into the street—dog—Dog! Watch your fucking dog! The owner yanked it back just in time while Wren shot them a glare over her shoulder before returning her focus to dodging cars and ignoring wet brakes skidding dangerously close to disaster at every turn.

Fuck this, I'm going to Golden Bites.

* * *

Wren pedaled through the rain-slicked streets, her legs burning with the kind of exertion that demanded attention, though she refused to give it. The surrounding city was a blur of neon reflections smeared across puddles, shadowy figures tucked into alleys, and the faint hum of something unseen but persistent. She veered suddenly to avoid a pothole—so deep it looked like it might swallow her whole—and barely kept herself upright as her tires threatened to skid out beneath her.

Ahead, the familiar strip of stores began to take shape in the dim light. It should have brought a sense of relief, maybe even comfort, but instead, something about it made her slow down. She couldn't put her finger on why until she was right there in front of it.

Golden Bites was gone.

She came to a halt so quickly that her tires sprayed water in an arc across the sidewalk. For a moment, she simply stared, blinking against the raindrops collecting on her lashes as though they were distorting what she saw—or didn't see. But no, it wasn't the rain that made this wrong.

The sign was gone.

The windows remained covered in their usual butcher paper, but that a printed sign had vanished entirely. Not stolen or damaged. As though it had never hung there at all.

Her first instinct was to grab her phone and capture this impossibility because that's what you did when reality felt like it might tilt out from under you: You anchored it with proof. Wren fished into her jacket pocket and yanked out the ancient flip phone that lived there like a relic from another era. Muscle memory snapped it open before her brain caught up to remind her what she already knew.

Of course there was no camera. Why would there be? This thing barely qualified as technology anymore; even calling it "functional" felt generous. Wren stared at the useless plastic rectangle in her hand and cursed softly under her breath—but not too loudly, because part of her hated giving this stupid thing the satisfaction of hearing just how much she despised it.

A notification blinked on its tiny screen—Maggie had sent the coordinates exactly as promised—but when Wren squinted at them, anticipation fizzling into confusion, another realization settled cold and heavy in her chest like a stone dropped into water.

No GPS app.

She stood there for a moment, unmoving except for the rhythmic drip of water soaking through every layer she wore—hoodie, jacket, skin—and pooling inside her sneakers. Then came the inevitable: rage bubbling up hot and bitter beneath all that cold dampness until it boiled over completely.

With a guttural yell—a sound that felt raw enough to scrape her throat—she hurled the phone as hard as she could across the sidewalk. It spun through the air in an absurdly slow arc before landing unceremoniously in a muddy puddle near the curb.

Wren didn't move right away; instead, she stood watching the ripples spread out like some dramatic effect from an old noir film until they stilled again and left behind... nothing impressive at all. Just an outdated phone lying pathetically intact in dirty water.

"Unbelievable," she muttered under her breath before trudging over to retrieve it from its watery grave.

To no one's surprise—not hers anyway—it still worked. The screen blinked back at her defiantly as if to say: *Is that all you've got?* There wasn't a scratch on its casing either; indestructible didn't begin to cover this thing's stubborn refusal to die.

Wren stared at it with a deep feeling of kinship before shoving it back into her pocket with more force than finesse.

"Piece of crap," she mumbled half-heartedly and turned back toward where Golden Bites should have been—might still be if only she could wake up from whatever strange dream this felt like—but deep down, she knew better than to expect anything different when she looked again.

It still wasn't there.

Of course not.

The rain flattened Wren's hair against her forehead. Golden Bites was gone—vanished without warning—and all it left behind was an abandoned building, a rising tide of questions, and something else. Something darker. Unease, maybe.

Wren tightened her jaw and stomped toward the door, grabbing the handle and giving it a sharp yank. It didn't move—not even a rattle of protest. She tried again, harder this time, because why not? Maybe persistence was the secret password.

Nope.

"Fucking locked," she muttered under her breath, her words lost in the drumbeat of rain. She leaned closer to the glass door, squinting through the water streaks running down its surface like tears. Thick butcher paper covered the windows from the inside, stretched tight over the glass like a barricade. She pressed her face closer on instinct, though she already knew it wouldn't help. No shapes, no shadows, nothing but paper and rain staring back at her.

Wren stepped back, swiping water out of her eyes even though it was pointless—wet was wet. Her fingers tapped absently on her helmet as her mind began to race. A pattern was forming in her head: coordinates, vanishing bakeries, locked doors that shouldn't be locked... She couldn't piece it together yet—it was like trying to solve a jigsaw puzzle in someone else's dream—but the edges were starting to take shape.

No use standing here.

Without further thought—or maybe too much thought—she swung onto Argo and pedaled around to the back of the building. The alley narrowed as she moved deeper into it, trash bags piled high on one side like unwilling sentinels. A crumpled soda can crunched under her tire before she skidded to a stop near the rear entrance. Dismounting in one motion, she propped Argo against the wall beside her. Just in case.

Her hand brushed over Argo's handlebars—a quick pat for luck or comfort or both—before turning toward the door at the back of Golden Bites. The handle squeaked faintly when she yanked on it—as if mocking her effort—but stayed firmly shut.

"Yeah," she hissed between clenched teeth before kicking the sturdy metal door for good measure. It didn't help anything except maybe her pride, but still.

Rain dripped from her sleeves and slid coldly down her neck as she stood there for a moment. Her clothes clung uncomfortably to soaked skin while water pooled around her boots. There wasn't anything more miserable than being both wet *and* stuck.

She fiddled with the strap on her helmet and slid it from her head. Wren stared at it like it might whisper advice if given enough time. Wren turned it over once in her palm before nodding at nobody in particular.

"Sorry about this," she murmured under her breath—not so much apologizing *to* the helmet as acknowledging that things were about to escalate in a way neither party had likely planned for.

She hopped back on Argo, pedaling furiously around toward the front of the building again—the long way round because apparently, the morning called for dramatic flair—and swung off once more when she reached those same stubborn doors. Rain continued its steady rhythm on everything around her: pavement sloshing underfoot; droplets smacking against cars parked along desolate curbsides; puddles rippling whenever stray gusts found them.

The street stayed dead quiet aside from all that—no movement beyond Wren herself—and honestly? That kind of silence wasn't reassuring anymore; it just felt wrong now instead.

Well... time to see if crime paid dividends tonight or just got you arrested soaking wet outside an abandoned bakery somewhere downtown.

Wren raised the helmet high above one shoulder before slamming it against one of Golden Bites' windows with all necessary force—and okay sure maybe some unnecessary frustration too while she was at it.

The glass broke with a sharp, satisfying crack, the fragments scattering like tiny stars against the wet pavement. Wren flinched at the sound, louder than she'd expected, echoing off the hollow streets. She turned her helmet upside down and shook it, watching as bits of glass tumbled loose and glinted faintly in the dim streetlight. That helmet was done for. She let it drop to the ground with a soft thunk, making a mental note to grab it before she left. Evidence like that couldn't stay behind.

The rain pattered steadily around her, masking smaller sounds, but not enough to settle her nerves. Wren scanned the street with quick, practiced movements, her head swiveling right, then left. No shadows darting behind windows, no hum of approaching engines—nothing but the quiet hiss of rain meeting asphalt. Her chest felt tight beneath her shirt as her pulse skittered unevenly.

She turned back toward the broken window and reached through gingerly, careful of the jagged edges framing the sill. The cold bite of glass brushed her sleeve as she fumbled inside blindly, searching for the latch. Her fingers slipped once... twice... before finally brushing against smooth metal. A twist to the left—click—and the door was unlocked.

Wren pulled it open slowly and winced at the groan of old hinges cutting through the silence. She stepped inside and let the door drift shut behind her with an unenthusiastic thud. It smelled sterile in here—clean in a way that didn't feel right. The sort of clean that came from scrubbing away something messy and real until only a hollow remained.

Her shoes squeaked faintly against linoleum as she moved farther into what used to be Golden Bites—or so she thought it had been. Days ago, this space had buzzed: food handed out through the pickup window, friendly chat with the chick behind the counter. Now it looked as if none of that had ever existed.

"Well," she murmured under her breath, surveying barren walls and blank countertops. "Shit."

Her voice bounced off emptiness, coming back to remind her how little was left here—no kitchen equipment or faded signs advertising specials taped haphazardly to windows; no color-worn booths sagging under years of use; not even stray napkins jammed into corners where mops forgot to reach. Instead there was just space—too much space—not merely empty but scrubbed clean of history.

She stopped in front of what should've been *the counter*, running a slow hand across its surface out of habit more than purpose. Cool and smooth beneath her fingertips—a deliberate kind of smoothness that told Wren someone had wiped this place bare with intent. No crumbs left behind. No streaks from hurried cleaning. Just nothing.

Her hand curled into a fist at her side before she even realized it had happened—fingers squeezing tight enough to make knuckles ache—until frustration broke free anyway: "Fuck!" The word ricocheted off walls and floors alike, filling all this nothing with noise for just a moment before fading again.

Wren let her fist fall heavily onto what should've held receipts or salt shakers or greasy fingerprints instead of pristine emptiness. The dull thud echoed back like mockery.

Pacing now helped burn off some of that restless heat building inside her chest—the same stretch over and over across ghostly floors wiped spotless by whoever had orchestrated this vanishing act so flawlessly it felt personal somehow.

No one throws together something like Golden Bites on a whim only to dismantle it in hours—minutes—without leaving even dust behind unless they know exactly what they're doing—and why they're doing it. This wasn't amateur hour at some hole-in-the-wall joint trying to dodge health inspectors; this was precision work born from deep resources and meticulous planning.

She crouched low near where tables might've once stood and studied every inch she could reach—the floor around her lit faintly by an overhead floodlight too dull to cast real shadows now—but not too faint for someone like Wren hoping against hope for scuff marks or scratches or dents heavy furniture leaves behind when dragged hastily toward trucks idling out back.

There were none. There never was. Ever.

Her lips pressed together tightly before curling upward—not quite a smile but close—as grudging admiration started swirling somewhere beneath everything else: anger still raw-edged; doubt creeping fast; exhaustion digging claws deep into muscles sore from too many long days ending like, well, *not this*. "You crafty bastard," she muttered softly under her breath.

Wren stood and brushed her hands against the damp fabric of her shorts, the rain leaving her clothes plastered to her like a second, unrelenting skin. The weight of it all sat heavy on her shoulders, though not in any poetic sense—it was just there, cold and pressing, like someone had slung a sodden blanket across her back and decided to leave it there for good. A pawn, she thought bitterly. From the very start, she'd been a pawn in someone else's game. The real question—the only question worth anything now—was this: How do I stop playing the game?

The rain outside didn't let up. It never did, not when you wanted it to. It hammered against the pavement with relentless precision, a steady rhythm that somehow made her thoughts even messier. Wren's mind churned through scenarios and theories that dissolved almost as quickly as they formed, dead ends breaking apart before she could fully chase them.

She shoved a hand into her pocket and wrenched out her phone. Her fingers fumbled over the keys before she managed to punch in Maggie's number. The ringing barely cut through the background noise of thought bouncing off every surface in her brain.

"Hey, babe," Maggie said, her voice thin and crackling through the tiny speaker.

Wren didn't waste time on pleasantries. "It's gone," she said flatly, pacing the length of the empty space around her. "Golden Bites. It's—" She paused, searching for words that matched the knot tightening in her chest but finding none sufficient. "It's just not here anymore."

"What do you mean the restaurant is 'not here'?" Maggie's confusion was evident even through the spotty connection.

"I mean," Wren said sharply, scuffing at the floor with one shoe where dust might've once existed if this place had ever been real enough to collect it, "it's gone. No sign, no kitchen, no frying oil smell hanging in the air—nothing. Like it never existed in the first place."

There was a sharp inhale on Maggie's end of the line. "Jesus, Wren." A pause thick enough for both of them to get swallowed by it. "That sounds like—"

"A set-up?" Wren snapped before Maggie could finish. Her voice came out edged in something between bitterness and exhaustion; at this point, what else could it be?

"Yeah." Maggie exhaled slowly this time. "What are you going to do?"

Wren ran a quick hand through her wet hair without thinking, grimacing when cold droplets slid down past her collarbone and soaked into her shirt further than gravity already had managed. "Cyclista," she said simply after another pause. "I need a GPS system for those coordinates you sent me earlier because so far? Useless."

"Wren..." Maggie started again; whatever came next had its edges softened by concern—or worry or doubt or whatever people let creep into their voices when they thought too much about outcomes they couldn't control.

"When am I ever not careful?" Wren cut in with forced levity that sounded hollow even to herself.

"I'm serious," Maggie pressed on as though she hadn't heard—or maybe didn't care enough about jokes right now to laugh at them properly anyway. "This is bigger than anything we thought we were dealing with."

"Yeah? Well," Wren shot back quietly but firmly enough that even she believed herself while saying it aloud this time: "They don't know who *they're* dealing with either."

There was another beat of quiet static before Maggie sighed audibly again: resigned but resolute somehow still underneath everything else packed tightly between unspoken words hanging where sentences ended prematurely unsaid instead.

"Just watch your back."

Wren smiled faintly despite herself. *She had to.* She snapped the phone shut, shoving it back into her pocket. The empty room seemed to close in around her, a stark reminder of how quickly things could vanish without a trace. Wren shook off the creeping unease and strode towards the exit.

10:42 a.m.

Wren shoved open the door to Cyclista, the forceful motion sending a cascade of water from her hair. Her helmet was long gone—tossed into a dumpster somewhere back on Third—and the purple strands clung to her face like limp seaweed. The sunglasses she hadn't bothered to remove did little to obscure her identity. As Wren stepped inside, every head in the room turned toward her, the click of her cycling shoes echoing against the concrete. The chatter stopped, replaced by a silence broken by the steady drip-drip-drip of rainwater splattering onto the floor beneath her.

She didn't slow down. She didn't acknowledge the looks. Marching past the dispatcher's desk without so much as a glance, she fixed her eyes on Willie's office door. Cold beads of water slid down her temples and over her jawline, tracing shivering paths across her skin before vanishing into the already-soaked fabric of her shirt. Her shorts clung to her legs; even her gloves felt clammy with moisture, a reminder of how thoroughly the storm had soaked through everything.

Wren reached Willie's door. No hesitation. No knock. Just one clean movement as she pushed it open and stepped inside. The door banged against the wall with a satisfying thud. Willie's head jerked up from his desk, startled at first—only for anger to replace surprise as his expression hardened.

"What in God's name are you doing here?" His voice was low and sharp, but it rose with each word as he shoved himself out of his chair. "The cops were just here looking for you!"

Wren raised one gloved hand—not to defend herself but to halt him mid-outburst—as drops trickled from her fingers onto his not pristine carpet. "I'll make this quick," she said evenly, though her voice carried a faint tremor that even she couldn't fully suppress. "Anne Cantu—was she ever a client here?"

Willie glared at her like she'd just asked if he kept bodies in his filing cabinet. He planted both hands on his desk, leaning forward in exasperation. "No," he snapped. "She wasn't. Now get out before I call them back."

"How do you know without checking?" Wren asked, standing firm despite the way water dripped from her chin and ran cold down the curve of her spine.

"Because I *did* check!" Willie barked, slamming one fist down on his desk for emphasis. His scowl seemed carved into his face now—deep furrows like trenches cutting across his browline. "The cops made me go through all our records when they were here."

He pointed toward the door with enough force that Wren half-expected him to dislocate a finger.

"Now get out!" he roared.

For a moment—just a moment—she didn't move. She let herself feel steady in that space despite how wrong everything felt: the tension radiating off Willie like heatwaves from asphalt; the weight of everyone watching just beyond this room; and most of all, the cold puddle forming beneath her cycling shoes as water dripped from every corner of her rain-laden clothing.

Drip-drip-drip.

Finally—finally—she turned away and left him there behind his desk, vibrating with frustration or rage or whatever emotion Willie liked best on days when things weren't going according to plan. Which was every day.

The courier area was no better than the office Wren had just left behind. Each step she took sucked some new tension into the space around her, coiling tighter and tighter until it felt ready to snap.

Eyes followed her every movement as though drawn by invisible strings they couldn't resist tugging on, no matter how much they wanted to look away or pretend they hadn't noticed anything unusual about their coworker dripping rivers onto Cyclista's once-clean floor.

"Anyone got a phone I can borrow?" Her words sliced through the silence, calm but unyielding in their clarity.

She scanned from face to face as murmurs gave way again to awkward shuffles and diverted gazes—the kind people offered when they didn't want trouble but suspected it might already be standing too close for comfort.

Massi was leaning lazily against his bike—or at least trying to give off that impression—but even he wasn't fooling anyone today. His usual grin was gone; instead, there was something tight about his mouth as he gave an apologetic shrug and shook his head.

"Can't help you," he said finally, softly even—but not so soft that Wren couldn't hear it clear as day over everything else in that moment: over their stares; over the drip-drip-drip continuing at its relentless pace; over whatever storm still raged in Willie's office two doors behind her. "It's not worth getting tied up in this mess."

Wren glanced around the room, her question hanging in the thick, uneasy air. "What about a spare GPS? Anyone?"

No one answered. The couriers exchanged nervous glances, their shoulders tightening in unison. Some fidgeted with their gear, others shifted their weight from one foot to the other like children caught stealing cookies from the jar. A few stared hard at the scuffed linoleum floor as if it might suddenly open up and swallow them whole.

Thanh moved closer, their bright hair a splash of color against the office's muted gray tones. They didn't say anything at first, just leaned in near enough that Wren could catch a faint whiff of cherry gum. Then, barely above a whisper: "Text me." There was a pause, deliberate but not awkward. "That way I'll have your number... in case you need help."

Wren gave a small nod and slid out her flip phone—a relic from another era that still felt alien in her hands. Her thumbs moved quickly over the keypad as she composed a short message. The phone gave off a soft, almost apologetic beep as it sent.

Thanh's phone buzzed faintly in their pocket, and they pulled it out to glance at the screen. A quick flicker of acknowledgment crossed their face before they quickly tapped out a message and tucked it away. *Avoid Main. Cops.*

The room hadn't changed much—it was still thick with tension—but Wren's eyes kept moving anyway. Scanning. Searching. And then she saw it: sitting almost forgotten on the edge of an old desk, sleek and unmistakable—a GPS unit. Her chest tightened at the sight of it.

"Who's GPS is that?" she asked, gesturing toward the device.

Before anyone could answer, Zak's laugh sliced through the silence—a sound so sharp and grating it made her jaw tighten instinctively. When he stepped forward, his smile was already in place: wide, cocky, just begging for someone to wipe it off his face. He reached for the GPS like it had been waiting for him all along and held it up just high enough to be obnoxious.

"This?" Zak drawled, tilting his head as though considering whether she even deserved an answer. "It belongs to the newbie." His smirk deepened as his blue eyes locked on hers like twin shards of ice. "And you can't have it, Wren. Not today, not ever."

Her hands curled into fists before she realized what she was doing. Wren unclenched them slowly and exhaled through her nose—a quiet hiss that she hoped sounded more controlled than angry. She felt rainwater seeping from her clothes onto the floor beneath her but ignored it.

"Come on, Zak," she said softly, keeping her voice steady even though every syllable tasted like restraint. "Don't be a dick."

For a split second—just one—Zak didn't move. Then he leaned forward until they were nearly eye-level and dropped his voice low enough that even whispers might seem loud by comparison.

"You know what else, Wren?" he said with deliberate slowness as though savoring each word like candy held too long on his tongue. He let the pause hang there before continuing: "Willie gave your address to the cops."

Her stomach dropped. She didn't think he'd had it.

Zak didn't stop there; of course he didn't stop there because why would he? He leaned back now but still kept that grin plastered across his face—a grin that seemed to grow larger when he added: "They're coming for you right now." He reached up with one hand and tapped an imaginary watch on his wrist twice for emphasis: "Tick-tock."

Wren stayed absolutely still for half a beat—not frozen exactly but suspended between fury and something colder than fear—and heard him chuckle softly when no words came out of her mouth right away.

She glanced at the others around them without turning her head much—didn't need to because no one was looking directly at her anyway—and saw exactly what she'd expected: pity on some faces; fear on others; indifference wrapped up tight like armor on most of them... but not one offering help.

A single word escaped under her breath before she could swallow it down again: "Fuck."

Her mind raced as fast as her pulse now—maybe faster—the two things competing viciously for control over how shaky everything suddenly felt inside of her chest cavity where rational thought was supposed to sit instead.

She needed to move; that much was obvious even in such chaos—but where? Maggie—that name burned through everything else clogging up space between rational thought & emotional impulse like smoke clearing after fire—but how far? How fast? With no GPS?

Wren stepped back from the group, her pulse thudding unevenly. She flipped open her phone with a snap and punched in Maggie's number, fingers fumbling over the keys like they had forgotten how to work properly. One ring. Two. Three. Straight to voicemail.

She slammed the phone shut like it had betrayed her. "Damn it," Wren whispered, low enough that no one else could hear. Her eyes darted around, skimming over the others in the room until they landed on Massi. He was by his bike, hands shoved into his pockets, head leaning to one side like he was trying to figure out what all the fuss was about.

When their eyes met, Wren mouthed "distract him" and flicked her head toward Zak. Massi blinked at her like she'd just asked him to juggle fire, but after a beat, he gave her one of those slow, reluctant nods that said *fine, but you owe me if the cops don't get you.*

Zak was already half-turned away, his posture stiff as he held a phone to his ear. *Who was he calling?* His voice carried enough for Wren to pick up snatches of what he was saying—"Yeah, she's here now... No idea how long..."—enough to piece together the full context. Not that it mattered; there wasn't time.

Massi strolled up to Zak with an exaggerated casualness that would have been laughable under different circumstances. He clapped a heavy hand on Zak's shoulder and grinned wide enough to distract a saint. "Hey man, you catch the game last night? That final play was wild!"

Zak didn't break stride in his conversation—didn't even glance at Massi—until he did. Annoyance flickered across his face as he lowered the phone just enough to growl out a terse warning: "Not now, Massi."

That's when Wren moved. She didn't so much think about it as act on instinct, lunging forward and grabbing the GPS off the table before anyone—including herself—could question whether this was a good idea or not. The device felt cold and smooth in her hand, heavier than expected but essential all the same.

She spun around and darted for the door. Her shoes slapped against linoleum in sharp bursts that echoed far too loudly in the sudden hush of the room behind her.

"Hey!" Zak's voice erupted like a gunshot. "That's not yours!"

Wren didn't look back.

The door banged open as she barreled through into the rainy chaos outside. The world was slick and gray—the kind of rain that soaked everything through in seconds flat—and yet she ran straight into it without hesitation, clutching the GPS like it might vanish if she loosened her grip for even a second.

Argo was where she'd left it, leaning against the curb and gleaming with fresh rainwater like some mythic steed summoned for exactly this moment. She swung herself onto the seat and started pedaling hard, legs churning as though powered by pure adrenaline alone.

The tires hissed against wet pavement, cutting through puddles that sent icy sprays up her shins and thighs—cold enough to make her teeth clench if she'd had time to notice. The handlebars were slippery under her grip as she tried to steer one-handed while fumbling with the GPS in her other hand.

It nearly slipped free at one point—a small jolt of panic sparking through her as she barely managed to catch it before it hit the ground—but Wren gritted her teeth and held on tighter this time. Her knuckles turned white around both the handlebars and the stolen device.

Somewhere behind her—distant but closing fast—she could hear footsteps pounding against pavement and an angry voice yelling something unintelligible over splashing rainwater.

She pushed Argo harder, legs burning now but refusing to slow down. Above everything else—the wet streets blurring past, Zak shouting behind her—the frantic drumbeat of her own heartbeat roared loudest of all.

"Come on, you little bastard," Wren muttered under her breath, her fingers fumbling as she finally managed to snap the GPS into its holder on the handlebars. The device flickered to life, casting a faint blue glow across her face. Gloom thickened the afternoon air, pressing down like a damp woolen blanket. Her pedaling lost a fraction of its rhythm.

Wren's gaze darted between the road ahead and the small screen. Her thumb hovered for a moment before she tapped in the coordinates from Maggie's text with quick, deliberate motions. Around her, the city morphed into a chaotic blur of rushing shadows—gray buildings, neon glares smeared across rain-slick pavement, traffic lights winking from red to amber to green. Cars honked. Voices rose in sharp bursts of irritation. She weaved through it all as though she were deaf and blind to anything but forward motion.

The GPS beeped sharply, jolting her focus back down to the screen. Coordinates locked. A single address blinked into view in clean white text.

Her breath hitched.

"The family courthouse?" she whispered aloud, the words barely audible even to herself. Her hold on the handlebars tightened.

No, that couldn't be right. Wren blinked once, twice—her pulse quickening with each flicker of her eyelids—but there it was again: precise, unwavering directions leading straight to *that* place.

Why there? Anne's cryptic USB, GPS games, family law—none of it made sense. Wren didn't do puzzles, not ones like this anyway. She hated that creeping feeling of knowing there was something she should have seen but hadn't yet put together.

But maybe this wasn't meant to make sense—not yet.

* * *

Her legs burned now with every push of the pedals—thighs tight, lungs searing—as she tore through intersections and swerved around jaywalkers without hesitation or apology. The city blurred past her in streaks of gray and blinding orange headlights. Her only constant was Argo beneath her—faithful in motion, steady in chaos—even as everything else around her seemed bent on colliding into destruction.

The rain had mercifully stopped, though Wren barely noticed. Her neck ached from all the swiveling, her eyes burned. She was pretty sure she'd traveled the entire route without blinking—the cops could be anywhere. Everywhere.

The courthouse rose up ahead like some ancient fortress conjured from steel and stone. Its severe lines and hulking mass carved into the skyline, blotting out what little light might have been left in the day. The sight slowed Wren's pace almost involuntarily as she neared the building's edge—a reflexive pulling back from something heavy enough to crush whatever stood too close. Not a cop in sight—not in uniform, anyway.

She eased Argo against a bike rack at the edge of the courtyard and fumbled with the lock for an extra second or two, more out of distraction than difficulty. Once satisfied it wouldn't budge without her approval, she turned toward the steps.

A fountain dominated the courtyard space ahead—water spilling dramatically from a carved gavel perched in triumph atop its pedestal. Wren almost laughed at that—the absurdity of it all—but instead let out a low exhale through her nose, biting down hard on any outward show of amusement or scorn.

Tourists orbited around it like moths drawn to some glowing irony they couldn't fully grasp: snapping pictures; posing beside justice personified in stone; babbling cheerfully in languages Wren didn't bother parsing right now. She stayed where she was for a moment at the base of those wide marble stairs—the kind meant more for grandeur than practical use—and resisted an urge to look over her shoulder.

The air felt charged somehow—stale sweat clinging beneath her cycling jersey; damp strands of hair plastered awkwardly against her neck; each shallow inhale bringing no relief, only more awareness of how close everything seemed now without being closer to answers.

Her eyes scanned instinctively across faces that weren't looking back at her: couples holding hands; families shepherding kids away from fountainside splashes; lone figures tucked into phone screens or wandering aimlessly with worn backpacks slung low on their shoulders.

Nothing familiar yet—and yet that absence didn't ease anything inside her chest either.

Wren stood in the open, her cycling gear plastered to her skin, damp with a mix of sweat and rain. She half-expected alarms to blare, a voice shouting through a megaphone: *"There she is! Get her!"* But no. The world around her carried on—no one pointed, no one screamed. The storm inside her churned unnoticed, as it always did. Life kept moving. It always did.

She took a slow breath, willing herself to stay grounded. The coordinates had brought her here—this family courthouse of all places—but why? What could this sterile and self-important building have to do with Anne? Or the USB? Or that empty restaurant? Her mind flicked through possibilities, each one wilder than the last: corruption, some tangled mess of justice, or maybe something simpler, like broken families trying to stitch themselves together in the courtroom upstairs.

A breeze swept past, cooling her flushed face and carrying the faint chemical tang of chlorine from the fountain nearby. Wren wrinkled her nose. Her eyes caught on the oversized stone gavel perched at the center of the courtyard—a caricature of authority if there ever was one. The sun slipped out from behind a cloud at just the wrong moment, scattering harsh light across everything and forcing Wren to squint against it. Her hand reached instinctively for Maggie's sunglasses—the ones she'd borrowed without asking (which Maggie would call "stealing," but whatever). Still there.

Fishing her phone out of her pocket, Wren typed quickly: "Anything besides GPS #s? Need clues. Courthouse now. WTF?"

She hit send and slid the phone back into her pocket before scanning the scene again through the tinted lenses. People milled about like ants on autopilot—women clutching legal documents with white-knuckled grips; fathers staring blankly ahead while their kids whined at their sides; lawyers moving in sharp-edged suits like sharks sniffing blood in water.

A snort escaped before she could stop it. She didn't belong here—that much was obvious—and not just because she was dripping rainwater onto pristine stone steps or because her arms were covered in bright tattoos that practically screamed "outsider." No, it was something more fundamental than that. The whole atmosphere reeked of domesticated conformity, and Wren... well, she wasn't domesticated. She flexed her arms—not enough to show off (or maybe just enough)—and felt a flicker of pride at how starkly she contrasted with these people.

"System drones," she muttered under her breath, watching as a cluster of students huddled around an enormous textbook two steps down from where she stood—all pressed khakis and carefully curated hairstyles, like they'd been assembled on an assembly line for mediocrity's sake. "Not a single original thought between any of them."

She shifted uncomfortably as some guy in a polo shirt barreled past and rammed into her shoulder without so much as glancing up from his phone. "Sorry," he mumbled automatically before continuing on his way—not even slowing down long enough to see who he'd bumped into.

Wren rolled her eyes and stayed rooted where she was while everyone else rushed forward like they had somewhere important to be (they didn't). This place wasn't built for someone like her—it never had been—but still, here she stood, waiting for answers that might never come and feeling more out of place by the second.

Wren stood at the base of the courthouse steps, watching the people flow up and down in a steady, unbroken stream. They moved like schools of fish—uniform, indifferent, mindless in their purpose. For a moment, she wondered what it would feel like to be one of them: invisible, indistinguishable from anyone else. Safer, maybe. Sometimes, blending in was better. Sometimes, standing out could get you killed.

Then again, she wasn't exactly the blending-in type.

"Tough luck," Wren muttered under her breath. "I'm here now."

She shifted her weight from one foot to the other and pulled out her phone. Still nothing from Maggie. The screen remained stubbornly blank despite her hopeful—and admittedly futile—habit of checking every few minutes. Wren tapped the device, as though sheer irritation could will it into lighting up with some critical piece of information. No such luck.

"Figures." She shoved the phone back into her pocket and let out a sharp exhale through her nose.

The courthouse steps buzzed with activity: lawyers in sharp suits clicking briskly along with briefcases swinging in pendulous rhythm; clerks juggling armfuls of files; a woman with cellophane-wrapped pastries barking into her headset about someone being late again. It was chaos in neatly pressed clothing, each person navigating their own small dramas without so much as a glance in her direction.

Which was fine by Wren. Mostly.

Her eyes roved over the crowd anyway, scanning faces and movements for... something. A sign? A clue? Maybe Anne's ghost descending from on high with some celestial evidence that Wren wasn't her killer? The thought brought an unbidden snort to her lips. Yeah, because that was likely.

The sun broke through lingering storm clouds overhead and hit the courthouse square like a hammer. The heat pressed against her neck and shoulders, still damp from cycling through earlier rain, and sweat traced an uncomfortable path between her shoulder blades. She shifted again but found no position that felt any less exposed or awkward—she hated standing still like this, hated waiting without purpose.

A trio of suits passed close enough that one of their swinging briefcases grazed her shin. Wren took half a step back and scowled at their retreating forms. "Assholes," she said under her breath—not loud enough to start anything but just enough for herself—and ran an absent hand through damp hair that had long since stopped resembling anything presentable.

The scrape of claws on concrete drew her attention downward. A pigeon strutted past her shoes, pausing briefly to cock its head in expectation before releasing a low coo of disappointment when she failed to meet whatever demand it had imagined.

"Don't look at me like that," Wren told it flatly. "I don't have any answers either."

The bird blinked once—offended or indifferent, she couldn't tell—before resuming its haughty waddle across the square and disappearing into the shifting tide of feet and wheels and noise around them.

Her hand brushed against the marker tucked into one pocket while another part of her brain whispered bad ideas—not suggestions so much as temptations:

Wouldn't it feel good? To write something real on all this polished marble perfection? To scrawl "WHAT THE FUCK?" right there beneath those pompous stone faces?

Wren stood frozen, caught in the limbo between action and retreat. The world spun on without her, oblivious to the storm brewing beneath her stillness. Everything around her hummed with normalcy—an ordinary day unfolding for ordinary people—while she floundered, drowning in her uncertainty and the gnawing sense that she was missing something vital.

What exactly am I supposed to be looking for? Her thoughts tumbled over each other, frantic and directionless. *What would a journalist even hide? A report? A USB drive? Where would she stash it?* Wren glanced around, teeth clenched. *Where would I hide it? Bikes... but bikes move. No bikes here anyway. Damn it. The fountain? Could Anne have hidden it in the fountain?*

She turned toward the water fountain, hope sparking faintly before logic smothered it. Wren began circling it, slowly at first, scanning its surface with desperate eyes. The water glistened under the harsh sunlight, shimmering until her vision blurred. She raised a hand to block the glare and leaned in closer, ignoring the curious stares of passersby who thought she'd lost her mind.

"Come *on*," she muttered under her breath, frustration rising like a tide threatening to pull her under as she completed another circuit around the fountain's edge. Her stomach sank when all she found below the rippling surface were scattered coins and soggy leaves.

Crouching now, Wren ran her fingers along the water's cool surface, tracing its curve like something might suddenly appear if she just touched the right spot. Her hands brushed smooth stone—nothing loose, nothing hidden—and came away wet but empty.

"Damn it." The words hissed between her teeth as she wiped her damp hand against her shorts.

Straightening reluctantly, Wren stood there for a moment as droplets slipped from her fingertips to rejoin the fountain's undisturbed pool below. Her gaze shifted upward toward the courthouse looming behind it—the massive stone gavel casting its shadow like some stoic overseer above everything happening on these steps—and glared at its sheer indifference. It offered no secrets, no guidance.

Just an empty monument to justice or order or whatever meaningless drivel bureaucrats thought might impress someone.

Wren stamped toward the far side of the fountain, anger bubbling hotter with each step until it threatened to boil over completely. She forced herself to stop and planted both feet firmly on the uneven stone path beneath her. From here, she stared directly at the family courthouse that towered above her like a fortress of ineptitude: its cold facade unyielding, its windows impassive mirrors reflecting nothing except sharp bursts of sunlight that made Wren squint in annoyance.

She scanned those windows one by one—a futile exercise—but couldn't stop herself from searching anyway. Maybe that's what Anne had done: stared up at this ridiculous building and somehow found meaning where none should exist.

The details carved into its upper levels faded into shadow too deep to decipher from ground level—not that any ornamental nonsense meant anything to Wren right now—but still... those carvings lingered there like smug relics of someone else's priorities.

Her eyes dropped lower again—to the entrance this time—where heavy wooden doors stood wide open as people drifted in and out like clockwork figures in some lifeless diorama. Nothing screamed out at her from those steps either: no flashing lights pointing toward hidden treasures or secret messages embedded in plain view among clumps of faceless strangers going about their days.

Just another building.

Another pointless monument in a city full of them.

Her fists tightened against her sides as frustration swelled again—sharp and cutting now—a scream coiling itself tight inside her chest but never quite escaping past gritted teeth. What *was* she missing? What had Anne seen here that kept slipping just beyond Wren's grasp?

Her gaze swept helplessly across every inch of that courthouse facade, lingering nowhere yet touching everything all at once until—

There.

A single brick snagged at this relentless loop playing through her head—not because it shouted significance from its perch—but because of how quietly wrong it seemed among uniform rows stacked meticulously alongside each other: plain beige bricks unmarred by difference except for this one split neatly by an unsettlingly thin black line running straight across its length—so subtle Wren wondered if she'd imagined noticing anything unusual at all.

Her fingers brushed against the marker in her pocket, the shape familiar and reassuring, though it offered little comfort now. She hesitated, her hand lingering there as if the mere act of holding it might steady her resolve. The mark on the brick was a message, sort of. Or a clue. She sniffed, running her free hand over her face, pausing midway as though the touch might clarify her swirling thoughts. For a moment, Wren stood still, caught in that fragile space between action and hesitation—between wanting to move forward and fearing what lay ahead.

"That has to be Anne's mark," she muttered under her breath. The words came out flat, carrying more doubt than certainty. Wren wasn't entirely sure who she was trying to convince. Herself, maybe? It didn't matter. There wasn't much left to lose.

She shrugged—an empty gesture more for show than anything else—and started toward the marked brick. Her steps were deliberate but casual as if she were just another part of the crowd ebbing and flowing around her. Her eyes flicked from side to side, scanning faces and corners with a precision born of being hunted. No one seemed to notice her or the brick wall that loomed ahead. Just life going on as it does: strangers milling about, eyes locked on their own problems.

The closer she got, the harder her heart pounded against her ribcage—not panic exactly, but something close enough to make her pulse quicken and palms dampen. There it was: a black line drawn on one of the bricks—not something sloppy or incidental, not some kid's aimless scribble. This was careful work, calculated in its placement and subtlety. You could walk past it a hundred times without seeing it unless you knew to look.

She stopped just short of the wall, pretending to admire something over her shoulder while peeking at the surrounding crowd out of the corner of her eye. Nothing seemed off: no lingering gazes or suspicious movements. Satisfied—or at least as satisfied as someone like Wren could allow herself to be—she turned back toward the brick.

Her fingertips touched the weathered surface lightly at first, tracing its uneven texture where this particular brick jutted out from the rest. Barely noticeable unless you were paying attention—and she was paying attention now.

The gap beneath her fingers confirmed what she already knew: this wasn't just about a mark on bricks—it was Anne's message.

She took a deep breath—the kind you take before breaking through some invisible barrier—and placed both hands on either side of the protruding brick. For a fleeting second, the absurdity struck her: standing here fussing with stone while people shuffled by none-the-wiser. But absurd or not, she pressed on because stopping wasn't an option anymore.

With a firm grip, Wren began to shift it side to side—testing first rather than forcing—but even that small motion sent grinding noises ringing in her ears like alarms embedded into stone. To anyone nearby they wouldn't register at all; for Wren though, each scrape felt deafeningly loud—a sound tethered straight into her nerves.

Slowly—agonizingly slowly—she worked it free millimeter by millimeter, gritting her teeth against both frustration and impatience. Dirt clung stubbornly to her fingers as tiny flakes rained onto her shoes with each tug and twist until finally—with one last tug—the brick gave way completely.

Wren froze then—not because anyone had noticed (they hadn't) but because that split-second after success always came with new dread: What now? She leaned in closer toward the dark cavity left behind where shadows pooled deep into cracks too narrow for light.

And there it was.

A small blue USB key nestled neatly inside as though waiting just for this moment—for *her.*

Relief swept through Wren before excitement could catch up—but briefly because relief came with tremors too subtle for anyone else to see but impossible for herself not to feel. Her hand hovered over that tiny object before she reached in quickly—decisively—her fingers curling around its cool plastic edges like closing around proof that something mattered after all.

Without wasting another second, she slipped it into her sock—not perfect security but better than leaving it exposed—and straightened up again as though nothing had happened.

To everyone around her? Nothing had.

Wren picked up the brick with what she hoped passed for ease. Her fingers trembled as she turned it, hiding the incriminating black line. She slid it carefully back into place, taking an extra moment to press against the edges until it was perfectly flush with the surrounding bricks. What had been inside and protected was now outside and glaringly clean. She didn't care anymore.

Her heart thudded in her chest as she stepped back to take in her work. She'd done it. The USB key was hers now, another piece of this maddening puzzle. But what did it mean? What truth, if any, sat locked away on it? Wren didn't know yet—couldn't know—but just holding it felt simultaneously like triumph and dread. Time to go home and find out what was on this bad boy.

She swung onto Argo, the bicycle's frame cool and familiar against her hands, and started pedaling away from the courthouse. The USB key pressed against her ankle inside her sock, its hard edge digging into her skin with every stroke of the pedals. She could almost imagine it ticking like a bomb, one in each sock, pushing her forward faster than her legs could carry her.

She made it a few blocks before the urge to share what she'd found became unbearable. Wren slowed to a stop, pulling Argo up beside a brick wall covered in faded concert posters that clung stubbornly to their corners while curling at their edges. The air smelled faintly of grease from a nearby diner, hot and heavy despite the cooling wind that ruffled her hair.

She leaned against the wall and fumbled for her phone. Her hands shook—not much, but enough that she noticed—as she typed Maggie's number and pressed call. A single ring buzzed in her ear. Then another. And then—

"Hello," a voice answered crisply. "May I help you?"

Wren pulled the phone away from her ear and frowned at the screen before bringing it back quickly again—yes, she'd called Maggie's number, no doubt about that—but there was something off about the voice on the other end.

"Mags?" Wren's voice came out thinner than intended, uncertainty leaking through.

"Yes," came the same crisp tone again. "Hello, may I help you?"

Her mouth parted as she stared at nothing in particular ahead of her—a jagged crack running through one of the posters—a cold feeling blooming deep in her gut like ink spreading in water. This wasn't right. This wasn't Maggie—not really—or if it was Maggie, then there was something fundamentally wrong with how she was speaking.

Thoughts churned in Wren's head like storm clouds gathering too fast: had someone else taken Maggie's phone? Was Maggie caught up in something worse than either of them had dared imagine? The cops had her address so... no... She stopped herself before finishing that terrifying thought but couldn't stop feeling its shadow over everything.

Her thumb moved instinctively before she even realized—the call ended abruptly mid-sentence without either side saying goodbye.

"Fuck." Wren hissed between clenched teeth and slammed her fist against the brick wall behind her—harder than she meant to—and felt a sharp sting radiate from her knuckles down to her wrist. But pain barely registered because all she could think about now—all that mattered—was that Maggie might be in danger.

Her world narrowed down to just that one fear: a fear so large it seemed almost impossible for anything else to exist around it anymore.

IO:53 a.m.

W ren's legs pumped as though they had a mind of their own, the muscles burning with an ache that somehow felt both unbearable and essential. Her breath came in sharp bursts, each one grating against her throat like sandpaper. The city roared around her—honking horns, screeching tires, the occasional yell flung from a passing car window—but none of it registered. Not really. Not until her phone rang.

Wren's heart thudded heavily as she stared at her phone, the screen blinking with Maggie's name. She hesitated before answering, her voice measured. "Hello?"

"Hey, it's me. You coming back to the basement soon?" Maggie's voice crackled faintly on the other end.

The basement? Wren frowned, her grip tightening on the handlebars until her knuckles paled. Since when did Maggie call it that?

"Yeah," she said evenly, though her fingers twitched against the phone. "I'll be home soon." She ended the call with a sharp tap, her pulse quickening as if someone might already be tracing the signal.

She exhaled through gritted teeth, the wordless pressure building in her chest spilling out in a low mutter: "Shit." Her legs pushed hard against the pedals as she veered into traffic, weaving between cars with precision. The wind lashed at her face and tangled her hair, but it wasn't just the frigid air that pressed at her throat. Something wasn't right—she could feel it, like a splinter lodged too deep to pull free.

The phone call echoed in her ears. "You coming back to the basement soon?" Maggie had said it so casually, as though "the basement" was a term they used all the time. It wasn't. It never had been. And that made Wren's stomach drop in a way she couldn't quite describe—not fear exactly, or not just fear, but something colder, something that curled tight like a coiled wire inside her chest.

Her hands tightened on the handlebars as Argo obeyed every command without hesitation or question. They moved as one down the congested streets, Wren weaving through traffic with a precision that flirted with reckless. A delivery truck pulled out too fast, its grill looming impossibly close for half a second before she veered left, cutting across two lanes of sluggish traffic and back onto the less-cluttered sidewalk. She didn't stop to acknowledge the startled faces of pedestrians or their angry shouts; there wasn't time for that now.

The blue USB key pressed against the sensitive skin of her ankle with each pedal stroke, its weight oddly disproportionate to its size—as if it carried more than just data inside its slim casing. Wren thought about adjusting it, maybe stopping just long enough to shift its position, but dismissed the idea almost as quickly as it formed. Stopping wasn't an option right now.

It was more instinct than anything else that made her glance over her shoulder at that moment. Just a quick check—nothing obvious back there, no shadowy figures weaving between cars or speeding after her on two wheels of their own—but still, something about it felt off. She couldn't shake the feeling creeping along her spine, dark and persistent like an itch buried too deep under your skin to scratch away.

She took the next left and then another after that, cutting down an alley so narrow it felt like slipping through the crack of a door just before it slammed shut. The scent hit her first: rotting garbage mingling with something metallic and sour—blood maybe? No, just rust—but it didn't matter because she was already halfway through when she heard herself gag involuntarily at the stench.

Wren emerged onto another street seconds later with a burst of speed that sent gravel spitting behind her like tiny projectiles. For a moment she thought she'd cleared it cleanly until the side view mirror of a parked car loomed too close for comfort. She overcorrected sharply, nearly losing control altogether before yanking herself—and Argo—back into balance at what felt like the last possible second.

Her thighs screamed in protest now; every muscle from her calves to her lower back burned with exertion as though they might give out entirely if she asked one ounce more from them. But Wren didn't stop pushing—not yet—and certainly not until she got home. Home being... what? The basement? That's what Maggie had called it anyway.

The word hung in her mind like smoke in a ventilation shaft: thick and cloying and impossible to clear away no matter how much fresh air you tried to let in afterward. Why had Maggie chosen those words? Was it code? A warning? Or was Wren just reading too much into things because everything lately felt precarious—like standing on a single thread stretched taut over an abyss?

She didn't have time to figure it out now. She tucked lower over Argo's handlebars and surged forward again into another knot of traffic waiting at yet another red light ahead of her. This time she didn't hesitate before swerving back onto the sidewalk—not caring about rules or right-of-way or even basic courtesy anymore—and pedaled past another cluster of startled pedestrians clutching coffee cups and shopping bags against their chests as though bracing for impact.

Wren gritted her teeth against both pain and frustration when she snagged a glimpse of herself reflected briefly in one glass storefront after another: sweat-soaked shirt clinging to every ridge and curve beneath; jaw set tight enough that it could cut stone; eyes darting everywhere at once while seeing barely anything clearly.

The corner was too fast. She knew it the moment her tires hit the loose gravel, skidding and sliding underneath her. For a split second, she thought she might recover—she always did—but then she caught sight of him. A man in a business suit, stepping off the curb, eyes glued to his phone, oblivious to the world.

"Watch out!" she yelled.

Too late.

The collision wasn't cinematic. It wasn't the slow motion of two bodies flying through the air, arms flailing for balance. It was messy and awkward. Wren hit him square on, and they went sprawling together onto the pavement in a tangle of limbs and momentum.

"What the hell!" The man scrambled to his feet first, brushing dirt and grime from his now-ruined suit. "You crazy bitch!"

Wren got up next, ignoring the sting of scraped palms and knees. Argo lay on its side next to her, the handlebars twisted at an odd angle. She grabbed her bike like it was a lifeline, checking it over with quick movements that were more habit than intent. A quick twist and Argo was good as—not new, but good enough.

"Fuck you," she muttered under her breath, not daring to meet his eyes.

"What did you say?" he barked, voice rising above the dull city noise.

But Wren was already back on Argo, pedaling away before he could get another word in. His angry shouts faded into the background as her heart thundered in her chest—not from exertion but from something deeper, sharper. Something was wrong with Maggie. Wren didn't know how she knew it; she just did. And she had to get home. Fast.

Her legs burned as she pushed herself harder, leaning into every turn like her life depended on it. When her street came into view, a flicker of relief tried to surface but failed to take hold. Everything looked normal—too normal—and that made it worse somehow. The quiet felt artificial, like someone had pressed pause on a scene that should still be moving.

She slowed Argo to a near crawl as she passed Fannie's window. The old woman who usually sat there knitting or scowling at passersby was nowhere to be seen. Wren told herself it didn't mean anything—Fannie could be napping or out playing cards with friends—but her stomach churned anyway.

Circling around to the back of the building, Wren dismounted and leaned Argo against the wall. The bike's frame was warm under her fingers—warm from the heat of her furious ride—but it didn't match the cold that had settled deep in her chest.

Her breaths came fast and shallow as she moved toward the door. She crouched low by the glass paneling, peering inside like a thief casing a house—though what she'd steal back wasn't objects but peace of mind.

And then Wren saw them.

Maggie sat at their tiny kitchen table. Her girlfriend's face looked ghostly pale, mouth set tight like she was biting down on every scream that threatened to escape her lips. Her eyes darted up briefly—just once—and even from here Wren could see fear swimming in them so clearly it made her own chest tighten.

Across from Maggie sat Dennis.

Dennis with his too-calm smugness that felt like nails scraping across skin you couldn't scratch raw enough to relieve. Dennis leaning back like he belonged there, like nothing about this situation should raise alarm bells loud enough to rupture eardrums.

Wren's whole body tensed when she saw what he held: a gun resting casually in one hand as though it were an accessory rather than an instrument of control and death.

Maggie clutched her phone in both hands under the table—trembling hands that made Wren want to storm inside without thinking twice about consequences—but Dennis didn't seem concerned about whatever message Maggie thought she might send or call she might make.

The sound around Wren shifted then—not silenced exactly but muffled somehow until all that remained was the heavy beat of blood rushing past eardrums too tightly wound for anything else to come through clearly. Her fingers twitched helplessly at her side, desperate for action—for *something*—but reason anchored her down when instinct screamed otherwise.

Wren's hand wavered, her fingers brushing the USB keys. She slid them under Argo's seat, her movements quick but clumsy, the small keys clinking faintly as they nestled into the shadows. The phone in her other hand felt colder than usual—like ice against her skin—as she brought it to her ear and pressed Maggie's number.

The line connected on the first ring, Maggie's voice crackling through both the phone and, faintly, through the glass door just ahead of her. "Hello." The word came out flat. Hollow.

"I'm home," Wren replied quietly, almost muttering. She didn't wait for Maggie to answer; she ended the call with a sharp tap and pushed open the door.

The air inside was thick—stagnant—as though it hadn't been disturbed in years. Both Maggie and Dennis startled at the sound of her entrance, their heads snapping toward her in unison. Maggie's eyes were wide—too wide—her expression caught somewhere between fear and... what was that? Confusion? Desperation maybe? Dennis's lips twisted slowly into something that might have tried to be a smile but failed miserably, landing instead on a scowl.

"What do you want?" Wren heard herself say. Her voice came out sharper than intended, each word coated in contempt as her gaze locked onto Dennis.

Her chest tightened, her pulse quickening into a steady drumbeat. She took a breath—or tried to—but it stuck halfway down.

Dennis rose from his chair with an ugly scrape against the floor, his movements deliberate. He didn't rush; he didn't need to—not when his gun remained pointed squarely at Maggie. "You know what I want," he said, his voice low but strong enough to fill the whole room. "Hand over what Anne gave you."

Wren stood frozen for half a beat—not long, but long enough that she knew Dennis noticed. Her mind scrambled: The USB keys tucked under Argo's seat. They had led here—to this moment—and yet she didn't feel ready for it.

Her fists curled tight at her sides. "I don't know what you're talking about." The words left her mouth before she had time to consider them, each syllable steadier than she felt inside.

Dennis tilted his head—a predator sizing up its prey—and took a single step forward. The gun didn't waver; his grip was steady in a way that made Wren's stomach turn.

"Don't lie to me," Dennis growled, each word cutting like barbed wire. "Anne had evidence—something big—and before she died, she gave it to you."

The walls seemed closer now—pressing inward—as though someone had silently moved them while no one was looking. Behind her, Wren could hear Maggie's breath coming fast and uneven like someone on the verge of hyperventilation.

"Even if she did," Wren said slowly, pouring every ounce of disdain into each word, "why on earth would I give *anything* to you? You tried to kill me."

For the first time since she'd entered, Dennis shifted his gaze fully onto her. His finger flexed against the gun's trigger—not pulling it exactly, just sending a message—and something flickered behind his eyes: amusement or fury or some toxic combination of both.

He smiled then—if you could call it that—a flash of teeth that looked more like a snarl. "Your girlfriend's life," he said simply, gesturing with the gun as if Maggie needed reminding of where it was aimed. "I already know."

Wren stiffened automatically at his words—the implication more chilling than any volume or theatrics could have been—but Dennis wasn't done.

"She told me Anne gave you something," he continued smoothly now, all false confidence dripping from every syllable like oil slicking pavement after rain. "A silver USB key." His tone hardened abruptly; whatever pretense of patience he'd been holding onto vanished in an instant.

"Hand it over."

Wren's mind churned, thoughts colliding as she tried to find an escape route that didn't exist. She glanced at Maggie, whose wide eyes and trembling lip made her look like a child caught in some other kid's doomed act of defiance. Her face was all fear and regret, and Wren couldn't blame her. Hell, if the roles were reversed, she'd look worse.

"It's outside," Wren said, summoning a steadiness in her voice that didn't reach her insides.

Dennis rose slowly, stepped closer, each movement deliberate, calculated. He didn't point the gun at her directly—he didn't have to. It stayed trained on Maggie, unwavering. "Go get it," he said, his tone laced with a calm that somehow made the threat sharper. "If you try anything stupid, she's dead."

The words hung there, thick and suffocating like smoke in a sealed room. Wren clenched her fists so hard the crescent moons of her nails dug into her palms. She knew how this played out—knew the odds weren't leaning in their favor—but all she needed was a sliver of 'maybe.' For now, she would have to settle for that.

"Fine." The word dropped from her mouth like a stone. Her jaw tightened as she added, "Just don't hurt her."

Dennis motioned with his eyes toward the door but kept his gun locked on Maggie. He followed closely as Wren moved toward it, his shadow stretching across the floor to swallow hers whole. She could hear every click of her cycling shoes against the floor—each one unnaturally loud in the silence that pressed down on all of them like a held breath.

Her hand hesitated on the doorknob for just a fraction of a second before turning it. She could feel Dennis standing right behind her, impossibly close; his presence radiated danger like heat off asphalt on a summer day. The sensation crawled up her spine and settled between her shoulder blades.

Stepping outside was momentarily disorienting—as though she'd passed from one reality into another misaligned version of it. The air was cool but carried no relief; it served as a cruel reminder that time hadn't stopped out here the way it had inside that room.

Argo leaned against the wall exactly where she'd left it: scratched frame, scuffed handlebars—an old warhorse that bore no judgment for its rider or the mess she'd brought with her.

She approached the bike slowly, hyper-aware of Dennis's scrutiny burning into her back through the open doorway. Her fingers dipped under the seat where she'd stashed it earlier—not shaking exactly, but not steady either—and after an agonizing second or two of fumbling, they closed around smooth metal.

The USB key caught what little light there was, winking up at her like it shared some private joke at her expense. Her hand closed over it tightly as if holding on too long might change what came next—might reverse time or rewrite fate or any other silly notion you entertained when out of options.

Wren forced herself back inside before hesitation could take root; there was no room for it now—not when Maggie's life depended on keeping Dennis happy enough not to pull that trigger.

She walked toward him deliberately and held out her hand—the USB resting flat on her palm—as though presenting some sacred relic to an impatient god. Dennis's eyes narrowed immediately; they flickered between Wren's face and the device as if trying to assess which one lied better.

"What's this?" His voice carried an edge sharp enough to cut stone.

Wren bit back several retorts before settling on one that wouldn't get anyone killed—yet. "It's what Anne gave me," she said evenly—or as evenly as she could manage under his gaze. "You know...the thing you've been waving that gun around for?"

His scowl deepened; suspicion carved lines into his forehead so deep they might never smooth out again. "How do I know this is real?"

Wren tilted her hand so more light hit it—a dark smear still clinging stubbornly to one edge of the metal surface despite every effort she'd made to clean it off weeks ago...no it had just been minutes, right? Either way, she hadn't been able to erase *that*. Not completely.

"There's still blood on it," she said finally, forcing herself not to flinch at how nonchalant the words sounded leaving her mouth—even if they made something twist deep in her gut just saying them aloud.

Dennis stared at the key for what felt like forever before glancing back at Maggie again without loosening his grip on either suspicion or weaponry.

Wren didn't move—not yet anyway—but every muscle in her body begged for action even when every rational part of her brain knew better than to oblige them too soon. There were still too many ways this could go wrong…and very few where any of them made it out alive.

Dennis leaned in, his eyes sharp as a hawk's, narrowing when they landed on the USB key. A slow smile spread across his face, cold and unpleasant, like something sour left too long in the sun. "Alright," he said, stretching the word out like it amused him. "That checks out. What's on it?"

Wren tightened her jaw, feeling her teeth press together almost painfully. She flicked her gaze to Maggie. Maggie sat frozen in her chair, all wide eyes and shallow breaths, her fear palpable even from across the room. Wren raised her chin, her voice measured but cutting. "You think I've had time to check? I've been a little busy *not* getting shot." She shrugged with a forced casualness that she hoped didn't betray the tension thrumming under her skin. "Dodging bullets sort of eats into your free time."

Dennis's smile vanished as quickly as it had come. His jaw tightened, and his eyes turned hard—dangerous—like storm clouds gathering on the horizon. "Watch your mouth," he said softly, which made it somehow worse than if he'd shouted. Then louder: "Hand it over."

He gestured with the gun—just a twitch of motion that made Wren's breath hitch despite herself. Her fingers tightened around the cool metal of the USB key until she could feel its sharp edges biting into her palm. The other key—the blue one—was still with Argo. Neither he nor Maggie knew it existed. Her mind raced as she scanned the room for something—anything—that might tip the odds in their favor.

She looked back at Maggie—a moment so brief it almost wasn't a moment at all—and their eyes met. Maggie looked terrified (of course she did), but even through her terror, there was something else there too: trust. Or at least hope masquerading as trust.

The tilt of Wren's head toward the stairs leading up was so slight it would've been imperceptible if you weren't looking for it. Maggie was looking for it though—or at least she saw it anyway—and after a beat that felt like forever but couldn't have been more than a split second, she gave an almost invisible nod.

Dennis reached for the USB key, his hand moving slowly—as if savoring what came next—but Wren was faster. She didn't hesitate because hesitation wasn't an option anymore; all those years navigating tight turns and split-second decisions on a bike had taught her that much.

Time to bet her life that in this neighborhood, at this time of day, he would not fire.

In one fluid motion—a flick of her wrist so quick and precise it felt inevitable—the USB key left her hand and sailed through the air before disappearing under the bed with a muted clatter.

"Are you kidding me?" Dennis barked, his calm veneer cracking like fragile glass as he dropped to his knees to retrieve it.

Wren didn't wait to see what happened next; there wasn't time for that kind of indulgence. Instead, she surged forward and grabbed Maggie by the arm—gently enough not to hurt but firmly enough that there was no mistaking what came next—and pulled.

"Move!" Wren hissed under her breath as she pushed Maggie toward the staircase with both hands.

Maggie stumbled at first (how could she not?), but Wren kept them moving forward anyway because stopping wasn't an option either—not now—not ever—not with Dennis behind them somewhere reaching for that damned USB key like his life depended on it.

The stairs creaked under their feet but for once Wren didn't have time to care about whether they were giving themselves away.

"Go!" she whispered fiercely when Maggie faltered again halfway up. Wren remembered Fannie had unlocked the door between the units, and was hoping she'd forgotten to lock it again.

Maggie's breath came fast and shallow—the kind of breathing people do when panic has its claws deep inside them—but then Wren felt Maggie pick up speed again even without another verbal nudge from behind.

They climbed higher while each step stretched endlessly forward like taffy being pulled too far yet somehow managing not to snap entirely apart beneath their feet.

Upstairs couldn't come soon enough.

Behind them, Wren caught the sharp sound of Dennis cursing, followed by the grating screech of furniture dragging across the floor. Her chest tightened, a cold weight pressing down. Time was slipping away too quickly, and she could feel it.

A split second of silence, and there he was.

Dennis's hand clamped onto her ankle with a grip that might as well have been iron. She hadn't even heard him coming before he pulled her backward, sending her sprawling. The world tilted wildly, her body colliding hard with the wooden stairs. The impact knocked the breath from her lungs in a harsh gasp, pain bursting through her ribs and down her back like fire running along a fuse.

"Maggie—go! Lock the door!" Her voice came out jagged, torn around the edges. She clawed at the steps in front of her, nails scratching against smooth wood as tiny splinters burrowed into her palms. She didn't care. She couldn't care.

Maggie froze for a moment—a heartbeat stretched too thin—her wide eyes betraying fear that screamed louder than any words could. Then she was moving, bolting up the stairs in a flurry of pounding footsteps that echoed sharply in Wren's ears.

Wren barely saw it coming—the dull thud of her head meeting a step sent stars spinning across her vision in bursts of white light. The metallic tang of blood settled on her tongue. When her vision cleared enough to focus, Dennis's face hovered just above hers, close enough that she could see every line etched there by anger... or worse.

Somewhere above them came the slam of Fannie's door followed by the distinct click of a lock sliding home. For a fleeting second, relief washed over Wren like cool water on blistered skin. Maggie had made it—she was safe now. But just as quickly as it had come, that feeling was ripped away. Safe meant alone and alone meant Wren was trapped here with him.

Dennis's fingers dug deeper into her leg, bruising with every movement. The pain sharpened something in her—it always did—and before she had time to think it through, her leg shot out with all the force she had left. Crack! His nose crumpled under the blow like brittle clay. Blood poured fast and thick over his mouth and chin as he reeled back with an animal howl.

Wren didn't wait to see what he'd do next; she couldn't afford to hesitate. Gritting against every flare of pain in her battered body, she scrambled backward on all fours up the stairs, putting inches but not nearly enough distance between them.

"Bitch!" The word tore out of him loud enough to shake dust from the stairwell walls as his rage boiled over again. He lunged at her even before he'd fully straightened himself, one massive fist swinging through the small space between them. She pressed herself flat against the wall at the last possible second—his fist caught her shoulder instead of its intended mark. It wasn't a direct hit, but pain still bloomed instantly under her skin.

She didn't stop moving this time—she *couldn't* stop moving now—and she slid under his arm with barely an inch to spare between herself and disaster. By sheer instinct or adrenaline or years dodging cars and people keeping her upright when every nerve in her body screamed otherwise, she pushed forward toward escape instead of freezing in place.

At the bottom of the stairs now and feeling ground beneath both feet again for what felt like the first time in hours rather than seconds, Wren spun sharply on one heel and drove a kick straight into his groin without mercy or hesitation. His scream cut through everything else around them—louder than footsteps or splintering wood or even blood rushing past her ears—but not loud enough to drown out what came after: silence.

He crumpled onto the landing like paper collapsing under too much weight, but Wren didn't dare assume anything yet—not safety, not victory—not until she was sure. He was a lightweight.

Her fingers touched the doorknob. Freedom was a twist away. Then—movement behind her. She ducked, a reflex more than a decision, and his fist crashed through glass where her head had been. A jagged shard embedded in his knuckles, blood pattering onto the scuffed wooden floor beneath them.

They stared at each other, gasping for air. His eyes burned with rage, a promise that this wasn't over. The steady drip of blood marked the seconds between now and whatever came next.

Wren's gaze swept the room, her mind scrambling for options. Her voice emerged steady, though her stomach churned. "Where's the USB?"

The question hit like a detonator. Dennis froze, panic flickering across his face. He opened his injured hand slowly, palm up, as though expecting the drive to materialize there despite the shredded skin and glistening blood. Nothing. Desperation overtook him as he checked his other hand with the same useless result. His head snapped back toward Wren, confusion and fear warring in his expression. His mouth worked soundlessly for a moment—a fish out of water—before he found no reply at all.

He hesitated, just long enough.

Wren didn't think; she moved. Years of threading her way on a bike through reckless drivers and chaotic city streets had trained her body to act before it could second-guess itself. She lunged forward, her hand latching onto his wrist like a trap snapping shut. Before Dennis could react—or maybe before he even fully registered what was happening—she thrust his bleeding hand toward his own face, shoving the jagged glass shard deeper into his flesh.

The sound that followed was part crunch, part wet pop. It turned Wren's stomach even as it sent Dennis reeling backward with a howl of pain that echoed off the apartment walls. His hands flew to his face instinctively, leaving trails of blood smeared across his cheeks as if tears gone wrong.

Wren spun toward the door, yanked it open hard enough to slam it against the wall, and fled into the light.

The cool air hit her like a shockwave, sharp against sweat-dampened skin. Her legs carried her forward without permission or direction, pure adrenaline dictating speed over purpose. Behind her came muffled curses interspersed with stumbling thuds—Dennis flailing in pain or fury or both—but she didn't look back.

She couldn't look back.

With every step putting more distance between them, Wren's thoughts caught up with her body—or tried to. Dennis was strong; she'd never doubted that. But strength wasn't enough on its own—it needed something to guide it: instincts honed by experience or discipline drilled into muscle memory or even just plain grit to push past pain when survival demanded it. Dennis had none of that. He couldn't fight through what hurt him; he folded under it instead.

Kind of pathetic when you thought about it.

Pain didn't kill you—that much Wren knew for sure after spending months trapped in that damn wheelchair years ago. Sitting still while everything else moved on without you? That was what did you in—every time.

So she kept moving now because stopping wasn't an option—it never had been—and let her legs propel her farther down the shadowed street until nothing but quiet lingered behind her and nothing but darkness stretched ahead.

11:45 a.m.

Dennis's footsteps pounded against the pavement behind her, each one a sharp reminder of the brief lead she'd managed to steal. Ahead of her sprawled freedom—or something close enough that she didn't dare slow down to question it.

"You're dead, bitch!" His voice was raw, shredded by rage and exertion, as though he'd dredged it up from a place too dark to imagine.

Wren didn't turn around. She didn't have to. She could picture him clearly enough: a lumbering tower of bruised ego and bad intentions, gun in hand, face smeared with blood from their basement scuffle. He was limping too. That part gave her some satisfaction—not much, but enough to keep her legs moving.

Dennis's shouts faded behind her, swallowed by the rush of wind in her ears as her speed picked up. The world narrowed into a single objective: forward. Maggie and Fannie were safe—that much she was certain of—and Dennis wouldn't risk shooting his gun, not with neighbors who could peek through curtains.

Her heart hammered against her ribs, but it wasn't exhaustion fueling it—not yet anyway. No, this was adrenaline's crueler cousin—chaos—that electric sting in your veins when danger wasn't past but wasn't quite at your heels either.

Wren let herself glance back once to confirm what she already knew: Dennis might've had shoulders wide enough to block the sun and fists like hammers, but his legs? Not so much. He was built for bulldozing through walls, not chasing bikes on foot. Watching him try almost made her laugh—and would've if laughing didn't require slowing down.

He turned suddenly and slammed against a car. His car.

Wren leaned harder into Argo's frame, urging it faster down the uneven street. The wind sliced across her cheeks—not gentle or refreshing but sharp-edged, like tiny knives reminding her that freedom came at a cost. Her thighs burned in protest as she pushed them past their limit.

And still—still—there was that feeling prickling at the back of her neck again. The kind you can't shake no matter how far you go or how fast you run (or ride). A heat crawling its way beneath your skin until there's one way to quiet it: look back.

She told herself not to do it. Told herself again that nothing good ever came from satisfying curiosity when survival was on thin ice—but habits are habits for a reason.

Wren tilted her head over one shoulder—and instantly regretted it.

The motion threw off Argo's balance; they wobbled together like a mismatched pair stumbling drunkenly home from a bad night out. Tires skidded sideways against asphalt slick with god-knows-what residue left behind by city living and neglect.

"Shit." Her nails dug into the handlebars while every muscle in her body screamed at once: *Don't fall!*

For one awful second—maybe two—it felt inevitable anyway. The pavement rushed up toward her like an eager lover readying its embrace.

But Argo held steady in that stubborn way only well-loved bikes seem capable of—a loyal creature unwilling to betray its rider's faith just yet—and when those tires found their grip again, Wren's momentum lurched forward instead of sideways.

That would've been good news if not for what came next.

The sound hit first—a low growl that rose swiftly into something more menacing: an engine revving hard enough to set teeth on edge followed by the screech of tires biting too sharply into pavement curves meant for casual drivers—not maniacs chasing women on bicycles around suburban streets at the lunch hour.

Dennis had wheels now and he wasn't wasting any time catching up.

Wren leaned closer into Argo's frame until they were practically one entity—a girl-bike hybrid fueled entirely by panic and spite—and squeezed every ounce of strength left out from lungs already tight and limbs that begged for mercy they wouldn't get today (or maybe ever).

Wren's heart slammed against her ribcage as the Tisker River loomed ahead, the road cutting off as though the world had decided to end right there and then. She had a millisecond, no more, to make a choice—left or right. Her eyes darted between the two paths, her brain throwing up possibilities she didn't have time to weigh.

Right. Steeper. Riskier. It just *felt* right.

She twisted the handlebars and leaned into the turn, trusting Argo to follow her lead. The tires squealed like they were protesting the decision, but they held their grip on the pavement. For now.

That was when she saw it—a flash of metal glinting in the corner of her eye. A car barreled toward her, engine roaring with unmistakable intent. Dennis. It had to be Dennis.

"Shit," she muttered under her breath, curling low over Argo's frame like instinct alone could make her aerodynamic enough to outrun him. Her legs burned as she pushed harder—too hard—but that didn't matter now. Speed wouldn't save her, not against a car. Not even on Argo, her trusty partner in this mess who felt more reliable than most humans she knew.

Her gaze flicked left: long rows of brick buildings pressed shoulder to shoulder without a single gap between them. No doors, no open windows, no mercy.

To her right—wait—a slim opening sliced between two graffiti-smeared walls, barely visible until now: an alleyway so narrow it looked more like a dare than an escape route. It wasn't much—maybe nothing at all—but it was something, and something was all Wren had left.

She didn't think, because thinking would slow her down. She veered sharply toward the gap just as the screech of tires behind her made it clear Dennis had caught on.

"Come on, Argo," she whispered—not quite a plea but more than an order—as though speaking to the bike might somehow make it sharper, faster, braver than it already was. "We've got this." In truth, she didn't know if *she* believed that.

The alley rushed toward her like it was shrinking by the second. Her chest tightened with every inch closer—it was going to be tight; so tight—but there wasn't time for doubt now. At the very last moment, Wren tucked in her elbows and folded herself small over Argo's sleek black frame.

The bike's tires hit the entrance with enough force that Wren felt every jolt in her bones as they clattered over uneven ground coated with grime from decades of neglect. She bit down hard against the vibration rattling through her arms as she fought to keep the handlebars steady.

Behind her came another screech—brakes this time—and a series of muffled curses that carried just far enough for Wren to catch their meaning: Dennis wasn't following anymore. The alley had won this round; his car was far too wide to squeeze through after her.

Not that Wren had time to bask in small victories. Her focus snapped forward again because naturally—and why would she expect anything else?—the alley wasn't empty or smooth sailing from here on out. Trash cans crouched like ambushes in every corner; broken furniture sprouted legs where no legs should be; crumpled bags spilled questionable contents across what barely passed for ground.

Then came the dip. A sudden drop at odds with everything else sent both bike and rider airborne for one sickeningly beautiful second that stretched forever and yet not long enough for Wren to process what was happening.

Her stomach flipped as gravity reasserted itself with enthusiasm bordering on cruelty; Argo crashed back down hard against loose gravel scattered like landmines across ancient asphalt. The tires skid left before catching themselves just shy of disaster.

"Steady, girl," Wren murmured under her breath—not quite calm but close enough—her fingers trembling against the handlebars as though Argo might sense nerves through touch alone and lose faith in both of them.

There wasn't room for relief yet—not here where every second demanded vigilance—but still: Score one for Argo and guts over horsepower and bad men in fast cars driven by worse intentions.

The engine's growl reached her ears from the right—too close, too loud. Wren didn't hesitate. She yanked the handlebars left, Argo obedient as ever, gliding past the garbage bin and onto an open stretch of asphalt.

The street ahead was unfamiliar. It gleamed faintly under the sparse light, its fresh surface unblemished by time or weather. Wren barely registered it before she turned left again, instinct overriding thought. The road tilted upward now—a slight incline, one that on a different day might have gone unnoticed. But today wasn't a different day.

Every push of the pedals felt heavier than the last. Her legs burned as she pressed harder, the velocity of the bike humming beneath her like a live wire, slicing through traffic with the precision of a blade. The hill stretched on endlessly, taunting her with every inch gained. Her speed dipped lower. Wren clenched her jaw and shook out her legs in short bursts, as though shaking could free them from the leaden weight creeping into her muscles.

She couldn't keep this up. That much was clear. A plan—she needed a plan. Somewhere to hide, some way to outmaneuver Dennis and his car before he closed in completely. But first, she had to crest this hellish hill.

Her breath tore from her lungs in sharp, uneven gasps, sweat tracing erratic lines down her face and neck. She forced herself to look up—eyes barely lifting past the handlebars—and there it was: Dennis's car roaring into view at the cross street ahead.

Argo responded like an extension of her body as she threw herself into action again, pushing harder despite every fiber of her being begging her to stop. Behind her, Dennis's engine roared louder with each second, a predator announcing its presence rather than stalking silently.

Idiot. Doesn't he know how obvious that is?

Wren dug deeper, forcing more power into tired legs that screamed in rebellion. Too slow—she was still too slow. He was gaining on her quickly now, his car a hulking shadow swallowing up the narrow margin separating them.

Almost there... almost there...

Dennis surged past first, his car brushing so close she felt the heat radiating off its engine—a scalding wave against the cool air whipping around her sweat-soaked skin. And then—bam! Pain exploded in sharp clarity as the side-view mirror slammed into her hip.

The strike jolted her entire body off balance, sending Argo careening wildly beneath her as tires skidded and fought for purchase on unforgiving asphalt.

For one fleeting moment, Wren hung between gravity and momentum—the world spinning violently around her as though trying to decide where to throw her next. And then it made its choice.

The ground rushed toward her.

Concrete loomed large—a merciless end to this chaotic flight—and she could do nothing but brace for impact, eyes squeezing shut against the inevitability of pain crashing down on top of everything else.

Instead of unforgiving pavement, Wren's body collided with rough brick. The wall greeted her unceremoniously, scraping against her skin as she slid down its jagged facade, friction sparking a fiery trail in its wake. Her descent ended in a graceless heap on the ground, where the impact robbed her lungs of air and left her momentarily stunned.

Pain arrived promptly, spreading its influence swiftly and without mercy. Her hip—the one that had taken the brunt of the mirror's assault—drummed with a deep ache that reverberated outward like ripples in water. Both palms throbbed and stung from instinctively breaking her fall against the abrasive surface, raw and trembling. As for her face—well, that was hot and sticky now, thanks to the same wall that had just introduced itself so rudely.

She tried to breathe. No easy feat. Each inhale felt like sharp claws raking across her ribcage, and when she exhaled, she tasted copper. Great. She'd bitten her tongue again.

The world tilted alarmingly as she fought the daze threatening to engulf her senses. Her vision swam in and out of focus; her ears rang with an insistent hum that wouldn't quit. The brick wall behind her was the only solid thing remaining—its harsh texture pressed into her back as though trying to keep her grounded in reality. Maybe it was doing her a favor after all.

Argo lay abandoned just a few feet away, its front wheel spinning idly as if mocking her predicament. For a fleeting moment in this mess of chaos and pain, she felt relief—a flash of gratitude that her bike had escaped harm. Argo was hers in a way few things were. And there it sat, waiting patiently for her to get moving again.

Ow.

Wren winced as she forced herself upright. Her head swam with protest at this sudden act of rebellion against gravity; the ground beneath her tilted dangerously before righting itself again. Tires screeched somewhere ahead, slicing through the fog in her brain like a siren snapping someone out of a daydream. Dennis had overshot his mark—his car skidded past the corner entirely and onto another stretch of road.

Her window was narrow but clear: Get moving.

Wren stumbled forward and grabbed hold of Argo's handlebars. Lifting the bike upright sent fresh shocks of pain ricocheting through every battered nerve ending in her body. It wasn't subtle about its displeasure either—it screamed at her with every motion, every breath, every ignored plea for rest—but Wren shoved it aside like an unwelcome guest overstaying their visit.

The slam of car doors behind her shattered any illusion of time to waste. Dennis wasn't giving up yet—that much was obvious—and neither could she. With a grunt that sounded more determined than defeated (she hoped), Wren swung herself onto Argo's saddle. Her body protested again but found itself overruled as she pushed off shakily down the hill that had been tormenting her moments before.

Gravity lent its hand eagerly, pulling her downward faster and faster until balance returned to those familiar wheels beneath her feet. The sharp wind clawed at everything it could reach—her hair, her scraped cheeks, even the edges of frayed nerves—but none of it mattered now.

"Good luck turning around, asshole," she muttered under her breath through gritted teeth.

The hill stretched out ahead like some divine reprieve from Dennis's relentless pursuit—a temporary salvation made sweeter by speed's intoxicating rush. She leaned in close against Argo's frame until they moved as one entity; wind shrieked past them both while tears formed involuntarily at the corners of swollen eyes from sheer velocity alone.

A car loomed ahead like a silent obstacle, its red brake lights glowing faintly in the haze. Not Dennis. Wren's pulse quickened, though she kept her line steady, her body taut with anticipation. At the last possible moment, she leaned into the handlebars and veered sharply to the right. The bike—Argo—responded without hesitation, skimming past the car so closely that Wren swore she could feel the heat from its engine. The driver honked, the sound sharp and indignant, but it faded quickly into irrelevance as she accelerated.

Another car now, blocking her path. This time, there was no pause, no deliberation. Wren tilted her weight to one side, her bike swaying as she slipped through a gap like water finding its course. A third car materialized in front of her, a bigger challenge this time—a hulking SUV with oversized mirrors and an air of immovability. Wren didn't blink. She crouched lower and sailed past it on the left, her movements so fluid it felt less like maneuvering and more like instinct taking over.

The Tisker River shimmered back into view just ahead, a sleek ribbon of dark water bordered by dull concrete banks. It stretched endlessly before her as though marking some elusive finish line she couldn't quite reach. Wren barely spared it a glance. She cranked Argo's handlebars hard to the left and hurtled toward the riverfront where buildings stacked high against each other blurred together like smeared paint in her peripheral vision.

Then she saw it—the gridlock—and something in her chest shifted. A surge of exhilaration bubbled up unexpectedly, reckless and unapologetic. Heavy traffic clogged the street ahead: rows of cars idling bumper to bumper, their tailpipes chugging fumes into the oppressive afternoon air. Her grin spread wide and unrestrained across her face as though this unyielding mass of vehicles was a gift dropped directly in her path. Gridlock meant Dennis couldn't follow.

Wren aimed straight for the narrow seam between two sedans resting too close for comfort. Without breaking stride or second-guessing herself, she threaded Argo through the gap with maybe an inch to spare on either side; it wasn't much room at all, but it was enough for her purposes. The horns erupted again—angry blasts of frustration—but they might as well have been applause for all Wren cared. Each honk seemed to fuel her further.

One by one, she slipped between cars with unfaltering precision: a minivan here, a truck there, an old sedan with peeling paint that groaned ominously as she scraped past its mirror (or nearly did). Her lungs burned with effort; every breath felt like dragging air through syrupy exhaust fumes thickened by the summer heat pressing down upon everything indiscriminately.

Argo responded beautifully each time—every shift of weight and turn of wrist translating perfectly between them—and for all its sleek lines and polished frame, Wren swore that today, Argo almost had a personality: quick-witted yet obedient when it mattered most.

She reached another bottleneck where two cars had parked too close together at odd angles—a trap for anyone else but not for Wren. She ducked low beneath one truck's side mirror; its chrome surface glinted briefly above her head before disappearing behind in an instant. Sweat poured down her face now—not just sweat but also streaks of dried blood from earlier scrapes mingling freely as they painted trails along her jawline.

Her focus sharpened further despite—or maybe because of—the growing ache in her hip pulsing steadily beneath layers of adrenaline masking it temporarily like some ill-fitting bandage soon to come undone.

The downtown core loomed up ahead at last: block after block of concrete rising into steel spires that pierced skyward unforgivingly over streets bathed mercilessly in sunlight bouncing off every reflective surface imaginable—glass windows glaring angrily alongside metal railings scorched hot enough to burn skin if touched too long.

The taxi swerved into her path out of nowhere. Wren didn't think—she just leaned hard to the right, her body moving on instinct. Argo's tires screamed against the asphalt, brushing so close to the curb she felt the scrape. The collision she braced for never came. She didn't hear what the cabbie yelled after her—not over the roar of her pulse or the wind whipping past her ears—but she figured it wasn't "Have a nice day."

Then she saw it: an alley wedged between two glass-and-steel giants, like someone had forgotten to fill in this one narrow gap when they'd built up the city. Wren yanked her handlebars left, darting into the jagged slash of shadow.

A rat froze mid-scamper at Wren's sudden arrival before deciding survival was better than curiosity and disappearing into the nearest heap of trash. The smell hit next: sour milk, rotting lettuce, something worse lurking underneath it all. A lesser person might have gagged. But Wren? She'd sprinted through worse.

She skidded to a shaky stop halfway down the alley, slamming one foot onto the ground to steady herself. Her hands fumbled for her phone before she'd even caught her breath, fingers trembling as they typed Maggie's number and pressed *dial*. It rang once. Twice.

"Wren?" Maggie's voice broke through on the third ring—tight and frayed at the edges.

"Oh thank fuck." Wren exhaled like she'd been holding that word in for hours. Her chest still heaved as relief started snaking its way through her veins. "You okay?"

The sound Maggie made wasn't quite a sob but wasn't not one either. "Oh god—oh my god, Wren." Her words came fast now, tumbling over each other like they couldn't get out quick enough. "Are you hurt? Where are you?"

"I'm fine." That was mostly true if "fine" allowed for scraped palms and lungs that still burned from exertion. "Really," Wren added when Maggie didn't say anything. "I lost him. Are you safe?"

"Yes. Fannie—God she is something else. She must be a prepper. Turns out she has this tiny room under her staircase. You'd never know it was there. I'm holed up inside with supplies." Maggie sounded scared—and suddenly Wren hated herself for making her feel that way again. "The cops haven't come by, but Fannie's keeping an eye out."

"Good," she said firmly. "I'm downtown somewhere. In some alley that smells like death warmed over."

There were tears now on Maggie's end; Wren could hear them even though Maggie tried to muffle them with sharp breaths and sniffles. "This is insane. Insane!"

Wren felt something tighten in her throat at that—not fear this time but something heavier in a different way—and she swallowed hard before speaking again, softer now: "Hey—it's okay." Her voice raw despite herself; apparently not all parts of her had gotten the memo about staying calm and cool under pressure. "I'm here. That guy? He couldn't catch me if I tied weights to Argo and gave him directions."

Maggie let out a shaky laugh that sounded more like surrender than amusement, but it was better than crying at least. "You're impossible."

"Yeah," Wren admitted without hesitation because denying it would've been pointless anyway—she'd heard it enough times from people who knew her well enough to mean it as both insult and compliment rolled into one. "But you love me for it."

There was silence then, heavy but warm somehow too—filled with all those unsaid things neither of them could find words for right now.

Finally: "Where can I meet you?" Maggie demanded.

"The Wheel Well," Wren answered after a beat—a courier dive where half-broken bikes hung from ceilings like trophies nobody wanted anymore but couldn't bear throwing away either because history mattered sometimes more than practicality ever did.

"I'll be there soon," Maggie promised immediately; no hesitation now because when had there ever been any when it came down to this between them? Then softer: "I love you so much."

12:02 p.m.

Wren pedaled hard as the Wheel Well came into view. Her legs, though burning, found a rhythm that pushed her forward with just enough steadiness to get her there. The sight of the converted garage—a haven she had grown to rely on—stirred something close to relief in her chest, though it was fleeting. She thought briefly about the helmet and sunglasses she'd lost during the day. Or maybe abandoned. She couldn't remember exactly what had happened to them and didn't care enough to piece it together now. The haze of adrenaline blurred most things into irrelevance.

She slowed as she neared the coffee shop, coasting the final few feet with a precision born of habit rather than effort. Argo's front tire bumped lightly against the rack outside, and Wren swung off the bike with all the grace of someone whose body was about to give up on them entirely. The sound of metal striking metal—her lock snapping into place—was oddly gratifying, even if it didn't reassure her as much as it should have. Argo had been good to her; losing it would feel like losing a limb.

It had never occurred to her until just now that all crashing and bashing might have dislodged the key. She slipped her finger under Argo's seat and lets out a breath as she grabs the blue USB key from the courthouse. Its new home was her sock.

Her legs wobbled as she stepped back from the rack, nearly folding beneath her altogether. She planted herself against Argo for support, sucking in deep breaths that did little to calm the fire in her lungs. It took a moment before her focus returned enough to take stock of her surroundings: twelve chairs clustered around mismatched tables under an awning that looked like it might collapse in a strong wind—a setup both practical and vaguely chaotic, much like everything else about this place.

Two couriers lounged at one of the tables nearby, balancing mugs in hands calloused from handlebars and brake levers. They were mid-conversation when they noticed Wren, their chatter halting as they took in her disheveled state.

"Damn, Wren," one finally said, shaking his head in mock dismay. "You look like you wrestled a dump truck and lost."

"You're gonna look worse," she shot back, though there wasn't much conviction behind it.

The other courier leaned forward conspiratorially, smirking. "You're not gonna tell us what you did this time?"

Wren dragged herself upright and waved a dismissive hand at them, too tired for explanations or banter. "You saw nothing," she said flatly, glad they didn't watch the news.

The first courier grinned but held up his hands in mock surrender. "Nothing at all."

Wren blew them a quick kiss without stopping, already halfway through the door by the time it registered as a gesture of thanks.

Inside, everything was just as cluttered as ever—a collision of caffeine and chaos. Six stools stood pressed around tall metal tables that had seen better days but still held their ground. Tools and bike parts were strewn across every available surface: wrenches balanced precariously on disassembled frames; wheels propped haphazardly against counters; bolts rolling aimlessly between coffee cups abandoned mid-repair.

The air smelled like something this place could conjure: rich coffee layered atop grease and rubber, each scent distinct but inseparable from the others. Wren inhaled deeply despite herself. It wasn't comforting exactly—this messy blend of aromas—but it was familiar, which was close enough.

Behind the counter, shelves sagged under neatly arranged chaos—rows of sleek helmets beside energy bars beside patch kits beside God-knows-what-else that someone might need at some point but never planned ahead for. Her eyes landed on the helmets first: glossy ovals in colors so bright they seemed to glow even under dim lighting.

She thought about grabbing one later—a cheap replacement for now—and noted how silly they all looked lined up together, like candy eggs waiting to be cracked open. For all their brightness, none could hide what she needed them to hide: purple hair that made her too easy to spot these days.

Still leaning against the counter, Wren let out a breath and reminded herself that hiding wasn't optional anymore.

"Wren? What the fuck?" a familiar voice chimed in, sharp enough to slice through the haze clouding her thoughts.

"Shhh. Not the name. Please."

"Jesus, Wr—woman! You look like you went one-on-one with a cement truck."

Wren turned slowly on the stool, her muscles protesting every movement, to find Jasper standing behind the counter, his hands frozen mid-pull on the espresso machine. His tattooed forearms bulged as he gripped the portafilter tighter than necessary, his expression vacillating between concern and disbelief.

"You should see the other guy," Wren rasped, her voice scraping against her throat.

Jasper barked out a laugh, shaking his head like she'd just confirmed his worst suspicions about her. "The usual?"

Wren nodded once, too tired to articulate more. Slumping forward, she let her elbows rest on the counter and pressed her weight into them, feeling something deep in her shoulder protest. She craned her neck and watched Jasper's methodical movements—he was annoyingly good at this; every action deliberate, controlled. He tamped down the espresso with a practiced flick of the wrist before sliding the portafilter back into place like he was some kind of coffee-conjuring magician. It was oddly hypnotic.

"And a lid," Wren added abruptly. Her eyes flickered toward the neat row of pristine helmets clipped above the barista station. "White."

He didn't respond but lifted an eyebrow at the request as he poured steamed milk over espresso, shaping an intricate rosetta without even looking down. Show-off. She watched him slide the cup across the glossy counter with unnecessary flair before adding a ceramic saucer beneath it like it mattered.

Her hand wrapped around the warm mug reflexively as if it might anchor her to something steady for once today. The heat seeped into her skin, cutting through some of the lingering chill left from where sweat had dried against her scraped-up back and shoulders. Her mind drifted—again—to earlier: metal scraping hard against bone; skin tearing beneath impossible angles; concrete rushing toward her face faster than she could brace for impact. The memory closed in like smoke curling up from under a locked door until she felt herself flinch involuntarily at its edges.

"Earth to woman." Jasper's voice cut cleanly through her spiraling thoughts like he had a talent for spotting exactly when someone was about to disappear inside their own head entirely.

She blinked up at him, startled to find he was leaning in closer across the counter now—too close—and staring at her with pointed curiosity that would've been irritating if he weren't so genuinely well-meaning about it.

"You okay?" he asked softly, his voice careful but probing around where she might've hidden answers she wasn't ready to dig up yet herself. "You look like you've seen a ghost or something... You know cops have been crawling all over town looking for you? Hit every rest stop from here to Bakersfield."

Wren barely managed half a shrug in response as she glanced down into her cup again where foam swirled around abstractly now—thoroughly unrecognizable compared to whatever pristine pattern Jasper had originally poured it into earlier. "Just beautiful," she muttered without bothering much conviction either way while letting herself sip deeply anyway because caffeine still worked wonders even when words failed outright.

The café door chimed faintly behind them then—and instantly shattered whatever fragile semblance of calm she'd cobbled together for herself just seconds ago—with its far-too-familiar metallic jingle that never failed somehow always sounded sharper whenever Wren stood right on edge already.

Her head snapped sharply toward where sound originated instinctively first before logic even got involved next—but thankfully... Not *him.* Just another courier this time: tall guy slinging messenger bags lazily across both shoulders simultaneously while fumbling awkward orders aloud into Bluetooth pieces nobody asked questions about anymore these days.

"Name's Reek," he said, extending a hand. "Heard you're in deep shit."

Wren let her gaze travel over him, taking her time, as if cataloging an exhibit at a museum she wasn't entirely sure deserved the ticket price.

His face was first: sharp cheekbones jutting out like warning signs under skin that seemed permanently smudged with grime—as if the city itself had decided Reek belonged to it and marked him accordingly. His hair was a mess of dark curls spilling out from under a cycling cap so battered it looked almost sentimental, like he couldn't quite let it go despite all it had been through.

And then there were his eyes—bright brown, alert in a way that set her on edge. They darted around constantly, scanning everything as though he couldn't trust the world to stay still for longer than a heartbeat. There was something behind those eyes too—streetwise quickness paired with something harder to name. A little weariness perhaps, or just the kind of knowing you didn't get unless you'd spent years balancing speed against survival.

The hoodie—black once but now closer to charcoal—was sleeveless, the frayed edges curling where the arms had been cut off. His arms, lean and ropy with muscle, were a gallery of inked chaos. The tattoos didn't match. Some looked like they'd been done in garages or prisons, all shaky lines and uneven shading; others were sharp enough to have cost real money, maybe even rivaling rent for a month.

His shorts hung loose and heavy on his frame—cargo shorts in what had been a crisp dark gray but were now an uneven patchwork of stains that told stories no one wanted to hear. The bulging pockets gave away their contents: tools of some sort, bike-related, though there could've been anything stuffed in there. Wren imagined loose bolts rattling against gum wrappers and spare keys that opened long-forgotten locks.

Then there were his legs—scarred and sturdy, each mark etched into his skin as if by a careless artist with asphalt for a brush. They told the tale of every spill, every near-miss, every inch of pavement he'd fought and survived on two wheels. Badges of honor? Maybe. Or just reminders that the streets didn't love anyone back.

She hesitated before reaching out to meet the hand he still held toward her—a little too steady for her liking. His palm was rough against hers, calloused in ways that confirmed what his legs and arms already hinted at: this was someone who lived his life outside soft places.

"Deep shit?" she asked finally, keeping her voice flat enough to skate across the surface without breaking through. "Who exactly told you that?"

Reek shrugged as he slid into the chair and invited her to sit with an unhurried kind of ease that made Wren think of water finding cracks in concrete. He leaned forward then, elbows resting on the table like they were old friends catching up over coffee instead of...whatever this was.

"You are Wren Hubbard," he said—not quite asking but not entirely certain either. His voice was low and rough around the edges, like gravel under tires.

Wren's eyes narrowed. Her chest tightened with a sharp pang of suspicion. "How do you know my name?"

A sickly smile crossed his face. "I spent seven years inside before they realized they had the wrong guy."

Reek reached into one of the many pockets on his jacket and pulled out a battered smartphone, its screen crisscrossed with tiny cracks like a spiderweb. His thumb swiped across the surface, the movements swift and confident. Then, without a word, he turned the phone toward her.

Wren's breath caught. Her own face stared back at her from the dim glow of the screen. The headline screamed louder than any voice: *Courier Wanted in Death of Local Journalist Anne Cantu.*

For a moment, everything inside her froze before flipping over itself in frantic motion. Her stomach twisted into a knot so tight it felt as though it might tear itself apart. She shoved the phone away with shaky hands, as if doing so would shove away the accusation itself.

"That's bullshit," she blurted. "I didn't do anything."

Reek raised his hands slowly, palms out, his posture one of exaggerated calm, like someone trying not to spook an animal. "Everyone has kinda nice things to say about you," he said, his tone way too casual for her liking. "I get it. Cops see you speeding by on your bike at just the wrong time, and suddenly you're guilty of everything under the sun. It's messed up."

Wren didn't respond right away. Her mind was spinning too fast, rushing through possibilities and half-formed plans that unraveled before she could grasp them properly. But one thing was clear: She couldn't sit here and do nothing. She needed to think—but more importantly, she needed information.

"Look," Reek continued, his voice softening in what she supposed was an attempt to sound sincere. "If there's anything I can do to help, just say the word. Us couriers gotta stick together, right?"

Stick together? Wren studied him closely. She wasn't sure if he was being genuine or playing some angle she couldn't quite see yet. Her tongue darted across her dry lips before she finally asked, "You got a laptop I can use?"

Reek shook his head almost immediately, which should've been discouraging but somehow wasn't surprising in the least. "Nah," he said as though delivering bad news about the weather instead of her possible salvation. Then he tilted his chin toward the repair shop beyond them and added, "But there's one in back—a loaner they keep around for customers or something. I can grab it for you if you want."

Wren hesitated longer than she meant to—long enough for doubt to start creeping in around the edges—but eventually nodded anyway. "Yeah," she said quietly. "Yeah... that'd help."

Reek unfolded from his seat with a loose-limbed ease that made Wren think of a switchblade flicking open—a comparison she didn't entirely like making but couldn't shake now that it had surfaced unbidden in her mind.

"No problem," he said cheerily as he started toward the shop entrance without waiting for further instruction or thanks from her. Over his shoulder came one last parting remark: "Sit tight—I'll be right back."

And then he was gone—vanishing into the depths of the repair shop just as easily as he'd appeared—and Wren was left alone with nothing but her thoughts and that cursed headline lingering behind her eyelids like an afterimage burned into retinas too slow to look away.

She drummed her fingers against the table absentmindedly—or maybe nervously; at this point she could barely tell anymore—and kept glancing between the door ahead and where Reek had disappeared moments earlier through another doorway altogether. Time crawled forward reluctantly—as if testing how much patience Wren had left—while anxiety pressed down on her chest like an overfull backpack she couldn't shrug off.

Her latte sat abandoned in front of her now—its heat already fading into lukewarm territory—and after staring at it without seeing it at all anymore anyway... she reached for it again and took another sip out of sheer habit more than anything else.

The warmth slid down her throat but did nothing to steady her insides this time—not even close—and still every second dragged on heavier than the last while uncertainty gnawed at whatever resolve she'd managed to scrape together thus far.

She needed information. She needed a plan. But mostly—and whether she wanted to admit it yet or not—she needed Reek to come back through that door holding what she'd asked for... instead of anything worse she hadn't dared let herself imagine yet but couldn't stop half-expecting anyway all the same.

The bell above the door let out a sharp chime, cutting through her reverie. Wren's head jerked up at the sound, her heart stalling mid-beat. There she was—Maggie, stepping into the Wheel Well. Her jacket hung awkwardly off one shoulder, her hair damp and clinging to her forehead in uneven strands. Disheveled, yes. But unharmed. Their eyes locked across the room, and for a moment, everything else—the low hum of chatter, the clatter of mugs, even Wren's own frenzied thoughts—dropped away into silence.

Wren was on her feet before she fully registered moving. Her body protested every step—the ache in her ribs, the stiffness in her legs—but she ignored it. She closed the space between them quickly, almost recklessly, until Maggie's arms were around her and they collided with a force that sent a flash of pain through Wren's side. She didn't care. Maggie didn't seem to either. Their lips crashed together with desperate hunger, hands trembling as they clung to each other's solid warmth, the metallic taste of tears mingling as they breathed in proof that Dennis had failed to claim his prize.

"You're okay," Maggie said, though her voice broke on the last syllable. Her arms tightened around Wren like she was afraid to let go. "God, I thought I'd never see you again."

"I'll haunt you forever." The words tumbled out before Wren could stop them. She leaned back just enough to look at Maggie's face—her flushed cheeks, her wide eyes rimmed with exhaustion—and then she kissed her again. It wasn't graceful or well-timed; their noses bumped awkwardly, their breaths colliding as much as their lips did. But it didn't matter. It never mattered.

When they broke apart, they were both gasping like they'd just surfaced from deep water. "I love you," Wren murmured, and even though her voice was barely audible over the din of the coffee shop, she knew Maggie heard it.

Maggie's hands came up to frame Wren's face; her thumbs moved gently across the creases at Wren's temples like they could smooth away all the worry etched there. "I love you too," Maggie said simply. "And we're here now—together. That's what counts."

They stayed like that for a moment longer, foreheads pressed together while everything else dissolved into static noise—the rattle of cups behind the counter, distant laughter from a corner booth—all of it faded under the thrum of their heartbeats syncopating against each other.

Eventually, reluctantly, Wren pulled back and laced her fingers through Maggie's. She led them to a small table by the window—Maggie following close behind as if she might vanish if Wren let go—and they sat down side by side instead of across from one another. Their chairs bumped together as their knees touched beneath the table's edge.

Maggie's gaze roamed over her now that they were sitting still—her eyes trailing from Wren's bruised knuckles to a scrape along her jawline that hadn't stopped stinging since yesterday morning.

Before Wren could respond—or ask anything more—a figure approached their table from the side. Reek moved with a twitchy energy—a battered laptop tucked under one arm and his eyes flitting between Wren and Maggie as if trying to piece something together about their dynamic without asking outright.

"Got it," Reek said, dropping the laptop onto the table with enough force that it made both women jump in their seats. He glanced at Maggie then and extended a hand toward her with what was supposed to be an easy grin but came off more like a grimace thanks to Reek being...well...Reek.

"Name's Reek," he said brightly—or as brightly as someone with perpetual dark circles under their eyes can manage—and then added with a curious tilt of his head: "You must be *the* girlfriend?"

Reek shook Maggie's hand, his grip loose while hers was firm. "Maggie," she said simply. "Thanks for helping Wren."

He dropped into the chair with all the grace of a slouch. "No biggie. I spent time in prison for a crime I didn't commit. I get it. And I'm always happy to help with something I can deny later."

Wren ignored him, flipping open the laptop with a snap and tapping her foot like the machine's slow boot-up was a personal insult. Her fingers dipped into her sock—she winced at the awkward angle—and emerged clutching the blue USB key like it might bite her. She tossed it onto the table where it skidded to a stop next to Reek's elbow, making a faint clinking sound against his coffee cup.

"What's that?" Reek leaned forward, eyebrows doing most of the heavy lifting in terms of showing interest.

Wren didn't bother looking at him. "Our ticket out of this mess," she said, though it sounded more like she needed convincing herself. She plugged the key into the laptop, her movements sharp and clipped.

The three of them huddled close, shoulders brushing as they craned their necks toward the screen in the cramped coffee shop booth. The air smelled faintly of burned espresso and overused cleaning supplies—a sharp mix that somehow made Wren's tension ratchet up another notch. When the USB drive finally loaded, Wren's heart gave one solid thud against her ribs before settling into an uneven hammering rhythm.

There it was.

One file.

A single text file staring back at them with all the smug indifference of a middle finger.

"Damn it!" Wren slammed her fist onto the table hard enough to send a ripple through their coffee cups and draw a few startled glances from nearby customers.

Maggie sighed and pinched the bridge of her nose, like this wasn't even in the top ten worst things about today. "We risked our lives for *one* text file? Again?"

Reek scratched at his stubble, his eyes flicking around the room, out the window, past the door. "I don't get it. So... what's inside? Is that not good?"

Wren glared at the screen as though sheer force of will could make another file (or twenty) magically appear on that damn USB stick. All that running, all that danger—for what? Her stomach churned as she clicked on the file and braced herself for another geocache location.

The text appeared almost instantly—just numbers—but Wren didn't have time to process because Reek suddenly stiffened beside her, his body going from slouched to coiled spring in less than a second. His gaze snapped past her shoulder to something outside.

"Oh no," he hissed under his breath but loud enough to make both women freeze mid-breath.

"What?" Wren asked without looking up, though every muscle in her body had tightened as if bracing for impact.

Reek tilted his head toward the window without moving anything else, like some amateur spy trying not to be obvious. "That jogger, it's his second time past us," he murmured through barely parted lips. "Pretty sure he's an undercover cop."

Wren felt her pulse spike again—today seemed determined to take years off her life—and shot Maggie a look across Reek's hunched form. Maggie met her eyes just long enough to confirm: yes, we're screwed if we don't move now.

"We've got to go," Wren said under her breath, already pivoting back toward the screen.

"Mags." Her voice was low but firm enough to snap Maggie into action. "Take a photo of this—quickly."

Maggie fumbled with her phone before raising it over Wren's shoulder to aim at the screen, hands shaking just enough to betray nerves despite how steady she tried to sound when she said, "Got it."

Reek hadn't moved; his eyes stayed glued to whatever he'd seen beyond the window as though he could ward off trouble by sheer vigilance alone. "Those numbers look like GPS coordinates," he muttered in what barely passed for casual observation given how tense his jaw had gotten.

Wren spared him half a glance but didn't slow down until Maggie lowered her phone and said more firmly this time: "Photo's clear."

Wren yanked the blue USB key from the laptop and shoved it back into her sock. Her hands moved quickly, almost on their own, as though they belonged to someone else—someone who wasn't shaking. She snapped the laptop shut with a sharp click, the sound louder than she anticipated, and turned to Maggie. Her voice was low but firm, like a wire pulled taut.

"Get Bridger," she said. "We're leaving. Now."

Maggie didn't ask questions. She never did. She nodded, her face pale but set in that way Wren had come to rely on, like granite beneath snow. Without a word, she started moving—smoothly, purposefully, gathering her things with quick efficiency that came out when it mattered most.

Wren's eyes swept the coffee shop as she rose from her seat. She scanned the faces—the barista with his earbuds in, the man tapping at his phone in the corner booth—as if one of them might suddenly snap into motion. Her gaze lingered just long enough to file each observation away before moving toward the door where their bikes were parked.

Reek stood by the window now, his silhouette stiff against the glass. He didn't look at her right away—as though looking would confirm something neither of them wanted to acknowledge—but when he finally did turn, his expression was grave.

"That jogger passed by again," he muttered under his breath. His voice carried an edge sharp enough to cut steel. "You need to go."

Wren felt a flash of gratitude—or something close enough to it—but there wasn't time for the luxury of words. "Thanks," she said quickly.

Reek's eyes flicked back to the street outside as though expecting it to shift beneath his gaze like water boiling over. "No reward yet," he said grimly, almost absently, "but once there is? Yeah. Then they'll all come for you." His lips curled into what might have been a smile or might have been exhaustion trying its best impression of humor.

He jerked his thumb toward the back of the shop without turning around. "Through there—repair area and out the back door. It's your cleanest shot."

Wren had already hoisted herself onto Argo by then—her bike as much muscle memory as machine—and felt its hard frame steady under her weight like an old friend bracing for impact.

But Reek's head snapped toward the street corner, and this time he swore loud enough for everyone in the immediate vicinity to hear him: "Shit." His hand rose instinctively like it could stop whatever was coming through sheer force of will alone. "Traffic's stopped. They're here—get out!"

That sent Wren moving before her brain even caught up with her body. She leaned forward over Argo's handlebars and angled toward Maggie with a quick nod that said everything words couldn't in moments like this: *Now.*

The repair shop was narrow and dimly lit with makeshift workstations that hadn't seen organization in years if ever—a graveyard of greasy tools and half-finished projects leaning against walls like forgotten corpses waiting for burial rites no one had time to give them anymore. Wren threaded through it all with precision born less from skill than necessity; Maggie stayed close behind her wheel, neither gaining nor falling back.

The heavy clang of the back door flying open hit Wren's ears along with sudden sunlight—or not quite sunlight but something brighter than what they'd left behind—and for one gut-twisting moment she blinked against disorientation so strong it made her feel seasick standing still.

Then she saw it: a police cruiser nosing its way slowly down the narrow stretch of road beyond them like a predator testing whether its prey would run left or right before committing fully to chase.

"This way!" Wren hissed over her shoulder without looking to see if Maggie was following—not because she doubted Maggie would but because there wasn't time for doubt either way.

She turned Argo hard—not smooth or graceful but urgent—and pushed off again down another twisting route between brick walls that echoed their movements back at them twice as loud as they actually were.

Behind her came Maggie's tires scraping against uneven pavement almost perfectly in sync with hers—a sound that somehow managed to be both reassuring and maddeningly fragile in its rhythm—and ahead lay only more shadows whose depths neither one could see yet but which waited all the same whether they slowed down or not.

They turned onto a narrow side street, their movements seamless, automatic. Wren bent low over her handlebars, legs churning as the bike surged beneath her. The wind cut through her hair—she never did get her helmet—but she welcomed it. It was better than the heat climbing up her neck, better than the way her chest felt like it might cave in.

Maggie rode just behind her left shoulder, close enough that their wheels nearly kissed on tight turns. She was always there, steady and unflinching, her face set in that same stubborn determination Wren had come to recognize in every ride they'd ever taken together. They didn't need to speak to know the plan—they'd learned to move as one a long time ago.

The city blurred past them in long streaks of color: gray asphalt, red taillights, yellow flashes of storefront signs. Occasionally, human shapes flinched out of their path—pedestrians shocked into motion by the sudden dart of two figures on bikes dodging between parked cars and potholes.

"We loop back," Wren said finally, glancing at Maggie without breaking stride. Her voice wasn't much louder than the wind whipping past their ears. "The Wheel Well—cops won't look for us there."

Maggie gave a small nod—just once—and banked hard as Wren took the lead again. The familiarity of the streets should've been a comfort, but today it wasn't. Today it felt like they were running out of places to hide, every familiar landmark blurring into something that felt less friendly with each lap they made around the block.

When they rounded the final corner and spotted the coffee shop ahead—the faded graffiti stretching across its brick walls—a flicker of relief curled at Wren's mouth like a grin trying to form.

It froze before it could take shape.

The black-and-white cruiser parked outside was like a splash of cold water on her skin—sobering and immediate. Her grip tightened around the handlebars until her knuckles went pale.

"Damn it," she muttered under her breath.

They stopped. Wren's eyes landed on Reek before anything else: his unmistakable frame leaning too casually against a lamppost, all limbs and jittery energy. He wasn't alone. His companion wore a badge and uniform.

Reek's head tilted up mid-sentence as though he sensed them before he saw them. His eyes locked onto Wren like magnets snapping together, widening in recognition faster than she could react. For half a second, neither moved—Wren gripping the bars so tight that she thought they might snap under her hands; Reek standing there with his mouth open like he'd forgotten what words were.

That moment ended with sharp precision as Reek's arm lifted and his finger shot out—a beacon aimed in the opposite direction. He said something—Wren couldn't hear it over the roar in her ears—but whatever it was hit its mark.

The officer turned almost mechanically in response to Reek's gesture. His hand moved instinctively to his holster as his narrowed eyes scanned down the street.

"Go," Wren said—or maybe shouted—but it came out raw and uneven, more jagged noise than word. And then they were moving up the street because there wasn't another option—not now—not ever really.

Wren's chest heaved as she and Maggie tore away from the Wheel Well, their bikes slicing through the restless churn of early afternoon traffic. Adrenaline surged through her, sharp and electric, but beneath it ran something colder, heavier—fear. Not the kind she welcomed when the stakes were high and the rush was its own reward, but the kind that sat like a stone in her gut.

She glanced over her shoulder—just a quick look, because she knew better than to linger—but what she saw made her stomach twist. The officer had seen them. Worse, he had drawn his gun, the barrel catching a flash of sunlight that made her throat tighten. But it wasn't just him.

It was Reek.

The wiry courier was running straight for the cop, his long legs eating up the pavement with a purpose that made Wren's breath catch. She could see it all too clearly now: his narrowed eyes, his clenched jaw, his unshakable focus on what he intended to do next.

"Mags, look!" Her voice felt thin against the roar of passing cars.

She turned back just in time to see Reek throw himself at the officer like some kind of deranged linebacker. The impact sent both men sprawling to the ground in a chaotic tangle of limbs. The officer's gun clattered against the pavement and spun out of reach, glinting once before coming to rest near the gutter.

Reek was already up again, waving his arms with frantic urgency. "Go! Don't stop—just go!"

Wren snapped forward, her hands gripping the handlebars so tightly it hurt. She ducked around a taxi on her left as Maggie mirrored her move on her right. The city unfolded in a blur of honking horns and screeching brakes, muffling whatever shouts chased after them from behind. Maggie was quiet—the kind of quiet that screamed focus—and Wren didn't dare break her own concentration either.

They darted past startled pedestrians who jumped back with startled cries and sidestepped carelessly flung car doors that threatened to cut their escape short. Her thighs burned as though they were being lit from within by molten fire, but she didn't ease up—not even a little. Every push of the pedals felt like a battle cry in itself. Distance—that's what mattered now.

"Left!" Wren shouted when she spotted their chance—a narrow alley cutting away from the main street like an afterthought.

The turn came fast; sharp enough that their tires squealed in protest but held firm as they veered into shadows painted by brick walls and faded graffiti. She let instinct guide her now, threading through gaps barely wide enough for their handlebars until they burst out onto another street entirely.

Traffic swallowed them whole again. Cars sped past without pause or care for two sweating cyclists merging seamlessly into their chaotic parade. Wren risked another glance back—not because she wanted to, but because she had to know—and saw nothing but commuters oblivious to what had just unfolded two blocks over.

Her shoulders sagged as she dragged air into her lungs, each breath raw and jagged against her throat. Relief flirted with her edges but didn't quite settle in—not yet.

"I think we lost them," she called out over her shoulder, though even as she said it, part of her braced for whatever might come next.

They pedaled on, their speed tapering until they blended seamlessly with the cyclists weaving through the morning streets. Wren's thoughts spun faster, a chaotic jumble of adrenaline and dread. Reek's intervention had bought them an advantage—but how much? And at what cost?

"Move! Fucking move!" The words shot out of her mouth before she could stop herself, directed at no one in particular—or at everyone. She glanced over her shoulder, catching a glimpse of Maggie pedaling hard to keep pace. Wren's stomach churned. *Come on, you're okay,* she told herself as much as Maggie. "Left!" she barked over her shoulder as they veered onto another street. "We need to change clothes."

The dollar store came into view just as Wren felt the first tendrils of real exhaustion gripping her muscles. Her brain latched onto the thought like a lifeline: *Here.* Maybe not safe exactly, but better than open roads and prying eyes. Her breath steadied just enough for her to yell back: "Here! Inside!"

By the time they reached the red light, she slowed Argo sharply and coasted alongside Maggie, who was breathing hard and flushed with exertion. "Where?" Maggie managed between gasps.

Wren didn't answer—she couldn't quite find the words yet. She yanked Argo to a stop right in front of the dollar store, tires shrieking against pavement as though echoing her still-frantic thoughts. One smooth motion saw her dismounting and striding toward the automatic doors without pause, all while gripping Argo like someone might snatch it away.

The fluorescent lights washed over Wren in a blinding glare as she entered, making her wince instinctively. The store smelled like new plastic shoved into old cardboard—cheap and stale yet strangely sharp all at once, its air heavy with artificial lemon cleaner that seemed determined to choke every other scent into submission.

Maggie came in seconds later with Bridger in tow, eyes wild but mouth silent. Her chest heaved visibly as she looked at Wren for direction without uttering a word—not trust exactly, but follow-the-leader desperation simmered there somewhere beneath those wide eyes.

The two of them stood still after entering—the kind of pause that lets you actually notice your surroundings for what they are: crowded shelves tottering under weighty piles of lurid packaging screaming for attention; discount signs plastered haphazardly like confetti; customers idling lazily beneath humming lights. A woman wheeled an ancient wire shopping cart filled with cat food past them and shot them a look—a narrowed squint that wasn't outright hostile but so piercing it might as well have been.

Wren scanned the aisles quickly. The layout was almost laughably predictable: Aisle 1 promised snacks healthy but only by legal technicality; Aisle 2 offered dubious kitchenware stacked precariously high; Aisle 3... never mind that now.

"What now?" Maggie whispered harshly behind her—not loud enough to carry but urgent enough to cut through Wren's fogged brain like static electricity sparking into life again.

She didn't respond immediately because just then—the cashier spoke up.

"Hey!" His voice carried from across the dingy space like an unwelcome announcement echoing too loud in a nearly quiet room full of strangers trying not make eye contact with one another—or maybe that was just Wren projecting onto everyone else present. "You can't bring bikes in here!"

Wren didn't even look back toward him—not intentionally rude but singularly focused on movement rather than confrontation—as though ignoring him might erase his existence entirely from memory afterward.

She spotted what she wanted: swinging double doors near the back corner labeled "Employees Only" in faded block letters peeling along their edges where grease or sweat stains had accumulated over years (decades?) unnoticed by management judging by smell alone nearby.

Wren guided Argo through the narrow aisle, her pulse still thundering in her ears. The hum of the overhead fluorescent lights mixed with the faint squeak of bike tires on linoleum, their glow harsh and unflattering, spotlighting rows of merchandise that seemed to dare anyone to find value in them. She glanced over her shoulder. Maggie trailed behind with Bridger, her expression a muddle of worry and bewilderment, like someone waking up in a strange room and trying to remember how they got there.

An employee stood ahead, stacking plastic owl lights into a pyramid. He didn't seem particularly interested in his work or much else for that matter. His eyes flicked toward them briefly—two women pushing bikes through a store wasn't exactly subtle—but his attention slid off them just as quickly, returning to the fragile tower of owls.

As they moved deeper into the store, Wren noticed the greeting cards first. Flimsy rectangles lined up neatly, their pastel messages of "Congratulations!" and "Thinking of You" feeling almost absurd in their cheerfulness. Balloons floated overhead, tied to racks brimming with cheap party favors. They bobbed gently in the artificial air currents like brightly colored jellyfish, their hues too loud and garish against the tension thrumming under Wren's skin.

"Careful," Wren hissed as Maggie's bike brushed a bin near the edge of an aisle. The handlebars caught just enough to tip it, sending a cascade of colorful candy wrappers spilling onto the linoleum tiles. The sound was comically loud in the otherwise quiet store. Maggie froze and looked down at the mess as though it might somehow put itself back together if she stared at it long enough.

Wren shook her head and pressed forward, weaving through aisles crammed too full for comfort. The aggressive scent of strawberry air freshener hung heavy in the air, cloying and synthetic, meshing unpleasantly with undertones of cheap plastic from bins stuffed with toys and cleaning supplies no one needed but everyone bought. Wren's eyes darted constantly now—not just at Maggie or Bridger but at everyone else in the store, at every corner they passed—seeking something, anything that might signal trouble before it reached them.

They reached the back section abruptly, Wren stopping so short that Maggie nearly stumbled into her rear tire. "What now?" Maggie whispered sharply. Her voice had dropped so low it was almost swallowed by her unease.

Wren didn't answer right away; her focus had shifted to a rack against the far wall. Cheap clothes hung limply from bendable hangers that looked ready to snap under even this light weight. The thought started small but grew quickly—a plan piecing itself together as if someone had slipped instructions into her mind without asking permission first.

"This way," she said finally, her voice steady even as adrenaline continued its relentless flood through her veins. She turned Argo toward the row of clothing without looking back to see if Maggie was following. The wheels of the bikes squeaked again—a sound that could have been mistaken for cartoonish except for how real everything felt right now—and drew a couple side-eyes from shoppers who clearly had their own problems but hated being inconvenienced regardless.

Maggie caught up fast enough but still looked puzzled as she came alongside Wren. "What are we doing?" she asked again, her words tight with barely contained frustration—as though she'd already guessed she wouldn't like whatever answer Wren was about to give.

Wren reached out, her fingers brushing against the fabric of a hoodie. Soft, synthetic, cheap. "We need to change how we look. Fast." She didn't wait for

Maggie to respond, turning to her anyway with an expression that left no room for discussion. "Got any cash on you?"

Maggie patted her pockets, her movements hurried but futile. Her hands stilled as she shook her head. "Nothing. You?"

"Damn it," Wren muttered, more to herself than Maggie. Her eyes flicked toward the nearest register, scanning for employees while pretending to examine a nearby rack of tank tops with garish slogans printed across them. "I'm tapped too."

Maggie made a noise, part hesitation and part light-bulb moment, then reached into her jacket pocket. Wren noticed the motion from the corner of her eye and felt a cold twist in her gut even before Maggie said, "I have my debit card on my phone—"

"No!" Wren's hand was on Maggie's wrist before the phone even cleared her pocket. She hadn't meant to grab her quite so hard, but she didn't let go right away either. "If the cops are watching bank transactions—and they will be—they'll have us pinged and picked up before we even leave this store."

Maggie froze under her grip for an instant before pulling back, wide-eyed and startled but not upset. If anything, the look on her face was something closer to impressed. "You've thought this through."

"Yeah. No," Wren said shortly, releasing Maggie's wrist but feeling a faint twinge where her fingers lingered against skin. Shaking it off, she returned her focus to their immediate problem and lowered her voice again. "One mistake and we're done."

She rubbed at a spot near her temple where a headache threatened to bloom until an idea began to take shape. Not foolproof by any stretch of imagination, but it might just work.

"Mags," she said at last, keeping her voice measured even though urgency hummed under every word now. "I need you to take both bikes outside and head for the corner down there." She nodded toward the glass doors and what little of the street beyond was visible through them. "Lean Argo against a pole so it looks natural—you get ready to ride if things go sideways."

Something about this didn't sit right with Maggie—Wren could see it plain as day in how tightly her brow knit together like she wanted to argue but didn't quite dare yet. "Sideways?" she asked instead.

"I've got an idea," Wren replied simply because explaining too much would waste time she didn't have if they wanted any real shot at pulling this off cleanly—or at all. She couldn't quite stop herself from smirking faintly either; force of habit when bluffing nerves into confidence, maybe. "Trust me."

Maggie hesitated exactly as long as Wren had expected she would—long enough for doubt or worry to wrestle briefly with trust and then lose—but after that moment passed, she nodded somberly. "Alright," she said softly but seriously while looking Wren directly in eyes like she intended those words not just as agreement but a promise too. Then added quickly: "Be careful doing whatever this is gonna be."

"Always am," Wren deadpanned with an almost automatic kind of ease despite neither truth nor humor being in those words anymore—but they exchanged no argument over such things either.

Wren watched Maggie wrestle both bikes toward the store's entrance. Argo's frame shimmered beneath the unforgiving fluorescent lights, its sleekness almost mocking the chaotic mess of dollar-store trinkets inside. Bridger trailed behind, solid and dependable, a bike built for endurance over speed, for journeys rather than split-second getaways.

The automatic doors slid apart with a hiss that was somehow both ominous and mundane. Maggie hesitated at the threshold, glancing back at Wren—her face a mix of concern and resolve, though which emotion outweighed the other was hard to tell. Wren nodded once, small but firm. That was all Maggie needed. She shoved the bikes forward and stepped out into the glaring sunlight.

The doors closed with an indifferent whoosh, leaving Wren encased in stale air-conditioning and the faint scent of cheap plastic. She exhaled slowly, letting her fingers brush against the nearest rack of hoodies. The fabric snagged on her skin—cheap and thin, trying too hard to mimic something better. For a moment she just stood there, grounding herself.

Wren started walking. Casual. Measured. The sound of her cycling shoes against the scuffed linoleum floor felt too loud somehow, but she kept her pace steady as she turned down an aisle brimming with toys. The bright colors hit her first—a swirling assault of primary reds, blues, and yellows plastered across shiny plastic packaging. Action figures with grotesquely exaggerated muscles stood frozen mid-pose beside dolls whose painted-on grins bordered on unnerving.

She reached for a squishy stress ball shaped like some bug-eyed cartoon character, squeezing it idly in her hand as her gaze flicked across the space. A store employee hovered a few feet away, vaguely restocking shelves with all the enthusiasm of someone counting down minutes to clock-out time. He didn't look up or acknowledge her presence—not even a flicker of interest—which suited her just fine. Wren placed the stress ball back where she'd found it and moved on.

Wren circled back to the hoodies, her fingers automatically reaching for one hanger after another as though searching for something that wasn't there. The hangers scraped across metal rods with an unpleasant screech that scratched against her nerves—like nails dragging over glass or an alarm no one else could hear but her.

Wren finally settled on two oversized hoodies—one black, one navy. The price tags dangled from the sleeves like tiny, judgmental signs, announcing to anyone who cared to look that these clearance-rack rejects were still ten bucks apiece. She let out a soft scoff. "Highway robbery," she muttered under her breath, but she didn't hesitate as she draped them over her arm. Beggars couldn't be choosers, and right now Wren was closer to begging than choosing. The hoodies would do.

She made her way toward the front of the store with what she hoped was a casual gait. The cashier was busy serving the next customer and the next customer and the next customer. Wren's palms began to sweat as her heart picked up its pace, each beat a reminder that she had no real plan—at least not one that would hold up under any serious scrutiny. Improvisation was the only option.

Then she spotted the security guard planted near the exit like an overweight watchdog. His uniform clung awkwardly to broad shoulders, the buttons on his shirt straining against their stitching. How had she missed him before? Her stomach tightened as she muttered another curse under her breath and tried to recalibrate. But recalibration wasn't exactly her strong suit.

The automatic doors slid open with a soft mechanical sigh, and a middle-aged man in a crisp business suit strode inside, his gaze glued to the rectangle of light in his hand. Wren's eyebrows lifted. He was so absorbed in whatever riveting email or stock report consumed him that he didn't even glance up as he crossed the threshold into chaos.

It was the chaos of Wren's mind—an idea not fully shaped but solid enough to work with—and before she could second-guess herself, she quickened her pace and angled toward him. Timing was everything here. A split-second too early or too late and the whole thing would crumble like... well, like what was about to happen next.

At the last possible moment, Wren twisted her body sharply and crashed into him, hard enough to send herself stumbling backward in an almost theatrical flail of limbs. "Oh my God!" she shouted, her voice loud enough to make heads turn across the store.

She didn't stop there—she couldn't stop there. Still off balance (or pretending to be—it hardly mattered now), Wren stumbled into a nearby shelving unit stacked high with neat rows of plastic storage containers. The metal frame shuddered under her weight, its stability clearly questionable at best.

Time seemed to slow down exactly when it shouldn't have. The first container teetered at the edge of its shelf before tumbling down, its lid popping off as it bounced across the linoleum with a hollow plastic clatter. Others followed—square, round, rectangular—all cascading down in a chaotic avalanche of mismatched plastic that skittered and rolled across the floor.

The noise was deafening in the quiet store—a cacophony of plastic percussion as containers bounced and spun. Her shoes slipped against the smooth surfaces as she fought for balance, arms windmilling wildly like some cartoon character on ice skates.

The containers skidded in every direction, rolling under shelves and displays. Wren hopped and dodged between the moving obstacles, each step threatening to send her sprawling. Somewhere distant—too far away for her liking—someone gasped audibly while another voice barked out something unintelligible.

"Hey! Are you okay?" The security guard's voice, deep and deliberate, carried across the store, each syllable slicing through the hum of background chatter. His footsteps—heavy, purposeful—thudded against the polished floor as he closed the distance.

The man in the suit—mid-forties, receding hairline, probably someone's insufferable supervisor—reached out instinctively to steady her arm. "I am so sorry," he said quickly, his voice tinged with panic and something that might have been guilt. "I didn't see you there."

Wren blinked a few times, as though trying to regain her balance. Then she drew herself up and turned toward him, unleashing what could best be described as a controlled storm. Her voice cut through the air, sharp and rising. "You pushed me!" she snapped, jabbing a finger toward his chest. "This guy shoved me into the shelf!"

The man's face twisted in surprise, his eyes flaring wide before narrowing in exasperation. "What? No! It was an accident—I didn't mean to—"

"Oh, don't give me that," Wren interrupted, her words quick and biting as though they'd been sharpened beforehand. She took a step closer to him—or maybe just closer to where anyone watching would get a better view of this spectacle—and added a venomous hiss: "You saw me coming and what? Decided to knock me aside like I don't even matter? Or is it because I look too queer for you?"

It wasn't clear whether Wren's hands were trembling from fury or adrenaline—or if it was just part of the performance—but either way, it worked. A couple walking by slowed their cart to watch. Someone near the stationary aisle craned their neck for a better look.

The businessman sputtered incoherently for a moment before managing to string together actual words: "That—that's absurd! I wouldn't do something like that! You've got it all wrong!"

"Wrong?" Wren spun on him fully now, her gestures wide, her tone laced with incredulous disbelief. She let out an incredulous laugh—not loud but enough to fill the space between them—and stared him straight in the eye. "Oh please," she said sharply. "Save your excuses." Her gaze darted briefly toward the growing audience before landing back on him.

The security guard finally reached her side then, placing one broad hand on her shoulder as though trying to anchor her down somehow. "Ma'am," he began in what was supposed to be a calming tone but came off as weary and annoyed at being roped into this mess at all. "Let's try to stay calm."

Wren shrugged off his hand without hesitation, taking another step toward the man in the suit now looking wildly uncomfortable but digging in his heels regardless. Her body language screamed defiance—spine straight as an arrow, shoulders squared—and yet there was something theatrical about it too, like she wasn't just addressing him but playing directly to an invisible jury.

"Calm?" she repeated with mock incredulity that morphed swiftly back into indignation. "You want me to stay calm after this jerk shoved me? What are we supposed to do? Just let guys like this walk all over us while they grin smugly about getting away with it?"

Her last statement hung in the air for maybe half a second too long before she added—quieter now but no less charged—"Or do you hate people like me too?"

The businessman's cheeks darkened from pinkish embarrassment straight into full-blown crimson indignation by that point. His mouth opened and closed once before he finally found words again: "Now just wait a second," he barked out stiffly. He tried straightening his tie—a reflexive gesture—but his hands fumbled awkwardly halfway through and instead he jabbed one finger vaguely toward Wren in frustration.

"I didn't push you," he started firmly but not quite angrily yet—more defensive than anything else. Then he paused briefly before adding: "...And I certainly don't hate anyone."

For half a heartbeat after saying it though—the pause giving room for doubt—it almost sounded like even *he* wasn't entirely sure whether anyone would believe him.

Wren's foot shot out, stopping just short of the businessman's shin. She missed him on purpose, but only by a hair. His reaction was almost too good: first his eyes went wide, startled, then narrowed sharply as his face turned a furious shade of red. He lunged at her with both hands, fingers clawing like he might wring her neck right there in the middle of the store.

"You little—"

The insult never made it to full bloom. A security guard, all bulk and booming authority, wrapped the man in a fierce bear hug from behind. "Sir! Calm down!" His voice reverberated off the tiled floors and fluorescent-lit shelves.

Chaos erupted. The two men staggered back and forth, stumbling into an endcap display of paper towels. Dozens of rolls tumbled to the floor and bounced in every direction, some rolling lazily like they were taking a Sunday drive away from the mess.

That was Wren's cue.

She didn't think. Thinking could come later—later when she wasn't clutching stolen hoodies like contraband gold bars and dashing for freedom. Her legs propelled her forward toward the exit as though they had a mind of their own. The automatic doors hissed open just in time for her to burst through them, sunlight smacking her face hard enough to make her squint.

Her head whipped around, scanning for Maggie. There she was—just where they'd agreed—hovering near the corner by their bikes, shifting her weight nervously from foot to foot. Wren raised her voice over the hum of traffic and pounding adrenaline: "Go!"

Maggie's face snapped up at the sound of Wren's shout. Her eyes widened in startled understanding before she threw one leg over Bridger and took off without hesitation. Her hair trailed behind her like a streaming banner as she pedaled furiously away down the street.

Wren sprinted to Argo. She reached it in three long strides, threw herself onto the seat and shoved off so fast her shoes barely found purchase on the pedals before she was moving.

The wind hit first—a sharp slap to her face that quickly turned into a full-on rush as she caught up with Maggie's zigzagging form ahead. Wren leaned into each pedal stroke, pouring herself into escaping as if speed alone could wipe clean what had just happened inside the store.

"What *was* that?" Maggie yelled over her shoulder as they flew down the street together. She didn't slow down; maybe she couldn't with how fast Wren was pushing behind her. Still, her voice carried enough panic to cut through the noise from passing cars and barking dogs. "What happened?"

Wren couldn't help herself. A sharp bark of laughter escaped her lips—loud enough to surprise even herself but impossible to hold back now that it had started. Her chest felt tight, not just from exertion but something else—something wild and irrepressible bubbling up alongside that laugh.

"It was *perfect!*" she called back between gulps of air, grinning so hard it hurt her cheeks but not enough to make her stop smiling. "I'll tell you later! Just keep going!"

They pedaled harder, weaving through traffic and pedestrians. Wren's heart raced, not just from the physical exertion, but from the thrill of their narrow escape. The stolen hoodies were stuffed unceremoniously under her jersey, a small victory in their ongoing flight from danger.

As they put distance between themselves and the dollar store, Wren's laughter faded, replaced by a grim determination. They weren't out of the woods yet, not by a long shot. But for now, they were free, two figures on bikes melting into the city's chaotic rhythm.

12:52 p.m.

Wren and Maggie sat slumped on a weathered park bench, their bikes propped haphazardly against the trunk of an old maple. The afternoon sun stretched shadows across the ground, while a breeze teased at the edges of Maggie's unruly hair. She clutched her phone in both hands, scrolling with a frown that deepened with every flick of her thumb.

"This is unbelievable," Maggie said, her voice tight and sharp. "You stumbled across a dead woman, got shot at, received a mysterious USB, handed it over to some lunatic threatening me at gunpoint, and now the police are looking for you in connection to Anne Cantu's murder. Oh, and let's not forget the small matter of finding the second USB drive at the courthouse. Wren, we are so far out of our depth I can't even see the surface."

Wren leaned back against the bench with the kind of nonchalance that shouldn't have been possible under the circumstances. She draped her arms along the backrest and tilted her face toward the sunlight, as though they were discussing nothing more pressing than what toppings to order on a pizza. A smirk crept onto her lips, slow and deliberate. "Don't forget my most daring crime," she said with mock seriousness. "The great hoodie heist of aisle five. Two whole hoodies—taken right out from under corporate America's nose." She glanced sideways at Maggie, grin widening now. "And until someone offers a reward for my capture, I'd say we're perfectly safe."

Maggie lowered her phone and turned to Wren with a look that could be described as incredulous exasperation—a specialty of hers when it came to Wren-related disasters. "This isn't funny." Her tone was clipped, her words spaced just enough for emphasis. "We are in serious trouble."

The smirk faltered but didn't entirely disappear as Wren sighed and reached beneath her jersey, pulling out two hoodies still dangling their plastic price tags like badges of dishonor. Without ceremony, she tore at one of the tags with her teeth and spat it onto the ground before inspecting the garment as if deciding whether it passed muster.

"I get it," Wren said finally, softer now but still unshaken. "It's crazy—we're crazy—but we'll figure it out." She held up both hoodies like a magician presenting options for an upcoming trick: black or navy? With a little wiggle of her hands meant to be enticing but landing somewhere closer to absurd, she added, "Besides, if there's anything more inconspicuous than dollar-store chic, I haven't found it."

Maggie hesitated before reaching for one—the black hoodie—her skepticism evident as she raised an eyebrow at Wren's continued irreverence. They slipped into their disguises without fanfare: Maggie's fit snugly over her frame while Wren's struggled valiantly against its new occupant. Fabric stretched tight across Wren's chest until it gave up entirely on covering her midriff.

"Well," Wren said after tugging fruitlessly at the hem for several seconds. Her voice was deadpan now as she struck an exaggerated pose worthy of a low-budget fashion ad: one arm flexed upward in mock triumph while the other rested on her hip. "I think sausage casing is my look."

It started as a snort but quickly escalated into full-blown laughter from Maggie—her shoulders shaking until she had to clutch at the too-large sleeves of her hoodie for stability. "Oh god," she gasped between fits of giggles. "You look absolutely ridiculous."

Wren dropped her pose and grinned unapologetically at Maggie before holding up both hands in surrender as if to say *guilty as charged*. Then Maggie tugged off her own hoodie and tossed it toward Wren in one fluid motion.

"Here," Maggie said lightly now despite everything weighing on them both. "That one's clearly your size—or whatever size this nonsense is supposed to be."

And somehow—for just a moment—the chaos around them felt like something far away instead of something closing in fast.

Wren turned to Maggie, her expression softening. "You doing okay?"

Maggie's laugh was thin and short-lived. It dissolved into a sigh that seemed to come from somewhere deep. "I think so? Maybe? My family's freaking out. Apparently, you're no longer a person of interest but now you are wanted for murder." She pulled out her phone, the screen lighting up with a seemingly endless stream of notifications. "My parents officially think you're Satan."

A sly grin crept across Wren's face. "Satan, huh?" She raised her hands and crooked her fingers into makeshift horns, sticking out her tongue in a way that was both absurd and strangely endearing. "Guess they're not entirely wrong."

Maggie shook her head, though one corner of her mouth twitched upward in a reluctant smirk. Wren dropped her hands and leaned back against the bench, staring off into the middle distance like she was trying to solve an impossible riddle.

"It's Dennis," she said finally, almost to herself. "It has to be Dennis. He kills Anne; I stumble onto his crime scene; now he's trying to tie up loose ends."

Maggie didn't reply right away. She stared at her phone but wasn't looking at it. Her brow furrowed, and she tilted her head, as though trying to get a better angle on a thought forming in the back of her mind. When she finally spoke, it was slow and deliberate. "There's more to it than that, Wren. Someone set this whole thing up—they contacted you about that delivery, remember? They wanted you at Anne's house at that moment."

"Yeah," Wren said, fingers drumming against her thigh in a quick, restless rhythm, "but who? Anne herself? Dennis? Some third party we haven't figured out yet? Like...the woman who gave me the food at Golden Bites?" She let out a sharp breath through her nose, shaking her head like she was trying to shake the puzzle loose from it. "This is like some twisted game of Clue—except the weapons are real."

"What if..." Maggie hesitated and lowered her voice until it was barely above a whisper. "What if Dennis is working for someone else? Like... I don't know... some crooked politician or something?"

Wren snorted—a short burst of air that sounded more amused than anything else. "Sure—but which one? Half this city's politicians couldn't pass a background check if their lives depended on it. Finding the right one'd be like finding a needle in a haystack—or worse."

Maggie blinked and then straightened up like something had clicked into place in her head. "Wait—" Her voice picked up speed as she spoke now, words tumbling over each other in excitement. "Remember how the mayor got those drug charges dropped last month? What if this ties back to him somehow?"

"Huh." Wren sat up straighter too now, leaning forward like the energy between them had shifted gears entirely. Her eyes caught on something distant but electric—an idea pulling into focus for the first time. "Okay—but we've got those coordinates from the blue USB I found at the family courthouse. Maybe they'll give us something solid to go on."

Before either of them could say more, Maggie's phone buzzed violently against the edge of the bench, cutting through whatever momentum they'd built between them. She glanced at it with all the weariness of someone who already knew what was coming next—and groaned loudly when she saw it anyway.

"It's my mom again," Maggie muttered under her breath before mimicking with dramatic flair: "'Honey! Come home before you get yourself killed!'" She let the phone drop into her lap and turned back toward Wren with an expression stuck somewhere between exasperation and amused resignation. "I swear," she added after a moment of silence stretched long enough to make room for both feelings fully, "she thinks you're going to drag me into some firefight or something."

Wren's grin was the kind that promised trouble, a flicker of mischief lighting her eyes. "Well," she said, stretching the word out, "she's not entirely wrong, is she? We did just make a run for it from a trigger-happy cop and that dollar store security guard."

Maggie's laugh started strong but fizzled out halfway through. Her expression shifted, something heavier pulling at her features. She turned to Wren, eyes narrowing with something caught between worry and fear. "Wren... be honest with me. Do you think—could we actually die doing this?"

For a moment, Wren's bravado cracked like thin ice under too much weight, but then she reached out, taking Maggie's hand in her own. It wasn't much of a grip—just enough to tether them both—and she gave it a single squeeze. "Listen," Wren began, her voice just a notch softer now, "I don't think you're in any real danger. If Dennis wanted to hurt you, he'd have done it right there at the kitchen table. No hesitation."

Maggie nodded slowly, though her lips pressed into a thin line like she wasn't completely convinced. Her gaze shifted—but not far. Just down to where Wren's shorts sat askew on her hip.

"Speaking of getting hurt," Maggie said carefully, leaning in closer now, "how's your hip? That mirror hit you pretty hard."

Wren shrugged in that casual way of hers, like nothing much ever phased her. But Maggie could see it—the way Wren's shoulders tensed at the question or how her jaw tightened just enough to give away the lie before she even said it: "It's fine. Barely hurts."

Maggie wasn't buying it for a second. She reached over without asking, fingers tugging lightly at the hem of Wren's shorts before pulling them up down enough to reveal the truth underneath—a dark purple bruise was blooming across her hip like spilled ink spreading over paper. Maggie froze at the sight of it.

"God," she whispered, her fingers hovering just above the edges of the bruise but never quite touching. "Wren... this looks awful. How are you even walking around like this?"

Wren chuckled low in her throat—not because it was funny but because it was easier than admitting the truth—and shifted her weight with the kind of care people took when every movement reminded them they weren't invincible after all. "Living always means pain," she said finally, grinning through what must have been at least half a wince. "That's how you know you're still alive."

Maggie rolled her eyes because of course she would—it was almost reflexive at this point—but there was a tug at the corner of her mouth too; part exasperation, part affection trying to pull itself free despite everything else going on around them. "You're ridiculous," Maggie said with a shake of her head before tilting it to one side as if considering something deeply profound—or deeply sarcastic; with Maggie, you couldn't always tell which until she spoke again: "You know there's another way to know you're alive though, right? Pleasure... Only living people get to feel that—don't you think that sounds so much better?"

Wren leaned in close, the faint scent of car exhaust clinging to her like an afterthought. "When it comes to you, Mags," she murmured, her voice low enough to be secretive or suggestive, "pleasure is always better."

The phone on Maggie's lap lit up, its insistent trill slicing through the quiet hum of the park. She glanced down at the screen, her jaw tightening as though bracing for a blow.

"It's Charles," Maggie said finally, her tone flat and unreadable.

Wren tilted her head, one eyebrow arching with what might have been curiosity or mild amusement. "Your dad? You wanna take it?"

Maggie's finger hovered over the screen before she pressed decline. The phone went silent again. "Not now," she muttered. "I can't deal with his lectures right now. Not today."

"Fair." Wren's lightness evaporated with a single word. Her expression shifted, grave but not unkind, the kind of seriousness reserved for moments that demanded unspoken understanding. "But soon, Mags—soon we're gonna have to turn that thing off." She nodded toward the phone. "If they're looking for you, they'll be tracking it."

Maggie stiffened almost imperceptibly before nodding back, more to herself than Wren. "Yeah. Okay... I just need to grab that photo first."

The USB sat between them on the bench like something clandestine and out of place—a small blue key holding answers neither of them had asked for yet. Maggie opened the image and held it up so Wren could see. The numbers stared back at them, stark and simple as secrets often are.

"Alright," Wren said softly, retrieving her GPS from Argo with deliberate care. She began typing in the digits while Maggie watched her face for clues to an answer they weren't ready to name yet. Wren's brow furrowed; then suddenly she blinked in surprise.

"An alley," she said finally, faint disbelief coloring her words, "Upper East Side." A pause thickened between them before she added with a wry grin: "Fancy neighborhood for a rendezvous."

Maggie bit her lip—a habit she'd tried to break—and looked down at the phone still warm in her hand. It wasn't hesitation exactly—not quite—but something closer to guilt wrapped up in practicality. Finally, she broke the silence: "I should let them know I'm okay... before we go dark."

Wren shrugged lightly but didn't argue, which Maggie appreciated in a way she'd never say out loud. "Good call," Wren said simply. "Just don't overthink it."

Her thumbs moved fast—too fast—over the keyboard as though slowing down might let second thoughts creep in. "'I'm fine,'" Maggie read aloud softly as though trying out the words for herself first. "'See you soon.'" Before doubt could settle on her shoulders or twist itself into knots around her chest, she hit send.

The phone made its cheerful whooshing sound before falling silent once more—a faintly mocking farewell to connection as Maggie thumbed down hard on the power button and watched the screen go black. She slid it into her pocket like stowing away something dangerous.

"You good?" Wren asked after a beat.

Maggie nodded again—this time sharper but no more convincing than before—and pushed herself upright from the bench as though moving forward physically would drag everything else along with it: thoughts, fears, hopes too fragile to name aloud.

"Yeah," she said finally, forcing steadiness into her voice even as something inside trembled. "Let's go see what's waiting for us."

* * *

Wren pedaled with a steady rhythm, the familiar motion grounding her even as her gaze darted from one shadow to the next. Her eyes were restless, scanning every alleyway that seemed to murmur hidden conspiracies, every darkened doorway that hinted at eyes watching like hawks. The weight of everything they'd endured clung to her like an overstuffed backpack, but the bike beneath her offered a strange sort of solace—an old habit turned lifeline.

Maggie rode just to her right, calm and upright, her helmet snugly in place as though they'd just set off for a leisurely weekend ride through the park. Wren couldn't help but glance at her and feel a pang of envy—or maybe it was admiration. Maggie always seemed composed, as if chaos might swirl around her but would never touch. Wren's own appearance told another story entirely: purple hair tangled and untamed in the wind, her clothes streaked with dirt and ripped at the knee from when she'd hit the pavement earlier. She felt like a living postcard of their wild day—Wish You Weren't Here.

They didn't rush; rushing drew attention. Instead, they melted into traffic, blending with delivery riders and commuters who all had somewhere to be and no time to notice two women on battered bikes. Wren glanced down at the GPS mounted on her handlebars. The screen glowed faintly in the dusk, its unwavering arrow pointing toward their destination—a set of coordinates that felt less like a promise and more like a dare.

The city thrummed around them, indifferent to their plight, as Wren felt her senses sharpen with each mile pedaled. But today, the usual thrill of navigating traffic was replaced by raw fear—this wasn't about making deadlines anymore, but survival, with Maggie caught in the crossfire beside her. Every sound made her nerves hum like live wires: brakes creaking, cars idling too long at stop signs, pedestrians lingering on sidewalks. The city she thought she knew so intimately had warped into a web of lurking threats, but still they pressed forward through the urban jungle.

A soft beep came from the GPS—time for a turn. Without missing a beat, Wren raised two fingers off her handlebars in a quick signal to Maggie before leaning into the turn onto a side street. The main road fell away behind them as buildings rose higher along their path, throwing shadows that stretched out in jagged fingers across cracked asphalt. Ahead loomed the upper east side: polished facades gleaming faintly under streetlights like they belonged to another world entirely—one she couldn't imagine stepping into even on her best day.

She kept pedaling through the city's veins, glancing back at Maggie who scanned their surroundings with wary eyes—corners bathed in shadow, fleeting faces in headlights' glow. Something swelled in Wren's chest despite it all: pride at Maggie's complete trust, evident in every silent exchange as they moved through this unforgiving cityscape. That trust was heavy, but for once it didn't feel burdensome.

They merged into humanity's current, becoming unremarkable faces in the crowd—their best chance at survival tonight. Wren's gaze never stopped moving: parked cars that might spring to life, the dreaded flash of blue-and-red lights that could shatter their safety. A distant siren made her muscles coil like springs, but they didn't stop moving—not yet anyway—and so neither did she.

The Upper East Side loomed ahead, pristine and imposing, a stark contrast to the grimy alleys Wren maneuvered them through. The air here was thick, steeped in the sour tang of rotting produce and damp cardboard. Somewhere close by, an engine revved, low and menacing, so Wren guided them seamlessly into a throng of office workers heading out for lunch. They slipped into the flow with ease, two shadows vanishing among a sea of hurried feet and tired faces.

Wren's legs pumped steadily. The urban maze was hers to command, her instincts sharper than any map or app, though the latter tried its best to keep up. Sirens wailed faintly in the distance, an ominous soundtrack that seemed ever-present in this city. They wove past street vendors who called out half-hearted pitches to disinterested passersby and under rusting fire escapes that hunched over narrow alleys like tired sentinels. A sudden flash of headlights ahead—a police cruiser idling at the corner—forced Wren to swerve hard to the right, steering them down a passage so tight that brick walls scraped against her elbows as she pedaled through.

"Recalculating route," chirped the GPS clipped to her handlebars. Its voice was unnervingly cheerful considering their circumstances. Wren glanced at the screen: a mess of overlapping lines and dead ends. She smirked, momentarily amused by its confusion. This wasn't its game; it was hers. The city wasn't some grid you could program—it was alive, breathing, twisting when you least expected it. And Wren had learned long ago how to read its pulse.

Their hoodies blended into the hazy twilight as they joined a stream of cyclists flowing like restless veins through the city streets. Couriers zipped past with insulated bags strapped to their backs; e-bike riders wove daring paths between cars; commuters with tired shoulders simply pedaled toward home. In this chaotic tapestry of wheels and motion, Wren and Maggie disappeared entirely—just two more silhouettes lost in the endless churn of bodies and steel.

They reached Miller Park without slowing down, entering its shadowed refuge like swimmers coming up for air after too long underwater. The canopy of trees stretched high above them, their branches tangling together as if conspiring to keep out what little light remained in the sky. Here, smells shifted—from acrid exhaust fumes to damp earth laced with fresh grass—and Wren let her shoulders drop as she inhaled. It wasn't safety exactly; it never was. But it was something close enough for now.

Maggie rode quietly beside her—she always did really, rarely speaking unless necessary—and her presence grounded Wren in this ghostly green silence. Wren's eyes stayed sharp despite the brief reprieve, scanning the shadows for anything amiss: a flicker of movement where there shouldn't be one or an unfamiliar shape half-hidden among the trees.

They emerged from the park eventually; they always had to emerge again. The city doesn't stop for long—it pulls you back in whether you're ready or not—and as soon as they left Miller Park behind them, its relentless rhythm consumed them once more. Streets swarmed with people and cars alike, everyone rushing somewhere as though their lives depended on it (and maybe some of theirs did). Wren led Maggie across intersections brimming with honking horns and darting headlights, weaving between vehicles like it was second nature—which it was.

The journey uptown blurred into fragments: side streets flashing by in narrow slivers; alleys darkening around them like closing jaws; Maggie's steady presence anchoring Wren even when everything else felt unsteady. The sounds grew louder too—blaring horns and distant sirens layering over each other until they formed a chaotic symphony with traffic's unending hum as its baseline.

So they kept moving because what else could they do? And as she steered them deeper into this labyrinth of concrete and steel that she could navigate with such certainty, Wren felt something both comforting and terrifying: she wasn't running blindly anymore.

The GPS on Wren's bike chirped directions with relentless precision, its robotic voice slicing through the din of the city. Each turn felt like a step deeper into some unsolvable riddle, the kind that tightened in her chest and made anticipation and dread blur into something indistinguishable. They were getting closer now—closer to what, exactly? That part wasn't clear. Answers? More questions? Wren wasn't sure which she wanted more, but she knew she had to have more.

"Your destination is on the right," the GPS finally declared, sounding far too smug for a piece of tech. Wren slowed Argo to a stop at the curb, Maggie pulling up behind her. For a moment, neither dismounted. Instead, they sat there straddling their bikes, scanning their surroundings like visitors to some uncanny museum exhibit, one full of expensive buildings and people who didn't seem to notice—or care—that two women were frozen by the edge of the sidewalk as though they were looking at something just out of reach.

Wren swung her leg over Argo and steadied herself against the handlebars, her eyes darting up and down the bustling street where the GPS had led them. It was your standard upper east side block: high-end boutiques with mannequins wearing price tags that felt like punchlines, trendy restaurants with chalkboard menus advertising things like "artisanal fennel soup." The kind of place where people moved in confident little waves, their conversations tripping lightly over topics like stock options and weekend trips to Montauk. None of them gave so much as a glance at Wren or Maggie.

Maggie climbed off Bridger next to her. She didn't say anything at first, but her expression—the tight line of her mouth, the way she ground her jaw—did all the talking for her. Finally: "This can't be it." Her voice was low enough to get lost in the swirl of traffic noise and footsteps around them but somehow still loud enough to carry all the frustration weighing on her. "How are we supposed to find anything here?"

Wren tugged off one cycling glove and ran her hand through hair that had long since given up any semblance of neatness—a move as much about thinking as anything else. "The GPS is accurate within thirty feet," she said after a beat, though there wasn't much conviction behind it. Her gaze kept sweeping over everything—the sleek storefronts, neatly pruned planters flanking doorways like sentinels, sandwich boards propped jauntily on spotless sidewalks—as if staring hard enough might force something obvious to materialize out of thin air. "Whatever it is," she added after another pause, "it's gotta be close."

Maggie exhaled sharply through her nose—not quite a sigh, not quite throwing in the towel either—and folded her arms across her chest. "But what are we even looking for?" There was a slight crack in her voice now—not frustration this time but something softer underneath it: doubt or maybe plain exhaustion.

"A USB key," Wren said without hesitation. "At least that's my best guess." She shrugged. "It could be something else—a report or a phone—but Anne has already given us two keys…" Her words trailed off as she scanned again, head dipping like someone trying to peek behind an invisible curtain.

The thing about places like this was that nothing looked out of place because everything was curated within an inch of its life—bricks scrubbed clean enough to almost sparkle in sunlight; window displays calculated down to every last fold in fabric or prop placement; even trash cans discreetly tucked into corners that wouldn't offend anyone's aesthetic sensibilities. And yet all that perfection nagged at Wren because too-perfect places had a way of hiding things right under your nose.

"It isn't inside anywhere," she thought aloud after another long moment spent cataloging planter boxes and polished doorknobs like clues someone might've left in haste. "Anne wouldn't have put it somewhere locked up—not if she wanted it accessible after hours." The sentence hung there briefly between them before Wren mentally added: *At least I hope not.*

Maggie let out another breath but straightened her posture—if disappointment had been creeping into her shoulders earlier, determination chased it away now. She gave Wren one curt nod and said simply: "Alright." The word landed heavy as concrete being laid down—not excitement exactly but grim resolve stitched tight together.

They started moving along the sidewalk then, side-by-side but not speaking much beyond occasional murmurs or tilts of heads toward things that caught their attention: trash cans stuffed with coffee cups and newspapers; stray bits of litter snagged against building edges or sidewalk grates; cracks between bricks wide enough that anything small could've been shoved inside without kicking up suspicion from passing pedestrians who had other places to be.

Every seemingly misplaced object became something worth studying—discarded paper scraps folded oddly enough that they might contain secrets (they didn't), locks scratched just faintly enough that maybe someone had tampered with them (no evidence), shadows pooling under benches where forgotten gum resided (disappointing).

It was tedious work—methodical and quiet—and yet neither woman stopped moving because stopping meant admitting they'd come all this way only for nothingness waiting for them here among boutique shops selling dreams wrapped in tissue paper skeptically passed between wealthier hands than theirs ever would be.

Wren and Maggie worked their way down opposite sides of the sidewalk, heads low, movements quick but deliberate. Wren checked under street furniture, her fingers brushing grit and grime, while Maggie probed along walls, her eyebrows furrowed in concentration. The city's usual hum now felt oppressive, every voice a threat, every glance heavy with suspicion. Each second that ticked by brought the possibility of Dennis—or worse, Dennis's friends in blue—spying them out in the open. When they reached the end of the block with nothing to show for it, Wren set her jaw. She wasn't done.

She tilted her head toward a row of old brownstones. "Those," she whispered to Maggie, her voice tight. They didn't need more words than that.

They split up again without ceremony. Maggie headed toward the storefront windows while Wren veered left toward the weathered brick facades. Her hands skimmed along the rough mortar as though it might give up its secrets if she touched it just so. The bricks were immovable, stubborn. Time was moving too fast now; she could feel it slipping through her fingers like water.

"Ugh!" Maggie's not-so-quiet yelp cut through Wren's focus.

Wren turned in time to see Maggie pull her hand back from one window frame with a look of utter disgust. "Fresh gum," she said through gritted teeth, wiping her palm furiously on the bricks. "That's nasty."

The corner of Wren's mouth twitched upward despite herself. "Welcome to treasure hunting in a big city," she said dryly. "Nothing but sophistication and glamor."

Maggie shot her a glare but said nothing as they went back to work. Wren circled a dented metal garbage can, scanning its dark interior and running her fingers around its rim—not that she expected anything there, but you never knew. Maggie crouched by a park bench nearby, tilting her head as though the underside might hold some hidden truth.

When Wren found nothing near the garbage can, she sank to her knees beside the bench Maggie had just left behind. The rough pavement dug into her legs, sharp little bites of discomfort. She ignored it, lowering herself further until one cheek was nearly pressed against the gritty concrete. Beneath the bench was darkness and disappointment.

Still nothing.

Undeterred, Wren crawled forward on hands and knees toward something else that caught her eye—a utility box bolted firmly into the ground at the curb's edge. She stretched out flat on her stomach now, feeling every scrape and sting from the uneven sidewalk pressing against her skin.

Her fingers reached underneath blindly at first—just cold metal and empty space—but then they brushed against something smooth. Something out of place.

Her breath caught as she shifted forward just enough to get a better grip, muscles straining with effort until finally—finally—she felt what could be a small container stuck beneath the box. Heart pounding in her ears now, Wren wriggled closer still and pried at its lid with trembling hands until it gave way with an audible snap.

A tiny object spilled free—a USB drive—and bounced once before coming to rest on the sidewalk near her face.

For a moment she froze on instinct, hand hovering like this fragile thing might vanish before her eyes if she moved too quickly. Then she snatched it up and pushed herself upright all at once, triumphant despite everything—the dirt on her palms, the ache in her knees that throbbed with every beat of her pulse.

"Maggie," Wren called sharply across the sidewalk as she held up their prize for both of them to see. Her was something close to relief as she added breathlessly, "I've got it."

Wren's fingers closed around the small green USB drive, her heart pounding in her chest. She didn't pause to admire the victory, though a flicker of triumph sparked deep within. Instead, she slipped the device into her pocket before thinking better of it. Too obvious. Her hands worked quickly, tucking the drive into her sock. It pressed cool and firm against her ankle—a strange comfort given what it might mean.

Her eyes swept the area, sharp and searching. Nothing immediately jumped out, but that didn't mean they were safe. Trouble had a way of lingering just out of sight.

"Maggie," Wren hissed under her breath. Urgent but quiet. No need to draw attention. "We need to go. Now."

Maggie looked up sharply, her gaze locking with Wren's for half a second before she moved. There was no fumbling, no hesitation—just smooth, practiced motion as she reached Bridger and swung her leg over the bike frame like she'd done a thousand times before. Wren was already moving too, Argo steady beneath her as she mounted with an ease born of muscle memory.

"What the fuck?" Wren spat as she looked at the empty GPS holder on her handlebars. She hit the brakes, causing Maggie to swerve and almost hit a post.

"Wren? What?"

"While we were on our little hunt, someone stole my GPS reader." She pointed at the empty holder because nothing was proof of loss.

"Shit."

"Yeah. Shit. Let's go."

The hum of tires on pavement cut through the otherwise muffled sounds of city life—distant chatter, a dog barking somewhere, the faint grind of machinery in the background. Wren pedaled forward, pulling ahead instinctively as Maggie followed close behind. They slipped off the sidewalk and onto the street with fluid precision, weaving between pedestrians who barely registered them as more than flashes of motion.

The USB drive pressed insistently against Wren's skin with every pump of her leg—a small but unignorable reminder of what they'd taken and what it could cost them. What did it hold? Wren hoped it was answers that would end their flight. Wren pushed those thoughts aside for now; they weren't helpful here—the time for pondering would come later, assuming there *was* a later.

For now, there was only movement.

The roads became a blur of sound and color as they threaded their way into traffic—honking cars, flashing lights, angry shouts from drivers who barely noticed cyclists unless forced to stop for them. Adrenaline coursed through Wren's body like an electric current, sharp and energizing and just shy of overwhelming. As much as she hated to admit it (even to herself), part of her loved this—the speed, the danger, the razor-sharp focus that turned every movement into instinct.

They zipped past startled pedestrians and swerving cars, making split-second choices at each intersection. Alleys were gambles—shortcuts or dead ends—but sometimes risks were all they had. The city's scents washed over Wren as they gained speed: exhaust fumes, fried food, perfume, sweat, and asphalt. This was her territory, and neither fear nor danger would take that from her.

Wren's mind raced as they rode—home wasn't safe with Dennis and his fellow cops hunting them. They needed somewhere quiet to check the USB drive. For now, she just grinned fiercely and kept moving, knowing that speed was their best defense.

Wren and Maggie pedaled in silence, their legs heavy, muscles groaning after a morning that had wrung them dry. Sweat had dried into a gritty layer over their skin, the dust of the streets clinging stubbornly, like evidence of something they weren't eager to relive.

As the Cyclista offices came into view, Wren's gaze swept the area, sharp and darting. No uniforms. No squad cars. That didn't mean they weren't around. Caution was its own kind of armor, and Wren wore it as snugly as her cycling shorts.

"Stay here with Argo," she said, swinging off her bike with swift precision. Her hand lingered on the handlebars for half a second—a gesture more out of reflex than sentimentality. "I'll check it out."

Maggie nodded once, her fingers tightening possessively around Argo's handlebars. "Be careful, babe."

Wren flashed a grin that looked cockier than it felt. Anxiety coiled in her gut, but no need to let Maggie see that. Confidence was half the battle—or at least that's what she kept telling herself. She stepped off the curb and sauntered across the street with a deliberate ease that didn't quite match her pulse rate.

She found a doorway tucked into the shadows of an old brick building and leaned back against its cool surface, letting it anchor her for a moment. Her phone was already in her hand—more instinct than planning—and it looked like something straight out of a salvage yard: cracked screen, dinged-up corners, held together by what could be described as sheer willpower. Like her. She tapped Massi's number and held her breath while waiting for the glitchy thing to connect.

It rang once. Twice. Three times—the universal soundtrack of impatience.

"Pick up, you stoner," she muttered under her breath, barely resisting the urge to bang the phone against the wall like some kind of retro fix-it method.

Finally: "Yo, what's up, wild child?" Massi's voice came through sounding equal parts amused and detached—standard fare for him—but today even his easygoing drawl felt like something solid to hold on to.

"Massi," Wren said, cutting straight to business and ignoring whatever teasing comeback he'd been ready to toss at her. "You at Cyclista? You busy?"

"Yes, and for you? Never." There was a pause before he added, more seriously now: "Everything cool?"

Wren glanced back toward Cyclista's unassuming entrance—a squat building with weathered signage that somehow always managed to look both inconspicuous and suspicious at the same time. No flashing lights outside. No uniforms loitering by the door or peering through windows. Still, she'd learned long ago not to trust appearances.

"Not really," she admitted quietly, lowering her voice even though no one was close enough to overhear. "I need your eyes for a minute—can you check outside? Make sure we're not about to walk into anything we can't walk back out of?"

There was a brief silence on Massi's end before he answered with a low whistle—not annoyance exactly but something close enough to make Wren feel worse about asking this favor.

"Cops?" His tone sharpened. "Yeah, yeah—hang on."

She heard muffled sounds: footsteps on tiles maybe, or something scraping faintly against wood—a chair being pushed back? A door creaking open? The mechanics didn't matter so much as what came next: waiting. That awful period where seconds stretched too long and left too much space for stray thoughts and creeping doubts.

She drummed her fingers against the brick wall—tap-tap-tap-tap—her mind churning in time with her nerves until finally—

"All clear," Massi announced at last, his voice coming through brighter now but still tinged with an edge she wasn't used to hearing from him. "No boys in blue anywhere near here."

Relief hit fast but didn't settle in immediately; it clashed too strongly with all that pent-up tension still working its way through her veins.

"You're sure?" she asked anyway because double-checking felt safer than not.

"Positive," Massi replied firmly this time. "You're good to go."

Wren exhaled slowly; only then did she let herself smile faintly—the kind without arrogance or swagger but just enough gratitude mixed into it.

"Thanks," she said simply before adding because old habits die hard: "I owe you one."

"You owe me like fifty," Massi shot back lightly—and maybe because he could hear something unspoken in her voice—or maybe because he just knew when not to push further—all he added after that was: "Catch you later."

The line went dead before Wren had time to respond again—and maybe that was better anyway.

Shoving the phone into her pocket (the fabric there already worn thin from doing this exact motion too many times), Wren gave one last glance toward Cyclista's door from where she stood—a quick sweep of everything visible until some part deep inside confirmed what Massi had already told her: It was clear.

Jogging back across toward Maggie and Argo felt easier now—not lighter exactly but steadier if nothing else.

"We're good," Wren announced as soon as she reached them again; there must've been something triumphant lingering in how she said those words be-cause Maggie responded first by snorting softly (exasperated) then smiling softly (fond).

Wren approached Cyclista's entrance at an unhurried pace, her gaze already fixed on Massi, who lounged against the doorframe like he had all the time in the world. A thin haze of smoke curled around his head, dissolving into the air. When she got close enough, he ground the joint under the heel of his sneaker, grinning at her with that lopsided smirk that always seemed halfway between charming and troublemaking.

"Well, if it isn't our very own brand of chaos," Massi said, shoving off the wall and falling into step beside her.

Wren returned his grin, though hers was sharper at the edges. "You know me. What would life be without a little trouble?"

They exchanged a quick fist bump before she stepped past him and into the space. Instantly, she was greeted by the unmistakable scent of Cyclista: bike grease mixed with stale coffee. Thanh's hair—dyed some fiery shade that looked almost neon under the dim lighting—caught her eye before anything else. It was impossible to miss.

"Holy crap, you're actually here," Thanh blurted as they bounded over, pulling Wren into a hug that nearly lifted her off her feet. "You okay? We've been worried sick."

Wren let herself sink briefly into the hug before pulling back just enough to meet Thanh's wide-eyed gaze. That was what made Cyclista different. They didn't see what others might—a danger or a liability—but someone who would ride through fire for them if need be. Whatever lines she'd crossed out there, whatever chaos she'd left in her wake, they weren't about to turn their backs on her now.

"Takes more than a bad day to knock me out," Wren said lightly. Her voice sounded steadier than she felt as she gave Thanh's arm a reassuring squeeze.

The soft chime of the door opening made Wren glance toward it just in time to see Maggie entering with their bikes in tow. Her heart did its usual two-part reaction: a tug of relief at seeing Argo—her bike, battered but remarkably intact—and then something softer, warmer when her eyes landed on Maggie herself.

"Alright," Wren said as she slipped a hand into her sock and pulled out a small USB drive, holding it up like a prize. "Gather round. We've got work to do."

But before anyone could move, another voice sliced through the moment like broken glass scraping across concrete.

"Hubbard."

Wren froze mid-step and turned toward the sound of heavy boots striking against concrete. Willie stood just outside his office doorway, his expression carved from granite and his scowl as sharp as ever. Any hope of sliding in unnoticed—or at least unchallenged—was officially gone.

"You think you can just stroll in here after everything you've pulled?" Willie asked, each word spat out like it burned on his tongue. He took another step forward, crossing his arms over his broad chest as his glare bore down on her like storm clouds gathering before rain. "Company property isn't yours to play with anymore—not after this mess you're dragging in here."

"Willie," Wren started—but before she could say another word, Massi threw himself into the fray with reckless determination.

"Boss," he said smoothly as he placed himself between them, hands raised like a referee calling for calm in an unruly crowd. "Cut them some slack, yeah? I'm sure there's more to this than we know."

Willie's eyes narrowed until they were practically slits. "I don't give two shits about explanations," he shot back sharply. "I want them gone."

Massi held his ground despite Willie's rising anger—a rare thing for someone who usually preferred to dodge conflict when possible—and pressed forward with quiet persistence.

"We take care of our own," Massi said simply but firmly, glancing once toward Wren and Maggie before turning back to Willie. "That doesn't change just because things got... complicated."

The pause that followed felt heavier than it should have been; for a second too long no one spoke or moved except for Willie retreating back toward his office door.

"No," Willie finally growled over his shoulder before slamming it shut hard enough to make several tools hanging nearby rattle ominously against the walls.

Wren let out a breath she hadn't realized she'd been holding and turned slowly back toward Massi only to find him watching her already—something quiet but understanding passing across his face without either of them needing to say much aloud.

She reached up and clapped him once on the shoulder—a gesture brief but full of gratitude—and gave him a small nod before turning back toward Maggie who waited patiently nearby with their bikes still propped neatly by her side.

"Alright," Wren said, her fingers brushing the edges of the USB drive like it might reveal its secrets if coaxed gently enough. "Let's see what kind of mess this little beauty's been keeping quiet."

Thanh shifted, their eyes darting back toward Willie's closed door as though it might swing open and swallow them whole. "You'd better hurry," they hissed, their multi-colored hair spiking in a way that mirrored their anxiety. "Captain Killjoy could make a call and start snitching any second."

Wren didn't bother glancing at the door. Instead, her gaze swept the room until it landed on Zak, who was leaning—no, draped—against the counter like he'd been sculpted there, coffee mug in hand. Casual as ever. Too casual, really. The way his eyes kept flicking toward the drive betrayed him.

"What's wrong, Zak?" Wren asked, her voice honey-smooth but laced with a sharp edge. "Forgot how to look inconspicuous when you're eavesdropping?"

Zak froze for half a second before taking an exaggerated sip from his mug. His cheeks reddened faintly beneath his practiced calm. "Just enjoying the theatrics," he said, feigning a lazy drawl that almost worked.

Massi cleared his throat loudly enough to cut through the moment and dragged Wren's attention back to him. "Look," he began, scratching the back of his neck like he hated where this was going but couldn't stop himself. "I'm just saying... maybe we're overcomplicating things? Why not just go to the cops? If you've got nothing to hide—"

Thanh nodded so quickly it was a wonder their head didn't snap off. "Yeah, wouldn't that just clear everything up?"

Wren laughed—a sharp sound devoid of humor or warmth. It startled in its bitterness. She shook her head slowly, dark hair catching just enough light to gleam like oil on water. "Oh, you sweet summer children," she said softly, mock affection curling around every word.

Massi frowned. "What are you talking about?"

Wren didn't answer right away. Instead, she leaned against the edge of the table and crossed her arms over her chest as though trying to hold herself together. When she finally spoke again, her voice had turned low and deliberate, each word cutting like glass through silence. "Tattooed queer bike courier with a record? Trust me—one look at me and they'll decide I'm guilty before I even step into their precinct."

"Wait." Massi looked confused now—confused but also wary. "A record?"

"Nothing big," Wren replied with forced nonchalance as she ran a hand through her hair like she was trying to smooth out thoughts instead of tangles. "Moving violations mostly... stupid shit like that." Her laugh came out quieter this time but no less bitter: "Not exactly parking tickets—not that it matters when they want me for murder."

The words lingered in the air too long after she said them.

Maggie stepped closer then—not hurriedly but deliberately—and rested a hand on Wren's arm like an anchor holding something steady against rough seas. Her voice was gentle but firm when she spoke: "Anne had a plan."

Wren looked down at Maggie's hand for half a beat before turning her attention back to the USB drive.

"She left USBs all over the city," Maggie said. "It seems—".

"Wait!" Thanh broke in suddenly anyway because apparently waiting wasn't their strong suit today—or any day probably—with excitement sparking in their wide eyes now instead of nerves from earlier. "That sounds just like geocaching!"

Massi blinked at them blankly while Zak raised one eyebrow without bothering to ask outright what that meant.

"Geocaching!" Thanh exclaimed again as though saying it louder would make everyone instantly understand (it didn't). They were practically bouncing now—actually bouncing—and speaking faster than anyone should after so much caffeine: "It's this real-world treasure hunt thing where people leave clues leading from one place to another until eventually—"

"They explode. We get it," Massi cut them off gently but firmly enough while holding both palms up briefly mid-air defensively before adding: "...kind of..."

Maggie nodded herself while redirecting conversation tactfully back into focus without breaking stride. "That's what we're thinking. Anne must have known something was coming. This was her insurance policy."

Massi exhaled sharply, dragging a hand through his perpetually messy hair. "Holy crap. So, what's on that drive you've got?"

Wren's grip on the small device tightened, her knuckles whitening as she turned it over in her hand. "If we're lucky? The last piece of the puzzle."

Her legs carried her toward the kitchenette almost on autopilot, each step a reminder of the day—a tangle of adrenaline and exhaustion simmering in her muscles. Cyclista felt like the only place left where she wasn't hunted—just bikes, friends, and the quiet, unspoken rule that everyone looked out for their own.

She reached for two chipped mugs, filling them with what passed for coffee here—thick, bitter sludge that smelled more burned than brewed. Maggie joined her quietly, plucking a pair of bruised apples from a bowl haphazardly shoved against the back wall.

"Breakfast of champions," Wren muttered, passing a mug to Maggie before draining half of hers in one go. Her lips twisted at the taste—more ash than caffeine—but at least it was hot.

The break room was hardly an oasis: a cramped space posing as functional, its mismatched chairs and sagging couch thrown together like an afterthought. Faded motivational posters hung limp on the walls—"TEAMWORK" adorned with a stock photo of rowers cutting through glassy water that bore no resemblance to this place or these people. Wren slid onto the couch and immediately regretted it when a spring jabbed into her spine. She shifted but resigned herself to discomfort, Maggie settling next to her close enough for their thighs to brush.

Massi clattered into an office chair missing one wheel, Thanh folded themself onto the floor and Zak loitered by the doorframe like he wasn't sure if he belonged or if he wanted out. He crossed his arms but leaned forward—the stance of someone pretending not to care too much.

"Alright," Massi said, his voice low and curious as his elbows planted on his knees. "Spill it. What's the deal with this USB?"

"Gimme your laptop," she said, wiggling her fingers impatiently. Massi reached out, snagged it, and swung back.

"Yes, my queen."

"Peon," Wren laughed because she needed to laugh. She retrieved the green USB and plugged it in.

"What's that?" Zak asked from so far back Wren could safely ignore him. With a few clicks, Wren had an answer.

"Ahh! Fuck me. More GPS coordinates," Wren snapped as she smacked the screen.

Massi snatched his laptop and petted it to calm it down after the slap.

"I'm sorry. Let me have it back. Easiest to check the location right now, while I have a connection," Wren said as she again wiggled her fingers like a queen.

Massi side-eyed her as he handed it back. "What about that GPS system I gave you?"

"Well first of all, it doesn't read USB keys," Wren said defensively. She leaned in low and added, "It was stolen right off my bike."

Wren took another swig of coffee—not because it helped but because it gave her a reason to pause—and then grimaced at the aftertaste clinging bitterly to her tongue. "I need a laptop to take with me," she said finally, placing the mug down with deliberate slowness. "This whole thing's been one long disaster for a couple of USB keys."

"It's the third USB," Maggie cut in softly.

Wren frowned, half-turning toward Maggie with narrowed eyes. "You sure? It feels like we've seen more than that. I can't keep anything straight anymore."

"I'm sure," Maggie said gently but firmly, her gaze meeting Wren's without wavering. "It's the third, babe. I've been keeping track."

Wren hesitated—then sighed and rubbed at her temples like even hearing that number was enough to exhaust her further. "Three USBs," she muttered under her breath. "Three clues." A pause, then a smirk tugged at one corner of her lips despite herself: "Three royal pains in my ass."

Zak shifted against the doorframe then pushed off entirely, taking three unhurried steps closer before stopping just within reach of the sagging couch's armrest. His eyes gleamed faintly as though he'd caught sight of something shiny in murky water—a steady glint of interest he wasn't bothering to hide.

"Let me see it," he said casually enough that Wren didn't buy it for a second.

She let out something between a laugh and a snort but didn't look away from him. "Yeah... right," she said slowly, drawing out each syllable as if explaining something self-evident to someone particularly dense. "And while we're at it, I'll toss in my bank PIN and bike lock combo too."

Zak shrugged but didn't back down; instead, he offered up what passed for charm—a half-smile coupled with raised eyebrows meant to suggest innocence despite his obvious curiosity. "I'm serious! Maybe I can help."

Her gaze sharpened on him now—not hostile exactly but far from friendly—and they stayed locked there for several beats longer than anyone else in the room seemed comfortable with.

Then Zak broke first, pulling a sleek laptop from his overstuffed messenger bag, her gaze sharpening. His movements were deliberate, almost rehearsed, and the too-bright smile plastered on his face made her stomach tighten.

"I've got my computer right here," he said, his voice teetering on the edge of forced enthusiasm. "You can borrow it. BORROW."

There it was. Too eager, too ready. Wren didn't take the bait. She leaned back in her chair, crossing her arms in front of her chest as if to barricade herself from whatever scheme Zak might be cooking up this time. Her mind drifted—unwillingly—to the alleycat race two months ago, to the image of Zak cutting her off at the last turn, forcing her to swerve hard into the curb, nearly throwing her from her bike. He hadn't even looked back. She'd scraped her knee raw and cursed him all the way across the finish line. That memory sat between them now, like a live wire humming with tension.

"That's awful generous of you," Wren said finally, her tone flat but laced with an edge. "Didn't realize you were feeling so charitable these days."

Zak's grin faltered for just a moment before bouncing back into place like elastic stretched too tight. "Come on, Hubbard. We're all in this together now. I'm just trying to help."

Sure he was.

Maggie's hand brushed lightly against Wren's arm—a quiet plea for restraint—but Wren wasn't quite ready to let it go. There was something about Zak's sudden cooperative streak that didn't sit right with her, like finding a gear out of alignment and knowing it would slip sooner or later.

"What's your angle?" Wren asked, leaning forward now, her voice low and steady. "Don't tell me you've gone all Team Wren all of a sudden."

Zak chuckled nervously and gave a shrug that might have seemed casual to anyone else in the room—but not to Wren, not today. "No angle," he said, holding up his hands as though declaring innocence. "This is serious. You need something and I can help."

"I'll bet," she shot back, raising an eyebrow but keeping her tone cool enough to mask the irritation building beneath it. "Kind of like how it was real 'serious' when you used me as a buffer during one last turn near the dumpster?"

Zak opened his mouth to respond—and closed it again just as quickly. His cheeks glowed red with frustration or embarrassment or both; Wren couldn't decide which.

"That was different," he managed finally, fumbling through his words like they were slippery rocks underfoot. "Okay? This isn't some petty competition." He gestured toward the USB on the table between them like it was some sacred artifact he'd sworn to protect.

"Stop the bullshit. What's on this USB?" Thanh suddenly blurted out in an uncharacteristic huff.

Wren took control of Massi's laptop again and opened the file on the green USB, then let out a low moan.

"More GPS coordinates," Wren spat as she copied them into the laptop's memory because at this point she trusted its memory much more than her own.

She pasted the numbers into a browser and ended up with... "Render Park, Maggie. We go to Render Park." Only after Wren had said it out loud did she wonder if it was a good idea. In her own defense, she closed the web browser, yanked the USB key out of the port and cleared the keyboard memory. Almost useless, but it looked serious.

"I guess we're going?" Maggie asked, shoulder slumping forward just a little, just enough that Wren noticed.

Wren pressed a kiss to Maggie's temple, her heart aching for her girlfriend's pain. But she couldn't blame her: a murder accusation was a murder accusation.

"Listen to me," Wren said, turning Maggie to face her. "You are not evil. You are kind, and brave, and so fucking strong." Wren pulled Maggie closer, her arm tightening protectively around her girlfriend's shoulders.

"Hey," Wren said softly, nudging Maggie gently. "We should get going. Still got a lot of ground to cover."

Maggie nodded, wiping her eyes with the back of her hand. "Yeah, you're right. They won't catch us if we just keep moving and find...whatever is at Render Park."

They stood up, stretching out the kinks from sitting on the lumpy couch. Wren turned to Massi and Thanh, her heart swelling with gratitude for their unwavering support.

"Come here, you big lug," Wren said, pulling Massi into a bear hug. He returned the embrace, nearly lifting her off her feet. "Stay safe out there, alright?" Massi's voice was muffled against Wren's shoulder.

She gave a quick nod, squeezing him tightly before pulling back. Thanh stepped in next, their brilliantly dyed hair brushing against her cheek as they hugged. It smelled faintly of some fruity shampoo—mango, or maybe papaya.

"You guys are the best," Wren said, her throat thick with emotion she tried to swallow down. "Seriously."

Thanh gave her one last squeeze before stepping back. Maggie was next, her arms wrapped around both of them in turn, her eyes still puffy but her smile genuine enough to offset it. "Thank you," Maggie murmured, the words so soft they almost disappeared under everything unsaid. "For everything."

Wren glanced over her shoulder as she grabbed her bag from the floor and caught sight of Zak lurking in a corner like some kind of brooding gargoyle. His earlier enthusiasm had curdled visibly, twisting into something petulant and sour. He glared at her like she'd stolen his last energy bar—or maybe his soul.

"Don't screw up my laptop," he snapped as she slid it carefully into her courier bag.

Wren arched a brow and shot him a look that landed somewhere between annoyed older sister and low-key amused. "Relax, Zak," she said, zipping the bag shut with exaggerated care. "I'll treat it better than you treat your bike."

If looks could kill, Zak might have committed several felonies on the spot. But Wren didn't stick around to find out—she just waved one last time at Massi and Thanh and followed Maggie outside before the air in Cyclista got any more toxic than it already was.

Their bikes were right where they'd left them. Wren's hand found the familiar curve of the handlebars, and for a moment, she just stood there, letting their solid weight press into her palms like an anchor after the chaos of goodbyes inside. She swung herself onto the seat, clicking her shoes into place as Maggie did the same beside her.

They pushed off together, pedaling until they hit their stride and pulled out into traffic. The wind threaded through Wren's hair like curious fingers as they merged into the cacophony of honking horns and whirring engines that made up the city's daily symphony. She glanced sideways at Maggie—always Maggie—and felt a rush of relief when she saw some of that tension fading from her girlfriend's shoulders.

"You holding up?" Wren called over the roar of passing cars.

Maggie turned toward her, a smile tugging at the edges of her lips—not a big one, but enough to make Wren's chest ache in that stupid way love tends to do when it catches you off guard. "Yeah," Maggie said, just loud enough to be heard above it all. "I think so. Let's just focus on what's next."

That was Maggie: steady even when everything else felt like it might shatter at any second.

Wren grinned back at her because how could she not? Her heart swelled with something warm and fierce—love mixed with an almost reckless pride—and she leaned into the familiar rhythm as they wove their way through streets filled with potholes and possibilities alike. They picked up speed together, two blurs moving as one through a city that never stopped moving too.

W ren's legs churned at a relentless cadence, the blacktop beneath her tires blurring as she and Maggie ducked and weaved through the labyrinthine streets of the city. It was one of those days when the sun seemed too eager, pouring down in bold strokes, creating sharp contrasts where shadows crouched low against crumbling walls. Around them, the city moved as it always did—rushed, indifferent—utterly uninterested in the small, frantic drama unfolding within this little pocket of urgency.

The noise was everywhere. The honk of impatient car horns layered over the holler of street vendors hawking their wares, each sound colliding and overlapping until it became the kind of dissonant melody that felt uniquely urban. Neon signs, garish even in their half-hearted daytime flicker, hung above grimy brick facades painted with decades-old graffiti. The glow didn't soften the edges but instead made everything look more surreal, as though someone had thrown a filter over a photograph that didn't need one.

The smells were just as chaotic—hot dogs from a corner cart mixing with the savory tang of falafel being fried somewhere close by. It would've been mouthwatering if not for the bitter undertone of exhaust fumes and something else indefinable yet unmistakable: city decay masked under layers of yesterday's garbage. Wren took it all in anyway, because there wasn't much choice when you lived in a place like this—it just came with the territory.

She glanced sideways at Maggie, her chest tightening in a way that had nothing to do with exertion. On any other day—and maybe even on this one—Maggie's face would've been enough to make Wren pause mid-step or pedal, just to take her in. The sun caught Maggie's hair just right now, turning it into something impossibly luminous—a moment that felt stolen from an artist's sketchpad. For just a second too long, Wren stared at her and thought about how Maggie managed to look completely composed despite everything. She kept moving forward, though; stopping wasn't an option. They didn't have time to process hurt feelings or broken messages from careless parents who should've known better.

They slid between cars like water fitting around stones, their tires humming over cracked asphalt riddled with dips and gouges—the kind that told stories if you cared to notice them. The burn started to creep into her thighs now—not unbearable but enough to remind her she wasn't made of steel even if she sometimes liked to pretend otherwise. Her muscles screamed for rest; she ignored them.

"Left on 34th?" she called out over the din without slowing.

Maggie nodded without hesitation, raising her voice just enough to carry above the roar. "Yeah! There's less traffic near the park!"

Traffic lights painted red halts across intersections like warnings they barely obeyed most times—but this time they slowed just enough not to tempt fate entirely. Balancing precariously on their pedals while waiting for green seemed almost absurd given their urgency, but what else could they do? Around them, life didn't stop or even slow down for fugitives tangled up in more than they could untangle themselves from alone.

The light changed before long—not soon enough—and they were off again. Wren leaned into every turn with precision borne equally of muscle memory and desperation, dodging every pothole like an old habit she'd never quite unlearned. Her bike hummed beneath her—a familiar companion on countless journeys that hadn't mattered quite like this one did now—and she swore sometimes she could feel it propelling her forward even when physics said otherwise.

For a fleeting moment—just long enough to inhale sharply through gritted teeth—she let herself believe they might make it out of this mess intact. Then reality crept back in quietly but insistently: They weren't couriers making routine deliveries; they weren't racing for medals or glory or anything resembling victory either.

They were running.

And there was no telling where—or when—it all might stop.

The graffiti-covered walls blurred by, a chaotic mosaic of rebellion and forgotten stories. Wren's gaze flitted from one tag to the next, each splash of color shouting for attention. A wolf, its maw open in a frozen snarl, seemed to howl against invisible chains. Further along, a butterfly, delicate yet defiant, stretched its wings as though daring the city to hold it back. The marks felt alive somehow—protests etched in vibrant hues against the gray monotony of brick and mortar.

They sped past a group loitering outside a diner clinging to life on this sun-warmed corner of the city. Cigarette smoke twisted upward like ghostly vines reaching toward some unseen promise. Their faces—fresh with youth but weathered by something far older—caught the strong light of mid-afternoon. It wasn't hard to guess what weighed them down. Fragments of their conversation slipped into Wren's ears as she passed.

"Layoffs again—"

"Rent's going up—"

"They're slashing programs at—"

Life seemed complex until it included death. The words dissolved into background noise, a rising tide of discontent that felt all too familiar. Wren clenched her jaw and pumped harder against the pedals. Her legs burned deliciously with each stroke—a fire that dulled the smoldering frustration rooted deep in her chest.

A horn blared close behind her, sharp and accusing. Without breaking stride or turning her head, she raised her hand and extended her middle finger skyward—a silent declaration that brought a quick grin to her lips. The rush was intoxicating: wind whipping her face, asphalt flying beneath her tires, adrenaline flooding her veins in waves that drowned out softer emotions like fear or doubt.

Maggie trailed just behind, her voice reaching through the hum of traffic. "Wren! Slow down a second!"

"Can't," Wren called back without looking. "We won't make it if we—"

Her words were cut short by the screech of brakes and shouts scattering in all directions as she swerved hard to avoid a pedestrian who had stepped blindly into the street. She wobbled for half a heartbeat before righting herself, body tense but unshaken.

The city buzzed around them, alive with its usual chaos: cars honking in agitation, engines growling impatiently at red lights that dared to hold them still. Each passing face seemed to carry an edge of suspicion or menace—or maybe that was just her own hyperawareness feeding illusions into the blur around her. Sirens wailed faintly somewhere ahead or behind; she couldn't be sure which direction anymore.

Wren glanced briefly at Maggie before refocusing on their path. Render Park was somewhere just ahead. It would provide shelter, food, water, anonymity and, most importantly, a skater park that offered free Wi-Fi.

A taxi swerved dangerously close from the right, its driver leaning on the horn as though scolding them for existing. Wren jerked left instinctively and snapped over her shoulder, "Watch it!" The driver either didn't hear or didn't care; his murmurs were swallowed whole by the cacophony around them.

For seconds—or maybe minutes—the world seemed wound too tightly, every detail standing out in sharp relief while simultaneously threatening to collapse inward under its own tension. Wren shook it off and kept pushing forward, letting the rhythm of motion take over where thought faltered. Each storefront they passed blurred into insignificance as Render Park loomed closer in her mind's eye, promising answers—or maybe just more questions.

"Almost there," she muttered under her breath—but whether it was meant for Maggie or herself didn't matter much now.

The entrance of the park rose ahead, a splash of green defiance against the gray monotony of the city. Wren's thighs ached with every turn of the pedals, her breath coming in uneven bursts, but she didn't slow. Maggie was just behind her—close enough that Wren could feel her presence without even looking back. It was strange how that worked sometimes, how the nearness of someone you trust could quiet a storm inside your head.

The park grew closer, and Wren had to remind herself to breathe. Everything felt magnified: the sharp bark of a dog chasing after a ball; the overlapping hum of voices from picnickers lounging on blankets; even the dry crackle of leaves skittering across the pavement reached her ears as though amplified. Her eyes darted from one corner to another, scanning for any anomaly, any clue Anne might have left behind. She didn't know exactly what she was looking for yet, but she'd know it when she saw it—or so she told herself.

At the park's edge, Wren swung herself off her bike. The sudden stillness hit her harder than expected—it was like stepping off a treadmill and realizing your legs were still trying to run. Her knees wobbled as she fought for balance, and for a second, she just stood there, gripping the handlebars tightly as if letting go might cause her to topple over. The weight of why they were here bore down on her chest again, heavier than before.

"All right," she said finally, glancing back at Maggie. Her voice came out steadier than she felt. "Let's do this."

Wren turned toward Render Park and let herself take it in. The mid-afternoon sunlight was working its magic across the landscape, breaking through the canopy of trees in dapples that shifted with every breeze. Shadows stretched long and thin across lush grass where children zigzagged between benches and picnic blankets like fireflies too fast to catch. Their laughter carried over everything else—a sound both piercing and warm at once.

Nearer to the playground, college students sprawled out lazily on a patchwork of ramps, rails and ledges that looked like they'd been thrown together by some stoner. A skater arced through the air before veering too wide and landing flat on his back. Groans and hoots all around. An older couple sat nearby on a splintering wooden bench—he scattering breadcrumbs while pigeons descended like royalty expecting an audience; she staring off into some distant middle space where memories lived.

The whole place smelled alive in a way Wren wasn't used to: grass trimmed too short but still damp with dew, flowers defiantly blooming despite being boxed in by traffic fumes and skyscrapers. She thought maybe fall was trying to make its presence known early; every now and then, one or two leaves would drift lazily downward before skimming across the ground like tiny skaters carried by an invisible current.

"Hopeless," Maggie said abruptly beside her. "We'll never find anything here." The words were soft but sharp at the edges—more frustration than despair—and they sliced cleanly through Wren's thoughts.

She turned toward Maggie then, noticing for what felt like the first time how much tension was etched into her face: lips pressed tight together, brows drawn low in concentration or doubt or both. Without thinking about it first—or maybe thinking about it too much—Wren reached out and laced their fingers together. It wasn't much, but it was enough.

"Not hopeless," Wren said softly but firmly. "Just... complicated." She gave Maggie's hand a small squeeze before letting go and retrieving Zak's laptop. It was still on and had connected to the internet quickly thanks to their proximity to the skate park.

Wren slipped the green USB into the port and checked the coordinates again. *Perfect.*

"GPS says we are within thirty feet." She paused for half a beat before adding with forced cheerfulness: "We've definitely done worse."

Maggie didn't smile exactly—it was more like something halfway there—but whatever answer lingered on her lips dissolved before it could form fully into words. Wren took that as permission to move forward.

Wren tucked the USB back into its snug little sock home and slid the laptop into her bag. Her heart pounded—a wild, almost painful rhythm—but she kept her face neutral, her movements casual. Just two friends out for a leisurely ride through the park. That's all anyone would see. That's all they needed to see.

The park's center came into view, and with it, its centerpiece. The fountain gurgled happily, spraying sunlight into shimmering droplets that hung in the air like tiny crystals. Three benches curved around it in a neat semicircle, their worn wood etched with the invisible graffiti of years and visitors passed—lovers' initials, restless hands, idle scratches. Nearby stood a metal tulip sculpture, shiny enough to serve as a funhouse mirror, bending and distorting the world in strange ways.

Wren's gaze flicked to the first bench. She gave Maggie a slight nudge with her elbow, tilting her head just enough to indicate where they were headed. Slowly, deliberately, they made their way over. No sudden moves. No obvious glances over shoulders. Just two friends out enjoying an afternoon at the park.

Wren leaned her bike against the bench. The frame let out a faint metallic clank as it met the worn wood. She glanced at Maggie again—just a brief exchange—and Maggie nodded before shifting her attention to scanning the surroundings. The park was alive with its usual buzz—kids squealing on swings, joggers thudding along dirt paths—but no uniforms disrupted the scene. Not yet.

Time to work.

Wren sucked in a breath and let her hand drift to the underside of the first bench. Her fingers moved deliberately over its rough surface, feeling for any bumps or ridges that didn't belong—hidden compartments or packages taped out of sight. Nothing. She moved to the second bench and repeated the process, then on to the third with growing urgency. Each fruitless search added another weighty layer of frustration pressing against her ribs.

"Anything?" Maggie called quietly from nearby, her eyes darting in every direction like she expected trouble to spring out of nowhere.

Wren shook her head sharply but didn't bother looking up. "Nada." She pushed back from the last bench and gestured toward the tulip sculpture without much hope. "Try that thing."

Maggie moved toward the tulip sculpture while Wren stayed rooted in place for a moment longer, letting her pulse settle—or trying to anyway. Maggie traced her hands along one of the tulip's metallic petals, her fingers gliding across its cold surface like she might coax it into revealing some hidden secret by touch alone. Twice she circled it—methodical and steady—checking every crease and fold of its design.

Twice she came up empty.

"Shit," Wren hissed under her breath as she straightened up and ran a hand through her hair in exasperation.

Her eyes wandered almost unwillingly back to the fountain at the center of the park—a proud bronze figure stood tall among cascading water jets, forever immortalized as some long-forgotten town mayor no one alive could likely name without help from Google or one of those plaques history buffs love. The sunlight played off his polished surface in arrogant flashes of gold and copper brilliance—the kind of glow that seemed to say: Look closer... if you dare.

Wren caught Maggie's eye, and in that fleeting glance, a silent exchange took place. Maggie raised an eyebrow, questioning, cautious. Wren shrugged, the universal gesture for "I've got this" or "Maybe I don't." It was hard to tell which.

The two moved toward the fountain with a mix of trepidation and resolve, as though daring the water itself to give up its secrets. Wren tilted her head, her voice just above the whisper of the splashing water. "Reckon there's something hidden in there? A baggie maybe? Or... I don't know."

Maggie didn't answer right away. Her eyes swept the water's surface like search-lights cutting through fog. The sunlight fractured on the ripples, sending dazzling flashes into their eyes. "Could be," she murmured finally.

Their steps slowed as they neared the edge of the pool. The fountain gurgled in cheerful defiance of their growing frustration. Wren circled it once—then twice—her gaze bouncing between the pool of water and the imposing bronze statue at its center. Maggie stayed put, rooted to the spot, but her eyes tracked Wren's movements like a nervous sentry.

"Anything?" Maggie asked, her voice barely carrying over the fountain's splash.

Wren didn't answer. Instead, she stopped mid-step, her brow furrowing as her eyes locked onto something.

"Wait." Wren's voice was different now—lower, focused. Her gaze sharpened on the statue's extended hand as recognition sparked somewhere in her mind. "Mags... I think it's not in the water at all."

Maggie followed Wren's line of sight until her own gaze landed on that same outstretched hand. Her expression shifted from confusion to alarm faster than Wren would have thought possible. A bit of green tape wrapped around one finger on that outstretched hand.

"You're not actually thinking about climbing that thing," Maggie said—not as a question but as a futile attempt to inject some sense into what was clearly already decided.

Wren turned toward Maggie with a grin that could be described as audacious. Mischief danced in her eyes, and she cocked one eyebrow like a dare personified. "When do I ever *not* climb things?"

Before Maggie could utter another protest or elaborate on why this was defi-nitely not one of Wren's better ideas, Wren was already stepping out of her cycling shoes and peeling off her socks. She handed Maggie the USBs they'd been carrying without ceremony, as if passing off something inconsequential instead of artifacts they'd gone through hell to find. Her bag settled onto Maggie's shoulder, and she stepped in.

The fountain's cool water lapped over Wren's toes as she stepped into it with-out hesitation—not because she didn't feel the chill (she did), but because letting herself hesitate wasn't part of her plan right now. A full-body shiver ran up her spine anyway when she waded deeper into the shallow pool.

"Wren..." Maggie hissed behind her, panic edging into her voice now as she glanced around at passing strangers stopping to stare at this sudden spectacle of footwear abandonment and fountain climbing plans-in-progress.

"Let 'em look," Wren shot back over her shoulder without even glancing around to confirm whether anyone *was* looking (they were). She reached for the statue with both hands like someone reaching for an old friend—or maybe an old nemesis—and added, "Keep watch down there, yeah?"

The bronze wasn't exactly welcoming under Wren's grip: slippery from decades of exposure to rain and city grime that no amount of maintenance had managed to completely erase. Still, this wasn't exactly uncharted territory for someone who spent years hanging onto her handlebars for dear life.

She found footing where others might have seen nothing more than decorative folds in metal: here in the exaggerated drape of a coat hem; there near an overly detailed boot buckle that made climbing strangely personal—as if she'd been studying this mayor longer than any history teacher ever had.

Her muscles burned almost immediately—not surprising given how little upper-body strength cycling actually required compared to hauling oneself up slippery bronze statues—but none of that mattered now. Above all else, determination drove each movement upward: handhold to foothold to whatever precarious bend or latch point she could use to inch closer to that outstretched hand and its little green ring of tape.

Somewhere below—a world away—it occurred to Wren briefly that Maggie must be pacing anxiously or wringing her hands or pleading silently for this ridiculousness to end already before someone came along who actually cared enough about civic statutes (or statues) to call them out for this obvious infraction against public decorum.

And yes—there were murmurs from those watching: quiet whispers punctuated by stifled laughter or camera shutters clicking discreetly from passersby who couldn't resist documenting what might turn out to be either heroics or humiliation—all depending on how this ended.

But none of it touched Wren—not really—because all she could focus on was getting closer and closer: the hand.

Finally, Wren hauled herself level with the statue's outstretched arm. Her breath came in short gasps, heart pounding a frantic rhythm against her ribs. And there, nestled in the upturned palm, was a small plastic baggie taped securely to his finger. Inside, a flash of red caught her eye.

"Bingo," Wren whispered, a grin spreading across her face.

With trembling fingers, she peeled the tape away and snatched the baggie. The red USB key inside felt like a lifeline, a tangible connection to Anne and the truth they sought.

Triumph surged through Wren's veins as she clutched her prize. She looked down at Maggie, ready to share in their victory—someone somewhere was already cheering them. But the excitement died in her throat as she caught sight of her girlfriend's face. Maggie's eyes were wide with fear, her gaze fixed on something beyond the fountain, her feet scuffling as her body tried desperately to run and her heart tried desperately to stay.

Wren's heart sank. She knew, even before she turned to look, that their moment of triumph had been painfully short-lived. Wren's heart leaped into her throat as she followed Maggie's eyes and spotted a familiar figure sprinting across the park. Dennis, his face contorted with rage, was closing the distance fast. His yells were not cheers at all.

"Shit! Maggie, we gotta move!" Wren yelled, her voice cracking with urgency.

In her haste to descend, Wren's foot slipped on the slick bronze. She tumbled backward, arms flailing wildly as she plummeted into the fountain pool. The shock of cold water hit her like a punch to the gut, knocking the wind from her lungs.

As she floundered in the shallow water, Wren felt the baggie slip from her grasp, carried by the fountain's gentle current.

"No!" she gasped, lunging for the precious package.

Her fingers brushed against the plastic, but it danced just out of reach. Wren scrambled, splashing water in all directions, her clothes now completely soaked and clinging to her body.

"Wren!" Maggie's panicked voice cut through the chaos. "He's almost here!"

Wren's eyes darted between the elusive baggie and Dennis's approaching form. She had seconds to make a choice—grab the USB or run. It felt like a thunderclap in her chest.

2:42 p.m.

Wren's fingers closed around the baggie, the plastic slippery and cold against her skin. Triumph coursed through her, sharp and hot, as she yanked it from the water and pulled it close to her chest. It wasn't much to look at—a cheap little sandwich bag—but right now it might as well have been a treasure chest sunk to the depths of some mythical sea.

"Got it!" she shouted, her voice rough from exertion, but the sound was swallowed by the roar of her own heartbeat.

Then Maggie screamed, and just like that, the moment splintered.

Wren turned to see Dennis charging closer, his face contorted into something monstrous—eyes wild, jaw clenched, a bull mid-charge. There was no reasoning in that face, no sign of humanity or hesitation. Just fury. Wren's stomach twisted.

"Shit."

She scrambled to her feet, water dripping from her clothes in quick rivulets that clung for a moment before splashing down into the fountain. Her shoes squelched as she wavered on unsteady legs, limbs numb from adrenaline. Maggie was there in an instant, grabbing Wren's arm and pulling her upright.

"Move!" Maggie barked.

They stumbled out of the fountain together, slipping on the wet stone before finding their footing. The bikes were where they'd left them by the park bench—an eternity ago, it seemed—and getting there felt like trying to run through molasses.

Dennis was gaining on them. She could hear him—the crash of his footsteps pounding against the pavement and his jagged breaths cutting through the air like knives. He didn't yell anymore. He didn't have to.

The moment they reached their bikes Wren didn't think—she just acted. She threw one leg over the frame and pushed off with shaky force until the momentum carried her forward. Maggie was just behind her.

"Go!" Wren shouted over her shoulder.

The pedals spun wildly beneath her feet as she pushed harder, harder still, each rotation bringing with it a little more speed but not nearly enough distance. The park blurred around them now—the orderly rows of trees became streaks of green; statues that had stood still for decades melted into gray smudges in her periphery.

Dennis's voice started to fade behind them as they hit the edge of the park and tore onto the street—a cacophony of blaring horns and screeching tires erupting immediately around them. Wren barely noticed. She narrowly avoided a taxi that swerved too close but didn't even flinch when its driver leaned hard on his horn.

Her lungs burned with every breath, each inhale more ragged than the last. Maggie was still beside her—still pedaling—but neither dared say a word beyond grunts of exertion. The city opened up before them like a living labyrinth: crossings to weave through, sidewalks teeming with spectators who leaped aside with curses as they sped past.

Don't look back.

That thought was all she allowed herself to grasp onto as she leaned forward over the handlebars, willing herself faster even when her legs felt like rubber bands stretched too thin.

Faster. Gotta go faster.

What did he think he'd do if he caught us? Drag me to jail? God. What an idiot—to think he could catch us while we're on bikes? But still—how did he find us? This goddamn city—it always felt alive somehow, breathing down your neck when you least expected it... claws ready to snag you if you so much as hesitated.

No hesitation now though. Focus forward—always forward.

It wasn't until she saw him—a man stepping into their path—that everything came crashing into sharp relief again.

He was ahead of them by a few yards—close enough for Wren to make out his face but far enough that he looked oddly serene against all this chaos around them: arms spread wide like someone welcoming disaster with open hands.

There was no time for anything else—not for second guesses or apologies or veering sideways into traffic that wouldn't stop even if it wanted too badly enough—and certainly not for mercy.

"Move, damn it!" Wren's voice cut through the city noise, sharp as a blade. The man didn't budge.

Her lips curled into something that wasn't quite a smile, more a mix of defiance and inevitability. The crash came hard and fast. Her bike collided with the self-righteous bystander, and he crumpled onto the pavement in a graceless heap—arms and legs splayed out like some broken marionette.

Wren regained her balance and glanced over her shoulder, not out of concern but with a fleeting smirk of superiority. "Idiot," she muttered, the word flat and dismissive, as though he were nothing more than an inconvenient pebble on her path.

She kept scanning until she spotted Maggie weaving around the fallen figure, ducking past him without so much as a wobble. Relief flickered through her—not overly sentimental, just enough to note Maggie was still on her wheels. Good.

Wren faced forward again, leaning into her pedals, willing herself faster. Her legs burned—a fire she was long accustomed to—and the wind tore at her hair as if trying to pull her backward. Around her, the city dissolved into vague shapes and flickering lights: traffic signals, neon signs, glass buildings reflecting the morning sun like shards of broken mirrors. Velocity was everything. It wasn't reckless speed; it was balance, an intricate dance between momentum and control, success and disaster.

The honking horns and screech of tires were still there, of course—they always were—but they receded into something distant now, background static to Wren's singular focus. Freedom wasn't far ahead; she could almost feel its edges brushing against her skin. But almost wasn't enough—not yet. She knew better than to believe in escape before you were truly clear of it all. There was still Dennis—the constant specter looming unseen but felt all the same.

"Left!" Wren called out sharply, yanking the handlebars toward a narrow alleyway before Maggie had time to question or hesitate.

The space closed in fast—walls rising high on either side, graffiti scrawled across them in vibrant chaos. She ducked instinctively under a low-hanging sign that swayed precariously overhead, its edges rusted and jagged like forgotten teeth. Too close.

Then they shot out into open air again—a chaotic street teeming with cars that seemed too loud and too slow all at once. A car screeched to an abrupt stop mere inches from Wren's back wheel; its driver leaned out the window to shout curses that vanished beneath the roar of their escape.

"Shit." The word hissed between Wren's teeth when she spotted a truck reversing blindly out of an alley ahead of them. Too tight to stop now—she swerved hard just in time to miss its hulking frame by what must have been millimeters.

The city wasn't done with them yet—it never was. Another obstacle loomed: orange cones and hastily placed barriers marked off what looked like an endless construction zone ahead. Wren didn't slow down—not even for a second. No time to think this one through. She aimed for a sliver of space between a dumpster and a pile of precariously balanced metal pipes, hoping physics wouldn't betray her this time.

The bike scraped against something solid as she squeezed through—metal grating against metal with an ear-splitting squeal—and sparks flew bright for one impossible second before she shot free on the other side like she'd just burst through some kind of portal. Angry shouts trailed behind them from workers clad in neon vests, but their insults blurred into irrelevance as quickly as they'd come.

"Where now?" Maggie's voice cut through the din—not panicked exactly but sharp with urgency because that was who she was: someone who trusted Wren would have an answer when it mattered most.

Wren's mind churned, fragments of strategies tumbling together but refusing to form a cohesive whole. The USB key pressed against her ankle, hot as a live ember. She couldn't forget it was there, couldn't forget what it might mean. Secrets she hadn't uncovered yet. Secrets someone wanted to kill for. They needed to find a place—somewhere quiet, somewhere invisible—just to pause and breathe.

Her eyes darted across the chaos in front of her until they snagged on something familiar: a neon sign glowing faintly through the haze of Chinatown's crowded streets. There was nowhere better right now.

"Follow me!" she yelled over her shoulder, cutting hard to the right.

Chinatown enveloped them immediately, its narrow streets bustling with life and noise. The air here was dense—pungent with the mingling odors of freshly gutted fish, tangy soy sauce and cleaning products. Vendors barked out prices in clipped tones while customers haggled back with equal ferocity. Lanterns strung overhead shifted in the breeze, their bright colors blurring together into smeared streaks like watercolor paint running down canvas.

Wren pushed forward without slowing, weaving between carts piled high with unfamiliar fruits, stacks of plastic crates, and oblivious pedestrians burdened by bulging shopping bags. Her bike rattled violently as it hit uneven cobblestones beneath the throng of foot traffic, every jarring shudder threatening to unseat her or rattle the frame apart entirely.

The alleys narrowed further as she continued deeper into the maze of Chinatown, branching into passages fewer maps remembered but Wren knew, having biked their snaking paths too many times before on her delivery runs. It wasn't ideal terrain—but it wasn't meant to be easy. That was part of why it worked.

Finally, after another sharp turn that sent a stack of empty wooden crates spilling behind them like discarded bones, the alley opened up into a small courtyard no wider than some living rooms Wren had been in before. She skidded to a harsh stop just shy of its center—and Maggie followed suit seconds later—both panting so hard it felt like their lungs might escape out their throats and collapse dryly onto the pavement between them.

"What now?" Maggie managed between quick gasps that hadn't transitioned yet from near-panic adrenaline toward something vaguely sustainable instead.

"There," Wren said, pointing. "We need to get off the streets." The pedestrian tunnel loomed ahead, a yawn in the concrete jungle. Wren jerked her handlebars and veered toward its entrance. She called back to Maggie, her voice frayed, every word scraped out of her throat. "It's a gamble. Best shot we've got."

They plunged into the shadowed opening. The sunlight vanished so abruptly it felt like someone had yanked a curtain closed. For a moment, everything was disorienting—the shift in light, the sudden chill in the air, the way the tunnel seemed to close around them. Their tires screeched against the slick concrete, sharp sounds bouncing off graffiti-scrawled walls until they couldn't tell where one echo ended and another began.

The tunnel devoured them whole, swallowed their noise until silence remained, pressed thick and heavy like cotton wadding in her ears. It was strange how quiet it became all at once—so quiet that Wren could hear the frantic rhythm of her own heartbeat pounding over the hum of fluorescent lights overhead.

Don't stop now, she thought, gripping her handlebars tighter. No hesitating. No looking back. Get through this first. Plan later.

The passage stretched ahead absurdly long, lit by buzzing fluorescents that gave everything an unflattering greenish tinge. Her legs burned with every push of the pedals, muscles clenching tighter with each stroke—sharp stabs of pain that didn't let up but didn't stop her either. She focused on the sound of their wheels spinning over the smooth floor; it became a kind of metronome for survival.

Maggie was still beside her—she could sense it without turning—and somehow that mattered more than anything else in this moment. If they were going down today, at least she wasn't doing it solo.

Wren resisted the urge to glance back—a quick look would cost precious seconds—but finally she risked it while keeping one hand steady on the bars. No Dennis in sight yet—not his hulking shape filling up the tunnel's mouth like something out of a nightmare—but that didn't mean he wasn't there somewhere, lurking just out of view.

The air down here tasted stale and sour, laced with exhaust fumes so old they'd lived here longer than most people had been alive. Breathing felt like inhaling industrial waste; every gulp stung her raw throat and seared all the way down to her lungs. Sweat dripped from her temples into her eyes—she blinked furiously against it but didn't bother reaching up to swipe it away.

Halfway through already? Maybe? Probably not—it looked closer because hope was shrinking distance into something manageable even when reality screamed otherwise.

Her mind latched onto the USB key again—that stupid little piece of plastic hiding secrets big enough to ruin or maybe save them all (but weren't those two things always connected anyway?). It weighed more than it should've in her mind—not physically but emotionally, metaphorically, some other adverb she couldn't focus on right now because Maggie was breathing hard behind her and she needed both hands on these handlebars and there wasn't time for metaphors when you were running for your life.

The crackle of tires skidding on grime snapped everything back into sharp focus as Wren came to an abrupt stop near what might've been halfway but also might not have been because time was slippery like that when adrenaline took over your bloodstream and made every second stretch or shrink depending on what you dreaded most.

Lights hummed above them like electric bees while shadows danced unevenly across graffiti-covered walls—all dripping letters and half-finished insults sprayed by vandals either too rushed or too scared to finish their thoughts properly before bolting for safety themselves.

Wren slid off her bike without thinking about it and planted both feet firmly on the ground while sweat pooled under her collar and trickled down between her shoulder blades unnoticed.

Maggie skidded to a stop beside her, chest heaving as though it might burst. They locked eyes for a moment—words unnecessary. They'd bought themselves some time, sure, but the question loomed large: Enough?

Wren leaned her bike against the curved wall of the tunnel. The frame clanged softly, the sound swallowed quickly by the thick stillness around them. She sank onto the narrow curb, concrete cool even through her sweat-soaked clothes. Maggie lowered herself beside her, their shoulders brushing lightly. For a second, maybe two, there was nothing but their breathing—loud, ragged gasps that echoed faintly off the tunnel walls.

Her heart hadn't quite slowed yet. It beat hard and fast in her chest, in her throat, in her ears, as though it had misplaced all sense of rhythm. Her hand shook as she reached into the bottle cage on her bike and pulled out a dented water bottle. She twisted off the cap with trembling fingers and took a long gulp. The water was tepid and carried that faint plastic bite that came from sitting too long in the sun. It didn't matter. At that moment, it might as well have been nectar.

When she finally stopped drinking, she handed the bottle to Maggie without a word.

Maggie nodded her thanks and drank deeply, so deeply that for a brief moment Wren worried there wouldn't be anything left for later—not that she would have said anything about it.

They must look like something out of one of those post-apocalyptic movies, Wren thought as she glanced at Maggie's streaked face and wild eyes. Matching dirt-streaked faces—or mostly matching—glistening skin, and clothes clinging uncomfortably to every inch of them. Yes, quite a pair, but no cameras followed them here in this grimy concrete artery under the city.

They were alone—it felt like they were alone. An odd sensation pressed on Wren's mind: the tunnel walls stretched into shadowy distance on both sides; beyond those shadows was more shadow until whatever boundary lay ahead felt unknowable. A place where light would feel inappropriate and out of context itself.

Wren reached down and felt the edge of the USB key tucked beneath her sock. It shouldn't have surprised her how small it was—barely larger than her thumb—but it did. Something so light, so utterly ordinary in appearance, had no right to leave destruction in its wake. She slid it out, holding it between her fingers like an artifact, turning it over to study the cheap red plastic casing. There wasn't much to see, but she couldn't seem to stop looking.

"What do you think's on it?" Maggie asked softly, her voice almost swallowed by the stillness of the tunnel.

Wren didn't look up. "No clue." She ran her thumb along the edge of the USB key like it might peel back a secret. "But it better not be more fucking numbers."

She leaned against the curved wall, letting her weight sag into the concrete. The cool surface pressed through her sweat-soaked shirt, chasing some of the heat radiating from her back and shoulders. Wren let out a slow breath and closed her eyes for just a second—long enough to feel the exhaustion sink its claws deeper into her muscles. Every bone in her body begged for rest, but there wasn't time for that. Not even close.

Dennis was still out there. Somewhere. She didn't need to remind herself of that; she could feel him, like a shadow stretching long behind them no matter how far they ran.

Wren's eyes opened again, scanning the tunnel ahead in both directions. Empty. For now. But tunnels were funny things—too quiet until they weren't, too safe until they weren't.

Her head thudded back against the wall as she tried to sort through it all. She tugged a hand through hair damp with sweat and grime, shaking out droplets onto the concrete floor below. "How'd he find us?" she muttered under her breath, though she already knew there wouldn't be an answer that made sense.

"Someone spotted us and called the police?" Maggie offered hesitantly from a few feet away. Her face was streaked with dirt that made the pale skin beneath stand out more starkly against her wild eyes.

Wren snorted sharply—mirthless, dismissive. "Sure," she said. "And maybe I'll grow gills next and swim us to safety."

The words hung in the air for a moment before sinking into silence thick enough to choke on. Wren glanced sideways at Maggie; she'd hunched forward, arms wrapped tightly across herself like they might hold cracks together before anything important spilled out.

"Sorry Mags, I didn't mean it like that," Wren said as she saw the hurt in Maggie's eyes. "If someone called the police, the police would have shown up. Not Dennis. How did *he* know where to find us?"

The faint tapping of Wren's fingers against her thigh punctuated the quiet as her mind churned—half adrenaline, half dread keeping her thoughts racing ahead of themselves without ever landing anywhere useful.

"What if," Maggie said, hesitating like she didn't want to finish but couldn't help herself, "what if he's been following us? Like… this whole time? So we could do all the work and he just has to steal the treasure?"

Her voice was barely more than a whisper—too soft for something so heavy—and yet Wren felt it hit square in the chest anyway. The idea burrowed in deep and sat there like a stone that wouldn't move no matter how hard she tried not to think about it.

For once, Wren didn't have a smart remark lined up. Instead, she just stared down at the USB key pinched between her fingers and watched as it caught what little light flickered along the tunnel walls—small and silent and utterly opaque.

Wren felt her jaw tighten, the muscles locking as if her body were bracing for impact. The thought had been lurking in the corners of her mind for a while now, but hearing Maggie say it out loud sent a ripple of unease across her skin. She could practically see Dennis in those shadows, always just out of reach, waiting. Her stomach twisted at the image, and for a brief second, she wanted to scream—loud enough to drown out all the creeping possibilities.

"Or maybe he has access to the city's camera network," Wren said, each word tasting bitter as it left her tongue. "Maybe I need a haircut to hide better."

At that, Maggie's eyes widened in alarm. Her breath hitched, and when she spoke again, the sound barely rose above a murmur. "Just wear a helmet, babe. It's the law anyway."

"I don't know what to think anymore." Wren cut her off sharply, frustration spilling over like a pot boiling too long on the stove.

She exhaled hard through her nose and reached into her courier bag. Zak's laptop was heavier than she remembered, its weight pressing against her palms in a way that didn't feel right. It wasn't just a laptop anymore—it was a burden, a reminder of shifting loyalties and fragile trust. She flipped open the lid and it glowed happily at her. She shoved the red USB key into the port with force. She hoped this was it, the information—evidence—that she needed to end this run.

The screen jolted to life. One single file blinked back at her, taunting in its simplicity. Wren's heartbeat quickened as she clicked on it. For a brief moment, hope flickered faintly at the edges of her thoughts—then dread snuffed it out like an unwelcome gust of wind. The contents began to load. She leaned closer instinctively.

And then she groaned—a guttural sound that seemed to rise up unbidden.

"You've got to be kidding me." The words hissed out between clenched teeth.

Maggie leaned in beside her, so close their shoulders brushed. "Let me guess," she said, already resigned. "More coordinates?"

Wren nodded tightly, grinding her teeth as if chewing through frustration might make it dissolve faster. "Yeah," she muttered bitterly. "Looks like Anne wants us running around the city chasing our tails."

Wren dug into her bag again and pulled out two protein bars—wrinkled but intact after weeks spent buried under gear and scraps of paper. She tossed one to Maggie without saying anything; Maggie caught it with an absent nod before tearing into the wrapper. They ate in silence at first—the kind that felt less like peace and more like tension stretching between them.

She tapped at the map app on the laptop and entered the coordinates. The next spot was well outside the downtown core, near an industrial area. "It's going to be a ride," she said as she turned the screen toward Maggie and took another bite from her delicious bar. "Take a photo."

The bar was dry and tasteless in Wren's mouth; each bite seemed to sap what little energy she had left rather than replenish it. She chewed mechanically while her mind wandered back to Dennis—Dennis charging across that park with his face twisted in fury, his voice barking orders sharp enough to snap branches from trees. The memory hit hard every time it surfaced, as though someone had slipped their hand into her chest and gripped her heart just tightly enough to hurt but not enough to stop its beating.

Wren swallowed thickly and took a long sip from her water bottle, though it did little to chase away the metallic taste fear left behind.

"We can't stay here much longer," Maggie said suddenly, balling up her protein-bar wrapper in one hand and tossing it toward her pack. Her eyes shifted toward the darkening street beyond them—a silent clock ticking down somewhere neither of them could see yet both could hear.

Wren's head jerked up at a sound, sharp and electronic, slicing through the stillness of the tunnel. The laptop—a ding that wasn't its usual chime and didn't belong here. It bounced off the damp walls, giving the impression it was everywhere at once.

"What the hell was that?" Wren asked, her muscles coiling, her body stiff like it was bracing for a blow.

Maggie leaned over and stared at the screen with narrowed eyes, confusion knitting her brow. "I don't know. I've never heard it make that sound before."

Wren opened the laptop and there it was: a message, bold and stark against the glow of the display. The words seemed benign enough—just a request to activate Bluetooth—but something about it felt wrong. Very wrong.

"Don't," Maggie said firmly, her hand darting out, fingers curling around Wren's wrist just as she moved to tap the screen. "Don't turn it on."

Wren froze. Her finger hovered mid-air, uncertain now. "Of course," she said slowly. "But what app even is this? I don't recognize—oh." Her voice faltered as she read aloud: "Lost-n-Founder?"

The name hung in the air like a sour note.

Wren frowned and squinted at the unfamiliar icon next to it—a generic shape with no personality or branding to give away its purpose. "Lost-n-Founder?" she repeated, testing the words on her tongue as though they might reveal something if spoken aloud. "What the fuck is that?"

Maggie shook her head quickly—too quickly—and there was something in her expression now: discomfort, worry. "I don't know," she said, her voice a little too defensive. "I've never heard of it, but it doesn't sound good."

A chill prickled along Wren's spine—not sudden or dramatic but slow and creeping, settling between her shoulder blades and refusing to budge. An app appearing out of nowhere wasn't just odd; it was ominous. And being on the run didn't leave room for coincidences.

"Lost-n-Founder. Sounds like a tracking app," Wren muttered under her breath, though saying it didn't make her feel any better about it. Her thoughts snagged on another possibility—one more personal and infinitely worse—and before she could stop herself, she added, "Dennis."

Maggie's head whipped toward Wren so fast that strands of hair caught on her face and clung there. Her mouth opened as though she meant to speak but forgot how for a moment.

"What?" she finally managed.

Wren ran a hand through her hair—a sharp motion more than anything else—and let out an irritated sigh through gritted teeth. "You heard me," she said quietly but with enough edge to cut glass. "Dennis could've put it there somehow."

"When? How?" Maggie demanded, clutching the phone tighter now like it might slip away if she loosened her grip by even an inch. Her eyes were wide—not scared exactly but raw in their intensity.

"I don't know," Wren admitted flatly because guessing wouldn't help right now and because saying too much would feed Maggie's spiraling uncertainty—the kind that could make this whole thing unravel faster than either of them could handle.

But they didn't have time for debates or hypotheticals or pointing fingers at ghosts from their pasts who may or may not have left breadcrumbs behind just to screw with them later.

She turned away from Maggie entirely because Zak's laptop chose that exact moment to explode into sound: shrill ringing that seemed both endless and instantaneously unbearable all at once—and amplified tenfold by their confined surroundings.

"What the fuck now?" Wren hissed through clenched teeth as adrenaline surged through her veins like gasoline meeting a spark. She slammed the lid and it didn't stop. She shook it and it didn't stop. She opened it again and it didn't stop.

Her gaze shot toward either end of the tunnel where shadows toyed with whatever light remained—and for one brief second silence seemed like something neither of them would ever hear again.

Wren yanked the red USB key from the port and shoved it down into her sock. The cold metal pressed against her ankle, sharp and unyielding, like a secret that didn't want to be hidden.

She glanced back at the laptop screen. The ringing continued, relentless and shrill, echoing in the cramped space of the tunnel. Each note seemed to vibrate inside her skull, growing louder. And then—silence.

Her shoulders loosened for half a second. Just half. "We need to go," she said, voice low but firm, tucking the laptop under her arm. "Now."

Maggie nodded. Her face was pale under the unforgiving fluorescent lights, her movements stiff as though fear had taken up permanent residence in her muscles. They scrambled to their feet, legs protesting after sitting too long on the hard concrete.

"What was that?"

A new noise. From somewhere further down the tunnel, too close for comfort. Wren froze. So did Maggie. For one suspended moment, it felt as though even time had stopped in its tracks.

"Go," Wren hissed through clenched teeth.

Her heart was already pounding as she swung a leg over her bike. It should have been automatic—after all, she'd done it a thousand times before—but now it felt foreign, like trying to remember steps in a dance when music no longer played. The handlebars were slick under her grip; maybe from sweat, maybe from something else entirely.

A shadow stirred at the far end of the tunnel. A chill spread across Wren's skin as Dennis stepped into view.

His bulk filled the narrow passageway, and for a split second Wren thought he might knock his head on the low entry if he moved wrong. The flickering fluorescent lights above made him appear larger than life—made everything about him seem harder: his jawline, his eyes, even his grip on the gun that dangled from his hand like an extension of his will.

"So this app actually works," Dennis said with a laugh that bounced off every concrete surface around them until it sounded like there were dozens of Dennises instead of just one. "Zak was right after all."

Zak had set them up.

"Hand over the USB," Dennis said now, raising the gun so no one could mistake exactly who'd be on its business end if things went wrong. "You know which one I'm talking about."

Wren's fingers tightened instinctively around the handlebars until they hurt, until she could feel bones pressing against skin with nowhere else to go. The USB key suddenly seemed unbearable against her ankle—like it wasn't just cold anymore but burning straight through her sock and into her skin.

Her eyes darted toward Maggie; she didn't need words to see how terrified she was. Her face said it all—pale and drawn tight with fear—and Wren knew what she had to do.

She took a deep breath that didn't feel like nearly enough air and pressed forward anyway, pushing off slowly, coasting toward Dennis inch by inch. Time felt stretched thin between each rotation of her pedals, between each heartbeat thudding loud enough in her ears to drown out everything else around her.

Behind her back, where Dennis couldn't see it, Wren waved once—twice—frantically toward Maggie in desperate silence: *Go. Just go.*

"Give it," Dennis said, his voice low and sharp, his finger curling tighter over the trigger. "Nice and easy."

Wren didn't respond. She kept her eyes locked on Dennis, but it took everything she had not to glance back. Her ears strained for the faintest sound of movement behind her, and then she heard it: the soft squeal of bike tires rolling against concrete. Barely a noise at all, but enough. Just enough.

Come on, Maggie, she thought, willing the girl to move faster, farther, away from this. *Please.*

Dennis advanced, one slow step at a time, closing the space between them with deliberate cruelty. His lips twitched into something that might have been a smile if it weren't so heartless. Wren's mind whirred uselessly, like the wheel of a bike spinning in place but catching on nothing. There had to be a way out of this. There *had* to be.

Her heart thumped hard against her ribs as though it were trying to escape before the rest of her could. Zak's laptop bumped against her hip—the thought struck like lightning—and suddenly she knew what she had to do.

She shifted her balance and gripped the laptop with both hands. One breath in—her last moment to hesitate—and then she threw it with every ounce of strength left in her body.

The laptop flew through the air in a clumsy spiral that felt like it took hours to complete even though it couldn't have lasted more than a heartbeat. It hit Dennis square above his brow with a dull crack that Wren felt more than heard. His head snapped back as though he'd been yanked by an invisible string.

"Go!" Wren shouted, already turning her bike.

She didn't wait to see if Dennis went down or if he recovered—it didn't matter now. What mattered was moving forward. Her legs pumped fiercely as she pushed herself into motion again, the muscles screaming from exhaustion but obeying anyway. The tunnel blurred around her; graffiti and grime dissolved into streaks of colorless gray on either side as speed took over.

Ahead of her was Maggie—smaller than she'd seemed before, hunched so low over her handlebars that Wren almost lost sight of her in the dim light of the tunnel. The girl was fast—faster than Wren would have expected—but not fast enough for Wren's liking.

Every turn of Wren's pedals sent fire through her thighs, but falling behind wasn't an option. She clenched her jaw and forced herself to go harder, faster—anything to close the distance between them. Her breathing grew louder in her ears until it drowned out everything else: the grind of tires on pavement; the faint rattle of a bike chain pulling slack taut; even the pounding rhythm of her own pulse faded beneath gasping breaths.

Then there was light.

Maggie hit it first—the end of the tunnel—as though breaking through some invisible barrier into another world. For half a second she was just a silhouette outlined by blinding daylight before disappearing completely from view.

Wren followed close behind but wasn't as lucky with her timing—her eyes watered instantly from the brightness after so much dimness underground—and for several long seconds everything was just white-hot light and disorientation.

"Right!" Wren yelled hoarsely when shapes began returning to form: Maggie veering sharply right ahead of her, tires screeching briefly before gripping asphalt.

Wren mimicked Maggie's move without thinking and felt gravel spit up beneath her own wheels as they made contact with sharper pavement outside the tunnel proper—a signal they'd officially left its confines behind them. Almost.

Crack.

The gunshot came loud enough that even inside herself—inside this storm raging between fear-induced adrenaline and sheer determination—it shocked clarity back into existence for one awful moment where sound echoed endlessly around them rather than staying safely buried far behind in the tunnel.

Wren's legs burned with every push of the pedals, a deep, fiery ache grinding into her muscles. Her heart thudded, a relentless drumbeat in her ears, drowning out most other sounds. The world around her was a smear of motion—too fast, too chaotic to make sense of. Up ahead, she caught sight of Maggie, hunched low over her handlebars, her shoulders jerking with each sharp intake of breath.

"Keep going!" Wren shouted, though her own voice sounded hollow and strained. She wasn't sure if Maggie could even hear her over the rush of wind and pounding adrenaline.

Maggie's head snapped up at the sound, her face pale and streaked with tears. For a moment, she looked frozen in place, as though she might stop entirely. Her fingers twitched on the handlebars like they might lose their grip at any second.

Wren pushed harder until she was close enough to reach out if she dared. "Maggie!" she yelled again. "Move! Now!"

They veered together, wheels skidding as they cut through the park's uneven paths and burst onto the street beyond. Cars honked sharply—angrily—but neither woman spared a glance in their direction. They wove between lanes recklessly, every movement automatic and reactive, powered more by instinct than thought.

The city loomed around them, a web of concrete and steel that seemed endless and suffocating all at once. Every turn they took was supposed to bring relief, but instead there was more road, more alleyways that led to nowhere. Wren's mind churned along with her legs on the pedals, replaying that single horrible sound—the gunshot—that still seemed to echo inside her skull.

Finally, an opening: Wren spotted a narrow alley between two crumbling buildings up ahead. She raised one hand briefly—signal enough—and led the way into the shadows. Both women dismounted their bikes hastily, their legs shaking beneath them like jelly threatening to collapse.

Maggie slumped hard against the brick wall behind her, folding in on herself as though trying to disappear entirely. "He shot at us," she said between sharp gasps for air. Each word burned as tears streamed unchecked down her face. "He actually fired..."

Wren didn't have words for that yet—not ones that would help anyway—but she reached out instinctively to steady Maggie's quivering frame with both hands. Her own fingers trembled as they made contact. "I know," she said quietly after a moment, trying to keep her voice steady for both their sakes. "But we're here now—we're okay."

Okay wasn't true exactly—they weren't safe and wouldn't be anytime soon—but it was what people said in moments like this.

The alley was damp and dimly lit by a faint glow from somewhere above—was the sun shining?—quiet except for the distant hum of traffic from nearby streets. Wren swept her gaze across it quickly: no doors ajar or shadowed figures lurking at the edges of vision—not yet anyway.

"We can't stay here," Wren added after another beat of silence stretched too thin between them. She crouched down so Maggie would meet her eyes if only for a second. "I mean it—we can't."

Maggie's breathing slowed marginally but did not even out completely; raw panic still flashed across her face.

Wren straightened back up and glanced toward the mouth of the alley where they'd come from before continuing: "We need to split up." She hesitated just, then forced herself onward: "It's safer this way—for both of us."

Maggie's eyes snapped wide, panic flaring in their depths. "What? No, we can't—"

Wren didn't let her finish. "We have to." Her voice was steady, sharper than she intended, but there wasn't time to soften it. "Go to Fannie's. She'll keep you safe until I figure this out."

Maggie shook her head so hard that a lock of hair fell loose from behind her ear. Tears glistened on her cheeks, catching the light as they traced trembling paths downward. "What about you? Where will you go?"

Wren forced a smile, though it felt thin and barely held together—like paper stretched tight over cracks. "Don't worry about me," she said, trying to inject some strength into the words. "I'll be fine." Fine. The word tasted hollow even as she said it. "Just get to Fannie's and stay put until you hear from me."

She reached out and squeezed Maggie's hand—a quick gesture meant to reassure but somehow feeling woefully inadequate. Then she stepped back, hesitating just a moment longer than she meant to. "Be careful. And Maggie?" Her voice softened now, almost breaking under the moment. "I love you."

For a beat, it seemed like everything was frozen between them—the two of them suspended in some fragile bubble that wouldn't hold much longer—but then Maggie's trembling hand rose, her finger pointing shakily toward Wren's shoulder.

"What?" Wren frowned, following Maggie's gaze. That was when she saw it: crimson blooming slowly through her hoodie in a dark, damning stain.

"Shit," Wren muttered under her breath. It was then that the pain hit her—sharp and searing, like someone had pressed a glowing poker against her skin.

Maggie gasped audibly as her face crumpled again, fresh tears spilling fast and unchecked down her cheeks now. "Oh god," she whispered, choked and barely audible. "You're hurt." She swallowed hard before adding, with visible disbelief: "He actually... he shot you."

Wren nodded once, stiffly. "And hit me this time."

"Hit you." Maggie echoed back at her helplessly, like saying it aloud might somehow make sense of it.

Wren reached under Bridger with shaking hands and fumbled with the latch beneath her bike seat until it gave way. She yanked out the small emergency kit. Before she could tear into it herself, Maggie snatched the kit from Wren's hands with trembling fingers that betrayed no less resolve for their unsteadiness. "Let me." There was steel under all that shaking—thin steel maybe—but enough to hold for now.

Maggie tore open the kit with a desperation that made even Wren pause briefly before nodding and letting her work. She watched as Maggie rifled through its contents with frantic efficiency until finally producing the roll of bandages tucked neatly inside.

The hoodie came off. The fabric of Wren's shirt peeled back with an awful tugging sensation that pulled another hiss from between her clenched teeth. The wound lay bare now: shallow but angry red and throbbing fiercely—a garish streak slashing across pale skin like some cruel artist had taken a jagged brush-stroke to canvas.

He'd shot a line right across her tattoo, splitting it open. *Bastard.*

Maggie's hands shook harder as she unrolled the bandage—so much so that Wren leaned forward as if to take over again—but Maggie shot her a look through tear-filled eyes and said firmly: "Don't move."

Her voice cracked halfway through wrapping Wren's shoulder anyway as another sob escaped despite efforts otherwise held tightly in check: "This is insane," she blurted suddenly between ragged breaths. "Dennis... he tried to kill us. He actually fired his gun at us. In broad daylight!"

Wren winced, the sharp sting radiating from the graze on her shoulder as Maggie began wrapping the bandage around it. "I know, I know," she said, her voice tight, though she wasn't sure if she was trying to reassure Maggie or herself. "Maybe someone saw us and called the police to rescue us!" The laugh came unbidden, brittle and ragged, spilling out of her throat and echoing back like something foreign until she noticed Maggie's hands freeze mid-wrap. Her face was pale, drawn tight in a way that sucked all humor from the air between them. "We can't stop now," Wren added quickly, less certain this time. "We're in too deep."

"Too deep," Maggie repeated softly, each word trembling on its own fragile fault line before breaking altogether. She began to speak, stopped, and tried again, her voice trembling. "Wren, this has gone too far. We have to go to the police—explain everything—"

"And then what?" Wren interrupted with more force than she'd intended. She saw Maggie flinch but pressed on anyway because stopping now, thinking now, would be worse. "What are we supposed to tell them? That we're running from a cop who opened fire on us in broad daylight? That we're caught up in some insane conspiracy tied to USB drives stashed all over New York City? They'd lock us up before we even finished our first sentence."

Maggie's fingers stilled against Wren's arm as if grounding herself there might steady the storm rising in her chest. Her eyes lifted, catching Wren's with an intensity that made it impossible for her to look away—not that she wanted to. The fear in Maggie's gaze wasn't just fear; it was heavier than that, tethered by something raw and desperate. Wren felt it lodge under her ribs and take root.

"I'm scared," Maggie whispered, barely audible at first but gaining strength as she said it again: "I'm scared, Wren. I've never been so terrified in my entire life."

In truth, neither had Wren, though she'd never admit it out loud. Swallowing hard against the lump forming in her throat, she forced her good arm to reach up and cup Maggie's cheek. Her thumb brushed lightly across skin still damp from tears Maggie hadn't yet wiped away. "I know." She hesitated for a moment that felt like forever. "I'm scared too." Her voice softened further as the words fell between them like fragile truths they both needed to hear but neither wanted to say out loud. "But we can't stop now. You know that as much as I do. Our lives depend on this—on keeping going." She faltered again before adding quietly, "If Dennis caught us... who knows what he'd do?"

Maggie nodded then—not quickly or easily but slowly and deliberately—as though piecing together shards of resolve she didn't realize were still within herself until now. Tears still traced faint lines down her cheeks, though they seemed to fade as she focused her trembling hands back on securing the bandage around Wren's shoulder.

"So... what do we do now?" The question came tentative and small but carried with it an openness that threatened to undo them both.

For a moment, Wren didn't answer—not because she didn't hear Maggie but because any answer worth giving stuck somewhere just shy of her lips where courage should've been growing instead of doubt.

"Mags..." Wren hesitated again before continuing in a rush of words she half-hoped might pass unnoticed if spoken fast enough: "You need to go home."

Maggie froze entirely this time—no trembling hands or half-finished sentences left lingering between them anymore—just silence so loud it filled every corner of whatever safe house they'd managed to scurry into like prey fleeing predators.

"It's not safe," Wren pressed on despite everything screaming inside of her not to say more—to let silence win for once—but she couldn't stop herself now any more than she could will away gravity itself when standing at the edge of something so profoundly irreversible. "It's not safe for us—together..."

"No." Sharp enough this time; clear enough this time; final enough this time.

Wren blinked slowly at Maggie's chin jutting forward stubbornly—her entire posture shifting under newfound strength neither woman had expected nor prepared for.

Maggie's jaw tightened, her chin tilting upward in that way that always signaled she wasn't about to back down. Her eyes locked on Wren's, shining with a defiance that made Wren ache with equal parts admiration and dread. "No," Maggie said, her voice steady despite the slight shake in her hands. "You need me out there. I spotted Dennis before you even realized he was in the park. You need me."

Wren opened her mouth to argue, but Maggie cut her off, her words tumbling out in a rush. "This isn't just about surviving anymore," she said. "It hasn't been for a while. Anne... Anne is dead because of him. God knows who else might be next—who else might already be gone." Her voice caught on the name, but she pressed on, relentless now. "We started this because it was the right thing to do. Because we couldn't look away from it, not like other seems to. And I'm not going to sit safe at home while people keep getting hurt—while *you* get hurt. Not when I could've been there to stop it."

Maggie took a step closer, her hands trembling before she clenched them into fists at her sides. "We're too close now, Wren. Every one of those USB drives gets us one step closer to taking him down for good, and if we split up now—if we let fear tear us apart—we might miss our chance to make all of this mean something." A pause, just long enough for her voice to soften, though her eyes stayed hard and unwavering. "I don't think I could live with that. With knowing that we were right there and didn't finish it because I walked away."

The silence stretched between them, heavy and thick as syrup. Wren's throat tightened as Maggie finally whispered, almost to herself, "I'm scared too. Scared doesn't cover it—I'm terrified. But there are worse things than fear."

Wren exhaled sharply and looked away for a moment, blinking hard at some indeterminate spot on the ground as if it held the answers she so desperately needed right now. She knew Maggie was right—of course Maggie was right—but that didn't make any of this easier.

When Wren finally looked back up, it was like something broke inside her—something fragile and tightly coiled that had been holding everything together by a thread until this moment. She grabbed Maggie by the shoulders and pulled her close, burying her face in the crook of Maggie's neck as she inhaled deeply. That familiar scent—distinctly *Maggie*—wrapped around Wren like a lifeline tossed into turbulent waters.

"I love you," Wren murmured into her girlfriend's hair, the words raw and uncertain, as though they weren't quite enough but were all she had to give right now. "God, I love you so much it scares me."

Maggie pulled back at that—not far enough for Wren to retreat but just enough so their eyes could meet again—and cupped Wren's face in both hands. Her touch was warm and steady where Wren felt anything but.

Their lips met then—not gently but with an urgency that made Wren forget everything else for just a moment: the danger they were still in, the weight of what came next, even the gnawing fear sitting heavy in her chest like a stone lodged there permanently. The kiss tasted of salt from unshed tears and something bittersweet Wren couldn't quite define—hope maybe, or desperation.

When they broke apart, both gasping softly for air like swimmers surfacing too quickly after being underwater too long, Maggie rested her forehead against Wren's and whispered so quietly it was almost lost in the space between them: "Promise me."

"Promise you what?" Wren asked hoarsely.

"That we'll never leave each other," Maggie said simply.

Wren closed her eyes for half a beat longer than a blink before opening them again and nodding solemnly. "I promise," she said quietly but firmly enough that it didn't feel hollow or rehearsed—it felt real because it *was* real.

As their fingers intertwined without either consciously realizing they were doing it—as though their hands had decided for them—Wren added softly but no less resolutely: "Together until the truth comes out."

They stood like that for a moment, drawing strength from each other in the way only shared fear and desperation could bind two people. Then Wren straightened, her shoulders squaring off as if bracing for impact. Her face shifted into something harder, sharper—a mask of resolve.

"Turn your phone on," she said, her voice steady now, as though the plan had been there all along, waiting for the chaos to clear. "We'll use the mapping app to find the next location. Once we've got it, the phone goes off and we're gone. Doesn't matter if Dennis can track us—he'll always be behind us." She paused, her lips twitching upward in a way that wasn't quite a smile. "But before we go, there's something I need to take care of."

Maggie pulled out the phone and fired it up, opening the photo and the map. Her fingers flew over the keypad. Numbers appeared on the screen one by one, glowing faintly in the dim.

Wren watched her closely, something unspoken passing across her face. Her brow dipped—a quiet question she didn't verbalize right away but couldn't quite hold back either.

Wren didn't ask where they were going. Instead, she exhaled slowly through her nose and tilted her head to the side, a slow motion that seemed almost deliberate—the kind of motion meant to intimidate an opponent before a fight begins. Then she turned toward Maggie, and this time the smile came fully into shape: slow and razor-edged, like the curve of a blade waiting to cut.

"Well," Wren said softly, words deliberate now as though tasting them first before letting them out. "First I have to see a guy. We're going to kick some ass."

The pedals churned beneath Wren's feet like something alive and hungry—their relentless spin locked in step with her legs' burning protest. The bike bucked forward as she pushed harder than she should have; every muscle screamed for mercy but found none in return. Up ahead, silhouetted against the city's hazy sprawl of buildings and blaring lights, loomed the Cyclista office: big open doors glowing faintly gold in early twilight—a shimmering promise of betrayal Wren couldn't ignore.

Sweat slid down her temple but didn't stop there—it pooled at her collarbone and soaked into fabric already damp from effort. It stung when it reached her eyes too; every blink was sharp enough to remind Wren that nothing about today would be easy—not breathing through bloodied airways or pedaling through streets still sticky with asphalt heat or facing what lay inside those Cyclista walls.

She tightened her grip on the handlebars instinctively—knuckles pale now against palms slick with sweat—and narrowed focus onto singular things instead: pavement cracks rushing under wheels or how far back Maggie might trail behind (she didn't dare glance back yet). But mostly? Mostly images lived unbidden within mind-space otherwise reserved for survival instincts...Zak's face among the most intrusive.

Zak was going to pay. And Wren was going to make sure of it.

Wren didn't so much enter the Cyclista office as invade it. Her bike screeched against the concrete floor, tires screaming in protest as she skidded sideways. For a moment, it looked as if gravity might get the better of her—one of those split seconds where time stretches just enough to make you doubt—but then, in a single motion, she let go of the handlebars. The bike slid out from under her, clattering harmlessly away, and Wren's feet hit the floor with a force that seemed to demand everyone's attention.

She didn't pause. The impact traveled up her legs, rattling through her bones, but she kept moving forward, the sound of each step punctuating the sudden silence that had engulfed the room. Her gaze locked onto Zak. He was frozen—statue-like—a mix of shock and fear creeping across his face. For just a beat, Wren wondered whether he hadn't seen this coming or whether he'd been foolish enough to think himself untouchable.

Her fist was already flying before either of them could blink.

The connection was immediate and brutal. A sickening crack echoed as her knuckles met Zak's nose, and for a brief second after impact, there was nothing but silence. Then came his scream—shrill and piercing—and the blood followed soon after, spilling from his nostrils like a faucet turned on too high. Zak stumbled backward, hands clutching at his face as though trying to hold it together.

"You rat," Wren hissed through clenched teeth. Her words weren't loud—they didn't need to be—but they were sharp enough to cut the air between them.

Massi had been slouched in a chair nearby, but now even he scrambled out of the way, sending his chair toppling over with a bang that barely registered in Wren's ears. Her focus remained steady on Zak.

Zak tried to retreat further, his movements jerky and uncoordinated. His wide eyes darted around the room in search of something—an exit, maybe hope—but there was none to be found. "Wren," he started weakly, voice trembling beneath the panic. "Just wai—"

Another punch silenced him.

This one found its mark in his gut. It wasn't elegant or precise—it didn't need to be—but it was effective. Zak doubled over instantly, an involuntary gasp escaping him as all the air left his lungs in one pitiful whoosh. His knees buckled from the blow, and in that moment he looked almost childlike—small and completely at her mercy.

Wren didn't give him time to recover.

Her foot swung upward in a swift arc and slammed into his leg with enough force to make even Massi flinch from the sidelines. The sound it made—something between a hollow thud and a sharp crack—ricocheted off the walls like gunfire in an empty canyon. Zak yelped again—a short burst this time—before collapsing entirely. His knee hit the ground hard enough that Wren felt it more than heard it; vibrations ran up from where he landed straight into her boots.

The room had descended into chaos by now—papers scattered across desks and floors alike, chairs askew from hurried retreats—but all Wren saw was Zak crumpled on the ground before her: beaten down but not yet fully broken.

Not yet.

He started rising.

Wren's kick connected solidly with Zak's chest, the dull thud of her shoe meeting his sternum accompanied by a wheezing gasp that forced its way out of him as though it had been trapped. He stumbled backward, arms flailing in chaotic arcs, until one hand collided with the edge of a desk. The desk toppled over, and the resulting clatter—a discordant mix of metal legs, plastic surfaces, and an avalanche of pens and paperclips.

Zak hit the floor but didn't stay there long. His movements were frantic, almost insect-like, as he scrambled to his feet. His breath came in short, sharp bursts that sounded too loud against the squeak and scrape of his shoes on the polished floor. For a moment, he seemed to hesitate—eyes darting around the room as though looking for something—but then his hand shot out toward a nearby folding chair. He gripped it with both hands, muscles straining visibly beneath his shirt, and let out a guttural noise as he hurled it toward Wren.

The chair hurtled through the air in what seemed like slow motion—an ungainly object rendered momentarily elegant as it spun toward her face. But Wren was already moving. Her hands rose instinctively, catching the chair mid-flight with a jarring smack that reverberated up her arms. There was no pause, no break; she pivoted smoothly on her heel, using its momentum to send the chair back where it came from. For a split second, time seemed to stutter—the chair's arc cutting across her vision like some kind of absurd pendulum—before it collided with Zak.

The impact was definitive—more than sound or movement; it was something you could feel in your bones even watching from afar. Zak crumpled under its impact just as Wren followed through, a blur now herself as she lunged after him. They hit the ground together in an awkward tangle of limbs and noise—the unmistakable thud of bodies against linoleum mingling with Zak's groaning breathlessness.

Wren pushed herself upright first—not entirely steady but quicker than Zak—and paused just long enough for her lips to curl into something that might have been called a smile if not for how predatory it looked. She reared back sharply, her forehead meeting Zak's face with brutal precision. There was no mistaking the sound this time: A wet crunch that came with horrifying finality, followed immediately by Zak's scream—a shrill note that sliced clean through whatever chaos still lingered from their clash.

"What in God's name is happening out here?" Willie's voice boomed through the space like a thunderclap breaking open the sky before a storm. The door to his office flew open so forcefully that its handle slammed into the wall behind it, leaving an undeniable dent—a perfect circle surrounded by cracked paint.

Massi appeared almost immediately after, shoes skidding on the slick floor as he rushed forward with both arms raised in what might have been a calming gesture if not for how panicked his expression looked. "Boss—no! Stay back," he said hurriedly, words tumbling over each other as though they'd been too long bottled up inside him and now couldn't escape fast enough.

Wren didn't acknowledge either of them. It wasn't even clear whether she'd heard them at all beyond some vague awareness tucked into the farthest corner of her mind. Her focus stayed entirely on Zak—a singular fixation that left no room for anything or anyone else. Her fists shattered whatever fragile silence Willie's entrance hadn't already broken: Each strike landed with sickening regularity—a rhythmic series of dull thuds punctuated occasionally by sharper cracks when knuckles found ribs instead of softer flesh.

Zak's gasps grew fainter with each blow until they morphed into something weaker still—little more than trembling exhales punctuated by pathetic whimpers barely audible over everything else. Wren kept going anyway—not because she didn't notice but because she did—and whatever drove her forward wasn't finished yet.

The bang behind her was deafening, rattling the walls and cutting through the haze of Wren's fury. She froze mid-swing, her breath catching as Maggie's hurried footsteps pounded against the office floor, each step a frantic heartbeat. Wren didn't need to turn to know it was her—she could feel Maggie's panic in the air, thick and suffocating.

"Wren! Stop!" Maggie's voice was sharp, urgent, slicing cleanly through the noise. Then came the hands—grabbing at her shoulders first, then snaking around her waist. Maggie yanked hard, surprising Wren with a strength that didn't match her frame. The pull dragged Wren back a half step, just enough to throw her off balance, her foot kicking out reflexively in the process.

The sharp toe of her shoe connected with Zak's groin. The sound he made—high-pitched and guttural—made everyone in the room flinch. His body folded in on itself like a puppet with cut strings, arms cradling his injury as he curled like a pill bug, gasping for air, his whimpers filling the sudden silence that settled like dust after an explosion.

Wren barely noticed Maggie tightening her grip from behind; she was too busy fighting against it. Her whole body felt coiled and ready to strike again. "You fucking rat!" she spat, pointing an unsteady but damning finger at Zak as he writhed on the floor. "You sold us out! You told Dennis where we'd be! He shot at us! We could've died!"

Across the room, Willie's face turned from red to purple, veins bulging angrily at his temples. His roar shook the room: "Get out of my office right now, Hubbard! Get the hell out!"

Massi was there in an instant, both hands pressed against Willie's chest like a human barricade. "Boss," he said firmly but not without strain, "we need to cool off here." He gave Willie a shove toward his desk—a gentle one but insistent—and stepped between him and everything else happening in the room.

"Wren," Maggie tried again, desperation creeping into her voice now as she tugged at Wren's arm like she might pull a drowning woman from water. "Let's go. Please. This isn't going to fix anything."

Wren's chest heaved with every breath she dragged in like it wasn't enough air, and her eyes stayed locked on Zak as though sheer force of will alone could level him further into the ground. "He almost got us killed," she repeated through clenched teeth, each word venomous and raw. "He's working with Dennis."

Zak let out another pitiful moan from where he lay on the floor—it was more a whimper this time—and that sound fueled Wren's rage more. She strained against Maggie's hold again even though her muscles already burned from exertion.

"Wren!" Massi called over from his spot near Willie, his tone shifting now—less about defusing Willie and more about getting Wren out of there before things got worse. "You gotta split. The cops are gonna show up soon, and you can't still be here when they do."

Her eyes flicked briefly toward Massi—just long enough for his words to register—but her focus snapped back just as quickly to Zak's crumpled form on the floor again. Her fists opened and closed almost involuntarily at her sides, knuckles torn and streaked with drying blood from blows that had landed minutes ago but still felt fresh under her skin.

Wren stood there for another moment longer than anyone expected—the tension almost unbearable around her—until finally Maggie gave one last desperate pull at her arm that sent them both stumbling toward the door.

Her rage didn't leave—it stayed there inside her like something alive and dangerous—but for now it simmered just beneath the surface instead of spilling over entirely.

Massi moved toward her, each step measured, unhurried. His hand landed on Wren's shoulder, light but steady—a strange counterpoint to the chaos that had been swirling moments ago. "Hey," he said, his voice low and calm, like someone coaxing a cornered animal. "You've made your point, Wren. Time to go."

His words seeped through the haze that had wrapped itself around her mind. She blinked hard, as though shaking off a bad dream, and for the first time she registered him standing there—Massi, smelling of weed and sweat, as familiar as a worn-out hoodie. Before she could say anything, he pulled her into a hug. Tight. Solid. Reassuring.

"Get out of here," he murmured against her ear, turning to steer her toward the door where their bikes were propped haphazardly against the wall. "Cops'll be here any minute." He took off his hoodie and wrapped it over Wren's shoulder like she was a little old lady in a care home.

It stank just like him.

Her feet obeyed without conscious thought, moving one step at a time even as her mind lagged behind. As she neared the door, she threw one last look back over her shoulder at Zak—sharp and venomous enough to cut glass—before stepping outside.

Maggie was already on her bike, hands gripping the handlebars so tightly that her knuckles had turned white. She sat perched and ready, her face tight with worry barely masked by mounting impatience. "Let's go," Maggie hissed quietly but urgently.

Wren didn't reply; instead, she swung a leg over her bike in one fluid motion and gave Massi a nod—not a goodbye or even thanks, just... acknowledgment—before lowering her head and pedaling hard. The pedals churned beneath her feet as she pushed forward, the tires humming against pavement with every turn of the crank.

The wind hit almost immediately: cool and sharp against her flushed cheeks, slicing through the sticky layer of sweat on her skin. It carried away some of the lingering heaviness in her chest—or maybe tried to—and blended into the distant sounds of Cyclista fading behind them: muffled shouting, breaking glass still echoing faintly in memory if not reality.

2:58 p.m.

Wren leaned back against the brick wall of the alley, a gritty texture pressing into her spine, and let her lungs work overtime to catch up. Her senses were greeted with its signature cologne: a sharp mix of ammonia and an ancient sewer that had just given up. Somewhere in the distance, sirens wailed—faint but persistent—a reminder that danger didn't disappear just because you couldn't see it anymore. The city around them pulsed with life, cars honking in frustration, engines growling. It all felt disconnected from this narrow sliver of forgotten space where they'd holed up.

Maggie had made herself at home on a pallet that somehow had escaped the filth. Pallets, Wren thought absently, were not meant to be dry—or comfortable—but Maggie adjusted as if she'd found a throne and went about rifling through her courier bag like it was Mary Poppins' carpet bag. A protein bar appeared first, then water bottles as if summoned by sheer willpower.

"Here," Maggie said, holding out one of each to Wren. "You look like you're about to pass out."

Wren took the offering with a grunt, unwilling to admit how much she needed it. Her body protested every movement—her shoulder burning with a steady throb where the bullet had left its mark and her knuckles raw from their introduction to Zak's face. She unwrapped the protein bar slowly and took a bite, chewing without interest but knowing her body would thank her later.

"Zak's chin was softer than his attitude," she muttered between bites. There was something satisfying about replaying how the scuffle had ended—with Zak on the ground looking both surprised and defeated. Small victories were still victories.

Maggie glanced toward the mouth of the alley, her brow furrowed as though expecting trouble to come hurtling in at any moment. "We've got to lose these hoodies," she said. "We might as well put up neon signs saying 'Hey, look! Suspicious people hiding here!'"

"I'm keeping Massi's," Wren said as she nodded faintly but didn't move right away. She wasn't sure what felt worse—the ache spreading across her shoulders or the fact that Maggie was right. With a small sigh, she set down the half-eaten protein bar and began peeling off the dollar store hoodie. The fabric clung stubbornly to her skin as though it had plans of its own—sweat and something thicker anchoring it in place—and the process took longer than dignity allowed.

The sound Maggie made when Wren finally got free wasn't quite a gasp; it was sharper than that—like someone had just slapped all available air out of her lungs. "Oh my God," she hissed. "Do you even realize...? Wren, your shirt is soaked in blood!"

Wren blinked down at herself as though it might explain things better than words could. The tank top—white when this misadventure began—was now marbled with dark red streaks and patches that were impossible to ignore. She shrugged one shoulder instinctively, regretted it immediately when pain flared up like static electricity running under her skin, and muttered, "None of it's new." It wasn't entirely true, but explaining felt unnecessary.

"Old? It looks fresh to me." Maggie's words came out soft but edged with something sharp, her fingers hesitating just above the stained fabric like it might lunge at her. The smell lingered between them—not quite metallic, not quite earthy, but enough to tie her stomach into a tight knot.

"It's fine," Wren said quickly, too quickly. She leaned in, her lips brushing against Maggie's in a kiss that felt more like punctuation than promise. "I'm okay. I swear. A couple of scrapes, maybe a bruise or two, nothing worth worrying about."

Maggie pulled back just far enough to study her face, trying to read between the lines Wren wasn't saying. "Wren—"

A finger pressed lightly against her lips, silencing her. "Shh. I said I'm fine." The smile that followed seemed rehearsed, but Maggie couldn't tell whether it was for Wren's benefit or hers. "Let's talk about what we're doing next instead. Turn your phone on."

Wren turned before Maggie could protest again, bending down and gathering the discarded clothes into her arms with a movement that felt rushed and clumsy. The fabric clung to itself in damp folds, darkened by the rain that hadn't quite washed away whatever else had soaked through it. Each step she took toward the dumpster was heavy with effort, her limp more pronounced now than before.

The lid shrieked on its hinges when she lifted it, cutting through the quiet of the alley and unleashing a stench that clawed at the back of Maggie's throat—rot and filth heated by hours of sunless decay. Without flinching, Wren tossed the bundle inside.

"So long, evidence," she muttered like it was a joke no one else would laugh at. When she let the lid fall back into place, it slammed with finality and left an echo hanging somewhere above their heads.

Before either of them could fill the silence that followed, Maggie's phone buzzed and chimed in quick succession—one notification after another stacking impatiently until everything else in the world shrank around it. She glanced at the screen.

"Voicemail." Her voice faltered before leaning into something harder. "From my dad."

Wren shifted her weight against the dumpster and crossed her arms loosely over her chest. "This oughta be good," she said with that same dry tone that could mean anything or nothing at all.

Maggie tapped in her code.

The voice on the other end was as familiar as it was unwelcome—a low hum of barely contained frustration wrapped tightly around clipped syllables: *"Margaret."* Even through the speaker's distortion, Charles Kline's disapproval landed heavy in the narrow space between them. *"I know you think Wren is innocent, but associating with a murder suspect? They're saying she killed that journalist."* There was something deliberate in his pauses, like he wanted each word to carry twice its weight before moving to the next one. *"Your mother's been watching this unfold all morning; she's beside herself—I don't need to tell you what this is doing to her."*

Maggie's chest tightened as she held perfectly still, though every instinct told her to stop listening.

"I need you to think this through." His voice rose now—not loud or angry but just loud enough to make each word press harder against whatever fragile sense of control she still had left. *"Whatever you believe about Wren's innocence... running like this?"* Another measured pause followed by a sigh long enough for Maggie to imagine him pinching the bridge of his nose like he always did during arguments he wanted to win without raising his voice. *"It makes everything worse."*

There was more—there always was—but Maggie's thumb hit stop before he could finish spinning whatever threat or ultimatum had been waiting at the end of his sentence.

For several seconds after Charles Kline's voice cut out completely, neither woman moved nor spoke. The air between them felt heavier now than it had in hours—a weight made up of too many unspoken things they both knew wouldn't stay unspoken much longer.

When Maggie finally looked up from the phone still clutched tightly in her hand, there was something raw behind her stare—hurt layered unevenly over defiance like neither one could fully decide who should take control first.

Wren pushed off from the dumpster and struck a melodramatic pose, one hand on her hip and the other resting just below her collarbone. "Oh, Margaret," she said in an absurdly posh accent that instantly grated, "won't you please come home and be my obedient little baby? Get a secretarial job—very respectable! Type up some memos, fetch coffee for your boss, and, most importantly, pretend you're not a lesbian?"

Maggie snorted before she could stop herself. The grin overtook her face almost involuntarily, breaking through the tension she'd been carrying like a weight all day. "Don't forget filing," she said, matching Wren's over-the-top tone with precision. "A truly good secretary must master the sacred art of alphabetizing."

Wren gasped and clutched at her chest like she'd taken a mortal wound. "How could I possibly forget?" she cried, eyes theatrically wide. "Without proper filing, society would simply collapse! Chaos in the streets! Anarchy!"

The alley echoed with their laughter, cutting through the stale air thick with smells they tried not to linger on. It was stupid—this was all stupid—but it worked. For just a moment, everything felt lighter than it had in hours.

When the laughter faded into something closer to silence, Maggie turned her attention back to her phone. Her thumb hovered over the screen as though unsure where to start. "While I've got this out..." she murmured, half to herself. Her fingers began moving with purpose now, tapping away. "I want to see if I can find out more about Anne." She frowned, adding under her breath: "Maybe then we'll understand what's coming next."

Wren stepped closer and perched on the edge of a wooden pallet stacked unevenly against the wall. She leaned in toward Maggie's shoulder until she could see the faint blue glow of the phone. "Anything interesting?"

"Hang on." Maggie's brow knit as her eyes scanned the search results. Then she nodded slowly. "Anne had her own podcast."

"No shit?" Wren shifted forward, her tone equal parts curiosity and disbelief. "What kind of stuff was she into?"

Maggie didn't look up as she scrolled further down the page. "Local politics... corporate misconduct..." She paused to read aloud from the list of episode titles: "'The Silent Partners: Dark Money in City Hall'... 'Secrets of the Shadows: Exposing Corporate Greed and Political Bribery.'"

Wren let out a low whistle that had just enough edge to sound impressed. "Well damn," she said softly. "Sounds like Anne wasn't afraid to dive straight into shark-infested waters."

She stayed quiet for a moment after that but shifted closer still until their shoulders were nearly touching. Maggie kept scrolling as Wren tilted her head to follow along—and then froze mid-motion when something caught her eye.

"Wait—hold up." Maggie sucked in a breath so sharp it could have cut glass before tapping hard at the screen with one finger like she couldn't quite believe what was there. "Holy cow." Her voice sounded like reverence—or maybe dread.

Wren looked up instinctively at Maggie's expression before following the direction of her finger on the screen.

"Look at this," Maggie said tightly.

Wren leaned in closer now too, reading aloud even as her heart started to beat faster: "'Behind the Badge: Uncovering Police Corruption in NYC.'"

Her voice faltered on that last word—not because it surprised her (it didn't), but because every syllable seemed heavier than it should have been.

They both went quiet for what felt like a long time until Maggie finally spoke again.

"No wonder Dennis wanted her silenced," she said evenly, though there was nothing even about how hard she gripped the phone now. Her knuckles had gone white against its edges.

Wren didn't respond right away but glanced sideways at Maggie instead—as though trying to gauge how much more either of them needed spelled out at this point.

It wasn't exactly news that taking swings at dirty cops tended to put you on someone's shit list—but somehow hearing it aloud made all those unspoken truths feel painfully real anyway.

Wren's stomach growled, sharp and insistent, a reminder of just how long it had been since they'd had anything resembling a proper meal. She glanced toward the mouth of the alley, where a flickering streetlight illuminated the corner convenience store like a beacon.

"Hey, Mags?" Wren reached into her messenger bag, fumbling around until her hand closed on her wallet. She held it out. "Think you could grab us something to eat? That place over there looks doable."

Maggie didn't move right away. Her eyes darted between Wren and the street beyond, hesitation clear in the tightness of her jaw. "Is it safe to use my card? Won't they be tracking us?"

Wren answered with a shrug that pulled at her shoulder, sending a jolt of pain through her arm. She winced but kept her tone light. "Probably, yeah. But by the time they figure out where we are, we'll be long gone." She paused, then added with a crooked grin, "And unless you're up for dumpster diving tonight, we don't have many other options."

Maggie's shoulders relaxed as she chuckled and took the card from Wren's outstretched hand. "Fine. Any special requests?"

"Surprise me," Wren said, leaning in to plant a quick kiss on Maggie's cheek. "Just make sure it's something solid—we've got a long night ahead."

As Maggie swung onto the bike and pedaled off toward the store, Wren leaned back against the cold brick wall and stared at her feet. She could still move them. All they had to do was stay ahead—stay ahead of Dennis, ahead of whoever else wanted them silenced for good.

Her gaze drifted back down the alleyway, where Maggie had disappeared into the streets. Wren let out a slow breath and thought about how absurd all of this was. This morning had started so normal—eggs and avocado, some vague plan about partying later; bullets hadn't exactly factored into any part of it.

Twice today she'd been shot at. Twice! One bullet so close it actually grazed her shoulder—a split second slower and it would've put a hole in her arm instead of leaving what promised to be one hell of a scar. That part wasn't so bad though; Maggie liked scars. She liked tracing them with her fingers like they told some secret story only she could read—always murmuring that they made Wren look tough, even badass.

But still—this wasn't what Maggie signed up for when she'd decided she was done with everything safe and familiar back home. Chuck and Karen would take Maggie back in an instant—they'd even smile while shipping her off to one of those hellhole conversion camps—but tough luck for them: Maggie wasn't going anywhere.

Because she was Wren's now.

Wren would keep her safe—not just from Dennis or whoever else was behind this mess—but from everything: bullets, betrayal, even Chuck and Karen with their saccharine smiles hiding knives behind their backs.

Safe.

It wasn't like there was anything left to lose anyway—not after what Dennis did to Anne. And whatever Anne had uncovered before she died? It must have been big enough to turn every cop within fifty miles against them too. Didn't matter though; whatever it was, Wren wasn't stopping now.

She couldn't stop now.

Maggie came back into view then, pedaling toward her with bags slung over both handlebars and hair catching bits of neon from the convenience store sign above them—a soft halo Wren swore only she could see.

Goddamn.

She looked beautiful—the kind of beautiful that made Wren's throat tighten just thinking about how lucky she was to even know someone like Maggie existed in this world.

The kind of beautiful worth risking everything for anyway.

She dismounted with fluid ease, her chestnut hair falling in untamed wisps against her damp forehead. "Dinner is served," Maggie declared, hoisting the crinkled paper bag aloft like a trophy.

Wren's stomach rumbled as if on cue. "My savior," she said, reaching out instinctively for the bag.

Maggie swatted her hand away, not harshly but with a teasing sort of authority. "Patience, cowgirl. We need to do this right."

She crouched down and began unpacking their modest feast—a handful of energy bars, a small bag of dried fruit, and two squished sandwiches wrapped snugly in wax paper. Maggie divided the haul with the precision of someone used to making do, carefully tucking half the protein bars into Wren's courier bag and the rest into her own.

"And now," Maggie said, her voice dripping with mock grandeur as she reached into the depths of the bag, "the pièce de résistance." She pulled out two bottles of electrolyte water like they were rare treasures plucked from an ancient hoard.

Wren didn't wait for further ceremony. She snatched a bottle, twisted off the cap, and drank deeply. The liquid was cold enough to send a sharp jolt down her throat—a bracing kind of relief that almost made her forget how dry her mouth had been just seconds earlier.

"Slow down," Maggie chided gently as she watched Wren gulp half the bottle in one go. Her tone was light, but her brow furrowed. "You're going to make yourself sick."

Wren lowered the bottle and gave a lopsided grin. "Yes, mom," she said, dragging out the word for maximum effect before rolling her eyes.

Maggie stepped closer then. Something in her shifted—her playful demeanor softened as concern crept across her face like a cloud blocking out sunlight. She reached up, cupping Wren's face in both hands with surprising tenderness. Her thumb brushed along Wren's cheekbone where the edges of a fresh bruise bloomed purple-yellow against her skin.

"You okay?" Maggie's voice had dropped to just above a whisper—low enough that it felt like something meant only for them and no one else.

For a moment, Wren simply leaned into the touch, letting herself fall into its warmth and care. It wasn't often that someone handled her so gently; she wasn't sure she'd ever get used to it. "Never better," she murmured finally—half truth, half plea—as something unspoken welled up inside her chest.

The kiss came naturally after that—not rushed or hesitant but steady, grounding. Maggie's lips carried traces of salt-sweet energy bar crumbs that tasted oddly perfect in the moment. Wren felt herself smiling into it despite everything—the ache in her limbs, the exhaustion sitting heavy in her bones—all temporarily forgotten.

When they broke apart, Wren lingered in the invisible bubble they'd created together. Her fingers brushed over her own lips briefly as though committing the sensation to memory before reality reasserted itself: They couldn't stay here forever.

She glanced at Maggie then—at those steady blue-gray eyes that seemed both fearless and unbearably fragile all at once—and felt something solidify sharp and sure inside her: *Protect this.* Protect *her.* The thought came unbidden but absolute.

"Let's check the GPS and go," Wren said. Diligently, Maggie turned her phone on, studied the route, and turned it off.

"We'll head west then south," Maggie said.

They pushed off together like synchronized swimmers breaking water's surface, slipping seamlessly into the rhythm they knew so well. The alley emptied them onto bustling city streets alive with late-afternoon energy—horns honking sporadically over distant chatter and soft strains of street musicians playing for spare change.

The sun hung low now—casting long golden streaks across glass buildings and asphalt alike—as shadows danced beneath their wheels. Wren rode ahead at first before they fell into single file to navigate an especially narrow stretch between idling cars and jaywalking pedestrians.

When they hit open pavement again—both lanes clear for just long enough—they veered back side by side without a word needing to be spoken about it: This was their version of normalcy amidst chaos—a fleeting pocket where everything felt almost controllable even when nothing actually was.

The city pulsed around them, frenetic and alive. Horns blared their grievances, engines growled in frustration, and pedestrians hurled words sharp enough to cut through the humid air. To most, it was chaos. To Wren, it was music—the untamed rhythm of her beloved concrete jungle, loud and unapologetic.

Her body protested with every push of the pedals. Muscles screamed, wounds stung anew with each jarring movement. And yet, Wren felt something else: a current humming just beneath her skin. The adrenaline leftover from the confrontation with Zak had mostly drained away, leaving behind a jittery afterglow that tingled through her arms and legs like static electricity. She drew in a lungful of thick urban air—scorched asphalt mixed with gasoline—and let it settle inside her chest.

The wind tugged at her hair as they gained speed, cool but fleeting against the warmth of the sun baking her shoulders. Ahead of her, Maggie veered around a slow-moving van. When Wren caught up to her at the next light, Maggie turned just enough to meet her gaze. They shared a fleeting smile—half camaraderie, half mischief—a wordless acknowledgment: this was their moment, their ride.

Maggie called out turns from memory in bursts of sharp directions that carried easily over the din around them. The comfort she had with the instructions she'd read was unmistakable; every lean into a curve or pivot at an intersection looked effortless. As they rounded a particularly tight corner—a left so sharp it seemed impossible not to skid—Wren caught herself grinning wide enough to make her cheeks ache.

This was it. This was living—not the kind you talk about wistfully but the kind you could feel buzzing in your blood and rattling your ribcage as you chased it down a crowded avenue on two wheels without a safety net. The ache in Wren's thighs argued otherwise; every burning muscle insisted she should stop or slow down or even consider quitting altogether—but that wasn't going to happen.

The city grid unfolded ahead of them like an unpredictable puzzle, full of veins carrying life and intersections sparking kinetic energy like synapses firing in some great urban mind. She'd ridden these streets for years as a courier—familiar with every dodgy crosswalk and pothole—but today felt different. Urgent. Important in ways she hadn't fully processed yet but couldn't ignore.

The pain sharpened now, digging deeper into her calves with each pedal stroke like claws scraping bone, but Wren welcomed it as evidence of forward motion—a reminder that she could still move despite everything that weighed on her shoulders and tightened around her chest like chains she refused to acknowledge aloud.

Maggie took another turn up ahead without warning, graceful as ever despite the squeal of protesting tires. Wren followed close behind, legs burning hot but steadying into rhythm while something resembling hope—or maybe just determination—pushed her onward past exhaustion.

The shift from city to desolation came like the slow dimming of a light. The energy of the crowded streets, with their churning cars and thrumming intersections, ebbed away block by block, until silence began to settle in its place. Wren noticed it first—not just the absence of sound but the absence of people—like they'd crossed an invisible barrier where human life had quietly withdrawn. The towering skyscrapers receded behind them, replaced by squat, tired-looking structures. The kind that leaned together as if conspiring to keep standing despite the years breaking them down.

Graffiti sprawled across the walls in wild bursts of color—vivid blues and electric yellows that were almost too bright against the peeling gray facades of abandoned warehouses. There was an odd artistry to it, Wren thought, though she wasn't sure if it made the place feel more alive or more forsaken. The air carried a damp heaviness now, thick with rust and mildew and something faintly sour, like stagnant water left too long in shadows. Wren breathed it in anyway, her nostrils flaring involuntarily as her gaze flicked to Maggie riding ahead. She didn't miss the tension in Maggie's eyes—the way her jaw stayed clenched tight, scanning every alley, every vacant doorway. The streets were emptier here, barren even, but that just meant fewer witnesses if Dennis or one of his lackeys finally caught up.

"Down Haverton," Maggie said over her shoulder, her voice low but urgent. "Then Hoops Street and south from there." She hesitated and added, "I'll want to check again once we're clear."

Wren slowed her pace until she coasted to a stop at an intersection where four roads stretched out like veins on a weathered map. She planted one foot on the ground and gestured around them with a sweep of her arm. "Check now," she urged, the words clipped but steady. "If Dennis is tracking your phone—and he's smart enough for that—we need to throw him off here." Her hand pointed toward each road in turn. "This is perfect. He won't know which way we've gone."

Maggie nodded silently and pulled alongside her, pulling out her phone with quick precision. It glowed briefly in the dimming light as she studied it—a flicker of technology against this hollowed-out backdrop—before she powered it down again just as fast. "Fillmore Manufacturers Building," she said quietly, slipping the phone back into her pocket. Her finger pointed southward down a long stretch of road ahead. "Thirty-six Lavigne Road. About two miles that way."

They started off again without another word, their wheels crunching faintly over broken shards of glass that scattered across the edges of uneven pavement. Each turn brought more signs of decay: boarded-up windows sagging inward like shut eyelids and fire escapes corroding into rusted skeletons clinging stubbornly to brick walls. Wren couldn't help cataloging it all—the slow erosion of what had once been solid and functional—thinking how time could make everything seem so fragile.

The streets around them widened gradually as they pressed on, opening up into an expanse where sound traveled differently: muted yet sharper somehow at the same time. The familiar bass hum of city traffic faded into echoes of something else—distant clanks and whirs from unseen machinery humming somewhere further out on industrial fringes.

Wren tightened her grip on the handlebars as she felt it—the texture beneath their tires shifting suddenly from asphalt to gravel, then dirt. The change was jarring at first: vibrations jolting up through her hands and forearms as tiny stones scattered noisily under each wheelspin. But she adjusted quickly, leaning forward into her bike's frame for balance while keeping pace beside Maggie.

The world around them emptied further still; no honking horns or distant chatter reached them anymore—just this brittle crunching sound beneath their tires, paired with their own labored breathing cutting through the heavy air like some makeshift rhythm they hadn't planned but couldn't quite escape.

Maggie pulled up next to Wren, their bikes gliding side by side now that the road had widened and emptied out. She reached over, her fingers brushing Wren's arm—silent reassurance, a shared acknowledgment of the storm they were pedaling into. Wren glanced at her partner, catching the mixture of wonder and unease on Maggie's face. It was like looking into a mirror.

Ahead, the Fillmore building.

They slowed as they approached. Wren's gaze swept over the structure—a hulking six-story warehouse, its walls covered in sprawling graffiti. The colors were bold and chaotic, defiant even, as if the paint itself was trying to fight off the decay creeping through the rest of the building. Rotting wooden beams framed windows shattered long ago, their jagged edges gaping like broken teeth. Trash was scattered haphazardly around the base—plastic bags caught on weeds, rusted beer cans sinking halfway into damp earth.

Wren swung off her bike and threw her bag to the ground with a grunt. "Fuck!" The word came out louder than she expected, bouncing off the warehouse walls before fading into silence.

Maggie dismounted too, her eyes tracing the height of the building. "It's huge." Her voice sounded small against the backdrop of it all. "How are we supposed to find anything in there? Let alone something as small as a USB key?"

Wren kicked at a dented soda can near her foot, sending it clattering across cracked pavement. "If it *is* a USB key this time," she snapped. Her voice was sharp enough to cut through steel. "Could be anything—a damn notebook, a stupid trinket—we don't even know what we're supposed to be looking for."

The frustration spilled over and out, words tumbling too fast to stop them. "Damn Anne and her sick little scavenger hunt." She aimed another kick at a piece of debris but missed. "Fuck Dennis with his itchy trigger finger." Her teeth clenched through the next ones: "Zak—that two-faced little bastard." She paused long enough for breath before finishing with venomous precision: "And your parents? Charles and Karen can go fuck themselves too, with their holier-than-thou bullshit."

The silence that followed hung heavy between them until Wren noticed Maggie watching her with quiet concern. That look—the one that said everything and nothing at once—made Wren bark out a laugh that didn't sound quite right even to her own ears. The sound ricocheted off crumbling bricks before falling flat against the ground.

"But you know what?" She turned toward Maggie then, eyes softer but still flashing with resolve. "I love you so goddamn much, Mags." Her voice caught on the last word before she steadied it again. "That's about all I can count on these days."

They walked their bikes slowly along the perimeter of the building now, scanning it like soldiers studying enemy territory before an ambush. The warehouse loomed above them—a decaying monolith wrapped in clashing stories: its graffiti screamed loud defiance, while time and neglect whispered surrender.

"This place is a disaster," Wren said, her voice barely rising above the crunch of gravel under their tires. She didn't add "fucking" this time, though it hovered in the air like unspoken punctuation. Why waste the energy? The wreckage ahead was emphasis enough.

They turned the corner, and Wren's eyes landed on a mountain of debris leaning against the building's base. Broken pallets and rusted metal sheets mingled with chunks of concrete, the whole mess forming a barrier that looked like it might collapse if you so much as sneezed on it. Above it all, a tattered banner flapped limply in the breeze, its faded letters struggling to spell out some long-forgotten promise.

"Look at this," Wren called back to Maggie, shaking her head. "Like a junkyard exploded and just decided to stay."

They kept pedaling. The shattered windows came next. Glass shards littered the ground, catching slivers of sunlight that made them wink like cruel little diamonds. Wren scanned each jagged frame as they passed, eyes narrowing as she searched for any sign of Anne's clue. Nothing yet—just broken glass and more broken glass.

"Those windows," she said finally, shaking her head again, "are basically my optimism right now. Completely shot to hell."

When they reached the back of the building, something else caught her eye: a doorway yawning wide open, its metal door hanging sideways from warped hinges. It creaked softly as the gusting wind pushed it back and forth—each sound grating enough to feel like nails down Wren's spine. Inside was darkness, faint figures of shifting shadows that hinted at more ruin awaiting them.

"Great," Wren muttered under her breath. Louder, she added: "Pretty sure this is an open invite for every squatter and stray dog from here to downtown."

They finished their lap around the building and coasted to a stop near where they'd started. Wren swung off her bike and approached a scatter of bricks spilled from the crumbling wall above. One sharp kick sent several pieces skittering along the ground; another crunch followed as stone fractured into smaller fragments across the pavement.

"This is useless," Wren said after a long moment, her frustration simmering beneath each clipped word. She planted her hands on her hips and surveyed their surroundings with something between exhaustion and resignation etched across her face. "How are we supposed to find anything in this chaos?"

She glanced toward Maggie then and saw that same weight mirrored in her partner's slumped shoulders—the kind of heaviness that made breathing feel more like work than instinct. They were both carrying it now: the doubt pressing down harder than these walls ever could.

And then something caught Wren's eye: a faint smear of neon spray paint on the battered facade ahead. She stepped forward until it came into clearer focus—a crude arrow sprayed in electric blue paint, pointing west like some makeshift compass.

"Hey." She nudged Maggie lightly with an elbow and tipped her chin toward the graffiti. "Look at that."

With renewed purpose—though not too much—they mounted up again and followed wherever it might lead. Around another corner of the building came more graffiti.

"What the hell?" Wren tilted her head, narrowing her eyes at the arrow scrawled in jagged black graffiti.

Maggie stood beside her, hands on her hips, studying it like she was trying to solve a puzzle. "It's pointing up. Roof, maybe?"

Wren let out a dry laugh. "Wonderful. I was just telling myself how much I hoped today would end with me scaling a deathtrap."

They turned back toward the doorway they'd passed minutes earlier, a gaping rectangle in the side of the building that looked less like an entrance and more like a mouth waiting to swallow them whole. Wren swung off her bike with stiff movements that betrayed her exhaustion. She leaned it carefully against the wall, watching as Maggie did the same with hers, though Maggie's stance seemed slower, more hesitant.

"Urban adventures," Wren said under her breath, throwing Maggie an exaggerated smirk as if to disguise the flicker of apprehension in her own chest. "Ready?"

Maggie gave a quick nod, though her face betrayed some lingering doubt behind the bravado. "Might as well be."

The smell hit them first—a damp, sour odor thick enough to taste on the back of their tongues—as they stepped through the threshold into what could be described as a cavern of decay. Sunlight poured reluctantly through broken windows high above, streaking across shadows like faint brushstrokes on a dark canvas. Dust motes floated lazily in the beams of light, undisturbed by time or activity.

3:31 p.m.

Their footsteps echoed across the concrete floor in uneven staccato beats—sharp taps swallowed quickly by hollow silence. The air grew heavier as they moved further inside, layers of damp rot mixed with something metallic and faintly acrid curling unpleasantly into their noses.

"Oh my God," Wren muttered, coughing as she waved uselessly at the air around her face. "It smells like my old apartment after a weekend away with no working fridge."

Maggie let out a small laugh that sounded more nervous than amused. "Honestly? This isn't that much worse than when you come home from work."

"Ouch." Wren placed a hand over her heart in mock offense. "Kick me when I'm down, why don't you."

"I love you, stinky girl," Maggie said with a giggle.

They pressed forward slowly—eyes adjusting to the dim light and scanning for hazards that seemed plentiful enough without looking too closely for them: jagged piles of splintered wood where pallets had once lived; twisted sheets of rusting metal; unidentifiable debris scattered like remnants of some long-forgotten battle. Wren stepped gingerly over something she didn't want to think about too hard and glanced toward Maggie, who was trailing just behind.

"There," Maggie said suddenly, pointing ahead toward the far wall where something caught what little light was left.

Wren followed Maggie's gaze and spotted it: a staircase made of metal so corroded it looked like one good gust could send it tumbling sideways into oblivion. It zigzagged upward like some exhausted skeleton clinging to the bone-thin walls for support.

"That's our way up?" Wren asked skeptically, taking an involuntary step back as though distance might make it look less precarious. "Perfect. Exactly what I was hoping for—a tetanus-ridden stairway from hell."

They made their way across the debris-strewn floor carefully now—the loose chunks of concrete and twisted rebar forcing them to step deliberately and occasionally stumble anyway. Wren cursed softly under her breath when one particularly jagged edge scraped against her shoe but didn't stop until they were standing at the base of the staircase itself.

She placed one hand lightly on its cold railing and stared up at its crooked ascent before setting tentative weight onto the bottom step. It groaned beneath her foot—a low sound that vibrated through the space—but held firm for now.

"Ladies first," Wren said with a grin that could have powered the streetlights. She swept her arm out dramatically, like she was unveiling a masterpiece.

Maggie didn't miss a beat. "Oh no. Age before beauty, remember?" Her tone was sweet enough to rot teeth.

Wren raised an eyebrow. "You're older than me."

"By, like, a year," Maggie shot back, waving off the accusation with an air of exaggerated nonchalance. "Butch before femme, then."

Wren rolled her eyes in mock exasperation and took the lead, heading up the narrow stairwell where each step groaned under her weight like it was auditioning for the role of creakiest staircase in a haunted house. Maggie followed close behind, her breath coming in quick, uneven bursts that suggested nerves more than exertion.

The higher they climbed, the quieter things got—not peaceful quiet but the kind that sits heavy on your chest and makes you hyperaware of every creak and shuffle. By the time they reached the fifth floor, Wren's thighs were staging a rebellion, and her forehead glistened with sweat. She paused to wipe it away with the back of her hand.

"Did Anne mention being a fitness trainer in any of her profiles?" Wren managed between gasps for air.

The top floor greeted them with silence, broken by the occasional whisper of wind through cracked windows. Dust motes hung motionless in thick beams of late-afternoon sun as though even they were too afraid to move. Wren squinted and scanned the space until she spotted what they were looking for: a hulking metal door tucked into the far wall like it hoped no one would notice.

"There." Wren nodded toward it and added with forced cheer, "Our ticket to the penthouse suite."

When they reached the door, Wren's hand hovered over the handle for a moment before she turned back to Maggie.

"Ready?"

Maggie nodded quickly—too quickly—her expression somewhere between bravery and unease. It wasn't exactly reassuring.

Wren took one last steadying breath and pushed open the door slowly. The hinges protested with a drawn-out screech like nails on chalkboard. Bright sunlight flooded in, making both women blink against its sudden intensity as they stepped onto the rooftop.

The expanse stretched wide before them—a bleak sheet of gravel shimmering under an unkind sun. Loose stones shifted beneath Wren's feet as she walked forward, revealing patches of cracked tar underneath that looked like battle scars earned from years of neglect. The air hit her hard: salty and sour all at once, sharp enough to wrinkle her nose.

"Well," Wren muttered, nudging at some gravel with the toe of her cycling shoe until it scattered across the rooftop's uneven surface. "This is charming."

Maggie didn't respond immediately; instead, she drifted toward the edge like someone drawn by an invisible string. She paused at the low parapet wall and peered down before letting out a low whistle laced with alarm. "Shit," she said softly. "That's a long way down."

"Hey!" Wren's voice cut through sharply as she hurried over to Maggie's side. Her concern came out sounding more annoyed than protective, but either way, it stopped Maggie from leaning any farther forward into oblivion.

The wind whipped across their faces mercilessly now—or maybe it had been there all along and they were just noticing it because there wasn't much else competing for attention up here besides old rusting vents and wires that cast jagged shadows across the gray expanse like skeletal fingers reaching out for something.

Wren let her gaze sweep over every inch of the rooftop as unease began coiling itself tightly in her chest like an over-wound spring. The soft crunch of gravel underfoot seemed deafening now in contrast to everything else—the silence above them almost unnatural after so much noise during their climb.

Her eyes narrowed as she walked slowly across the surface, scanning it all for anything—everything—that might be out of place.

"What exactly are we looking for?" Maggie asked. Her voice was nearly carried away by a gust of wind, the kind that felt engineered just to make her question whether shouting was worth the effort.

Wren didn't look up. She ran a hand through her hair, mostly out of habit. "Hell if I know," she replied. "A USB? Another clue? Or maybe Anne just wanted to watch us sweat it out and laugh from wherever she is now. Maybe that's her grand joke—get us scrambling around rooftops for nothing." She paused. "Wouldn't put it past her to have given me the wrong USB key entirely. This could all be some elaborate geocaching prank, and we're just the punchline."

The roof stretched out before them like an abandoned wasteland—gray gravel as far as the eye could see, punctuated by rusting vents and warped metal chimneys. They moved in slow circles, scanning for anything that might stand out against the monotony. The sun pressed down relentlessly, and Wren could feel beads of sweat gathering on her brow before sliding down into places she didn't want to think about.

"This is like looking for a needle in a haystack," Maggie muttered after what felt like hours but had been less than ten minutes.

Wren kicked at a loose clump of gravel, sending it scattering noisily across the rooftop. "More like looking for a needle in a pile of other needles," she said. "Same color, same size... Oh, and they're invisible too." She let out a breath that came dangerously close to being a growl.

They kept moving, their shoes crunching over gravel with every step. The sound echoed in the stillness, unsettling somehow, like they were trespassing on something they weren't supposed to disturb.

"This is stupid," Wren said under her breath as she reached one of the larger ventilation ducts and gave it a solid kick out of sheer frustration. It responded with a low groan, flakes of rust tumbling to the ground like bits of burnt autumn leaves. As if mocking her effort.

Maggie crouched near one of the chimneys and peered into its dark opening. "What if it's hidden inside one of these things?" She didn't sound particularly confident; more like she was grasping at straws.

Wren snorted without turning around. "Oh sure," she said. "Because if I had sensitive information to hide, my first thought would be, 'You know what's perfect? A chimney full of bird shit.' Genius plan."

They pressed on, methodically circling the rooftop with all the enthusiasm of people dragging themselves through an endless line at airport security. Every warped vent or suspicious-looking patch of gravel became a possible hiding spot for half a second before being dismissed just as quickly. Wren's eyes darted from one object to another until she stopped in front of a particularly warped duct that seemed barely capable of holding itself together.

"Hey Mags," she called over her shoulder, resting her hand lightly on its twisted edge. "Think this thing's about to take a swan dive off the roof?"

Maggie shot Wren a look, her brow furrowed with disapproval. "Don't even think about it," she said, her voice sharp but measured. "We're not here to play Jenga with rusty metal."

Wren let out a low sigh, her eyes rolling skyward before she moved on. She crouched down, her fingers brushing against a stubborn clump of weeds that had somehow managed to claw their way up through the gravel. The resilience of it gave her pause—it was remarkable, really, how life could insist on existing in a place like this—but the moment passed as quickly as it arrived. Wren grabbed the weeds by their roots and yanked them free, shaking the dirt loose from their base before tossing them aside. Beneath: more gravel. Of course.

"Nothing," she muttered, the word heavy with resignation. She wiped her hands on her jeans. "Just dirt and gravel. Always more fucking gravel."

The sun was merciless now, pressing down like an unyielding hand on the back of her neck. Sweat gathered at her hairline and began its slow journey downwards, tracing a path along her spine until it met fabric already damp and clinging to her skin. She paused just long enough to swipe at her forehead with the back of her hand, leaving behind a streak of grime that she didn't bother to notice.

"This is hopeless," she groaned, straightening up and gesturing toward the endless expanse of rooftop stretched out before them. "We could waste days here and still find nothing."

Maggie didn't answer right away—she rarely answered immediately—which added to Wren's growing frustration. Instead, she was crouched near the edge of the roof, head tilted in quiet concentration as her fingers carefully parted another patch of weeds. Wren watched as Maggie sifted through a mix of roots and rocks with practiced precision, probing deeper into the gravel layer beneath.

"Anything?" Wren asked finally, though even she could hear the wariness beneath her own tone—hope creeping into places where she wasn't quite ready for it to return.

Maggie sighed through her nose and shook her head, letting one last handful of gravel fall back to the ground in reluctant surrender. Her shoulders slumped under an invisible weight. "Just more rocks."

For a moment they stood there in silence, both women caught between frustration and exhaustion as the heat pulsed around them like something alive. Wren ran a hand through damp hair that was sticking to the back of her neck and turned slowly on her heel to take in their surroundings again—the rooftop with its scattered rusting chimneys and crooked vents casting thin black bars onto gray gravel. In spite of herself—or maybe because this was all starting to feel so maddeningly pointless—she thought there was something almost beautiful about it: this strange landscape of decay standing defiantly against time.

"Maybe we're thinking about this wrong," she said at last, breaking the stillness with words that sounded hesitant even to her own ears. Her gaze narrowed as it swept across the horizon for what felt like the hundredth time that day. "What if it's not in the gravel? Or underneath some vent? What if we're not asking the right questions?"

That's when she spotted it—a hint of white against the greasy, soot-black metal. For a moment, Wren thought it had to be her eyes playing games with her again. Gravel dust, maybe, catching the light in just the right way. But no, not this time. She squinted and leaned in closer. There it was, plain as day: a white envelope, smudged and crumpled, clinging to the side of the air duct like a stubborn band-aid.

"Maggie!" she called out, her voice breaking somewhere between excitement and urgency. "Over here!"

She could already hear Maggie's footsteps crunching across the gravel before she saw her, quick and purposeful. Wren shifted her weight onto the duct—carefully at first—and reached for the envelope. Her fingers grazed its edge but couldn't quite catch hold. Just barely out of reach. Of course.

"Great," Wren muttered under her breath, gritting her teeth. She stretched farther, ignoring the duct's metallic groan beneath her weight. "Come on, you piece of crap," she hissed. The words were mostly aimed at herself.

With one last lunge, her fingers snagged the envelope—success!—but in that same instant, success turned traitor. The duct beneath her let out an ear-splitting screech like a wounded animal before collapsing entirely. Wren tumbled backward with all the grace of a sack of potatoes and landed hard on the gravel.

"Wren!" Maggie was there almost immediately, crouching beside her and grabbing for her arm like someone checking to make sure she still had all four limbs intact. "Are you okay?"

Wincing, Wren brushed shards of gravel from her scraped palms and tried to ignore the sting creeping up her backside. "Fine," she said, though her backside loudly disagreed. "Just my pride." A beat passed before she added wryly, "And my beautiful, beautiful ass."

She held up the envelope as if it were some sort of prize trophy recovered from a battlefield. "I got it," she declared. She tossed it almost carelessly to Maggie.

Maggie didn't look nearly as triumphant as Wren felt; instead, she frowned down at the envelope like it was something much worse than just a piece of paper taped to an old hunk of ventilation metal. Turning it over in her hands, she squinted at it suspiciously.

"It's not a USB," Maggie said after a long pause, shaking her head like that fact itself made no sense whatsoever. Her voice carried a note of confusion that Wren didn't particularly like hearing just then.

"What is it?" Wren asked—though what she meant was *why do you look like that?* Because Maggie wasn't one to frown so intently over nothing.

"It's soft," Maggie said after another beat of silence, holding it up to the sunlight at just the right angle so that something inside shifted faintly against its paper prison walls.

Wren felt herself leaning forward unconsciously. Her stomach twisted with anticipation—or maybe dread; sometimes they felt too close to tell apart. Maggie finally spoke again: "It's paper... I think."

Now Wren frowned too because *paper* wasn't exactly what they'd been looking for or expecting or even remotely prepared for at this stage in their desperate guessing game about what came next.

"For a second," Maggie added lightly—but even in its lightness there was something uneasy about her tone—"I thought it might be drugs or something." She laughed faintly but without humor.

Wren rolled her eyes but said nothing because frankly? That idea didn't seem entirely off-base considering where they were and *who* they were dealing with these days.

Her fingers twitched almost involuntarily toward the envelope now resting delicately in Maggie's grip. She wanted—no needed—to know what was inside right this second because, whatever it was? It had to be important enough for someone to go through all this trouble hiding it up there in such an obvious-not-obvious place.

But before she could say anything—or reach out with those itching fingers—a voice sliced through the air so sharply that Wren felt herself flinch even before turning toward its source.

"I'll take that," the voice said smoothly—not loud but loud enough—with just enough bite around its edges that you knew immediately who it belonged to before you even looked.

Wren froze.

Her blood went cold—and not metaphorically either; no, really cold—as though someone had replaced it with ice water flowing straight through every vein in her body right at that very moment.

Slowly—because fast movements suddenly didn't feel wise—Wren turned toward where she already knew Dennis would be standing: gun steady in his hand (of course) and that cruel little smile plastered across his face like he practiced it in front of mirrors every morning just for moments exactly like this one.

"Well," Dennis drawled lazily as though he were commenting on nothing more serious than today's weather forecast while casually pointing his gun directly at them both now standing motionless beside broken ductwork debris scattered all around their feet.

"This just keeps getting more interesting."

Wren's heart hammered in her chest as Dennis raised the gun, the barrel unwavering in its aim at Maggie. The air on the rooftop felt stifling, heavy with heat and tension. It pressed down on her like a lead blanket, the sun above relentless and merciless.

Dennis tilted his head, his voice low and sweet with venom. "Hand it over, sweetheart," he said, each word slow and deliberate. His gaze stayed locked on Maggie, never straying for an instant. "Nice and easy now."

Wren's muscles coiled, ready to move, ready to fight—but the gun kept her frozen in place. The sight of that barrel pointed directly at Maggie's chest was enough to root her feet to the hot concrete beneath them. She didn't dare breathe too loudly. Not yet. Maggie's hand trembled violently as she held onto that dirty white envelope like it was her lifeline. Or maybe a death sentence.

"How did you find us?" Wren spat through clenched teeth. Rage clawed at her insides, but fear wrapped icy fingers around her throat, choking it down.

Dennis laughed—a sharp, brittle sound with no humor behind it. The kind of laugh that makes your stomach twist. He shifted on his feet, the gravel underfoot crunching loud enough to cut through the thick silence between them. "You thought you were clever," he said smoothly, almost casually, but his words carried a bite sharp enough to draw blood. "After you clocked me with that laptop? I decided to drop by Cyclista for a little chat." A smirk curled at the edges of his mouth, cruel and smug. "Had myself a nice talk with Zak. Again."

"Poor little Zak," he said softly but with enough malice packed into those three words that Wren felt something in her gut twist like a vice grip tightening up all over again. "Crying like a baby when I got there." He chuckled darkly before adding almost conversationally: "You did a number on him though—I'll give you that much credit." Then came one final smile—cold and razor-thin—and those last four words hung thick in the air between them: "Gotta admit—I'm impressed."

The words hit like a punch to the gut. Zak. That spineless coward.

The ground beneath Wren felt unsteady for a moment as her mind raced to catch up. Zak had betrayed them—of course he had—but hearing it still sent fresh anger coursing through veins already stretched too thin.

"Anyway," Dennis said, his voice dripping with smugness, "once he stopped crying like a baby, he couldn't wait to help me out. Opened up that laptop you so generously threw at my head. It was ruggedized, of course. You bike messengers love your tech to take a beating, don't you? Real handy for me. Turns out, you're not as clever as you think you are. There was a temp file saved—a neat little copy of whatever you'd been digging into."

Wren felt her mistake in her chest, heavy and sudden, like an anchor plunging into deep water. She'd been so caught up in running, in escaping from one disaster to the next, that she hadn't stopped to think about covering her digital tracks. Rookie mistake. Amateurs screwed up like this—left windows open when they should've locked them tight.

"Zak recognized them as GPS coordinates pretty quick," Dennis went on, his grin widening enough to show the uneven line of his teeth. "You mentioned something about 'em back at Cyclista while you were busy turning his face into hamburger meat. And now? Well..." His arms opened in mock grandeur, the gun still steady in one hand. "Here we are. Funny how things just line up sometimes, huh?"

Her gaze slid toward Maggie without meaning to. Her lover's expression was carved out of equal parts terror and bitterness—an ugly cocktail of emotions that Wren didn't need a mirror to know she shared. She'd screwed up big time, and it wasn't just her neck on the line.

The crunch of gravel under Dennis's boots pulled Wren back to reality as he took a deliberate step closer. The sound echoed in the empty space around them, somehow both sharp and muted at once. His gun stayed trained on Maggie—it hadn't wavered by more than a breath since he'd entered—but it was close enough now that even a shallow inhale from Maggie might brush against the barrel.

"Now," Dennis said with exaggerated patience that might've been funny if it didn't carry the promise of violence beneath it, "how about you hand over that envelope before things get messy?"

Wren's mind worked faster than her pulse as she scanned for options or exits or anything that didn't end in disaster—or worse. Her eyes shifted between Dennis's gun and Maggie's wide-eyed terror; neither sight gave her much confidence.

"How'd you even know we were up here? Not somewhere else in the building?" she asked suddenly, stalling for precious seconds while ignoring the dryness creeping into her throat.

Dennis snorted like the question amused him more than it annoyed him. "Didn't," he said simply. "But I saw your bikes out back. Figured you couldn't be far." He jerked his chin toward the stairwell behind him like it was obvious—as though their carelessness had practically rolled out the welcome mat for him. "Then I came inside and heard your voices bouncing around this dump." He shook his head in mock disappointment before adding, "Place is emptier than your heads. Sound carries."

Wren kept any flicker of reaction buried deep under layers of guilt and frustration. Another rookie mistake stacked neatly atop the first one—the kind she could practically hear her old crew mocking her for if they were around to see this mess.

"Now," Dennis added flatly, all humor drained from his tone like blood from a wound, "hand it over before I lose my patience."

"Asshole," Wren muttered under her breath, though the word came out weak, deflated.

Dennis turned toward her, raising the gun almost casually, as if he had all the time in the world. His lips curved into something that might have been a smirk or a grimace—it was hard to tell—but before he could utter whatever line he surely thought would land with impact, Maggie moved.

She bolted.

The envelope stayed clutched in Maggie's trembling hand, her knuckles so white they seemed to glow against the rust-colored grit of the rooftop. The gravel shifted beneath her sneakers with every step, sounding like breaking glass and threatening to spill her forward onto her knees.

"Maggie!" Wren's voice cut through the air—or tried to—but it was no match for the wind. The word broke apart and scattered before it could reach its target.

Dennis swore—loudly, violently—and then he was after Maggie, his gun still raised. His strides were long and unrelenting, purposeful in a way that made Wren's stomach tighten.

And then she was running too. She didn't remember deciding to move; her body had overridden any internal debate. Her feet pounded against the rooftop, muscles stretching and protesting with every step as she chased after them both.

A sharp crack split the air.

Gunfire.

The sound seemed to echo endlessly in Wren's ears even as Dennis surged forward without hesitation. Maggie stumbled but didn't fall—thank God she didn't fall—and then ducked behind one of the rusting ducts that jutted up from the rooftop like jagged teeth.

The smell of gunpowder was sudden and acrid, burning Wren's nostrils and twisting her stomach into knots. She could taste it now too—sharp and metallic—and it made her want to gag.

Maggie zigzagged ahead of them, weaving between ductwork and old chimneys with a kind of frantic energy that was almost methodical. Wren wanted to believe there was a plan buried somewhere in that chaos—that Maggie had worked out some way to escape or turn this around—but all she saw was desperation.

Dennis wasn't slowing down. He tore after Maggie like an animal chasing prey, his breath coming quick and ragged now but his pace relentless. The distance between them was shrinking fast.

Wren pushed harder, ignoring the fire spreading through her lungs and legs. She was close enough now that she could see beads of sweat trailing down Dennis's neck, glistening in the fading sunlight, close enough to hear him curse under his breath with each step.

She didn't think about what came next; there wasn't time for that now. She lunged at him with everything she had left.

The impact was sudden and violent. They hit the gravel together, Dennis landing hard with a grunt as Wren clung to him like her life—or maybe someone else's life—depended on it. Gravel scraped at her palms; an elbow jabbed sharply into her ribs. Pain exploded through her side, but she kept holding on.

Dennis twisted beneath her and managed to get one solid kick off—a brutal strike to her stomach that left her gasping even as her body tumbled across the rooftop. Her arms flailed against nothing as she hit the ground awkwardly—gravel biting into exposed skin—and came to a stop on her side.

Wren tried to rise immediately, but nothing obeyed: not her legs or arms or even lungs, which seemed incapable of taking in air just yet. Her vision tilted dangerously as she remained grounded where Dennis had left her.

She forced herself to lift her head anyway—just barely—and saw him already back on his feet again like nothing had happened at all. He adjusted his grip on the gun without missing a beat and resumed his pursuit of Maggie like an unstoppable force winding forward.

And Maggie?

She was running out of space.

The edge of the roof loomed closer with every step: a low wall crumbling at its topmost edges but still sturdy enough for someone determined—or reckless—to climb over it if they wanted badly enough.

Wren's heartbeat rose into a frantic drumbeat in response—as though it could somehow will itself across that rooftop and into Maggie's chest instead—to slow hers down or stop whatever terrible choice was forming behind those determined eyes now locked on where sky met earth below.

"Maggie, wait!" Wren's voice came out hoarse, barely more than a rasp. She didn't think Maggie could hear her over the wind, and maybe that was for the best.

Sixty feet ahead, Maggie sprinted across the gravel roof—her legs churning with an urgency that seemed both reckless and inevitable. She was heading straight for the low wall at the building's edge, the envelope clenched in her hand like a lifeline.

Wren stood paralyzed near the roof access door, her heart hammering in time with Dennis's heavy footsteps. He was closing in on Maggie from the left, no more than thirty feet behind her. His rasping breath carried across the roof like that of a predator closing in on its prey.

The wind tore at Maggie's hair as she charged toward certain disaster. The edge loomed closer with every stride she took.

Finally, Wren's body caught up with her racing mind. She launched forward, weaving between the hulking shapes of ventilation units. Her legs felt like cement blocks, her lungs burning with each sharp breath. She hadn't caught her second wind yet—or was it her third or fourth? Didn't matter now. All that mattered was reaching Maggie before Dennis did.

Dennis maintained his pursuit, even as he raised his gun again. Another crack split the air like a whip. Wren flinched instinctively, hearing the bullet ricochet off a ventilation duct to her right, but Maggie didn't even look back.

Wren's feet found their rhythm as she ducked low under pipes and leaped over debris. She cut diagonally across the roof, taking a more direct path than Maggie's panicked zigzag. The gap between them began to shrink as Maggie arched away from the edge, circling back toward the center of the roof. For just a second, Wren thought maybe they had a chance.

Maggie glanced over her shoulder, eyes wild and wide when she spotted Wren just yards behind her. It was a look more desperate than hopeful—a last-ditch gamble without any guarantees. She held out the envelope.

Even before Wren realized what she was doing, her hand shot out and grabbed it mid-stride. The paper crinkled against her palm as though protesting being passed so suddenly between hands—it felt heavier than it had any right to feel.

Dennis roared behind them, changing direction abruptly when he saw the exchange happen right in front of him. He lunged for Wren now instead of Maggie—his fingers outstretched like claws grasping for prey.

If life were fair (and they all knew it wasn't), Dennis would've caught her then—his speed against hers wasn't even comparable—but Wren didn't pause or hesitate long enough for him to get close enough this time.

Instead, she veered sharply away at just the right moment—channeling her namesake—so his momentum carried him forward past her... skidding across loose gravel near what once been sturdy footing but clearly wasn't anymore.

And then he slipped.

It wasn't dramatic like in movies where someone screams 'No!' loudly—it happened too fast yet slow-motion-like simultaneously somehow while reality sped onwards regardless.

Time didn't exactly slow, but it played one of those awful tricks where the most terrible details came into sharp focus: Dennis's arms flailing like he was trying to fight off a swarm of invisible bees, the way his right foot skidded uselessly on the gravel, the sheer, cartoonish wideness of his eyes as he realized there was nothing left under him. For the briefest moment, he hung there, caught in some cruel loophole where gravity hadn't quite made up its mind yet. And then it did.

Dennis went over the edge without so much as a gasp for air, just a strangled noise that wasn't quite a scream. Wren heard his hands scrabble desperately against concrete until—somehow—they caught on the crumbling parapet. His weight yanked him downward with such force that bits of old stone and dust rained down like brittle pieces of stale bread. The structure groaned in protest, its decay laid bare under the strain of one man's life hanging from it.

Wren didn't move. She couldn't. Her feet felt bolted to the rooftop, her breath caught somewhere between her lungs and her throat. The envelope in her hand—yes, she still had that stupid envelope—was a crushed mess now, but she barely noticed. All she could see was Dennis's face below her, twisted and panicked, his fingers clawing at a ledge that seemed determined to give up before he did.

The parapet groaned again—the kind of sound you don't forget because it lodges somewhere deep in your stomach. More chunks broke away, tumbling downward into nothingness. Wren heard Maggie yelling something beside her—or maybe she just imagined it—but all she could focus on was Dennis's scream, raw and jagged like something primal ripped straight out of him. And then that awful realization hit: the parapet wasn't going to hold.

Wren didn't remember running to the edge with Maggie; one second she was frozen solid, and the next, her legs were moving on their own. Gravel crunched underfoot—funny how loud such a small sound could seem when everything else felt muted—and then there they were at the ledge, peering down at what was left.

The parapet had completely given way now; it looked less like a structure and more like broken teeth in an old man's mouth. Dennis wasn't hanging anymore because Dennis wasn't there anymore except six stories below them where the sun cast long shadows across an industrial wasteland. Wren saw him—a crumpled pile that didn't look much like a man—before she even realized she was looking.

"Holy shit," Wren muttered under her breath, not sure who she was talking to or if she'd even said it aloud.

Maggie screamed behind her—sharp and high-pitched before cutting off abruptly, like someone had yanked the cord on a blender mid-spin. She stumbled back from the edge as though the sight alone might pull her over too. Her hand slapped over her mouth so hard Wren half-wondered if it hurt.

"Don't," Wren said instinctively, reaching out to steady Maggie even though her own knees felt about ready to give out. "Don't look."

But it was too late for that—for both of them.

4:17 p.m.

The warehouse district stretched out around them—rows of exhausted buildings leaning into each other for support like they'd been left behind by progress decades ago—and further out still was the glittering skyline of downtown, shimmering faintly as though this tragedy belonged in another world entirely. Wren tried to focus on anything else besides what lay six stories below—tried to count windows or trace power lines or whatever—but no matter what direction she looked in, her attention kept jerking back down to Dennis.

Or what used to be Dennis.

"Is he...?" Maggie's voice trembled, thin and unsteady, like it might break under its own weight.

Wren blinked, hard, but the world refused to come into focus. Shapes bled into one another, colors ran together, and the edges of her vision pulsed as though unseen hands were crumpling the picture in front of her. She felt the midday sun pressing down on her shoulders—not warm, not comforting, but sharp and punishing, a constellation of pinpricks against her sweat-slick skin.

She tried to ground herself in sound, but that was no better. The city had gone quiet—not silent exactly, but subdued, muffled. Somewhere far off there was still the steady thrum of traffic and snatches of conversation carried on waves of heat, but they felt unreal now, hollow echoes of a world she wasn't part of anymore. Her ears hummed with static. Beneath it she could make out her pulse—steady at first, then quickening—a distant drumbeat pounding faster and faster until it swallowed everything else.

"Wren?" Maggie again. A voice that sounded like it came from underwater.

Wren shook her head once, as though that might clear it, and then again harder when it didn't work. Her knees cracked as she bent forward over the edge to look down at six stories of nothing ending in Dennis splayed out on the pavement below.

He hadn't moved. Wren blinked again to be sure—but no, he was as still as before. His arms were flung awkwardly above his head; his legs were bent at angles they weren't made for; his entire body sprawled across sun-baked concrete like some grotesque chalk outline before anyone bothered with chalk. She focused on the dark patch beneath him, spreading outward in uneven tendrils that found their way into every jagged crack and crevice in the pavement.

She let out a breath she hadn't realized she'd been holding and heard herself mutter: "Yeah. He's not getting up from that." The words sounded strange—hollow somehow—and she wondered if maybe someone else had said them instead.

It took another second—two perhaps—for reality to settle over her like a weighted blanket: Dennis was dead. The killer cop who had chased them across town like a predator closing in on prey was gone just like that—no dramatic final showdown, no last-minute redemption arc—just gone. One moment he was there with gun raised and lip curled back into something that wasn't quite a smile or a snarl; the next... Well.

Her stomach clenched hard enough to make her gasp quietly through gritted teeth before stepping back from the ledge with legs that felt less like legs now and more like props hastily cobbled together with sticks and string.

"We need to go." Wren turned toward Maggie and grabbed hold of her arm—not gently but not violently either—because Maggie wasn't moving even though she needed to move immediately if not sooner.

But Maggie didn't move and didn't speak either—not right away anyway—and when she did finally speak again it was slow and deliberate: "We can't just leave him there." She wasn't looking at Wren now but down at Dennis like maybe if she stared long enough things would start making sense or stop hurting or both.

"Yes," Wren said sharply before softening—more for herself than Maggie although maybe for Maggie too because guilt always seemed louder when you didn't say kinder things aloud after snapping harsher ones instead—"Mags... we can." Pause here followed by inhale followed by sigh followed by softer still: "You know what he would've done."

A siren broke through everything after that—the heat haze—the pulsing noise—the stifling quiet—all cut clean through by one sharp wail climbing higher fast enough already without waiting around much longer so no waiting around much longer now obviously either.

"That's our cue," Wren said, her voice low but firm as she tugged on Maggie's arm. "C'mon, babe. We gotta go."

Maggie hesitated, just for a second, her gaze lingering on the edge of the rooftop. Then she nodded, and they turned together, their fingers knotted tightly as they ran across the rough concrete of the rooftop. The city lights blurred below them, distant and indifferent.

Wren's thoughts scrambled, a chaotic jumble barely held together. A cop. He's a cop. Dead cop? No, he can't be dead. Can he? Damn it, fuck this! He shot at us—what about the bullets? Could we find them? Can they trace them to Dennis? What if he's alive? Call an ambulance—no, don't call. Shit! If he's dead... Goddamn it, does that make us cop killers? COP KILLERS? What the hell happens now?

Her pulse thundered in her ears as one thought crashed into another like waves against rock. The envelope. That stupid envelope. What was so important that it was worth dying for—or killing for? Did we even look inside? Couldn't think about it now. Where do we go next? How much time before someone finds him—minutes, hours? Hell, maybe years if we're lucky. No, not years—don't be stupid.

Wren glanced at Maggie beside her. Maggie's face was streaked with tears she wasn't bothering to wipe away anymore. Her shoulders shook with muffled sobs as they ran hand in hand across the rooftop. Wren wasn't crying—not even close—and that tiny fact pricked at her like a thorn buried under skin. Was something wrong with her?

"Fuck," Wren muttered under her breath, more to herself than anyone else. "Maggie... oh God, Maggie." Each tear rolling down Maggie's face felt like another stone added to the weight crushing Wren's chest. This is on me—every last bit of it—and now you're here in my mess. You shouldn't have to deal with this.

She squeezed Maggie's hand tighter and quickened their pace toward the rooftop exit door ahead of them.

A warm breeze kicked up as they paused at the door, carrying with it the gritty tang of tar and exhaust from the streets below. Wren inhaled deeply without meaning to—it burned in her throat but steadied her for just a moment.

"Fannie." The name surfaced like an answer whispered underwater—a fleeting clarity amid chaos—but no, Fannie wasn't an option—she is just an old lady. Maybe Massi or Thanh... No time to think about it now.

"Let's find somewhere safe first," Wren finally said aloud, pulling open the door and hurrying down the dimly lit stairwell two steps at a time with Maggie close behind.

"We need to call someone," Maggie said suddenly as they reached ground level. She fumbled with her phone, hands trembling so badly she nearly dropped it.

Wren spun around sharply and grabbed Maggie's wrist before she could dial anything. "Wait."

"What?" Maggie blinked up at her through tear-clumped lashes, confusion etched deep into her expression now mixed with exhaustion and fear.

Wren tightened her grip; not enough to hurt but enough to make sure Maggie heard every word that followed.

"Think about it," Wren said carefully though her own words felt heavy and jagged in her throat. "He was a cop—a dirty one, sure—but still a fucking cop." She exhaled hard through clenched teeth before continuing: "Do you want to stick around and try explaining this?"

Maggie froze in place for what felt like an eternity before shaking her head weakly but saying nothing.

"It doesn't matter that it was an accident!" Wren pressed on when Maggie didn't respond right away. Her voice softened but stayed sharp enough to cut through whatever hope lingered between them: "Think about us, Mags—two queer girls running from this shitshow versus a badge and uniform-backed 'thin blue line.' How do you think *that* plays out?"

For once—mercifully—Maggie didn't argue back; instead she slipped her phone back into pocket silently while nodding numbly toward wherever Wren decided they'd go next because honestly neither had answers anymore except maybe just keep running until footsteps stopped feeling like hammers nearing executioner gallows trails too closely behind.

"We have to check," Maggie whispered, her voice an unsteady thread that barely reached Wren over the rush of blood pounding in her ears.

Sweat trickled down Wren's spine, soaking into the fabric of her shirt until it clung awkwardly to her skin. She nodded once, stiffly, as though afraid that any more movement might shatter what little composure she had left.

The stairs blurred beneath Wren's feet as she plunged downward at a reckless pace. The hollow slap of her sneakers echoed off concrete walls, each step reverberating like a drumbeat in the narrow stairwell. Somewhere behind her, Maggie kept pace—ragged breaths and scuffed footfalls tracking Wren's descent like an anxious shadow.

The image replayed in fragments behind her eyelids: Dennis lunging toward her, wild-eyed and erratic; a sharp sidestep and then his body tipping backward. Over the edge he went like he weighed nothing at all. By now, she'd run through it at least a dozen times in her head, always returning to the same conclusion: It had been an accident. Honest.

Her legs burned as they rounded another landing, but she didn't slow—not with five flights still separating them from whatever waited below. The rest was noise: Maggie gasping for air behind her; sweat dripping down into one eye and blurring half her vision; questions chasing themselves in circles inside her skull until they blurred together and become nothing.

Another turn of stairs and still no answers—their descent felt endless now, spiraling deeper into some unseen void where logic crumbled under its own weight and left only fear standing in its place.

She glanced back at Maggie, whose face was set with a grimness that didn't quite belong there. Maggie wasn't built for this—Wren knew that—but here she was, following Wren into the chaos that would greet them outside that door. Wren felt a flicker of something—guilt, maybe—and made herself a promise she wasn't sure she could keep: Maggie would get through this unharmed (physically, anyway).

They reached the final step, and Wren pushed open the door. The sunlight hit her full force, sharp and relentless, making her eyes sting and water. She blinked and rounded the corner to the front of the building where Dennis lay sprawled on the ground. One look, and it was clear: motionless body, blood pooling like spilled ink on dry earth. He was gone.

Her stomach clenched as she took it all in again: his closed eyes, his chest still as stone. The blood seeped outward in dark tendrils, soaking into the cracked asphalt beneath him. The air reeked of copper and heat—the tang of blood mingling with the humid stink of sun-baked pavement. Wren's stomach heaved at the smell, but she forced herself to stay upright.

Behind her, Maggie made a sound—something between a sob and a gasp—and fumbled with her phone. Her hands shook so badly that Wren half-expected it to slip free entirely. "I'm calling 911," Maggie said, her voice cracking like brittle glass.

Wren turned sharply and grabbed Maggie's wrist before she could press anything. Her skin felt damp and ice cold all at once—a dissonant combination that instantly unsettled Wren. "No," she said forcefully.

Maggie flinched at the contact but met Wren's gaze with wide, tear-filled eyes. Panic radiated off her in waves—her breathing too fast, her voice trembling as she started to stammer something unintelligible about help or duty or hope. But none of that mattered now because Dennis wasn't clawing his way back from this.

Wren tightened her grip and swallowed hard against the dryness in her throat. "Mags," she said quietly but firmly, "he's dead." The words came out heavier than expected—like lead dropping from her lips. She blinked hard once before continuing: "He's gone; there's nothing we can do."

Maggie froze at those words—it was as though they'd sucked all movement from her body—but after a second or two, she shook her head violently, as if to reject what she'd just heard outright. "But we have to do something," Maggie whispered at first before her voice rose in volume and urgency: "We can't just—"

"Maggie." Wren cut through her rising tone like a blade slicing cleanly through fabric. Her own voice came out harsher than intended—not from anger but from fear coiled tight in her chest like a spring ready to snap loose at any moment. "Just give me a second to think."

She let go of Maggie's wrist and ran one shaky hand through her sweat-damp hair while trying—and failing—to push back the rising tide of panic threatening to drown them both. You couldn't think straight when fear clawed its way up your throat like this; you needed space to breathe.

Wren kept her eyes on Maggie, watching the way her emotions flickered across her face like a reel of film she couldn't pause. The envelope in Wren's pocket felt heavier with each passing second, as though it carried more than just paper, as though it could somehow pull them both under if they didn't move. Her fingers tightened around Maggie's wrist, harder than she meant to, but Maggie didn't seem to notice.

"Listen to me," Wren said, her voice low and steady, like she was trying to talk down a spooked animal. "We can't call anyone. Not now. Not without thinking this through."

Maggie's eyes darted toward the body—Dennis's body—and then back to Wren. Her lips parted like she was about to speak, but nothing came out at first. She swallowed hard, and when she finally did find her voice, it wavered. "It was an accident," she murmured. "We didn't mean for this to happen."

Wren exhaled sharply. She wanted to say something comforting—something that would make all of this easier—but instead what came out was sharp. "You think that matters?" Her words hung in the air, jagged and unkind. "Maggie, look at where we are." She gestured toward Dennis's lifeless form with a quick flick of her head. "He's a cop—a dead cop. Who lied and said I killed Anne. How do you think that's going to go for us?"

Maggie flinched like the words had hit her square in the chest. Her face paled even more, which Wren wouldn't have thought possible until now. She stepped back as though putting distance between herself and the truth might make it less real. "Oh god," she whispered.

Wren glanced around the lot. The sun was brutal overhead, baking the pavement until the air seemed to shimmer above it. Everything felt too bright, too exposed. In the distance, the faint cry of sirens reached her ears—not close enough to panic yet, but getting closer. Her pulse kicked up another notch.

"We have to go," Wren said, tugging lightly on Maggie's arm, willing her to move.

Maggie stood firm, feet planted like roots had sprouted from her heels and anchored her in place. "We can't just leave him here," she said again, quieter this time but no less stubbornly. "It's not right."

The words made Wren want to scream—not at Maggie exactly but at everything: at Dennis for being dirty, at herself for not seeing this coming, at the whole goddamn mess they were now tangled in—but she forced herself to take a breath instead.

"Mags," she said softly now, measured but firm. "I know it's messed up—I do—but we don't have time for 'right' or 'wrong.' He tried to kill us. He killed Anne." She pressed a hand against her pocket where the envelope sat folded and fragile yet somehow heavy enough to change everything. "Whatever's in here... It was worth killing for."

She saw Maggie flinch again and hated herself for pushing so hard—for putting that fear on her face—but they didn't have time for anything else.

Wren patted the pocket again absentmindedly as if checking that it hadn't disappeared in the last few seconds—that some cruel twist hadn't erased their only clue. "We need answers," she continued quietly. "And we can't get them if we're locked up... or worse."

The silence stretched between them before Maggie spoke again, barely more than a whisper: "Where will we go?"

It was such an innocent question—one Wren wished she had a good answer for—but there wasn't time for second-guessing right now.

"Not home," Wren replied after a moment's hesitation; that much she knew for certain. Home wasn't safe anymore—not with Dennis dead and his connections undoubtedly hunting them already—and if they hesitated any longer... Well, hesitation wasn't an option either.

"We'll figure it out," Wren added quickly, gripping Maggie's hand tighter and giving it one last tug before stepping forward herself—forward into whatever came next because going back wasn't an option anymore either.

"Fannie," Wren said, her voice cutting through the tense silence like a blade. The thought had come to her suddenly, unbidden but sharp, like something that had always been there, waiting for her to notice. "We'll go to Fannie's place. She has that spot under the stairs—the one you stayed in? She'll know what to do."

Maggie's wide, frantic eyes met hers, the panic ebbing at the mention of their landlady. Fannie Severina wasn't everything you'd want in a landlord—she had a tendency to show up unannounced—stoned out of her head—and offer unsolicited advice—but she was loyal. And if you were someone she cared about, fiercely so.

Maggie nodded, her lips parting in a shaky exhale. "Okay." She said it again, like she needed to convince herself. "Okay. Let's go."

Wren glanced back at Dennis's body—a crumpled heap now devoid of the anger and menace it had once possessed. A tangle of feelings churned in her chest: fear, yes; anger too—hot and raw—but also regret scratching faintly at the edges of it all. There wasn't time for any of that right now. Not if they wanted to survive this.

"Wait," Wren said sharply, already scanning the ground around them.

She spotted it quickly: a stray piece of plastic wrapping—some discarded remnant of someone's snack—and moved toward it with purpose. Her gaze flickered downward as she crouched, noticing how her own shadow stretched long and thin over Dennis's motionless form. The smell hit her again—a metallic tang mixed with something heavier, riper—and she swallowed hard against the bile that rose unbidden in her throat.

The plastic was brittle in her hands as she wrapped it carefully around her fingers and steeled herself for what came next. She didn't need to look at him again. She didn't want to look at him again. But here she was—leaning down until his scent filled her nose and his lifelessness loomed large in front of her like some grotesque monument to all the mistakes they'd made tonight.

She wrapped the plastic around her hand and slipped into his pocket. There. Cool metal: his phone. Careful not to let any skin touch it—not even by accident—she pulled it free.

"What are you doing?" Maggie hissed from somewhere behind her; Wren could hear the disbelief crackling under each word.

"Calling 911." Her voice came out flat, clipped. She didn't bother turning around. "On his phone."

"But—" Maggie started.

"So they don't trace it back to us," Wren interrupted quickly, not giving Maggie time to finish whatever argument or protest she was trying to form.

The screen lit up when Wren—using the plastic wrap as a barrier—pressed the button, bathing her face momentarily in pale blue light. For a second, nothing registered except relief—it worked—but then... then she saw it.

The lock screen image wasn't what she expected: some default wallpaper or maybe even an innocuous personal photo—Dennis and a dog or a sunset or whatever normal people put on their phones these days. What stared back at her instead made Wren freeze where she stood.

It was her.

Not Maggie—but *her*. The woman from Golden Bites.

Her hair was different in the photo—slicked back into a severe bun—and the casual civilian clothing had been replaced with something far more telling: a police uniform pressed so crisp it looked starched to perfection. Her expression was as cold as ever—hard lines etched into sharp features—with none of that observing-from-a-distance detachment left in her gaze now. No, this photo was different; this photo demanded attention.

"Holy shit," Wren breathed softly—to herself more than anyone else—as comprehension clawed its way through the chaos swirling inside her skull.

Behind her, Maggie must have noticed something shift because suddenly she was right there too—close enough that Wren could feel Maggie's breath on her shoulder as warm puffs of shared panic filled what little space existed between them both now.

When Maggie saw the screen for herself, every ounce of color drained from her face all at once like someone had flipped some internal switch labeled *normal human function*: OFF.

"Oh my god," Maggie whispered after what felt like forever but couldn't have been more than five seconds tops—her voice trembling on each syllable though no one could blame her under circumstances like these.

"Is that his wife?" Maggie trailed off briefly before finding strength enough—or maybe desperation enough—to finish: "She's a cop?"

Wren nodded stiffly but said nothing until finally dragging herself out from wherever shock had tried pinning her down moments earlier.

"Not his spouse. He only ever ordered delivery for one person." A pause heavy enough hang weights off words yet still brief enough keep momentum alive added next bit hastily almost angrily: "Maggie. It's the woman from the restaurant. From Golden Bites. The one who said 'good luck' or some shit. It's the same woman."

Wren's heart pounded like it wanted to escape her chest. She kept her breathing steady—shallow but steady—and tried to ignore what she had just realized. "We're in even deeper shit than we thought." Her voice came out low, raw. "This isn't just about Dennis. There's someone else in on it. Her."

The phone felt heavy in her hand. Wren stared at the black screen, her frustration bubbling over as her thumb hovered uselessly above the glass. It wanted a passcode. Or a fingerprint. Damn it all. "Well, he still has those," she said, though even as the words left her mouth, they felt flimsy and thin.

Her fingers shook as she dropped to one knee beside Dennis's body. For a moment, she thought she might gag, but there wasn't time for that. Focus. She placed the phone carefully on the ground near his limp hand, taking deliberate care not to leave prints.

"What are you doing?" Maggie whispered behind her, barely audible but vibrating with panic.

"Unlocking the phone." Wren didn't bother looking back at her, didn't spare a second to soothe Maggie's mounting fear. Instead, she reached for Dennis's hand with her plastic wrap. His hand had changed since—well, since whenever it happened—and now it felt all wrong: waxy, rubbery, already too much like something dead and not nearly enough like something that used to be alive. Wren hesitated for half a second before gripping his index finger and angling it toward the sensor.

The screen lit up almost immediately—too easily—and Wren blinked down at it as though surprised that it had worked at all. Her relief was fleeting.

Her thumb hovered over the icons on the screen before she opened the keypad and dialed 911. The sound of ringing filled the air around them, sudden and jarring against the silence of the warehouse yard.

"911," a cool voice answered on the other end. "What's your emergency?"

Wren swallowed hard and forced herself to speak lower than usual—gruffer too—not quite trusting how convincing she'd sound through nothing more than improvised plastic wrap over the speaker. "There's a man lying outside the old Fillmore Manufacturers warehouse at thirty-six Lavigne Road," she said quickly, each word clipped and pushed out before she could second-guess herself. "He's not moving—I think he's dead."

"Can you tell me if you see any signs of breathing or movement?"

"No," Wren answered without hesitation, clutching onto whatever illusion of calmness she could muster. She tried to paint a picture for them: disjointed details given with just enough reluctance to sound authentic while still keeping them from asking too many questions. "I didn't get too close... there's blood."

The operator remained steady; they always did—or at least they pretended to—while people—unlike Wren—unraveled on their end of the line. "Alright," they said after a beat that felt longer than it was. "We're dispatching an ambulance and police now. Can you stay on the line?"

Wren didn't answer.

Instead, she lowered the phone back onto the ground near Dennis's lifeless hand—the call still active—and let their distant voice drone on in muffled bursts as though it existed in some other plane entirely.

"We need to go." Her voice came sharply then—urgent but just quiet enough not to carry far—and with one quick motion, she grabbed Maggie by the arm.

They started backing away together—Wren first, pulling Maggie along with cautious steps—until Dennis was no more than a shape crumpled against concrete. The operator was still talking faintly from somewhere behind them; their words were soft now but persistent, tethering itself futilely to empty air as Wren led them farther and farther into shadow.

Her mind raced ahead of their feet as they retreated: turning over questions she couldn't yet answer in full but would have no choice but to soon enough. What now? What next? Who else? None of it clear yet except for this much: they needed distance—from Dennis; from whatever tangled mess tied him together with whoever *she* was; from everything else that might come if they stayed too long in one place.

They needed Fannie.

Wren jammed the plastic wrap into her pocket, where it crinkled against the envelope she'd stuffed there earlier. Her hand shot out, grabbing Maggie's wrist, yanking her away from Dennis's lifeless body. They didn't look back. The gravel crunched loudly beneath their feet as they darted around the back of the warehouse, the sound amplified by the unnerving stillness all around them.

Their bikes were right where they'd left them, leaning against the old brick wall that had long since lost its original red hue. Wren's fingers trembled as she reached for Argo's handlebars. Her breath came quick and shallow, and she muttered a curse under her breath. Then she froze. The envelope.

Her hand instinctively went to her pocket again, pulling it free. It felt heavier now in this moment than it had when she'd hidden it there earlier. With a sharp rip of the seal and hands still unsteady, she unfolded a single sheet of paper.

"What is that?" Maggie asked, her voice too loud in the quiet as she leaned closer to get a better look.

Wren frowned at the document, scanning its words over and over as though repetition would somehow make them clearer. "It's—uh—it's some kind of contract," she said finally, keeping her voice low. "For this company... Elite Enforcement Training Solutions? EETS? Looks like they provide police training."

Maggie wrinkled her nose in confusion. "That's it? That doesn't—why would Dennis...?" She trailed off but didn't finish the thought aloud.

"I don't know." Wren shook her head slowly, the words on the paper blurring before her eyes. "None of this adds up."

But then came the first faint wail of sirens—a distant cry that quickly grew louder—and both girls jumped as if jolted by an unseen wire.

"Shit," Wren hissed under her breath, shoving the paper back into its envelope and stuffing it into her pocket with one swift motion. Her mind was spinning now, barely keeping up with what was happening or what needed to happen next. "We've gotta go."

They grabbed their bikes and bags without another word and took off down an old footpath that cut through the vacant land—a remnant of workers taking lunchtime shortcuts toward civilization—pedaling hard and fast enough to kick up clouds of dust behind them. The cool air stung Wren's face as it whipped past, but it did nothing to ease the fire now spreading through her legs with each push of the pedals. She didn't dare slow down. It was adrenaline keeping her upright now—not logic or planning, just raw fear—and every muscle in her body screamed at her to not stop moving until those sirens were far behind them.

The railroad tracks stretched out ahead of them, the sirens behind fading until they became little more than a murmur on the edge of hearing. The overpass loomed like some forgotten relic, its hulking concrete structure casting long, jagged shadows that seemed to claw at the earth. As they ducked beneath it, the sudden drop in temperature hit them—a stolen moment of cool relief before the sun would reclaim its hold.

Their bikes clattered and jolted over the uneven ground near the tracks. Wren winced as her teeth jarred together with each bump, but she didn't ease up on the pedals. Slowing down felt like something only fools or people with no sense of self-preservation would do right now. A thicket of brush and low-hanging branches rose up before them, and they were swallowed by it without hesitation. Branches clawed at their faces and arms, leaving invisible welts that would sting later. There was no time to stop and care about that now.

When they broke through to the other side, Wren blinked and took in their surroundings: an industrial graveyard, forgotten and unmourned. Decaying factories stood as silent witnesses to an era that had long since passed. Rusted machinery jutted out from weeds like bony fingers reaching for a sky that had already turned its back on this place. In the distance, as though belonging to another world entirely, the city skyline bristled with life and promise—or at least with a direction to flee.

Wren's lungs screamed with every breath, but stopping wasn't an option. She could feel the envelope stuffed in her pocket pressing against her hip like a lead weight. It wasn't just paper anymore—it had transformed into something live and volatile, something dangerous. What exactly had they stumbled into? Why was this piece of paper worth killing over? It didn't make sense—none of it made sense—and her brain spun uselessly as she tried to stitch fragments of logic together while still pushing herself forward.

She dared a glance at Maggie riding beside her. Maggie's eyes met hers for just a second—long enough for Wren to see her own fears mirrored back at her. Long enough for her to know there was no comfort in company when neither of them had answers.

5:19 pm

Wren and Maggie turned onto their street, their legs heavy, their breaths jagged and uneven. It felt as though every muscle in their bodies had been wrung out, left trembling and raw. The bikes wobbled beneath them, the effort to stay upright almost too much. The sun was lower, slipping to the horizon, leaving streaks of burned orange and deep purple brushed across the sky. The shadows stretched long and thin, reaching for them like lazy fingers.

As they approached the building, Wren caught a flicker of movement in her peripheral vision. Her gaze lifted instinctively to Fannie's window. There she was, framed in the soft glow of her living room lamp, her face pinched with worry. Fannie was waving frantically now, her hands shadowed against the glass, her urgency like a jolt through Wren's already frayed nerves.

They dismounted their bikes slowly—too slowly—and Wren almost buckled when her feet hit the ground. Her legs felt unsteady, like they might collapse under her at any second. She steadied herself against handlebars slick with sweat and exchanged a brief glance with Maggie before they stumbled toward Fannie's front door. The transition from the thick, clinging heat outside to the cool stillness inside was abrupt enough to make Wren shiver.

Fannie was waiting for them just inside the door. Her small frame seemed even smaller somehow—folded in on itself—and her hands trembled as she gripped the edge of the doorway.

"There was a police officer here," Fannie said without preamble. Her voice quivered on the edge of panic—or maybe fury; it was hard to tell which. "A woman cop. She was looking for you."

Wren's heart stuttered in her chest, that half-second skip enough to send a flood of dread through her veins. "What did she look like?" she asked quickly.

Fannie didn't hesitate. "Tall," she said. "Broad shoulders. Hair cut short—dark hair—and eyes sharp enough to cut glass." A pause, then: "She looked serious."

The description hit like a punch in the gut: unmistakable. Wren could practically see the grainy photo they'd stared at on Dennis's phone. She swallowed hard, her throat suddenly dry and tight.

"That's her," she murmured, more to herself than to anyone else.

"Officer Barber?" Maggie said quietly, as if naming her out loud might summon some new disaster.

Fannie nodded grimly. "Yes," she confirmed. "That's what she said when I asked her name—Officer Frances Barber."

Wren closed her eyes briefly before opening them again to meet Fannie's intense gaze.

"She said you're wanted for murder." Fannie's voice cracked on the name but pressed forward regardless: "And Maggie is wanted too—for helping you. Aiding and abetting."

The words landed like blows—one after another—and Wren felt something inside of her curl up defensively against their weight. She glanced over at Maggie and saw that same weight reflected back at her: wide eyes full of disbelief and terror; lips pressed into a thin line as though holding back tears or screams or both.

Wren forced herself upright then—forced air into lungs that didn't seem particularly interested in cooperating—and reached instinctively for some measure of control amid the chaos threatening to engulf her entirely.

"Did she say anything else?" The question came out hoarse and uneven; she barely recognized it as hers.

Fannie hesitated for a moment. "Just that they'd be back with a warrant. I wouldn't let them into your place without one. But something is off. Usually, the cops come in pairs when it's something as important as murder. But it was just her, and she was pissed."

Wren ran a hand through her damp hair, the strands sticking to her fingers like the thoughts clinging to her mind. "It's so screwed up, Fannie," she said, her voice quieter now but no less firm. "We didn't kill anyone. You have to believe that. But proving it? That's a whole other story."

Maggie moved closer, her hand reaching for Wren's and holding tight. "So what do we do?" Her words wavered like a bridge about to give, but the pressure of her fingers against Wren's was steady.

Wren squeezed back, grounding herself in that small, fierce point of contact. "We can't stay here," she said finally. "Every second puts Fannie in more danger."

Fannie was already shaking her head before Wren even finished speaking. "What kind of talk is that? You girls aren't going anywhere. We'll get through this."

But Wren didn't waver this time. Her grip on Maggie's hand tightened as if to keep herself anchored while the rest of her untethered. "No, Fannie," she said softly but without hesitation. "You've done enough—more than enough—but if we stay, it'll bring trouble right to your doorstep. We need to go." She pushed forward. "Now."

Fannie's lips quivered as she reached out with trembling hands and rested one gently on Wren's arm. For an instant, that fragile touch nearly shattered Wren's resolve. "Oh, my dears," Fannie said, her voice raw and uneven like fabric tearing at the seams. "You can't just leave. Not like this." She hesitated, glancing toward the window as though expecting trouble to burst in at any moment. Then, lowering her voice: "It isn't safe out there."

Wren swallowed hard against the knot forming in her throat. The older woman had become more than just a landlord; she was family in every way that mattered—kind eyes, steady hands cooking meals for them long after they were supposed to fend for themselves—but none of that changed the truth.

Wren let go of Maggie's hand and stepped back, distancing herself from both women as though that would make what she had to say next any easier. "There's more," she began haltingly before forcing herself onward. "It isn't just about Anne anymore." Her heart thudded painfully against her ribs as she added: "A cop is dead."

The words hit like stones dropped into still water—jarring yet rippling outward until they filled every inch of space between them.

Fannie's face froze mid-expression—the attempted reassurance wiped clean by sudden shock. It took two tries before she managed to speak again: "What did you say? Who?"

Wren stared at the floorboards beneath Fannie's kitchen table as though the answer might be carved there instead of sitting heavy on her tongue. She closed her eyes—just for a moment—and then released it all in one breath: "Dennis. The cop who shot at me." Another pause hung hollow between them before she finished quietly: "He fell off a building."

She could feel Fannie stiffen beside her even though neither moved nor spoke for several seconds after that revelation landed with unnerving finality.

"Lord Almighty," Fannie whispered finally—though whether it was prayer or curse wasn't entirely clear—and swayed where she stood like someone who'd just been punched in the guts but refused to fall down.

Behind them came sharp footsteps—the sound of Maggie bolting down the stairs with no particular destination except *away*. A sob echoed faintly from deeper in the house, and Wren flinched instinctively at its rawness—as though it had claws sharp enough to tear straight through skin and bone.

She leaned heavily against the wall beside her now-empty chair; it offered little support but somehow seemed better than standing alone with nothing solid behind her anymore.

"Listen here," Fannie said—not loud exactly but commanding all the same—and waited until Wren looked up at last into those still-kind eyes masked by worry lines etched deep over decades lived hard but full nonetheless.

"That girl hasn't given up on *you*," Fannie continued plainly as though delivering something obvious yet profound all at once—truth wrapped neatly around compassion until barely distinguishable apart. "So don't—for God's sake—give up on *her*."

Wren let out a bitter, unexpected snort. The sound startled her as much as the words that followed. "Yeah? Could've fooled me. She hates me right now, Fannie. And who could blame her?"

Fannie shook her head slowly, the movement deliberate and unyielding. Her eyes, sharp and filled with something that felt too much like certainty, held Wren's gaze. "No, child. That's not hate. That's love—love that's scared and hurting. I know what it's like."

Wren barked a laugh, harsh and humorless. "You have no idea what the fuck this is like," she snapped, though the words tasted bitter the moment they left her tongue. Guilt coiled tight in her chest, but she couldn't stop herself now; exhaustion had cracked something open inside her. "We're fugitives, Fannie. Wanted for murder. How the hell can you understand that?"

Instead of flinching or stepping back, Fannie leaned closer. Her grip on Wren's shoulder tightened—not painfully, but firmly enough to root Wren in place—and something flickered in the old woman's expression. It was fire, unmistakable and fierce, flashing through features softened by age yet strangely ageless in that moment.

"I understand it perfectly. I'm living it," Fannie said.

The words hit Wren harder than she expected, their weight heavy enough to stall whatever retort had been building on her tongue. She stared at Fannie—really looked at her—and for the first time saw past the layers of soft cardigans and silver hair to something harder beneath. The lines on Fannie's face shifted under Wren's scrutiny, suddenly deepening into etchings carved by years Wren had never thought to ask about.

"1972." The year came out measured but steady, like each syllable had been waiting decades to surface. "Carl and I—we weren't Fannie and Carl back then." She gave a small pause, as if testing whether Wren would follow where this was going. "We were Edith and Arthur Brown."

The names hung in the air between them like smoke from a long-extinguished fire.

Wren blinked, frowning as she grasped for any familiarity in those names or this story, but none came. She opened her mouth to say something—anything—but Fannie spoke first.

"Active members of the Weather Underground," Fannie said evenly.

There was a beat of silence before Wren managed to stammer out: "The Underground?" The words felt flat as soon as she said them—too weak for what was already starting to build inside her chest.

Fannie chuckled dryly, though there wasn't an ounce of humor in it. "Ah," she said, shaking her head so that strands of silver hair caught the light just so, "to be young enough not to know the Weather Underground."

Wren wanted to respond—to push back against whatever strange turn this conversation had taken—but again found herself unable to do anything except stare. It was as if she were watching someone peel back layers of a painting she'd always assumed was complete only to find whole other scenes hidden underneath: vivid strokes of color and violence replacing familiar shades of whimsy. The frail old woman who made organic herbal tea was nowhere to be found now; instead sat someone with steel in her spine and stories buried deep beneath her skin.

"We were radicals," Fannie continued after another measured pause—her voice quiet but far from fragile. "Revolutionaries trying to change a world we believed needed changing. Does need changing." Her gaze grew distant for a moment before snapping back into focus on Wren like a spotlight narrowing on its mark. "We bombed government buildings... staged protests... fought against injustice wherever we found it."

"Bombed?"

"Bombed. And yes"—her tone sharpened now—"we were fugitives too." The faintest trace of a smile curved her lips then—not smug but knowing—as if daring Wren to argue otherwise. "Wanted by the FBI... just like you are now."

Wren stared at her as though seeing an impossible illusion come to life before her eyes—the cracks between what was real and what couldn't possibly be widening faster than she could patch them together again.

She tried—tried hard—to reconcile this image of Fannie (no... *Edith?*) with everything she thought she knew about the woman who sat across from her now: cranberry scones on Sunday mornings; needlepoint pillows with cheerful sayings embroidered on them; stories about her travels told with soft laughter over steaming mugs of chamomile tea.

And yet here they were—with truths dropping like stones into water too still for comfort—and suddenly those delicate lines on Fannie's face didn't look soft anymore but sharp instead: not wrinkles born from age but scars shaped by choices made long before Wren had ever come into being.

"Weather Underground?" Wren repeated, the words coming out barely above a whisper. The name tugged at something in the recesses of her mind, an echo from a history class she hadn't thought about in years, its details hazy and half-formed.

Fannie nodded slowly, the corners of her mouth curling into a faint, almost wistful smile. "I'm not surprised you don't know, dear. It's ancient history for someone your age." Her gaze drifted, her expression softening into something distant, like she was staring through time instead of the modest living room they sat in. Then she took a measured breath and looked straight at Wren. "There's something I need to tell you." Her voice was calm but carried an undercurrent that made Wren's stomach tighten.

"We were young," Fannie said softly. "Idealistic. Angry. Carl and I thought we could change the world—" She paused, her fingers twitching against the fabric of her skirt—"by any means necessary."

The room squeezed in tight around Wren, or maybe it was inside her chest that everything was constricting—hard to tell which. This woman with flour-dusted hands and kind eyes who fussed over overwatered ferns and left homemade bread at their door... this woman had been a bomber? A radical? It didn't compute.

"Holy shit," Wren finally breathed out, slumping back against the wall like it was the only thing holding her upright.

Across from her, Fannie just sat there in that same worn armchair by the window with its crocheted throw draped over one side as if nothing monumental had just been revealed. But something about her posture changed—a slight straightening of the shoulders—and for the first time since Wren had met her, there was steel in Fannie's expression.

"The FBI," Fannie said after a long moment, practically spitting out the letters like they tasted bitter on her tongue, "didn't exactly appreciate our methods." Her lips pressed together into a thin line before she added quietly, almost to herself now: "I can't say I blame them anymore." She looked down at her hands folded tightly together in her lap—knotted fingers twisting against one another like they were trying to wring some invisible burden clean away—and then back up at Wren with a faint shrug that somehow managed to be both resigned and defiant at once.

"At the time..." Fannie trailed off briefly before shaking her head as though trying to rid herself of cobwebs or ghosts. "At the time Carl and I thought we were doing what needed to be done."

Her fingers stilled in their restless knotting for just an instant when she mentioned Carl's name again: "They're still after us—even now—all these decades later." A flicker of something raw passed across her face then: grief maybe or regret or both woven so tightly together you couldn't separate one from the other even if you tried.

"It's just me now," she said after another pause so long it almost felt like maybe she wouldn't finish what she'd started saying at all. Her voice dipped in those last few words but steadied again as she continued without waiting for Wren's reaction (though Wren didn't have anything coherent to offer anyway).

"We went underground after things got too hot," Fannie said simply. "We changed our names," Fannie said again softly like repetition might make it simpler somehow; "took up new jobs... built new lives." Her gaze swept slowly across this space—the walls painted pale yellow three summers ago when she'd insisted sunlight should live indoors too.

"They're still looking for me," she said, her voice low and steady. "You can look me up if you want, my real name. I'm there, plain as day. On their lists." Fannie leaned back but didn't let go of Wren's gaze. "That's why I'm careful. Always have been. That room under the stairs is there for a reason. You think I'm just some harmless old woman, but trust me—there's a lot you don't know."

Her hand reached out then, wrapping around Wren's with an unexpected firmness that made it impossible to pull away even if she'd wanted to. The skin of Fannie's hand was paper-thin and covered in faint blue veins, but her grip was as steady as her words. "Now you know," Fannie said simply. There was no surprise in her tone, no grand gesture or proclamation of relief—just the quiet weight of someone who had carried a secret for too long.

Wren stared at her, trying to fit this new version of Fannie into the one she'd known before—the one who baked muffins, offered unsolicited advice about keeping plants alive, and tutted at the news like it was all some predictable soap opera. That Fannie and this Fannie didn't match up.

Then she laughed.

It wasn't a forced laugh either; it bubbled out of her, warm and sure, filling the small space between them like sunlight breaking through an overcast sky. Fannie looked younger suddenly—or maybe Wren had just been looking at her wrong this whole time. "You should've seen them," Fannie said with a shake of her head, the laughter fading into something softer now—a wry sort of pride coating her words. "Coming into *my house*. Poking around like they'd find something. But they didn't know who they were dealing with." She shrugged like it had all been inevitable anyway. "It was easier to disappear back then—no phones tracking your every move or whatever nonsense you kids deal with now."

Wren blinked once. Twice. Her brain felt slow—too slow to keep up with what Fannie had just unraveled in front of her like it was nothing more than a stray thread on an old sweater.

Fannie leaned in closer, lowering her voice until it barely rose above the hum of fluorescent light overhead. "Thing is," she said, "you've always got to have an escape plan. Always." She gave Wren's hand two firm pats before withdrawing hers and resting them softly on her lap. "In case things take a turn on you—and they always do eventually."

Those words hung there for a moment before something clicked inside Wren's chest—not loudly or dramatically—but quietly in that way new doors opening sometimes sound: faint hinges creaking open after years of neglect.

"I think… I think I might have an idea."

Fannie nodded, understanding without needing to know the details. She pulled Wren into a tight hug, her frail arms surprisingly strong. As they parted, Fannie's eyes sparkled with a mixture of pride and mischief.

"Go on now," she said, giving Wren a gentle push towards the stairs. "Go get the woman you love."

Wren felt a surge of energy course through her, their situation suddenly feeling a little lighter. She hugged Fannie once more, quick and fierce, before heading towards the stairs. As she descended, each step felt more purposeful than the last. The seed of an idea was blooming in her mind, fueled by Fannie's unexpected revelation and unwavering support.

Wren took each step down to the basement with care, her legs heavy as though the day's events had somehow attached themselves to her ankles. The door creaked open, and the room that normally felt like a safe harbor now seemed stifling, the air thick and unmoving, as if it too bore witness to the earlier argument. She spotted Maggie on the bed, her slender frame folded in on itself, trembling with sobs.

Wren didn't speak. Words felt inadequate here. She crossed the room in a few soft strides, climbed onto the bed, and slid her arms around Maggie. The strands of Maggie's hair clung damply to Wren's fingers as she stroked them back from her face. That familiar scent of shampoo mixed with the salt of fresh tears. Wren held her tightly and let the storm pass.

Maggie's sobs began to ebb, small hiccups replacing the full-bodied cries that had wracked her moments before. She nestled closer into Wren's chest, aligning herself instinctively with its rhythm: inhale, exhale, repeat. Their bodies fit together like an old habit, a weave of arms and legs drawing warmth from one another. The silence stretched pleasantly now, disrupted by Maggie's occasional sniffle or a shaky breath that hadn't yet evened out.

Wren kissed Maggie's temple at first, then found her lips—a kiss laced with salt and apologies neither needed to speak aloud. It wasn't just a kiss; it was a declaration of something unspoken but understood: solidarity through the mess.

"I'm sorry," Maggie murmured against Wren's mouth, her words breaking apart as though afraid they might dissolve entirely. "I just…"

"I know," Wren said simply, brushing her thumb across Maggie's damp cheek. There wasn't anything else to say; there didn't need to be.

After a while—minutes or maybe an hour—they unwound themselves from each other. Wren stood first and padded toward the small kitchenette on bare feet that barely made a sound against the cold linoleum floor. She opened the fridge door and stared inside before pulling out an apple.

"Apple or orange?" she asked over her shoulder.

"Apple," came Maggie's reply, small but steady.

The crunch of their first bites filled the quiet until Maggie set hers down and reached for the envelope sitting on the counter nearby. Her fingers hesitated at first but then slid under the flap to pull out its contents—a single page. Her brow pulled together as she scanned the top page.

"Elite Enforcement Training Solutions," she read aloud slowly, frowning as though tasting something bitter on her tongue. Maggie said nothing else but grabbed her phone from where it lay on the table and began tapping at its screen with quick precision. Wren watched as Maggie bent over it intently, her face bathed in cool light from the display. That faint glow sharpened every line of worry etched into her expression—it made those lines almost permanent-looking in a way Wren didn't want to dwell on for too long.

"Got something," Maggie whispered eventually without looking up, though there was an edge to her voice now like she wasn't quite sure whether this was relief or more trouble ahead. She turned the screen toward Wren, who stepped closer until their shoulders brushed lightly—an accidental reminder that even here, even now in this murky in-between space where answers were scarce and questions abundant—they weren't facing it alone.

The press release glowed on the laptop screen, its corporate jargon stark and lifeless against the harsh white background. Wren's eyes skimmed over phrases like "innovative partnership" and "cutting-edge training techniques," her mind stumbling to make sense of them. It took a moment before the significance clicked: the police department had signed a contract with a company called Elite Enforcement Training Solutions.

"This is it," Maggie said, her voice a strange mix of excitement and something closer to dread. She tapped the edge of the envelope resting on the table in front of her, as though trying to drive the point home. "The contract we found—it's this one. A copy of what they're talking about."

Wren frowned, her fingers drumming softly on the table. "So what? Elite trains cops? How does that even remotely justify killing Anne?" Her voice was sharp, but behind it lurked an exhaustion she couldn't shake, like her body was still catching up to everything she'd learned—or thought she'd learned—over these past few days.

Maggie didn't answer immediately. Instead, she hunched over her phone, her brow furrowed in concentration. "I think...If I'm right about this..." she began, trailing off as her thumbs flew across the screen, "...then this is big. Millions of dollars, according to the press release."

A familiar chill crept down Wren's spine at those words—big wasn't good. Big was never good. The pieces were starting to fit together in her mind, but the image they formed wasn't just incomplete; it was unsettling in ways she couldn't yet articulate. She pulled herself back into focus and glanced over at Maggie, whose face had flushed with determination.

"Hang on," Maggie muttered, more to herself than to Wren. Her eyes narrowed as she tapped at her phone with renewed urgency. "I'm checking something—WHOIS records for the website."

Wren's breath caught in her throat. The room suddenly felt too quiet—the kind of silence that amplifies small noises until they start to feel unbearable. The ticking from the kitchen clock sounded louder now, each tick cutting through Wren's thoughts like a metronome counting down to something inevitable.

Then it came—Maggie's sharp inhale, like she'd just stepped into freezing water.

"What is it?" Wren asked, but Maggie didn't reply right away. Instead, she looked up from her phone with an expression Wren couldn't quite read—shock? Disbelief? Maybe both.

Finally, Maggie spoke, her voice barely above a whisper: "Dennis Owen."

"Dennis? My Dennis? Killer cop Dennis?" The name landed between them like a dull thud—heavy and impossible to ignore. For a moment, Wren couldn't move. Her chest tightened as an image flickered unbidden in her mind: Dennis lying motionless, his lifeless eyes staring back at nothing. She gripped the edge of the table almost without realizing it; when she glanced down at her hand, her knuckles were white.

"What does that even mean?" The words gripped the sides of her throat, refusing to be spoken. She stared helplessly between Maggie and the laptop screen before letting her gaze settle on the contract lying on the table—the missing piece they hadn't known to look for until now. Then back again to Maggie's phone.

"Dennis owns—what—a website?" The realization hit mid-sentence, throwing off her rhythm as understanding dawned on her face. She spoke slower now but no less urgently: "Dennis…a cop…owns a website that offers training…to other cops?"

"That's it," Maggie said firmly, sitting up straighter in her chair as though bracing for something unseen. "That has to be it—it's all about money."

For several long seconds, Wren could only stare blankly at Maggie while turning those words over in her mind: conflict of interest. It all sounded so clinical when laid out like that—simple even—but somehow none of this felt simple anymore.

"And that's worth killing someone over?" she muttered at last under her breath but not quietly enough for Maggie to miss it.

Wren turned toward the small television perched on the kitchen counter and pressed its power button almost absently. Its screen flickered weakly to life as static-filled sound filled what little silence remained in the room.

"TV now?"

"News channel. Just keeping up. Anything else about EETS?" Wren asked as she lowered the volume on the TV.

Wren leaned against the kitchen counter, her eyes darting between the television and Maggie. The news anchor's voice droned on in the background, a constant reminder of the world outside their small apartment.

"Shit, Mags. What the hell do we do now?" Wren ran her fingers through her hair, tugging at the roots in frustration. "We've got no idea who knows what. For all we know, the entire fucking police force could be in on it. Maybe this EETS shit is completely legit and has nothing to do with anything."

Maggie bit her lip, her brow furrowed in concentration. "Let's go through what we know. Anne investigates corruption and she's dead. Dennis killed her—we think—and now he is dead. He was definitely corrupt. And we've got this contract that somehow ties it all together."

Wren nodded, taking the paper and spreading it on the kitchen table. The paper crinkled under her fingers as she smoothed it out.

"Hold up," Wren muttered, her eyes scanning the document. "Look at this."

Maggie leaned in, her shoulder brushing against Wren's. "What am I looking at?"

"The signatures," Wren pointed. "See here? That's Frances Barber's name. And over here... Dennis Owen."

Maggie's eyes widened. "Holy shit. Dennis signed on behalf of EETS, and Frances for the police department."

"Three point five million dollars." Wren whistled low. "That's a hell of a lot of money for 'specialized training'."

The gravity of their discovery settled over them like a heavy blanket. Wren felt her heart race, the implications of what they'd stumbled upon hitting her full force.

"So, Dennis owns the company," Maggie said slowly, "and Frances signed off on the contract from the police side. That's gotta be illegal, right?"

Wren watched as Maggie's eyes lit up with understanding. The pieces of the puzzle were finally falling into place.

Maggie's voice dropped lower, barely louder than a breath. "Murder. Conflict of interest. Fraud. Maybe bribery too, depending on how deep this goes." Her fingers hovered just above the paper, tracing invisible patterns across the contract lines. "That's exactly what this is. Cops selling services back to their own department for that kind of money? It's dirty. And it's big."

Wren nodded slowly, her pulse quickening as her mind scrambled to piece it all together. "You think this is what Anne found out? The thing that made Dennis kill her?"

"It has to be," Maggie said, her gaze fixed on the inked signatures, as though staring long enough might help her see what Anne had seen. "This is the kind of thing that could ruin careers—ruin lives. And let's be real: what cop do you know wants to end up behind bars with the very people they put there?"

Wren leaned back in her chair, the realization sinking in like lead in her chest. "But if it's this clear-cut, why didn't Anne just... go public?"

The question hung there for a moment while Maggie chewed on her bottom lip, a habit Wren had noticed always meant she was thinking something over hard. "There has to be more to it," Maggie said finally, her voice quieter now but no less resolved. "Something we're not seeing yet. Anne wouldn't have gotten herself killed over something this... obvious."

"Maybe she didn't have a chance," Wren offered, though even as the words left her mouth, they felt wrong—too simple. She shook her head and rubbed at her temples as if trying to massage clarity into existence.

The room fell into silence then—the kind that pressed down on you without mercy. Somewhere in the background, the TV muttered faintly to itself—a laugh track echoing through a punchline neither of them could hear or care about.

"We can't just sit on this," Maggie said after what felt like an eternity, breaking the quiet with a firmness in her voice that didn't quite match the flicker of fear Wren caught in her eyes.

"And do what?" Wren shot back almost too quickly, frustration sharpening every syllable. She dragged both hands through her hair until it stuck up like static wires. "Who are we supposed to tell? For all we know, every single person in that damn department is neck-deep in this."

"There has to be someone," Maggie said again, almost stubbornly now. Her fingers tapped an uneven rhythm against the edge of the paper before going still entirely. "Internal Affairs? Or maybe even the FBI?"

Wren shook her head without looking up, rejecting both ideas outright even before she fully processed them. "You should ask Fannie what she thinks of them," she muttered bitterly under her breath.

The quiet returned briefly—just long enough for doubt and desperation to settle back into its familiar corner of the room alongside them—when Wren suddenly sat up straighter. A thought sparked at the edge of her mind and bloomed into resolution almost immediately.

"Fannie," she said aloud before hesitation could talk her out of it.

Maggie blinked at her, surprised by both the name and the way Wren's voice carried sudden determination where none had been moments earlier.

"Fannie will help."

Maggie stared at her, brow furrowing as confusion etched itself across her face. "Fannie? Little old Fannie? How could she possibly help us? Why would she help us?"

Wren leaned forward, elbows on her knees, fingers laced tightly as though holding herself together. Her eyes glimmered with a strange mix of excitement and apprehension. "There's something about Fannie you don't know," she said, lowering her voice like someone might overhear. "She's not just our sweet old landlady. She has a past, Maggie. A past that might be exactly what we need right now."

Before Maggie could respond, the television yanked Wren's attention away. The sound of the news anchor's voice punched through their conversation, sharp and unforgiving. Wren fumbled for the remote, her hand trembling as she turned up the volume.

"This just in," the anchor said in that deliberate cadence reserved for tragedies and scandals. "The body of a police officer has been discovered inside an abandoned warehouse..."

6:40 p.m.

Wren found herself perched on the edge of Fannie's floral-patterned couch, her knee bouncing like it was trying to shake loose from her leg entirely. She glanced sideways at Maggie, who couldn't seem to stop pacing small circles into the worn carpet by the window. Across from them, Fannie sat primly in her faded armchair, her slight frame almost swallowed by it. Her eyes flicked nervously between the two women and the TV screen that hummed quietly in the background.

The news droned on—mere background noise to fill the heavy silence—but for Wren, it wasn't just noise. It was a reminder of every wrong move they'd made, every error compounding into something they might never crawl out from under. Her mind whirred in loops, trying to find answers where none existed yet.

Then came the buzz—sharp and sudden like a hornet trapped in glass—and Maggie froze mid-stride. The phone lit up in her hand, and whatever she read there made all of her crumble at once. Shoulders hunched forward; lips trembled; eyes glistened beneath lashes already wet with unshed tears.

"It's my sister," she whispered thickly, choked words barely able to pass through tightening vocal cords. Then stronger: "She says... she says I've shamed them all. Disappointed the family."

Wren felt something twist deep inside her chest—not quite anger but not far from it either—a raw ache that burned hotter for every crack she saw forming in Maggie's composure and couldn't fix fast enough.

"Hey," Wren said softly as she reached out and tugged Maggie down onto the couch beside her. Arms wrapped instinctively around her girlfriend's shaking form—stronger than Wren believed herself capable of most days—and pressed lips near Maggie's ear sharply but gently adding: "Who cares about them? Fuck 'em." She gestured vaguely toward nobody in particular before tightening her hold again like a protective cocoon against shame itself whispering venom now replacing comfort was felt necessary directly yet vaguely directed "Fuck THEM."

Maggie's shoulders trembled as she buried her face into Wren's shoulder. The room seemed to hold its breath, the only sound Maggie's muffled sobs blending with the faint, steady hum of the television.

Then Fannie gasped, a sharp intake of breath that shattered the stillness. "Girls, look!"

Wren's head turned toward the screen before she could think. Her own face filled the frame, pale and wide-eyed, staring back at her like some distorted mirror. Then Maggie's face appeared alongside hers. Her chest tightened; her stomach flipped. Somewhere outside the roar in her ears, the news anchor was speaking.

"The public is urged to assist in locating Wren Hubbard," came the clipped, professional voice, every syllable slicing through her like shards of glass. "She is wanted for the murder of journalist Anne Cantu. Her companion, Margaret Kline, is also wanted as an accessory after the fact."

"Shit." The word slipped out in a whisper. Wren tightened her arm around Maggie instinctively, holding her close like it might protect both of them from what was unfolding on the screen.

The broadcast cut to another image—a face Wren recognized. Officer Frances Barber stood like a monument to authority, stiff posture, expression carved from stone, eyes glaring straight into the camera. Straight into Wren.

"We will not rest until these women are brought to justice," Barber said with cold finality. She didn't blink. "They are dangerous and must be apprehended."

Dangerous. Wren wanted to laugh, but there was no air in her lungs for it. She felt hollowed out and sick at once, heat rising behind her eyes while ice settled in her chest. Dangerous? No—this wasn't justice; this was theater.

Maggie turned toward Fannie. "We can tell them about the contract," she said, desperation bleeding through every word. Maggie lifted her head, hope flickering weakly in her tear-streaked face—too fragile for all this weight they carried. "Yeah," she said quickly, almost too quickly. "Then they'll believe us. Right?"

Fannie didn't answer at first. She just stared at both of them with that worn-out gaze she so often gave now—the one that said she'd lived long enough to see too many ways things could go wrong—and finally shook her head once, slow and deliberate.

"You're accused of murder." Fannie's voice wasn't harsh—it was careful, as though saying it gently might soften its meaning somehow—but it was firm enough to sting anyway. "That doesn't just go away because you found corruption or signed contracts or have proof."

Maggie wiped at her eyes with trembling fingers and sat up straighter now despite everything weighing against her shoulders. "But we're innocent." Her words were fiercer now than Wren had expected—still shaky but growing steadier with each syllable like someone trying to climb a crumbling staircase one careful step after another. "We have proof of their corruption," Maggie went on firmly this time—determinedly—as though sheer belief alone might force something good into being where nothing good existed anymore.

"Doesn't that count for anything?"

Another pause hung heavy between them before Fannie exhaled audibly through her nose—not quite exasperation but not far from resignation either—and leaned forward toward Maggie.

Fannie shook her head, the movement slow and deliberate. "It's not that simple, dear. They've framed you for murder. That's a whole different ball game."

Wren felt her chest tighten, as though the air around her had thickened. Murder. The word clung to her like smoke, curling into every corner of her mind. It wasn't just corrupt cops now; the entire city would be after them, and there was no undoing what had already been set in motion. Her hand brushed against the contract in her pocket, and for a moment it seemed impossibly heavy, like it might drag her down if she held onto it any longer.

She looked up just as Fannie straightened. It happened gradually, yet undeniably—like watching an old jacket shrugged off to reveal something far sturdier beneath. Wren had only ever known Fannie as fragile, stooped by years of hard living and harder memories, but now that frailty seemed to dissolve entirely. Her spine was rigid, her chin lifted, and when she spoke again, the quaver in her voice was gone.

"Listen closely," Fannie said with an edge of steel that hadn't been there before. "Living on the run ain't easy, but it's doable if you're smart about it."

Wren blinked, trying to reconcile this version of Fannie with the one she thought she knew. She leaned forward; whatever came next didn't feel like advice—it felt like survival itself being handed to her.

"What's smart?" Wren asked.

Fannie's mouth curved into a faint smile—not warm exactly, but measured and knowing in a way that sent chills down Wren's spine. "First thing," she began evenly, "you've gotta become someone else. New names, new stories, new IDs. You blend in—be forgettable. Ordinary. Don't give anyone a reason to look twice at you." She paused, tipping her head as though testing Wren's reaction before continuing with an almost dismissive wave of her hand: "You can buy what you need online or print your own—hardly anyone bothers checking anymore."

The words sank in slowly, like stones into water leaving ripples behind. Wren nodded without thinking and glanced toward Maggie sitting across from them at the table. Maggie's expression was taut—equal parts fear and something else that flickered briefly behind it: fascination.

"Next," Fannie said calmly but firmly now, "you cut yourself off completely from anything digital—phones, social media accounts, credit cards—all of it has to go. Use cash for everything from here on out."

Wren stiffened instinctively; her fingers brushing against the frayed outline of the burner phone tucked deep in her jeans pocket—a device that had carried so many desperate calls and whispered plans over its battered plastic keys until now...Easy part with it. Knowing she'd have no way to reach out when all its buttons were silent? She pressed harder against the phone for just another second before easing back again.

Fannie wasn't finished yet—her voice was lower now as though they were conspirators sharing something unspoken: "And speaking of trails..." Here came another hint—a flicker—of that mischievous glint returning briefly beneath Fannie's sharp eyes "...you'll want false ones—all kinds scattered everywhere—to throw 'em off your scent completely."

Wren's grin spread slowly, almost involuntarily. This wasn't the usual kind of advice that came with a knowing smile or a pat on the back. No, this was survival distilled into a masterclass, delivered by someone who had clearly walked the tightrope herself. For the first time since Anne's death, since Dennis's fall, Wren felt something unexpected: hope.

"You've been sitting on this for a while, haven't you?" Maggie asked, her voice soft as she sat down beside Wren. Her hand found Wren's and gave it a squeeze—not too hard, not too light—just enough to ground them both.

"Fannie," Wren said, her tone carrying an awe she rarely let slip, "you're an absolute fucking genius."

Fannie didn't react to the compliment. If anything, her sharp eyes sparkled with something between amusement and determination. She leaned back in her chair, letting her fingers drum lightly against the armrest in a steady, deliberate rhythm.

"Stay mobile," Fannie began. Her words were clipped but clear, with a confidence that made Wren sit up straighter without realizing it. "Never stay in one place too long. You think you're safe because no one's come sniffing around yet? Wrong. Keep moving. Switch locations before they even know where you are."

Wren nodded even before the last word left Fannie's lips, her mind already darting from one possibility to another. She cast a quick glance toward Maggie and caught the look in her girlfriend's eyes—terrified and resolute all at once. It mirrored how Wren felt: split down the middle between two impossible states.

"And disguises," Fannie added, as though she were ticking off items on an invisible checklist. "You don't just run; you disappear. Hair color? Change it. Clothes? Don't stick to any one style too long. Even your walk—change how you carry yourself." She gave Wren a pointed look that felt more like a challenge than advice. "Speaking of hair? That dye job has to go. Never dye your hair bright again. Grow out the mohawk."

Fannie tapped the side of her head. "Your beautiful violet eyes, honey. More obvious than your hair. Buy some tinted contacts online and wear them when you are out in public. Brown. Boring but reliable. Switch to sunglasses to let your eyeballs breath."

Instinctively, Wren reached up and touched her hair—bright and bold and unapologetically hers for as long as she could remember. The thought of letting her natural color creep back wasn't just unsettling; it felt like peeling away part of herself. But even as the protest rose to her lips, she swallowed it back down. Fannie was right.

"Next," Fannie continued without missing a beat, "you're going to need allies—but not many." She punctuated that last part by holding up two fingers like it was gospel law. "People you trust implicitly—the kind of trust where you'd put your life in their hands without blinking—but don't let them become crutches. Use them sparingly."

Maggie squeezed Wren's hand again, firmer this time, as if to say she understood their lives were about to change forever but they would face it together nonetheless. Wren's mind flitted briefly through the names of potential allies: Fannie, Massi and Thanh came first. Maybe even Reek if she could track him down—his alliance ran deeper than his questionable nickname suggested.

"You're also going to want big cities," Fannie went on, leaning forward now as if proximity would drive the point home deeper. "Anonymous populations where no one asks questions or remembers faces they've seen once or twice." Her voice dropped then—not softer so much as heavier with meaning—"And learn how to survive out there with nothing but wits and what you can carry on your back."

A silence followed those words—not awkward or expectant but one that let them settle deep into the bones of anyone listening.

Wren stared at her hands for a moment before lifting her gaze toward Maggie—and then back to Fannie again. The weight of everything ahead pressed against her chest like an incoming storm gathering speed—but there was something else beneath it all too: a flicker of exhilaration threatening to break through like sunlight from behind thick clouds.

She glanced down briefly at Maggie's hand still gripping hers and gave it a squeeze of her own this time—a promise unspoken but understood between them both.

They weren't alone in this fight.

Not anymore.

Wren leaned against the arm of the sofa, arms crossed, watching as Fannie's eyes lit up with something between mischief and steely resolve. The old woman leaned forward, her voice dropping to a low whisper that seemed to carry decades of hard-won experience.

"And if things heat up too much—if it gets too dangerous—head for Canada. It can be a safe haven." She paused, her gaze sharp, calculating. "Just don't use the border crossings. You might have to cut through the woods or slip across some back road—stay off their radar entirely. You girls are smart. You can do this. Stay smart, stay safe—and keep moving until they have forgotten all about you. Fifty, sixty years, maybe." Fannie laughed and shook her head. "Maybe."

Maggie let out a soft laugh, her head shaking in disbelief even as her pulse quickened. "You'll never guess," she said finally, unable to suppress the grin spreading across her face, "what I was looking up earlier today..." She straightened up, energy buzzing through her as she looked Fannie directly in the eye. "There's an 800-mile bike trail—yeah, seriously—a bike trail that goes all the way from New York City straight into St. Catharines in Canada. No highways, no major roads, just forest and back roads and... you know... nothing."

Fannie blinked at her for a second as if trying to take it all in. Slowly, a smile crept across her worn face, one that carried more than a hint of approval. "Well," she said with a touch of admiration in her voice. "Well, I'll be damned. Looks like fate's handing you girls a golden ticket."

But then something shifted—the spark in Fannie's eyes dimmed as her expression turned serious again, her voice sharper now, more urgent. "Before you go," she began, fixing Wren with a look that could have steadied an army mid-retreat, "give those bastards one last thing to chew on. Send out that contract—to everyone—right now."

The words hadn't even finished leaving her mouth before Maggie sprang into action, fingers flying over the keyboard like they were fueled by pure adrenaline—or maybe pure rage. It was hard to tell sometimes with Maggie.

"On it," Maggie snapped, not looking up from the ancient desktop computer that wheezed faintly under the sudden burst of activity. "Downloading privacy software now... setting up a VPN... I'll make it look like we've already skipped town—say we're heading to Texas or something."

Wren nodded distractedly as she paced back and forth behind Maggie's chair, unable to stay still while energy coursed through her veins like an electric current. Her thoughts felt wild and scattered but sharpened at the same time—a paradox she couldn't quite explain.

"It's time," she said out loud to no one in particular—or maybe herself—before focusing on Maggie again. "We need to tell them everything we know." She stopped pacing long enough to plant both hands on the back of Maggie's chair and lean closer. "Create fake accounts," she said sharply. "Find journalists—bloggers too—from everywhere—America, Europe... wherever people will listen." Her breath hitched for half a second as she added softly but firmly: "This has to spread."

Maggie didn't answer—not verbally anyway—but her silence wasn't troubling; it spoke volumes louder than words ever could have at that moment. Her eyes remained glued to the phone's screen as files opened and closed in rapid succession—email drafts being composed with online artificial intelligence software to keep the writing style plain; anonymous accounts created there—all moving too fast for Wren to follow.

Wren forced herself to stop pacing long enough to watch Maggie snap quick photos of the contract with her phone—one angle after another until every detail had been preserved and cataloged in some digital archive for later use—and then shift seamlessly into taking screenshots of the EETS website while also cross-referencing WHOIS data.

"Okay," Maggie said, her voice taut with a nervous intensity. "I've got everything ready. The emails are drafted, but I haven't sent them yet." Her eyes flicked up to Wren's for a brief moment before darting back to the screen. "Are we really doing this?"

Wren placed a hand on Maggie's shoulder, feeling the coiled tension beneath her fingertips. The muscles there were wound tight, like a spring on the verge of snapping. Outside, the world was still and silent, but in this small room, what they were about to do pressed in on them from every angle. Wren tried to smile, or at least muster something close to reassurance, but instead she said, "This is... honestly the best I've felt since I left for work this morning." She almost laughed at how absurd that sounded.

Maggie didn't look up this time. Her fingers moved quickly over the keyboard, filling the room with the rhythmic tapping of keystrokes. The sound wasn't loud—more like a soft background hum—but it carried with it an urgency that made Wren's throat feel tight. Occasionally Maggie murmured under her breath as she worked, her lips forming half-words that never fully escaped.

"To Whom It May Concern," Maggie read aloud after a deep breath, her voice quiet but steady as her fingers slowed just enough for punctuation. She didn't need to say it aloud—Wren could already see the words taking shape on the screen—but somehow hearing them made it all feel more real.

"I am writing to expose a grave injustice and corruption within the local police department." Maggie paused there for a second before continuing, each word deliberate and sharp, like she was carving them into stone rather than typing them on a keyboard.

Wren nodded without realizing she was doing it. Her hand stayed on Maggie's shoulder—it felt important somehow to keep that connection—but now her grip shifted as though bracing herself for what came next.

"Officer Dennis Owen, in collusion with Officer Frances Barber, orchestrated a plan to silence investigative journalist Anne Cantu and cover up their illegal activities."

The facts fell into place one by one. The murder, the set-up, the USB keys and geocaching, the death of Dennis. It wasn't as though Wren didn't know these things already—she'd lived through them, hadn't she? But seeing it laid out so clearly like this made it harder to breathe. Her free hand found its way to the back of her neck as if trying to rub away the cold prickle that had started there and was spreading down her spine.

Maggie's fingers hovered above the keyboard, her breath shallow. "It's ready," she said, her voice barely audible, as though speaking too loudly might shatter the fragile air around them. She turned to look at Wren, eyes wide, face pale. "Should we send it?"

Wren didn't answer right away. She stared at Maggie, everything pressing down like a hand on her chest. Unlike Maggie, though, Wren thrived in pressure. Always had. She took a slow breath in through her nose and steadied herself. "Do it," she said finally, her voice calm but firm. "Let's blow this wide open. Set it for two hours from now. That gives us just enough time."

"Time for what?" Maggie asked, finally turning her head to meet Wren's gaze again.

Wren allowed herself a small smile—a rare and fleeting thing these days—but there was no warmth in it, just adrenaline and resolve. "We've got plans," she said lightly, almost teasingly if not for the undertone of urgency that cut through her words like glass. "We're going banking."

Maggie blinked at her like she hadn't heard correctly—or maybe hoped she hadn't. "Banking?"

"We'll hit a bunch of ATMs for cash advances on our credit cards," Wren said as though explaining something obvious to a child—but without malice or condescension; there wasn't room for that between them anymore. Then she added: "Cash from our debit cards." Her violet eyes flashed with something sharp and unyielding as they locked onto Maggie's brown ones again. "All of it—savings accounts drained, cards maxed out. Across the city heading south, like we are going to Texas."

Fannie's voice broke the silence, perfectly calm, as if they weren't all balancing on a knife's edge. "Smart thinking, girls. You'll need to be quick. Drop the cards on the street, let some strangers pick them up, and watch as the cops start chasing their tails."

Wren met her eyes and didn't flinch. "Speaking of cops... Fannie, you know they'll come looking for you, right?"

Fannie didn't blink—she laughed, a full-bodied sound that managed to both settle and unsettle them. "Me? Oh please. I've already got my performance all worked out. 'I'm sorry, officer. What was that? Two girls living here? Oh no no, I think it was just a girl and a boy—at least, that's how I remember it. But if you say so... my memory isn't what it used to be.'" She tossed her head back like she was already rehearsing for an audience. "You know, I pull that same act every time a cop pulls me over for speeding. They already think I'm some doddering old loon. This is going to be a riot!"

Maggie grinned and darted forward before Wren could stop her. She threw her arms around Fannie in a hug that seemed half gratitude, half admiration. "Fannie," Maggie said through her smile, "you are something else."

Wren turned her gaze toward the hallway where Argo and Bridger leaned against the wall like sentinels standing guard. The sight of them—scuffed frames, worn tires—made her chest tighten. Leaving them behind wasn't just practical; it felt like abandoning old friends who'd carried them through too much to count.

"We'll get new bikes from Massi," Wren said finally, her voice quieter now. "He can strip down Argo and Bridger for parts, maybe make use of what's left of them. We'll take whatever boring bikes he's got—that's what we need anyway." She swallowed hard before adding, "Our babies will have to sacrifice themselves."

Maggie hesitated for a moment before nodding slowly. Her hand brushed against Bridger's handlebars in a small farewell gesture. "I don't want to say goodbye," she murmured, almost to herself. "But if it keeps us ahead of them... it's worth it."

Fannie clapped her hands together suddenly, breaking the heaviness in the room like snapping a twig underfoot. "I've got some oversized panniers lying around," she said brightly. "They're ugly as sin but roomy enough for half your lives—or at least whatever you can still carry."

And then everything shifted into motion.

The hallway blurred into the basement apartment and back again as Wren and Maggie darted between the two spaces like hummingbirds drawing nectar—quick but deliberate, never wasting a move or moment. Essentials piled up faster than they could decide what stayed or went: clothes shoved hastily into crumpled bags; toiletries tossed together without rhyme or reason; small objects held in their hands for long seconds before being tucked away or set aside forever.

The urgency thickened the air until there was no oxygen left for doubt or hesitation—but woven tightly beneath that urgency was something softer and far more difficult to ignore: loss.

Normalcy wasn't just slipping through their fingers—it had already slipped past them without so much as a goodbye.

They carried the last of their belongings up the narrow staircase to Fannie's apartment, each step pulling at Wren in a way she didn't entirely understand. Maybe it was the finality of it all. Maybe it was something else. Either way, her throat tightened as though her body had decided on its own to mark this moment. This was it. The end of one life, the uncertain start of another.

Fannie stood in the doorway, her arms open wide, her eyes shimmering but holding back. Wren and Maggie stepped into her embrace at the same time, their movements uncoordinated but instinctive. Fannie's voice broke softly—not a sob, not yet—but enough to spill over them like a fragile kind of armor: "Take care of each other." She held them tighter for just a second longer and added, "Stay safe."

Wren pressed her forehead against Fannie's shoulder and closed her eyes. "We will," she murmured. Her voice didn't sound like her own—it felt heavy and caught somewhere in her chest.

Maggie pulled back first, swiping at her cheeks with quick, almost impatient movements. She looked up at Fannie like she wanted to memorize her face, then said, "We'll find a way to reach you. We will." Her voice wavered on the last two words, but Maggie being Maggie, she didn't let it linger.

They stepped away eventually—too soon and not soon enough—and walked their bikes toward the door. Fannie's—now their—bags were strapped down haphazardly but securely enough for now.

At the threshold, Wren hesitated, gripping Maggie's hand without meaning to but also completely meaning to. Fannie handed Wren a pair of cheap sunglasses—the kind meant to be disposable and cool. It worked. She smiled crookedly—watching them go couldn't have been easy for her either.

"Thank you," Wren wanted to say out loud but didn't. Instead she held onto that thought as tightly as she held onto Maggie's hand and swung herself onto the bike seat.

Maggie followed suit, glancing back before they started pedaling away. Wren didn't know how long Fannie stayed there in that doorway watching them leave—for all she knew, Fannie could still be standing there even now—but she refused to look back again. Once was enough.

The air was cool against Wren's face as they rode side by side down the familiar street. Her legs moved automatically, but everything about this felt too fast and too unsteady—like falling before you had time to decide whether or not you should jump. Her heart pounded in rhythm with the tires on asphalt: fear with one beat, exhilaration with the next.

They were fugitives now—or maybe they already had been and now understood what that meant. But Wren still had Maggie beside her and a plan ahead of them—flimsy though it might be—and decided that for now, for today at least, that would have to be enough.

Day 285

Wren braced herself against the windowsill, the wood rough beneath her palms, her gaze fixed on the empty street below. The amber glow of twilight settled over Victoria's skyline, soft and hazy, a quiet so profound it still felt foreign to her. Two hundred and eighty-four days ago, quiet like this was unthinkable—a luxury for other people, people who weren't running. Now it stretched out before them, strange and tenuous, as if it might vanish if they let their guard down for even a second.

She didn't hear Maggie approach—no, Sophie now—but she felt her first: a warmth at her back, as constant and familiar as breath.

"Penny for your thoughts, Riley?" Maggie's voice wrapped around her softly, the edges smoothed by the new accent they'd adopted like a poorly fitting coat.

At that, Wren turned, a slow smile curling across her face. "Just thinking about how far we've come." She leaned her shoulder against the window frame, savoring the sound of it: Riley Brooks. Her name now, and hers alone. "Do you remember that first night on the road?"

Maggie's chuckle rippled through the little room like smoke in still air. "How could I forget? That abandoned barn." She shook her head at the memory. "Jumping at every creak like it was coming for us."

Wren let out a small laugh herself but didn't add anything to it. They both knew how far they'd come from those nights of shivering under cobwebbed beams with nothing but their fear to keep them awake. The dingy apartment they now called home wasn't much—just four walls that always smelled faintly of mildew no matter how many candles Maggie burned—but it was theirs. For cash. No questions asked.

She glanced around the cramped space, taking in its mismatched pieces: a battered old radio perched on the counter that sometimes seemed as ancient as the news it sputtered out each morning; the scuffed-up table with uneven legs where they mapped out contingencies only to shred them later just in case; the mattress on the floor that had felt like actual decadence after months spent sleeping wherever wouldn't crush their bones by morning.

Wren crossed the room and threw herself down onto that very mattress with a melodramatic sigh. "You know," she said, half to herself but loud enough for Maggie to hear, "I never thought I'd actually enjoy this kind of life."

Maggie didn't answer at first but soon followed her over, settling onto the mattress until their shoulders touched lightly. Her presence was steady—always steady—and Wren leaned into it without thinking.

"Even with all of it?" Maggie said after a moment, her voice careful. "The fake names? The constant looking over our shoulders? The cash-only hustle?"

Wren turned her head, catching just enough of Maggie's profile to make out her features in what little light remained—the line of her nose, the curve of her lips. She studied them for a beat because she could do that now.

"Yeah," Wren said finally. Her voice came out quieter than she expected. "Even with all of it." She caught Maggie's eye then and smiled faintly before finishing: "Because I've got you."

Maggie held her gaze for a moment too long before breaking into one of those smiles that wrinkled up at the edges like old photographs folded in half too many times. "Sap," she said softly enough that it didn't sound like teasing.

It still made Wren grin anyway—grin and look away before Maggie could see how much she loved hearing that word from anyone else but especially from her.

They stood together in the hush of their sanctuary, the muffled symphony of city life spilling in through the cracked window. A car horn blared faintly, a dog barked once then twice, footsteps clicked against pavement far below. The world churned on outside, ceaseless and indifferent, but in this small, dim room, time held its breath.

Wren let her thoughts drift—unbidden yet familiar. To the frantic nights when sleep evaded them like prey too quick to catch. To the drawn-out days where every shadow could hold discovery. To the close calls that had sent their hearts hammering one moment, their sighs of relief emptying out the next. And yet—because there was always an "and yet"—there were kindnesses too. Stranger smiles and helping hands when they didn't expect it. Views that snuck up on them with their quiet beauty and took their breath away. Whispers of strength found not in themselves alone but in each other, intertwined as tightly as fingers clasped in the dark.

"We made it," Wren said softly, breaking the silence without meaning to.

Maggie's fingers brushed hers first before slipping between them completely, warm and steady. "Yeah," Maggie replied, her voice a low hum like an engine idling. "We did. And we'll keep making it, right?"

Instead of answering outright, Wren squeezed her hand—a slow press that said everything they both needed to hear. "Damn straight," she added anyway after a beat, because sometimes words helped too. "Riley Brooks and Sophie West against the world."

The last light of day softened into something thinner and darker, shadows stretching long across the walls of their apartment as though reluctant to let go of shape entirely. Outside those walls, they were fugitives—a label stamped onto them like an expiration date—but here? Here they were just Riley and Sophie. Nothing more complicated or threatening than that. And for once—for now—that felt like enough.

The mattress creaked faintly as Wren lay back onto it, her fingers moving absently over Maggie's arm in lazy spirals that didn't quite form anything specific but might've felt like stars if you squinted hard enough at them.

"Hey, Mags," she murmured finally after they'd let silence settle again and stretch comfortably between them for who knew how long. "Remember that email?"

Maggie turned toward her without fully sitting up yet—a half-shift that brought her closer but kept things easy somehow all at once. "Of course I do," she said after a pause just long enough to recall it fully instead of on command like some rote memory test back in school or wherever else people tried to measure thoughts neatly like that anymore anyway. "It was..." She hesitated briefly again before settling on: "Our Hail Mary."

Wren snorted faintly—not unkindly though—and grinned crookedly up at nothing specific except maybe ceiling cracks now barely visible in twilight gloom above them both. "Some pass," she echoed dryly but not without affection either—if affection could live safely wrapped inside sarcasm (which it could sometimes if handled right). "Blew everything halfway to hell and back."

They had watched it unfold from a safe distance, staring at the headlines on borrowed screens while their digital time bomb went off exactly as planned. News outlets pounced like jackals to carrion, tearing hungrily into revelations of corruption and conspiracy, each more damning than the last. The frenzy was almost cartoonish in its intensity—microphones shoved in faces, cameras flashing as though trying to blind their prey into confession.

"Frances whatever-her-name," Maggie muttered. Her voice carried that strange mix of satisfaction and unease that had become all too familiar. "Who'd have thought she'd fall so hard? It was... spectacular."

Wren's breath hitched for just a second before she forced it out again. Spectacular, she thought bitterly—what a word for it. Her mind tripped back to Dennis lying on the cold concrete, his body splayed unnaturally, his vacant eyes wide open to nothing at all. "Dennis went down pretty spectacularly too," she said finally, her tone hollow but sharp around the edges. "Like, *literally*." A weak attempt at gallows humor, and though she wouldn't admit it aloud, the taste of it soured her mouth every time.

Maggie reached out and squeezed Wren's hand gently. There wasn't a need for words; they both felt Dennis lingering like the sword of Damocles: they were cleared of Anne's death by Dennis's gun, but Dennis's death still hung over them.

For weeks now, they'd followed Frances's implosion through snappy news clips and shaky social media videos shot by overeager bystanders with smartphones held aloft like beacons. Frances Barber—the badge-stripped officer turned pariah—had been paraded in shackles past flashing bulbs, her face locked somewhere between defiance and resignation. The trial promised fireworks—or so the commentators liked to say—but Wren found it hard to imagine anything more incendiary than what had already gone public.

"It's weird," Maggie said after a while, her words slow and measured as though testing them for logic first. "We did what we set out to do—blew it all up—and yet here we are. Still... hiding."

Wren nodded without looking over at her. She knew exactly what Maggie meant—how victory could taste so much like ash when you were chewing it down from a crawlspace or behind blackout curtains in some rented room too small to feel secure but too big to feel safe either. It wasn't fair, of course—not after everything—but fairness had never been part of the bargain.

Wren watched Maggie out of the corner of her eye, amazed at how much they had changed in just a few months. Once, they had been easy to notice—distinctive, as Maggie liked to call it. Not anymore. Now their looks were carefully calibrated to be unremarkable. Maggie's thick long hair was gone, replaced by a dull, mousy brown cut into a style that was neither long nor short nor anything worth remembering. Wren's own once-vivid locks had grown out, fading into their natural sandy blonde like a forgotten photograph left too long in the sun.

They had adapted—out of necessity more than choice. Survival demanded it. They'd learned how to slip quietly through the cracks, navigating a world of cash-only transactions where each folded bill felt like a tiny rebellion against the system that hunted them. Maggie worked as a personal trainer now, her no-nonsense demeanor attracting clients who paid under the table while enjoying the affordability that came with it. Wren spent her weekdays fixing bikes in a cramped repair shop, her fingers deftly restoring life to broken chains and bent wheels while she kept her head down and her tattoos covered—she was going to have to find a trusty artist to work some magic. Or maybe something homegrown, maybe Maggie could learn.

On weekends, she swapped grease for dirt, landscaping under wide skies that offered a kind of freedom she hadn't realized she craved—the anonymity of open air and honest sweat.

Fannie kept them tethered to the world they were trying so hard to elude. Encrypted messages zipped back and forth between them like whispered secrets, each one carrying just enough information to guide or reassure them without giving away too much. They'd grown skilled at disappearing into the background—at leaving no trace other than faint impressions on borrowed mattresses or tire tracks on back roads—and Fannie's instructions helped keep it that way.

Sometimes Wren couldn't help but think about what they'd left behind—the lives they used to have—and those memories came with a sharp sting. But just as quickly as nostalgia crept in, it was overshadowed by something stronger: pride. Whatever else could be said about their situation, this life—the tiny apartment with its mismatched furniture and sagging couch—was theirs.

She turned toward the window and let her gaze drift past the glass. Outside, nothing looked remarkable: power lines sagged over rooftops; cars idled at an intersection; laundry flapped on a distant balcony like surrender flags no one would ever notice. Still, her mind wandered back along the road that had brought them here—a zigzagging trail across three states so riddled with close calls and restless nights that sometimes she wasn't sure how they'd managed it at all. And then there was Canada.

That border crossing stuck with her most of all. The unmarked dirt road cutting through wild fields had been both a gamble and their salvation—a dusty lifeline leading into another world entirely. She remembered gripping the wheel tightly as though sheer force alone could ensure their safe passage; remembered holding her breath as if exhaling might alert someone to their presence; remembered looking over at Maggie and seeing both fear and hope etched into her face like two sides of an unfinished coin.

The ocean was the first thing Wren noticed. That vast, beautiful ocean. Ontario had been fine, the prairies endless and predictable, but Victoria—it felt alive in a way the rest of Canada hadn't. The misty mornings curled around them like something tangible, and the salty sea air, sharp and persistent, scraped away layers of their past every time they breathed it in. Victoria didn't care who you were or where you'd come from. It was a city of transients, wanderers, locals who minded their business. There were colorful houseboats bobbing in the harbors and winding coastal roads that seemed to lead nowhere specific but always offered a view worth stopping for. Wren wasn't sure if they belonged here exactly—they still felt like visitors—but it didn't seem to matter. Victoria accepted them anyway.

Maggie had adjusted better than Wren had expected. She thrived on routines, and this new life gave her plenty to settle into: clients to coach, meals to toss together in their cramped kitchenette, tiny rituals that made each day feel solid and real. Maggie's strength was quieter than Wren's—always had been—but it showed up in ways that often took Wren by surprise. A steady hand when Wren's faltered. A smile over morning coffee even on the days when everything else felt unbearable.

They'd both changed so much in the past 284 days—Wren could count each one if she tried, though some blurred together now as exhaustion and fear mixed into an endless reel of survival. They were harder people than they'd been before all this started, but there was something softer underneath too, a fragility that existed because of how much they now leaned on each other.

Tomorrow would bring its own battles, unknown and unrelenting. The risk of being found was always there, a quiet tension woven into the fabric of their fragile calm. But Wren saw them as more than fugitives now. They were partners, bound by love and resilience. Whatever came next, they would face it head-on, driven by the fire that had brought them this far.

Wren turned from the window, her gaze settling on Maggie. In that stillness, one truth shone clearly: whatever trials waited for them, they had already claimed the most precious victories. They were here, they were together, and they had reclaimed their freedom.